A SKULK OF FOXES

Richard Sutcliffe

Eloquent Books

Eloquent Books
An imprint of Strategic Book Group
P.O. Box 333
Durham CT 06422
www.StrtaegicBookGroup.com

ISBN 978-1-60911-794-8

To my wife, Marilyn Floyde, our children, mine, hers and ours, Rebecca, Ben, William, Olivia, Eleanor, their equally wonderful consorts and the growing tribe of grandchildren.

Acknowledgements

There are many people who deserve my gratitude for their help in bringing this book into existence.

All the folk at my publishers have been ever helpful and encouraging.

My wife, Marilyn, and my daughter-in-law, Kelly Whitfield, were brave and loyal enough to read early drafts and offer sound suggestions.

Caro Trustram who has a small and lovely gîte in Santa Lucia outside Vejer de la Frontera in Andalucia welcomed Marilyn and me last winter and that is where the bulk of the first draft was written.

When disaster struck and my computer blew up on me, my son, Ben, and his wife, Kelly, bought me a new laptop. Without this generosity, I may well have given up.

CHAPTER . . .

1

"I shall have more to say when I am dead"
(Edwin Arlington Robinson "John Brown")

Commissaire Jean Luc Renard had never seen such a viciously damaged body and he was greatly relieved when he was able to come outside into the yard having left the abattoir of a living room to the pathology team. His assistant, Capitaine Duvallon, was bringing up his breakfast next to the old piggery. Renard was close to doing the same but his seniority obliged him to exercise fortitude. Beyond the sagging farm gate, in the lane, a policewoman was tending to the bread lady who, making her usual Monday morning call at the house, had first discovered what was left of her former customer. It was unlikely that she would be up to completing her rounds today even though her initial hysteria had now subsided into white faced silence.

"Sorry about the puking, boss."

"Your sensitivity does you credit, Jérôme. We shan't have many Monday morning starts like this. Never again let's hope. According to the bread woman, the victim is René Guyard. She thinks he's in his late eighties or maybe even early nineties. An old guy anyway. We'll get some poor sod from his family to formally identify the body but that will be later when it's been tidied up a bit—if that's possible."

Duvallon gave an involuntary glance towards the front door.

"We'll need to find out more about him. Shall I kick off at the Mairie and nose round in the village a bit?"

"Yes, why not, Capitaine. There's no point trying to keep this to ourselves. I saw the postman with the bread woman just now. She'll have blurted out what she stumbled across and I expect, like most country postmen, he thinks he's Reuters and the France 1 newsroom all rolled into one. They'll know about it in Paris by now never mind here in the village."

Renard suspected that his colleague was finding a reason to avoid having to go back into the house when the initial forensic work was completed. He also imagined he would head straight for the nearest café to settle his innards with a coffee and cognac. After all, he was only in his thirties and not long in the Murder Squad. Even before today's grim episode, Renard had thought him to be on the delicate side for a Serious Crimes officer. But time would tell and, in any case, why shouldn't he get the leg work started. Duvallon's timing was precise for as he squeezed through the gate and made for his car, not even pausing as he passed the police woman and the traumatized bread lady, the attending medic called from the door.

"I'm ready for you, Commissaire. We're just about done in here and before we get the body on its way, we'd better go through my first impressions."

"Yes, well okay. Let's make it quick. We can go through things out here in the yard, can't we?" Renard asked hopefully.

"It is gruesome in there I have to admit but we have to be by the body so I can explain things. I'll keep it quick and then we'll come back out here to finish things off."

Renard breathed deep and stepped through the low doorway back into the nightmare. He stayed as close as he reasonably could to the door and looked round the room which, as had ever been the case with these old farm dwellings, served almost all the owner's daily and nightly needs. In the middle of the room was a table and around it four rush-seated chairs. His gaze turned to this last of all and reluctantly, for this was where the body was sitting.

"So, Commissaire, what I can tell you from my initial examination is on the whole pretty obvious from what you yourself can see. I have one or two thoughts that I can offer you, subject to verification when I get him on the slab of course."

"Fine, fine, my dear Frédo," as Docteur Frédérique was known to all his colleagues and also, it was rumoured, to his good lady wife even in moments of high passion, "but let's get on with it and then we can finish off, as you said, outside."

"It goes without saying that we have here a case of murder and a most brutal one at that. I am not yet sure precisely which injury actually killed him. There are several possibilities. You will have noted that the throat has been deeply severed. From the incision, I would hazard that this was done with a hobby knife—you know the sort of tool one uses for cutting carpet and the like—and this could certainly have killed him in itself. I'm surprised there isn't more blood from a neck wound such as this one though and so it could be that he was already dead when the throat was slashed. A sort of coup de grace, so to speak. There have been a number of heavy blows to the head and face as well as a deep bruised cut to each shoulder. I believe further examination will show the skull has been fractured by one or more of the blows. Again death could have been caused by this alone. As for the weapon used for this part of the attack—Come closer, Commissaire, come closer, please do," Frédo beckoned and grinned wickedly. "You will see that there is a wooden handle protruding from the upper abdomen. Do you see it? When we are able to remove it, I am sure we will find that it is the sort of implement that is used for chopping kindling or lopping small branches. Not being a countryman myself, I can't tell you the precise name. A weighty, long, thick blade with a sharp edge is mounted on a stout wooden handle. Were we in Africa, I should call it a machete. I believe he was beaten about the head and shoulders with it. The stab to the abdomen could also have led to the death of the victim, although this would have taken some time. It would have been a question of bleeding to death rather than a vital organ being penetrated so far as I can judge from the position and angle of the machete. Finally, that is to say for the moment finally, if you see what I mean, we come to the hands. They have been nailed to the table as you will not have failed to observe. Given the advanced age of our victim, the shock of the heavy nails penetrating the hands could have been fatal. Unless his heart was sturdy indeed, he could equally have died from the trauma of having three fingers removed. As you can see two of the three amputated digits are on the table. Unless you come across the missing one when you are digging around, we will have to assume it was taken away by the killer or killers. It could have been taken as a trophy, I suppose. If that is so, then we are dealing with someone sick in the head. In any case just the sheer loss of blood from the various wounds would have been enough to do for him."

Frédo paused briefly as they both looked at the corpse in silence and then went on.

"Now, my dear Commissionaire, my additional reflections on the matter . . ."

"Could I please hear those outside, if you don't mind?"

"Of course, Commissionaire, how thoughtless of me."

Renard believed that Docteur Frédo could never be termed as 'thoughtless' and he knew only too well that Frédo was enjoying his discomforture at having to be in the room. They stepped out into the yard and back in to the sunshine much to the detective's relief.

"So then, my dear colleague, let me have your thoughts and you can take the body away and I can get on with finding the bastard who did this."

"Yes, indeed, Commissaire, you are right. Such a crime demands that the guilty should pay. First—and please don't think that I am playing the detective for that is clearly your role—I would suggest that you should perhaps have put an 's' on the end of the word 'bastard'. As I see it there may have been more than one killer. Even allowing for the victim's advanced years, he would still have had strength enough to make it difficult for a single attacker to nail his hands to the table. That all depends on the order in which the various assaults on the body took place, of course. He could have been incapacitated by the blows to the head first. But then, why the nailing when the old boy was probably already out of it? Anyway, in my view, you may have to reckon on at least two assailants, one to hold him down and one to do the nailing."

A thought came unbidden to Renard. The old man must have been sat facing the smoke darkened picture of the Madonna which hung on the wall opposite the fireplace while the nails were hammered in and when the machete was thrust into him. Although he would now have described himself as having no religion, the early years of his Catholic upbringing made it inevitable that Renard should think of the Crucifixion and of the legions of Martyrs who had populated his childhood nightmares. He just hoped that the victim had been a believer and that, if the final thing he saw on this earth had been the picture of the Madonna, it had granted him some sort of peace.

" Second," continued Docteur Frédo, "given the plurality of wounds which necessitated no fewer than three weapons, the carpet knife for the throat, the machete for the head, shoulders and belly and a hammer for the hands, the attacks took place over a period of time. This was not a quick death. That means to me that it is highly probable that the foremost purpose of the attacks was torture."

"And," the Commissaire took up, "torture may indicate that they were after extracting information."

"Or maybe exacting vengeance. Or giving a warning to someone else . . ."

"As ever," Renard interrupted, "I am most grateful for your help and insights but if there is nothing more, you could perhaps . . ."

"Ah yes, the body. Indeed. Think of me, Commissaire and the next few enchanting hours I have ahead of me. Will you be in attendance, dear colleague?" Frédo asked with another smile that also verged on malevolence.

"I will try my best not to think of you and what you have to do. I've told one of the local officers to be at the autopsy. I must speak to our bread lady. What about the time of death? Any thoughts?"

"I can't be too precise at this stage. But let's see. It's now Monday morning and what are we? Eleven o'clock. Given the state of the body, I should think we are talking about no earlier than very late on Saturday evening, perhaps even the next day. Let's say not after ten or eleven o'clock on Sunday morning, shall we?"

"Thank you for that. No doubt you will have a more accurate idea when you have done the post mortem?"

"As ever, I shall do my best for you—Oh I say by the way, I take it you will see to the removal of the other body, Commissaire?"

"What do you mean 'other body'?"

"Oh didn't I say?" Frédo grimaced at Renard and then paused to achieve maximum impact before continuing. "There is a large black dog of confused race lying in the nettles at the back of the house. Stone dead. Skull split—the machete no doubt."

"But . . ."

"I'm sorry. I can't risk contamination of our evidence. You understand. My chaps will see to the removal of the human remains only. I'll be in touch as soon as I have completed the autopsy. Good luck with Fido!"

The Doctor pleased with the fine timing of his announcement, chuckled all the way back to his car.

Renard moved off after him to the front gate to talk to the bread lady but spoke first to the policewoman.

"Could I ask you, Officer, do you like dogs . . .?"

"Oh yes, Sir! I've always had a dog at home. The one I've got now is a . . ."

"In that case, my Dear," Renard broke in, "there's a little job you could do for me . . ."

CHAPTER...

2

*"In marriage, a man becomes slack and selfish, and
undergoes a fatty degeneration of his moral being".
(Robert Louis Stevenson "Virginibus Puerisque")*

"Please don't go on and on about yourself being an Estate
Agent and delving into all the ins and outs of selling properties when we are with our friends. I never imagined and
would not ever have contemplated being married to a bloody
Estate Agent. I'd rather you were something really naff like
a teacher or even something out and out grubby like a car
salesman. Why can't you just say you are retired and let them
forget what you do for a job?"

Tom considered a range of replies but opted to concentrate on getting the Clio home safely rather than to engage
in verbal tennis. But Jenny was not to be ignored and sent
down another forehand cross-court drive.

" It's not as though my friends feel they need to grub
around demeaning themselves having to grovel to all and
sundry just to earn a few euros. I mean come on Tom, how
can you go on about it ad nauseam?"

" Look! It's pretty late. I've had too many scoops of dubious red wine and you've certainly done more than your bit
for the Chablis winegrowers' cooperatives. Let's leave it out
until tomorrow," proffered Tom by way of an innocent lob,
albeit with a heavy touch of top spin.

Jenny spotted the top spin.

"I had four glasses all evening and it wasn't Chablis. The
Walkers only ever serve up Aligoté as you should know. You
are always going on about the red they give you. If it's so
bad, I don't know why you insist on troughing so much."

Tom could have said that it helped him to endure the conversation which was served up with the drinks; he could have

said it gave him the strength to bear being a bloody Estate Agent; he could have told her to piss off. Instead, he kept all these to himself and concentrated on steering the Clio round the series of sharp bends that cut through the forests of the Morvan Park towards their house. Jenny, too, lapsed into silence and Tom wondered if this meant she was about to nod off which was the usual conclusion to a drinks party and a late drive home in the dark.

The headlights cut into the night and, as he took the corners, panned off into the undergrowth and trees, first to one side and then to the other, giving a more spectral glow to what, had it been daylight, would have been an almost painfully bright green. Tom was struck again by the wild impenetrability to each side of the lane and thought, as he habitually did, of the Resistance days here in the Morvan, of ambush, of treachery, of violent death and yet, he supposed, they must have been willing participants in that ultimate and deadly adventure. Certainly, more elemental than being a bloody Estate Agent . . . To a large degree he bridled at Jenny's hauteur at his 'profession' because he was not over proud of what he did either. What she didn't seem to recognise was that his grubby trade brought in a necessary addition to their pensions.

"Oh, my God, Tom! Look! Just look at that!" Jenny's shriek tore him from his musing.

She was not dozing after all.

Tom pulled to a halt because some fifty metres ahead of them, a line of wild boar was crossing the lane. First came mum or dad, huge at the shoulder, gingerish in the glow of the lights, trotting off without any apparent panic into the undergrowth followed by a single file of babies, macassins, still wearing their juvenile stripes. The eighth and last was clearly a runt and was being urged along by snout-shoves from the other parent. Then they were gone, swallowed up in the dense undergrowth. Tom and Jenny were silent, smiling broadly at the lane ahead and then at each other wishing to share their sense of wonderment.

"That's why we are here, Tom. It's just fantastic. How many of our friends in England have seen anything like that? I must email Carole tomorrow."

"It makes it all worthwhile, doesn't it? Even being a bloody Estate Agent, I suppose?"

Jenny was too moved by the sight of the wild boars to wield her racket in response and the last five minutes of the journey home passed by in silence.

They pulled up in front of their house on the pink gravel and heard the dogs barking behind the closed but not locked front door. They never locked the house unless they were to be absent overnight. Nor did they lock up the cars. Whether this was because they really didn't need to or whether it would allow them to boast of the lack of crime here to any of their English visitors, they never actually analysed. But certainly, it figured in the list of what was so wonderful about living here and it was one of the reasons which they gave to these English acquaintances for never regretting their move abroad.

"I'll just take the dogs for a piddle. Do you want to put on the kettle, Jen? A cup of weak instant for me."

"Right ho," said Jenny as she was swept aside by the hairy torrent of dogs which poured out as soon as the door was opened just wide enough to allow them to burst through.

The three dogs described several frenetic circles around them and disappeared into the night barking at imagined intruders. Tom followed them as far as the field beyond the swimming pool primarily to enjoy an illicit cigarette and certainly not because the dogs needed him to accompany them. They could after all manage to empty their bladders and bowels without any human assistance. Tom did not smoke in front of Jenny, a convention which had begun when she had given up the weed some six years earlier. She disapproved of his continuing weakness and he was not proud of his habit. But he did succumb to it in private and, although she was aware of his peccancy, she chose not to nag him despite her worries about his health. Tom stubbed out the Gauloise when it was only half smoked and felt a childish sense of self righteousness, a frisson of pleasure at this slight exercise of self abnegation.

The two Briards soon returned and pressed against him, one each side of his legs like living bookends, and growled to encourage the Spaniel who was charging and barking her way through the surrounding woods. He would have to wait up for her return. The chance of another smoke perhaps?

Jenny gave him his steaming instant coffee and announced that she was going up. This meant that she would 'check her emails' in her study before using the bathroom and finally retiring with her latest book by some female writer which Tom, out of petty male defiance, would refuse to read when she had finished it. Why he would not read her books he had never sought to explain to her, certainly not in any coherent way. This was largely because he knew that he was prejudiced by a vague sense that the world of the novel had been usurped by women writers but that when pushed, he would not have enough statistics at his disposal to support his stance and so his prejudice would be laid bare to Jenny and she may possibly be able to demonstrate that his position was ill-founded. He liked to use statistics when he was arguing a point with Jenny. It seemed such a male technique. Naturally he did not care to reveal that he had prejudices since he also laid claim to being logical, another great property he attributed to the male gender. Put more simply, his refusal to read her books was a brick in the wall of his resistance to Jenny's feminism. In order to counter it, he had felt the need to erect his own edifice of masculinism and exclusively reading male writers was one of its footings.

He heard Jenny go into the bathroom upstairs and he went out on to the rear terrace for his second smoke, calling for the Spaniel just for the camouflage this gave him. The stars were out in their millions and after the heat of the day there was even a slight chill to the night air. An almost perfect moment had it not been for the mild uprising acidic reminder of the rough red wine he had quaffed that evening. Jenny was right. He had over indulged but then even one glass of Harry Walker's usual stuff, a genuine *'gros rouge qui tache'* as the expressive French phrase had it, would have had the same effect. He wished he could refuse Harry's red wine in the manner of Nigel Barnes who would loudly and dismissively demand Evian water instead. Still, it had not been the worst way to spend a Monday evening—odd night for a get-together though. The Brits in Saint Val usually congregated at one or other of their houses during the weekends. It was as though they were holding on to the patterns of their former lives in England—work during the week and play on Friday evening through Saturday and Sunday—despite very few of them being gainfully employed now they were in France. So why not a Monday 'do' after all.

He knew the Spaniel was sitting just out of the reach of the terrace lights watching him but he would only become tetchy if the dog failed to return when he had finished his Gauloise. Eventually, the animal would re-appear and he would bed down the three dogs, clean his teeth and read himself to sleep with his current piece of testosteronabilia. Jenny would already be deeply asleep. The Aligoté would have driven her into the arms of Lethe or wherever else her habitual vivid pattern of dreams was to unfurl this night. One thing was sure. He would be given chapter and verse of her dreams the next morning.

As he finally made his way upstairs armed with a glass of water and a Rennie just in case, Tom mused once again on the fact that unless a party was held at his and Jenny's place, there were never any French people in attendance. This led him on to considering how little effort any of the others put into learning French, let alone using it. Some of them positively avoided any circumstance in which they would be forced to use the language although Nigel Barnes would have a go in the right situation. On the other hand, just the other day, he had heard Steve Brown say "Cheers" instead of "Merci" and "Wotcher mate" instead of "Ca va" or even "Bonjour". This, he thought, was just appalling. But, Tom admitted to himself in a moment of unusually honest self appraisal, he enjoyed being the best French speaker by far of the Brits in Saint Val. It gave him a position of importance in the small expatriate community since in almost all the contacts between them and local tradesmen or officialdom, they had to call on his help. The fact that he had been the agent when each of the Brits had acquired their property only reinforced this position since, by being so involved, he knew quite a lot about their personal backgrounds. He even knew which of them had property loans and for how much, as well as their precise ages and how long they had been married and if they had been divorced. All of these details had figured on the sales contracts. Even more gratifying to Tom was that the local people, up to and including the Mayor of the Commune, were happy to involve him in their dealings with the Brits. These ruminations gave Tom a feeling of worthiness and as he turned out the light, he knew he would fall asleep easily, particularly as he had taken the precautionary antacid drink he had brought upstairs and it appeared to be winning the battle inside him.

Perhaps if the expatriates had not so hermetically sealed themselves off both socially and linguistically, if Tom and Jenny Fox had had a postal delivery that Monday morning so that Tom hadn't missed out on his daily chinwag with the postman, if the bread woman had not abandoned her round leaving the two or three Brits who used her services with no baguettes or croissants, then one or more of them would have heard of old Guyard's mutilation and death on the day his body was discovered rather than, as was the case, not until Tuesday morning.

CHAPTER . . .

3

I pass, like night, from land to land;
Have strange power of speech.
(Coleridge— "The Rime of the Ancient Mariner")

Tom thought of Tuesday mornings as the real start to his working week as all the estate agencies, the notaires' offices and the banks were closed on Mondays. He was fond of what he considered to be perpetually long weekends. He loved the slow start to the week. But now it was Tuesday, there would be telephone calls starting soon and emails from over the weekend to open. So doggedly following the instructions which his wife had written out for him because of his technical dimness, he had downloaded and printed off the day's Guardian crosswords—Cryptic for him and Quick for Jenny. They would attack the puzzles as usual over breakfast. His eager anticipation at matching wits with Araucaria or Paul, if he was lucky and today's puzzle was by either of his favourite compilers, was interrupted by the ferocious barking of the dogs followed by their hurtling across the graveled area in front of the house and off along the winding lane which connected the house to the outside world. This meant only one thing. Someone was arriving. Jenny fled upstairs to complete her toilettage and dress while Tom went out to see who was paying them a visit—not yet eight o'clock either!

Advancing slowly down the drive was a blue vehicle which, as it got closer, Tom recognised as a police car. He felt immediately edgy. He had never discussed the question with Jenny or with any of their Brit neighbours but he was fairly convinced that they all viewed the gendarmerie with some suspicion not untinged with fear or, at the very least, apprehension. Their last uniformed visitors had been the

Fire Brigade selling their calendar at the end of November. He'd even felt uncomfortable at their presence too and they did not carry weapons. That was perhaps it. Carrying guns as the gendarmes did all the time was a step un-British too far. He found himself hoping the dogs would behave themselves. He didn't fancy having to apologise for muddy paw marks on pristine uniforms. It was already bad enough that the Briards were herding the police car and the Spaniel was snapping at the wheels. Tom imagined that the police men would be getting angry.

The car drew up on the graveled apron.

"Please. Just a moment, if you please. I'll shut the dogs in the house," said Tom leaning down by the passenger window. By some rare miracle the dogs heeded his command to 'get in the house!' and he shut them inside with the smug glow of a dog owner obeyed.

Two men in plain clothes emerged from the vehicle. The uniformed driver remained behind the wheel. Tom began to ask himself if this was one of those occasions on which the protocol of a handshake would be dispensed with but his dilemma was answered by the elder of the two men advancing with hand outstretched.

"Do I have the pleasure of addressing Monsieur Fox? Excuse us but we are obliged to ask you one or two questions if you do not mind. May I present myself and my colleague? I am Commissaire Renard and this is my assistant Captain Duvallon."

"Please, Commissaire, Captain, come and sit on the terrace."

As Tom had expected, the two policemen were impressed by the terrace and swimming pool with the massive granite walls which retained the hillside above the pool. That the renovations never failed to impress people almost made up for the fact that the investment had taken Tom and Jenny to the outer edge of financial wisdom. Tom felt a little more self-assured here. He had recovered from being put on the back foot by the over exuberance of the dogs' welcome. He would have felt less calm however if he had been able to read Captain Duvallon's mind. For him, this swimming pool, these granite walls only spoke of money and reinforced his view that the English with their wealth and seemingly easy access to credit were pricing locals, including himself, out of the housing market.

"So, gentlemen, can I get you something to drink? Coffee perhaps? It won't take a minute. The machine is already on."

"I think perhaps not, Monsieur Fox. I have recently taken my breakfast and I am sure that my colleague has not missed out on his coffee and tartines. I think rather that I should like to put my one or two questions to you as I have already said, without delay. Are you able to follow what I am saying? You are after all English . . ."

"Thank you, Commissaire. I understand completely and rest assured that if I do not follow you fully then I shall tell you at once but I don't usually have any problems."

The Commissaire did not fail to pick up on the Englishman's irritation at this questioning of his linguistic competence but at the same time he had to admit to himself that first impressions indicated that he spoke very correctly and almost without an accent. Nevertheless, he determined to make no allowances for his not being French and if the Englishman did get snarled up then so much the better. Commissaire Renard was not averse to enjoying any advantage he could take when he was putting his questions. He continued but now his delivery was quite deliberately much more rapid.

"So then, first of all, I should explain what brings us here on this so lovely a morning. I am sorry to have to tell you that one of your neighbours, Monsieur Guyard, has been found dead."

"My God! Poor old Guyard! How? When? Did you know that we bought this place from him? We know—knew—him very well."

"I am afraid I can't say anything about the circumstances of his death for the moment and yes indeed I have been made aware that you bought your house from him. In fact that is why we are here talking to you."

"Well if you are making enquiries, it is more than likely that the poor old soul didn't die of natural causes. You don't have to be Descartes to work that out, do you?"

"Nor Thomas Hobbes nor John Stuart Mill, I suspect."

Renard was pleased at throwing these two names into the conversation since now Monsieur Fox would know that he too was not without education. He was clear that Fox suffered from what his father had identified in Renard himself as 'intellectual pride' and which his father had considered to be a weighty sin. So if Fox intended to show off his European cultural awareness then the Englishman would have to expect Renard to do the same. The language and intellectual context of their engagement had been defined.

He vouchsafed that indeed Guyard had not died of natural causes.

For his part, Tom was thinking of chucking in Bergson and Sartre but recognised just in time that this would have been a childish move too far. In any case, it was quite possible that Renard would be able to produce a more impressive parade of philosophers than he could. He had always felt considerable awe that French school pupils studied Philosophy as a compulsory part of their Baccalaureate and so he opted for modest discretion rather than to pursue cultural cock-fighting. At least he could strut his linguistic superiority, unchallenged.

"Poor old chap! Mind you he was a good age. I seem to recall from the paperwork of the house sale he would have been 93 next birthday. Sometime in October isn't it? Yes, as I say, we bought this place from him. It had been left to him by some distant relative or other and he already had his own place of course. Even so, I really had to work hard to persuade him to sell. You will forgive me, gentlemen, I am sure, if I say that there is a type of French person who feels happier having land and buildings and actual cash in the hand rather than funds in the bank. They prefer what is tangible perhaps."

"You are referring to peasants, perhaps," Duvallon intervened rather sourly.

"Yes, I suppose I am. Those who live in the country at any rate. It's in the blood, I imagine."

"Be that as it may, perhaps you could tell me, Monsieur Fox, when you bought the house and you came to move in, what state was the place in? I don't mean the state of repair. I don't mean what renovations you have had to do. What I mean is, had the buildings been emptied of their contents or had he left the place full of rubbish?"

"I must admit that we were a bit taken aback by the muck that had been left in the property and in the yard as well, I have to say. But I've got used to that sort of thing since then. You know that I am a bit of an Estate Agent and I've learned that it is quite usual—especially with old farms—for places not to be cleared out properly by the vendors. Occasionally, among all the rubbish, you come across a few interesting items . . ."

"Exactly so. Could I ask you about these 'interesting items' that you came across?"

"Well, there were some rusty old farm implements—scythes, saws, chicken feeders and so on. We cleaned up a lot of them and painted them with anti rust. We put them on the walls of the lower barn for decoration—and there was one piece in particular which I suppose I should have given back to Guyard. But I didn't. I just kept it in return for all the clearing up we had to do, I guess. I came across a First World War French infantryman's helmet and, as I say, I just hung on to it . . ."

"The Spoils of War you might say, Monsieur Fox. What I really wanted to know was whether you came across any old papers . . ."

"What sort of papers? Personal things do you mean?"

"I don't want to be too specific but . . . in fact, why should I not be more precise? What would interest me in particular is anything you came across that was in English."

"In English? What do you mean? Do you mean handwritten items or printed materials?"

"Just anything in English. I can't put it more simply than that, Monsieur Fox."

"I don't think we found anything in English. There were lots of old local newspapers . . . No. I'm pretty sure all we found was in French. It would have stuck in our minds if there had been anything in English naturally."

Jenny emerged on to the terrace and advanced to shake hands with the two policemen.

"Ah Jenny—let me introduce you. Commissaire, Captain, this is my wife Jenny. Jenny, this is Commissaire Renard and this is Captain Duvallon."

"To what do we owe the honour of your visit?" Jenny asked, her nervousness at the presence of policemen on her terrace translating itself into excessive formality.

"I am afraid, Madame, that it is a very serious matter which brings us to your lovely home. We have just been talking to your husband about Monsieur Guyard. I regret to say that we are investigating his death."

"The Commissaire was asking, Jenny, if we had come across anything written in English that had been left here when we first moved in," Tom intervened.

"Oh, Tom! How very dreadful. How did he die, Commissaire? Poor, poor Monsieur Guyard . Was it an accident? What happened?"

Commissaire Renard glanced over at his colleague and almost imperceptibly shrugged his shoulders. But however slight the gesture, it was enough to indicate to Duvallon that his boss was going to tell these English people more about the circumstances of the death provided that he, Duvallon, had no objections. An equally minute movement of but one of Duvallon's shoulders was sufficient to signal his agreement to the disclosure.

"Monsieur and Madame Fox, I am very sorry to have to tell you that the brutality of Monsieur Guyard's death leaves us in no doubt whatsoever that he was the victim of a most vicious murder."

"Oh my God," chorused the Foxes.

Neither would have admitted that their immediate and genuine feelings of sympathy for the old man were followed very rapidly by other less noble thoughts. He couldn't stop himself wondering how such an event would affect the price of houses in Saint Val and she couldn't help asking herself if she could assume the role of quasi official bearer of the news to the rest of the Brit community. It was as if the Commissaire was able to see straight into Jenny's mind, for he added:

"I understand that there are a number of British people living in the commune of Saint Val. It would most certainly do no harm if you were to let them know what has happened. You might also feel able to tell them that we shall be calling on them in due course."

Thus Jenny felt she was rather more than 'quasi'. If she played it right, she might even be able to encloak herself with the threatening mantle of officialdom when she announced to her compatriots that they should expect a visit from the law.

"Of course, we will no doubt need to speak to you again. For the time being, however, we shall leave you in peace. Thank you for your help and Monsieur Fox I must complement you on the level of your French language skills. It must be strange and not a little gratifying to pass from the speech of one land to that of another with such facility."

"You are too kind, Commissaire. But I have to say that if one comes to live in another land then one has to do one's best to speak its language, absorb its culture and so on."

"That is no doubt true. But it is equally valid to retain an essential element of one's own nationality. Isn't that what our wonderful political leaders think they mean by multiculturalism. But that is a discussion for another day and different circumstances. I am afraid that policemen should be neither political nor social commentators—especially when they have a murder to solve."

As the police car gathered speed away down the drive, Tom found himself thinking that he might well enjoy spending time in Renard's company—especially when he didn't have a murder to solve. Jenny, wearing an appropriately solemn face, was already heading for the telephone. As for Renard, he was idly wondering when it would occur to Tom Fox that, in fact, they shared the same name.

CHAPTER . . .

4

"Frogs Eat Butterflies, Snakes Eat Frogs,
Hogs Eat Snakes, Men Eat Hogs"
Wallace Stevens (Title of a Poem 1923)

Tom stood in front of his house and looked out across the valley at the wooded hills of the Morvan. The countryside had a special quality of inducing a state of reverie, a frame of mind usually associated with calm contentment. But now Tom took in more the darkness under the trees than the sunlit clearings between them. He was conscious of the menace which lay beneath the surface beauty of this wild area. He felt all too aware of the struggle for survival which the creatures living here in these forests had to undertake each day. His mind moved on to the people who lived here. Not the incomers but the real locals who had been born of locals. How could it not be that over the generations they had absorbed into their very spirits this struggle for life and this familiarity with death which was daily played out around them? Compared with the incomers, were they not more intimately involved with death and killing? They did not buy oven ready chickens at the supermarket. They wrung necks, slit throats, plucked feathers themselves. Tom had seen the aftermath of the slaughter of a pig in a French neighbour's barn. He had fortunately missed the actual dispatch but had seen the buckets of blood reserved to make black puddings, the cloven skull which would become brawn, every part of the animal butchered to meet its allotted culinary destiny. Of course, in theory, in principle, philosophically, Tom approved of such efficient husbandry. In reality, he could not have brought himself to perform any such butchery. In like manner, in common with all the incomers that he knew, he considered the locals' dedication to hunting through the winter open season as barbarous. The woods at those times sounded like the Battle of the Somme. Death was visited upon the deer, the wild boar, the bird life so fervently, it seemed to Tom, that it was a miracle that enough specimens survived into the following spring to create new generations ready for the slaughter of the next winter. He could accept intellectually that there was perhaps a rightness about it all, that the attitudes of the incomers who enjoyed with gusto such delicacies as terrine of wild boar were less honest than those of the locals. It was just that he could in no way participate in the slaughter. But at the same time he also thoroughly enjoyed the delicious end products. So he thought of himself too as less than honest. He was aware that however much he strove to become more French in outlook, he would forever be an alien when it came to actually participating in turning animals into food products.

Speaking of food products, he guessed it was about time he was leaving for Avallon as he always had lunch at the Cheval Blanc with Maître Lemaître, his notaire friend, on the first Tuesday of the month. In addition, he needed to call in at his favourite butcher who had been hanging some venison for him. Bambi had been divided into cook sized pieces and vacuum packed and so would not risk offending his sensibilities.

Jenny too would be going into Avallon. Once a week, she and a friend took one of their aged neighbours, Jean François Casson, to do his shopping at the supermarket. It was a trip which demanded careful preparation in making sure who was to participate. Whilst members of the Brit community took it in turns to accompany Jenny in escorting the old man to the shop, none of them wished to take him on their own. This was not because he represented any sort of threat. It was just that he spoke with a very robust Burgundian accent and this, combined with his semi toothlessness, made him very difficult to understand even for those with a fair range of French language skills like Jenny. When they took Casson to the shops therefore, they preferred to go mob handed. He could then chunter away to himself while his escorts needed only from time to time to utter a noncommittal 'Yes' or 'Really' to him and chat for the most part to each other. Despite the linguistic isolationism which prevailed, the Brits continued the trips in the sure and self satisfied belief that they were furthering anglo-french relations. Certainly, Casson found it helpful and he would have not have been able to rely on his French neighbours since he did not speak to most of them and they did not speak to him.

On this occasion, Jenny was to be joined by their hostess of the previous evening, Peggy Walker, a woman, like Jenny, of a certain age. She possessed the social quality of talking a great deal without saying very much and often about people or places or events which were a total mystery to her audience. Jenny would be able to concentrate on driving and be bathed in the flow of Peggy's undemanding if frequently unfathomable monologue, occasionally directing a brief phrase in Casson's direction mainly to let him know that she remained aware that he was there in the back of the car. The arrangement was that she and Tom would meet up at the Walker's house when they had both returned from Avallon. Tom had reluctantly had to make do with the Clio so that Jenny could use their much more spacious Passat.

When Tom got to the Cheval Blanc, it was with some surprise that he found his friend Lemaître sitting at a table with Commissaire Renard. Lemaître, seeing Tom pause and sensing that he was hesitant at joining them because he felt perhaps that they wished to be alone and was about to make his excuses to leave them, exercised his unfailing charm, rose from his chair, took Tom by the elbow and steered him to the table.

"My dear Tom. I did not have time to forewarn you. I don't often get the opportunity to have lunch with my pitiful cousin and I did not think you would mind—despite the fact that he is a gendarme, I think you will find him bearable, the poor chap. Let me introduce you."

"Charles, there is no need. We know each other already. The Commissaire called on me at my home this very morning. In fact, I might even believe that he is following me."

"Monsieur Fox, please accept my assurances that I am not following you. No one would go so far as to invent having this old reprobate of a notaire as a cousin, simply to maintain contact with you. Could I offer you an apéritif? Charles and I have ordered a Kir. What about you?"

"Well, I have to drive after . . ."

"Please Monsieur Fox. My cousin and I get together so rarely, the occasion demands that we take a celebratory drink or two. For today, you will be under my protection. I am sure that Charles here will tell you that he has never been picked up and asked to blow in a bag. Between you and me, his registration number is a far better safeguard than diplomatic plates. Not that he has ever thanked me, of course."

"'Then, I will join you in a Kir with great pleasure," Tom responded although, in reality, the combination of the sweetness of the cassis and the fizziness of the Crémant de Bourgogne made Kir one of his least appreciated tipples.

"And as for the drinks with the meal, Tom, you will be my guest because I am in charge of selecting and paying for the wine. If the police can pay for our apéritifs, then it is the very least that the law can surely do. No arguments from you or from Jean Luc."

Having partaken of previous meals with French friends in similar circumstances, Tom was quite sure that the cost of drinks would far outstrip that of the food and he felt quite safe in asking Sonia, who was hovering with her pad, to give him the bill for their meals. He was not being mean in any sense. It was merely that in this way he could ensure that he paid his fair share without any risk of being caught up in the macho competition to outspend the others when it came to selecting the drinks.

As it turned out, they all chose the same food—Assiette Gourmande as a starter, a faux filet, a ripe Epoisses and a Honey and Walnut tart—a menu that would ensure that Tom at least would not be requiring an evening meal. Charles Lemaître, as Tom had predicted he would, did them proud, selecting a Meursault-Charmes for the entrée and a couple of bottles of '98 Corton Clos du Roi to accompany the steak and the cheese.

"So, Tom," said Lemaître, when the ritual of the ordering was completed, "I have just taken on a house for sale which I think might interest your English. It's very well priced too. Remind me to give you the details before we depart."

"I don't know why you always call them 'your English'. I don't think of them as mine. Surely we should call them 'ours' as we are all making a few euros out of them—except for you, that is, Commissaire. I expect that Guyard's house will be coming up too although, of course, one does not wish to talk of such things when he has so recently died . . . I'm sorry but I just can't help wondering. It is after all my job and I do have a particular interest in anything that comes on to the market in Saint Val. I expect there is family somewhere around though."

"I am not sure. I do in fact deal with his affairs but I have never been aware of any relatives. There is nothing like the sniff of an inheritance to bring them out of the woodwork though. So I should not be surprised if someone comes knocking on my door."

"Well if they do," Renard interjected, "I shall most certainly be keen to see them."

"And if there are no relatives," continued Lemaître, "the property will revert to the State and in due course it will go up for auction."

"Whatever the state gets for it, it won't scrape the surface of what Guyard has no doubt drawn by way of pension over the years. This is France after all—a ship slowly sinking under the weight of its social commitments. If it were a private concern, it would have been declared bankrupt years ago," Renard expressed the habitual refrain of the French.

Because he knew better, Lemaître contented himself with a secretive smile

"If only you knew how lucky you are still to have a medical service and let's not forget you still have an education system. Rejoice in them while you still have them and thank your stars that Thatcher was not French."

"I always thought it odd that Mitterand was so attracted to her or so it has been said. How was it he described her?" asked Renard.

"He said she had the eyes of Caligula and the lips of Marilyn Monroe," Lemaître quoted.

Tom had always been astonished that Mitterand could have found Mrs Thatcher in any manner attractive. Perhaps the unconvincing socialist had merely been seduced by her aura of power. Perhaps it was as inexplicable in its own way as the love-hate relationship between the French and the English was in general. Whatever the reason, it is most certainly highly unlikely that she would have reciprocated any passion he might have entertained for her. Nevertheless, Tom found himself needing to expunge from his mind emetic images of a heavy lidded Mitterand moving towards a bed with a Union Jack for a cover and upon which lay a naked, beckoning Mrs Thatcher. He eventually cleared this unsettling image of Entente Sexuelle from his mind only by invoking the words of Lord Kitchener in a message quoted in the Times of 19 August 1914 and addressed to the troops of the British Expeditionary Force 'You are ordered abroad as a soldier of the King to help our French comrades against the invasion of a common enemy . . . In this new experience you may find temptations both in wine and women. You must entirely resist both temptations, and, while treating all women with perfect courtesy, you should avoid any intimacy. Do your duty bravely. Fear God. Honour the King'. What could she have been thinking of? Had the Empire sunk to this? Most certainly not! Get dressed, Madam! Tom recognized that the wines were having a provocative impact upon his imagination.

The three of them concentrated on their food and gave appropriate little moans of pleasure at the excellent wines which were disappearing steadily.

At length Tom expressed the view that it was almost obscene to be drinking such fine wines on a Tuesday lunchtime. Charles Lemaître chastised him for this very British attitude and added that the same sort of thinking made love-making in the hours of daylight sinful to the British but all the more piquant to the French. Renard added that he would always tend to serve modest wines on important occasions but that it was divinely appropriate to serve up great bottles when it was least expected.

"I must say, Monsieur Fox, that I have never met any other English person who speaks French so well as you. I am full of envy," said Renard

"He has helped me out a lot with my English clients. It has been invaluable. It has not only saved a lot of time but it has also been reassuring to them," Lemaître added.

Tom basked in these compliments and mumbled suitably modest disclaimers. He took the opportunity to remind the two Frenchmen that he had not always been an Estate Agent and that he treated it very much as a part time occupation. He explained that it brought in a welcome top up to his pension.

"So what did you do before you came to France, Monsieur?" Renard quizzed.

"I was in local government. I ended up as Deputy Director of Education in West Sussex."

What he did not say was that he had narrowly missed getting the top job when the previous Director had retired and that this had been such a disappointment to him that he had negotiated an early retirement. He could also have added that his wife was of the view that the role of Estate Agent was beneath him. She herself, if she had been a less discrete woman, would have pointed out that the trauma of missing out on the senior post had marked Tom deeply. She believed that the episode was at the root of his need constantly to validate himself, to demonstrate that his life was still meaningful and influential.

"An impressive career indeed," was Renard's brief response.

They reached their coffee at last and with a supreme act of common sense decided against a digestive drink. Glowing and heavy, they made their way to the car park where they shook hands and Renard's parting shot was

"Don't be surprised, Monsieur Fox, if I make contact with you tomorrow."

Tom drove off with all the excessive caution of one who knows he is over the limit to meet up with Jenny at the Walkers' house and wondered not for the first time why it was that when French people said his name it sounded very like 'fucks'.

CHAPTER...

5

"How few of his friends' houses would a
man choose to be at when he is sick."
Boswell (Life of Johnson, Volume 4, page 181)

It may have been the suppressed images of the concupiscent Thatcher but it was far more likely that it was the previously imbibed wonderful wine now being so rudely assaulted and stirred up by the acerbic stuff pressed on him by Harry Walker which was causing Tom to feel bilious.

As arranged, he had arrived at the Walkers' to find Jenny helping her hosts to quaff their habitual Aligoté. They appeared to have been meeting the challenge with some success as there were already three empties on the table and Tom just hoped that Jenny had eaten something to soak up the alcohol. Harry was opening another bottle and Tom's guts churned in anticipation.

"Now, this is really what I call taking the rough with the smooth", he volunteered, confident that his remark would pass over them, unnoticed.

"Jenny has told us about Guyard, Tom. We think it's just dreadful. Right here in our village as well! Who would have thought it?" Peggy said, confirming Tom's confidence that they would not pick up on his less than oblique criticism of their wine.

"Guess what, Tom?" Jenny asked and then paused as if she expected him actually to guess what she was going to impart to him.

"We are making an attempt on the Tuesday afternoon four man Aligoté swigging record, perhaps," hazarded Tom

"Don't be silly, Tom. Try to be serious!"

Peggy dived in and took over from Jenny.

"When Jenny and I went round to collect old Casson, well, guess what. He'd got his door locked and he wouldn't come out. He said he didn't want to go shopping—well, at least we think that's what he said anyway. In the end he slipped a shopping list under his door with a couple of twenty euro notes and Jen and I brought him back what he wanted. And, Tom, do you know he wouldn't open the door to let us give him his shopping. He wouldn't, would he, Jen? We had to leave it on the step. What do you think is wrong, Tom? Do you think he's ill or something?"

A slight hesitation by Tom, who was astonished that she did not seem to have recognized the old man's unwillingness to join them on the shopping trip might have had something to do with his being upset at the news of Guyard's death, gave Peggy licence to carry on in full swing. In any event, Tom knew that even after just a glass or two, his neighbour's questions were inevitably rhetorical. When she was in drink no one was required to respond anyway.

"Well, I know what I think," she continued. "It's this terrible news. I just had to ring Susie because of course they met old Guyard at one of your get-togethers when they were over last year and she was shocked I can tell you, even though she doesn't live here. Just think about Casson and what he must be thinking."

So she was not totally devoid of sensitivity or imagination, Tom recognized with some relief.

"I tried to ring Joy as well but there's no answer and you know them. They don't have an answer machine. I don't know why not. You'd think in this day and age everybody would have one," Peggy ploughed on.

Tom and Jenny looked at each other seeking help at identifying 'Susie' and 'Joy' but in vain.

"I should think she's right," Harry took up. "I expect the poor old bugger reckons now that Guyard has gone, he's the only old timer left round here. It'll have shaken him up no end, I'll bet. 'Am I next?' That sort of thing, you know what I mean?"

"I'm sure they are right, Tom" continued Jenny. "I expect he is ever so sad. You'll just have to go and see him, Tom. See if there is anything we can do."

"Look," said Tom, "I'm perfectly sure that you are all correct. Casson has got to be very upset. I don't know whether I have ever spoken to you about what apparently went on towards the end of the war."

"Oh Tom," Jenny sighed. "Not the bloody war again. You're always on about it!"

"No. No. Just listen, Jenny. It might well be connected. We just don't know. Well anyway, according to Casson, he and Guyard were in the Resistance together. They are—or 'were' I suppose I ought to say now—more or less the same age and when they got orders, on the very same day in fact, to report to the police station in Quarré les Tombes for transportation to Germany to do forced labour for the Nazis, they both decided to leg it. That is the reason most young men joined the Resistance in those days. It was to avoid going to Germany. Casson wasn't too forthcoming on the details but he gave me to believe that things went on during those days that don't bear too much digging into. He told me a few things though and he also said that the reasons some people round here still don't speak to each other even now come from those days. In any event, it is more than likely that he is the last of the veterans who are still around and that is bound to make him feel a bit vulnerable simply because of his age. Add it all together though and it could be more than that. It could have something to do with what went on back then— or, more likely, what has continued to go on since then. If that is the case, then maybe he will be feeling he might be in danger as well."

"But all that happened so long ago, Tom," said Jenny.

"Guyard's murder was not long ago at all. We haven't been told when it happened exactly but it must have been in the last day or two . . . That means we've had a current murder and from what Casson has told me, there were killings then. He didn't just mean between French and Germans either. I got the very clear sense that there were French going after other French as well. He was a bit vague of course. I didn't get any names or any specifics. But that would be typical, wouldn't it. Everybody knows that a blanket of silence was thrown over what happened especially towards the end of the war during the period of the Liberation. The French seem to have decided that silence is better than opening up old sores. Well, so far as I am concerned, it would be no surprise if the sores had carried on festering. It's the same locality, the same Saint Val and for sure, at least some of today's players, the families who live round here now, have to be descended from people who were involved then."

"I suppose you are saying that it may not be a very good idea to go and see him," said Harry as he did the rounds with the wine

"No, that's not what I mean at all. I fully intend to go and see him. Try to find out what's up but not today. I think it would be wise to sleep on it. In any case, I have had too much to drink to be going anywhere this afternoon. But what I'm really trying to get over to you is that we could be out of our depth. I don't think any of us can imagine what it must be like never to have lived anywhere else but Saint Val, to be tied here because this is where your family home is, this is where your land is. Just imagine how differently old Casson—and poor Guyard for that matter when he was alive—must view this area. They must have such a sense of the history of the place. Many of the things we see and assume have always been here, they have seen come into being. When we see a ruined barn we just see a ruin but, in their mind's eye, they must also see the sound working building it used to be. The people who used to work these barns and who died before we ever arrived here in Saint Val simply do not exist for us. For them, though, the memory of all these people is alive. What am I trying to say? Oh God, I've had too much to drink. I suppose I am trying to share my feeling that we just have no sense of the living past of this place, we Brits. We have no conception of the complex links that exist between one family and another. We don't care a toss about a few square metres in the corner of some field, a few bushes at the edge of some wood. But for them even a patch of scrubland seems like a matter of life and death. There, you see, I've said it 'life and death'!"

"Surely he wasn't killed over a bit of land. Is that what you think? Have a top up, Tom," said Harry, hovering over his glass with the beginnings of unsteadiness. "It'll all come out in due course. You may be right. It could all be to do with a sodding piece of land. I can't really see what you're on about with the bloody war though . . ."

"No. No, Harry. I don't just mean the war. That's only part of it. How can I describe it? Look! We all love this part of the world. I guess we all feel pretty lucky to live in such a beautiful place. God knows, my breath just gets taken away by some of the views around here. But for them, it's more than that. Much more. I'm sure they see the beauty but they also know by instinct what each square metre is good for, what will grow best on it and on top of that they know who owns each of those square metres. We're Brits and we lost that umbilical connection with the land generations ago. We're all townies living a sort of rural dream which we imagine used to be the reality in England. Well, I don't think it has been like that in England for generations. We just think it was. When I chat to elderly locals about a piece of land they may be thinking of selling—not because they want to but because they need the cash or even sometimes because they simply can't farm the land anymore because they're getting past it and they can't bear seeing it unproductive—they still put a value on the parcel of land according to its position in the valley, according to how much sun it gets, according to whether there is a stream passing through it. In other words, Harry, they put value on it as a living thing capable of growing crops or feeding animals. It's what the French call "terroir" and there's not really a word for that in English. When I show an English buyer a piece of land the only value he is interested in is the price in euros per square metre, whether it can be built on and, if so, what price can it be sold on for. For the French the land is somehow part of themselves; for us, it's just something to buy and sell. It's a commodity just like everything else we get our bloody hands on."

"Hang on, Tom! You're getting carried away again. You're always the same when you've had too much," Jenny interrupted him, aware from past experience of Tom in his cups that he was winding up for a lengthy harangue. There was every chance that he would shift from opinionated generalisations to personalized criticism in all likelihood aimed at her but even, God help us, at Harry perhaps. "It's always the same with you. You think the French are perfect and you can't see any good in the Brits."

"Of course the French are not perfect. It would be potty to claim that. In fact, they are learning mighty fast from us about land values and about making money without getting their hands dirty. Can't blame them either. Anyway, sorry, a bit of a hobby horse of mine."

"Well at least if the coppers are thinking on the same track as you, Tom, they won't be bothering us. They'll be looking for the killer among the French," said Peggy.

"They'll probably not even want to see us, Peg," Harry took up

"There's something I ought to have told you Jenny. When I met up for lunch with Lemaître, he had his cousin in tow. You'll never guess who his cousin is!"

"How on earth should I know?"

"Well, you've met him—and very recently too."

"Tom ! Don't be annoying! Who is this bloody cousin!"

"He's the Commissaire de Police, Renard. He's actually Lemaître's cousin. Incredible don't you think?"

"I don't see why it should be so incredible. I mean it's not as incredible as if his cousin had been, say, Jacques Brel."

"No. You are right. It would have been entirely incredible if I had just had lunch with someone who died thirty years ago. Anyway, we did push the boat out a bit. God knows how much Charles forked out for the wine but it was the tops."

"Before you start, I don't want any comments on my wine, thank you very much, Tom, You don't have to drink it if it's less up-market than you're used to," Harry intervened, remembering Tom's critical comments on several previous occasions.

"I am sure I shall suffer for it Harry but I'm past caring now. Pour us another one, old chap, unless, of course, you can lay your hands on some of your rough red instead of this death by Aligoté. I am really not feeling too good at all . . . Perhaps a change of grape will do the trick. But on the whole, I think I had perhaps head off home . . . Discretion and valour and all that . . . Stomach . . . Need to get home, Jenny . . . Fast."

Jenny who in truth was feeling rather squiffy herself made her excuses by claiming she ought to follow Tom home to make sure he was alright. When her Clio, Tom having opted to use the Passat, had edged into the lane, Jenny wondered whether she should have gone home with Tom. He always seemed to be able to drive after a serious session. She felt she was aiming rather than steering her car but the challenge of the drive was minimal since she saw not a soul during her five minute journey home.

Back at the Walkers' house, Harry was not very happy. He had worked himself up in anticipation of Tom making sneering comments about his wine and the swift departure of the Foxes had left him high and dry.

"I can just see it. Bloody Fox is so keen on smarming up to the Frenchies, he'll fetch up getting the police interested in us Brits. You heard him! He's already had lunch with that copper. He's so up himself showing off his poxy French, they'll think all his chattering is covering something up. Next thing we know they'll be sniffing around in our affairs."

"And Harry Warry wouldn't want the coppers coming round here, would he?" Peggy mused filling her glass once more.

"No, Peggy Weggy, I fucking wouldn't and if you weren't so ratted neither would you!"

"Calm down, Harry. Have another drink. Relax. There is nothing we do here that we need to worry about."

"Yes. You're right. They'll surely not want to dig around years ago back home, will they?"

Harry Walker would have been even more on edge if he had but known that Commissaire Renard had telephoned Europol headquarters in Lyon that very afternoon while they and the Foxes had been swilling wine. His purpose had been to request through them the cooperation of the police authorities in Britain in discovering whether there was anything in the pasts of the Brits who lived in Saint Val which ought to be of interest to him in his present enquiries. Tom would not have been terribly happy either as his name figured prominently in Renard's list of persons who were 'of interest' to him.

CHAPTER...

6

"O woe, woe, People are born and die. We
also shall be dead pretty soon. Therefore let
us act as if we were dead already."
(Ezra Pound "Mr Housman's Message" 1911)

Quite remarkably, Tom Fox did not feel that he was suffering from a hangover the next morning. He was not so sure about Jenny though. She was still in bed and he was not even convinced that she would drink the cup of tea he had taken up to her. Still less was he persuaded she had registered that he had told her he was popping around to see Monsieur Casson. So he took the precaution of leaving her a note on the kitchen table. As usual the dogs pursued his car as far as the main road but halted there and looked forlorn as he accelerated away up the hill. He just hoped they would go home and not hang around in the road for although no more than a dozen vehicles passed by each day, he was well aware that the dogs had no inkling of road sense and would be quite likely to stand their ground and wag their tails if a car approached. He was not anxious enough however to stop and escort them almost a kilometre back to the house.

When he drew up outside Jean François Casson's ancient farmhouse, the first thing he noticed was that there was a stack of publicity leaflets stuffed in his letter box next to the gate. As Tom knew, 'Le Pub' was always delivered by the postman on Tuesdays and so Casson had not been out to clear the box for twenty four hours at least. The second thing which struck him was that none of the shutters had been opened. Even under normal circumstances, this would have worried Tom because he knew Casson to be an early riser and he was, after all, a very old man. Now, because of

Guyard's murder, just across the valley, it seemed ominous indeed that there was no sign of life. His first impulse was to get back in his car and leave someone else to discover whatever had gone on. Despite his trepidation, however, he found himself looking under the plant pot where Casson always left his keys. They had gone.

What persuaded him to knock at the door was less that this was what he wanted or felt he ought to do than the thought of trying to explain to Jenny or, if it came to it for that matter, to the Police, why he had got as far as the door and had then backed off.

"Jean François! Are you there? It's Tom. Tom Fox. I've come to see if you are alright. Hello! Are you there, Jean François?"

There was no reply and he knocked again. This time, he thought he heard someone moving about inside the house. If he really had heard someone, it need not necessarily be Casson. It could even be the murderer, a thought which almost prompted him to dash back to his car and disappear. What stopped him was Casson's frail voice.

"Yes, I'm here. What do you want?"

"I just want to see that you are alright."

"I'm alright. I just want to be left alone."

"My friend, just open the door will you? I need to see for myself that all is well."

"How do I know that there isn't someone else there besides you? I know you're there because I can recognize your voice. But that doesn't mean there isn't somebody else with you, does it?"

"Look! It's just me here. There's nobody else. Believe me! We're all worried about you."

Tom recalled similar exchanges that had gone on with Jenny's mother across a locked bedroom door in the early stages of her Alzheimer's and he could not help wondering if perhaps the shock of Guyard's murder hadn't driven Jean François over that same edge from which there seemed to be no return. As a last recourse, he decided to try a threat or two.

"I'm very sorry, Jean François, but if I have to go away without seeing for myself that there is nothing wrong with you then I shall just have to come back again and this time I shall bring a policeman with me—and maybe even your Doctor. You don't need me to tell you what she will do if she thinks you are not coping on your own, do you? So, for the last time, open the bloody door, Jean François!"

There was a delay during which Casson must have been thinking his prospects over and then, at last, Tom heard two bolts being drawn back and the key turning in the venerable lock. The door was opened just wide enough for Casson to peer out and ascertain that there was nobody else around. Casson took Tom's sleeve and pulled him into the house. He quickly shut the door and locked it behind them. To Tom's surprise, Casson took him into a hugging embrace.

"Thank you for coming to see me. You mean well. You are a good neighbour."

Tom realized at once that the old man had not gone off his head. He was just very, very frightened and that at least was something that they could talk about whereas, as he recalled all too well, with dementia there was no longer any link between sense and words at all.

"It's very dark in here, Jean François. Don't you want to open the shutters?"

"No. There's enough light for me. It's fine."

"Just open them while I am here. You can always shut them when I go. It's pretty chilly in here you know and it's going to be a lovely day outside. Let some sunlight in."

"You didn't see anyone hanging around out there then?"

"Not a soul. It's as quiet as the . . ." Tom realized in time that it would not be terribly sensitive to say it was 'as quiet as the grave'. "No. There's nobody about. I can be sure of that," he added.

Casson, after what seemed a long period of internal debate, finally said

"I'm not opening them. You can though if you insist but you'll have to shut them again before you leave."

Tom realized that in order to open them, one had first to open the windows inwards and then lean quite a way out to secure the shutters against the wall of the house and this meant exposing oneself for some time to anyone out there. He was catching Casson's fear. There was no-one anywhere near the house unless they were hiding in one of the outbuildings or behind a wall. Tom told himself to pull himself together. Why should there be anybody hiding on the premises?

"So what is it, Jean François? Have you seen someone out there?"

"No. Not yet. They're bound to come though. Ever since Jeannot, the postman, told me about Guyard, I've been waiting for them. When the English women came about the shopping, I thought that was it. Then, last night, it was almost dark, somebody came knocking, claiming to be from the police. Well I know all the local coppers and it wasn't one of them. So I didn't open the door."

"But, Jean François, this is to do with a murder. It's out of the hands of the local station. There are police around but they're from the 'Police Judiciaire' in Auxerre or maybe even from Dijon as far as I know. There is no way you would recognise them. You did answer the policeman's questions at least, I hope."

"Well, I didn't let him in and I didn't say much. I didn't think he was a copper, you see. He asked some pretty stupid things. He wanted to know if I was Jean François Casson. Well it's bloody obvious isn't it? If he was from the police he would have known that, wouldn't he? All he had to do anyway was look on my letter box. My name's on there. Come to think of it, will you take my name off the box when you leave? The postman knows it's mine and why should I let anybody else know this is where I live?"

"What else did he ask you that you didn't want to answer, Jean François?"

"He wanted to know if I knew René Guyard, where I was on Saturday night and Sunday morning, if I'd seen any strangers around. So I told him he was the only stranger who had been here. I think I said I'd heard of Guyard and I couldn't remember where I was over the week-end. He got a bit angry after a while and thumped at the door. It had come on to piss down with rain, you see, and he must have been getting wet through. But I didn't let him in and he went away after a while."

"You know, Jean François, it really was a policeman in all likelihood. There are at least two of them investigating Guyard's murder. The boss is a chap called Renard and he has someone called Duvallon in tow. They'll be back without any doubt and probably this morning if I'm not mistaken. You are just going to have to talk to them. If I were you, I would tell them as much as you can. I mean it's absolutely potty pretending you hardly knew Guyard. Even I know that you knew him very well indeed. You went to school together; you had even been in the Resistance together. They'll be well aware of that. As for claiming you can't remember where you were during the week-end, they just won't accept that. You are just storing up problems for yourself by not cooperating with them."

Casson went into his shell and seemed a long way off. Minutes went by and finally he responded.

"Yes, you're right. Me and Guyard go a long way back but there are things we were involved in that are best left alone. There is no way I can tell the police about all that."

"If you are saying what I think you are, you've got it into your head that whatever you got up to together in the past may have had something to do with his killing and you have managed to persuade yourself that you are in some way in the same sort of danger. That's why you've locked yourself in your house, of course. Am I right, Jean François?"

"It seems pretty obvious to me. We've spent our lives, Guyard and me, waiting for our retribution. Now it's come."

"Don't you think being on your own, not seeing anybody from one day to the next, locked in your house that you could be building things up in your imagination? Reading between the lines, you're probably reckoning it's to do with something that happened when you were in the Resistance together and if that is the case and this is, as you believe, a matter of 'Retribution', then why on earth did it not happen sooner? If I am on the right track you are talking about an event that happened over sixty years ago. Why wait until now? Answer me that!"

"I can't," Casson replied, after another long moment of self absorption. "I know what I know, that's all."

"Look, Jean François whatever it is that seems to be filling you with a sense of guilt, this talk of retribution, whatever it is that you believe is putting you in danger, don't you think that if you brought it out into the open . . ."

"Open, open!" Casson responded angrily. "You don't know what it's like here. You're a stranger. You and all the other Brits, you don't know what it's really like. It's not 'open' here. We don't do it like that. You lot are all trying to lead lives where there are no shadows, no hidden secrets. You're about swimming pools, sun terraces, getting drunk together, talking shallow nonsense. It's just not like that for those who belong here. We know that things don't go away just by bringing them into the open."

Tom was stunned by the vehemence of Casson's outburst and by the dismissive view he held of the expatriates of Saint Val. He had never seen him like this before. He was accustomed to a much more benign person. His first reaction was to argue the case on behalf of his compatriots but as he began to rehearse his riposte, he recognized at once that he agreed to a large degree with what the old man had said. Indeed, he had made more or less the same judgement about the Brits to Jenny on more than one occasion. On one point, however, he disagreed. One of his pet theories was that, in fact, many of his fellow expats did have secrets to hide or at the very least life in England had for some reason become unacceptable and this explained, in part, why they had moved to France in the first place. All the same, he felt he had to continue trying to persuade Casson to unburden whatever was causing him such deep disquiet.

"You're right. Of course, you're right. Just talking about things doesn't make them disappear. But just think about this! You talk about retribution. For this to happen, there has to be an avenger and whoever that person is, he has to be stopped; he has to be caught and put away. If you are right about Guyard's death being somehow connected with what you and he were involved with in the past, you need to tell the police as much as you can about it all. Only then will they have a fighting chance of catching whoever murdered Guyard and who, you believe, might now be after you."

"You make it sound very easy. But suppose the past was just as horrific as what has just happened. What will the police make of that, do you imagine? In any case it's not our way to suck up to the authorities."

"I expect that they will be far, far more interested in clearing up Guyard's death than in something that went on all those years ago. In any case, there is bound to be a statute of limitations in France so even in the most unlikely event of their wanting to pursue you for whatever went on all that time ago, the law simply won't allow it."

"It's not just that. Not just the punishment of the law. Everybody would know what had happened and would be horrified."

"It seems to me you have the choice between your secrets coming out or continuing to exist locked in your house, racked with guilt and fear. I know which I would choose especially since I would be helping to apprehend a murderer—always assuming your guilty secret really is at the root of things. Not that for one moment I go along with your thinking on this."

It seemed to Tom that the old man was pondering hard about this choice and he thought it was perhaps the right moment to make his getaway and to leave him to mull things over alone. When he had repeated to Casson that he wouldn't be surprised if the police were to turn up at his house once more during the course of the morning, he was not just trying to frighten Casson into opening up. He himself was fully convinced of this likelihood now that he knew what sort of reception the old man had given them and he did not particularly wish to be there when they arrived. He did not want them to think that he was poking his nose in, that he was playing the detective, as it were, although that was precisely what he was doing and he was sufficiently free of self-deception to admit this to himself.

He had not taken more than a step or two towards his car than he heard Casson closing his shutters, which Tom, feeling very bad about his negligence, remembered he had been asked to do, and locking and bolting his front door. He did not however forget to remove the bit of card with Casson's name on it from the post box. He had only driven a few hundred meters up the hill when a police car passed him travelling in the opposite direction.

CHAPTER . . .

7

'L'esprit français est de ne pas vouloir de supérieur. L'esprit
anglais est de vouloir des inférieurs.' (de Tocqueville,
'Voyage en Angleterre et en Irlande de 1835')
(Author's translation : "The French attitude
of mind is to wish no-one to be superior. That
of the English is to want inferiors.")

As Tom drew up in front of his house, Jenny was waving the
telephone at him. He heard her say
"Hold on a second please. He's just got back."
Tom scowled and mouthed
"Who the hell is it?"
Jenny shrugged, shook her head and mimed that she did
not know. It was a source of constant annoyance to Tom that
she rarely ever bothered to determine callers' identities and
it was with a grumpy 'Allo, oui' that he took up the call.
Jenny gathered from Tom's end of the conversation that the
caller was ringing him in his capacity as an Estate Agent
and this was enough to drive her tutting back into the house,
leaving him pacing to and fro, as was his wont when he was
on the telephone, in front of the house.
"I do not know why I do this job," said Tom as he came
into the kitchen to put the telephone handset back on its
base.
"Well, you know my feelings about your noble profession,
darling. Why do you do it indeed?"
Rather than launching into their too often rehearsed arguments about his job and the need to earn income, Tom went
through the content of the call to demonstrate to her and, at
the same time, perhaps, explain to himself the irritation with
which it had left him.

"They weren't even ringing from the UK. They are already here and they want to look at places tomorrow. Tomorrow, if you please!"

Tom would usually have had a few days notice of the arrival of potential purchasers and this allowed him to select half a dozen properties which might suit their requirements. More crucially, it gave him time to check whether places were still available and whether the price had changed. As his French vendors didn't often take the trouble to let him know if they had sold through another agent or if they had reduced the asking price of a place which wasn't attracting clients, such checking was important. Otherwise, he would be risking possible embarrassment in front of his potential purchasers. He did not enjoy appearing less than totally efficient and the lack of warning this last minute telephone call gave him meant that he was condemned to spend the rest of the day, and the evening too no doubt, ringing round to the owners of the properties he would be picking out for a visit.

"And that's another thing! They didn't seem to have a fucking clue what they are looking for!"

"Do you prefer old places? Beams, stone walls that sort of thing? Or would you be interested in newer properties?"

"Doesn't matter really."

"How many bedrooms do you need?"

"Dunno . . . Two maybe."

"How much land would suit you?"

"That's not an issue."

"Do you want a place in town, in a village, rural, remote?"

"That depends."

"Depends on what?"

"Whether we like it maybe."

"Right. Do you want somewhere that's ready to move into? A full renovation job? Somewhere that just needs a bit of DIY?"

"We could consider anything, really."

"What about your price range—I'm sorry but I have to ask?"

"Just show us what you've got. We'll let you know about price if and when."

There were only two criteria which Tom gathered were essential and these were that the property had to be in or near to Saint Val and, if at all possible, was being sold by English owners. This second requirement Tom found somewhat bizarre since English vendors would be sure to bump up the asking price at least to its reasonable limits and no doubt beyond. After all, their attitudes had been conditioned by familiarity with the UK property market. On the other hand, it could be the potential purchasers simply felt it would be easier to deal with English speakers.

It seemed to Tom that his best strategy would be to sort out the couple of places in Saint Val he already had on his books and then see what his contacts among the Immobiliers in Avallon had available as well. He shouldn't forget Lemaître either as he often had old houses which were part of the estate of his late clients and which the inheritors wished to dispose of. He thought momentarily of Guyard's house but recognised that it was far too soon to be considering that one. There were still scene of crime tapes sealing off the property and there was no doubt a policeman watching over it. It would also be quite interesting and possibly great fun too to ring round the English inhabitants of the village to see if any of them were thinking of selling up. At the very least, it would make a juicy snippet to share with Jenny especially if he got a bite from one of them. He could always bait the hook with hints of 'money's no object', 'absolutely desperate to buy in Saint Val' or 'you might be surprised how much your place would fetch'. He may as well enjoy himself by satisfying his nosy-parkering tendencies because he was pretty much convinced that people who had so little clue about exactly what they were looking for were almost bound to turn out to be 'time wasters' and he had had plenty of those already. So if it was to be a wasted day then why not have a bit of gentle amusement at his neighbours' expense. Tom had many pet theories and one of them was that people who rang up out of the blue, particularly if they were on holiday and most especially if they were having a wet day or two, would turn out without exception to be 'time wasters'. It would be interesting too to discover whether the murder in the village would put intending purchasers off the area. Still, he would find that out the next morning when he had agreed to meet them in front of the war memorial in the village square. That was a bit odd as well, he reflected, that when he had started to give them directions to the meeting point, he had been cut short by their assertion that they knew their way there. He realised also that he had neglected to discover their names. Come to think of it, he didn't even know what sort of car they were driving not that this would make recognition particularly difficult since the village square was hardly seething with traffic. He hadn't found out where they were staying either so if they did not turn up or if, despite their assurances, they lost their way, he would have no means of getting in contact with them. He hadn't even got their bloody telephone number and when he tried to find it in his list of received calls he discovered that it was withheld. Tom just hoped that they would not let him down.

He was about to start ringing round his English neighbours when Jenny asked him if he had remembered that he had to take her to Montbard early on Saturday morning to catch the TGV which linked up with the London bound Eurostar at Lille.

"It's just that if you're going to get involved with taking people to view houses, please don't make any commitments for Saturday morning."

"I'm taking them around tomorrow which, in case you have lost track of the days, is Thursday."

"I know what day tomorrow is, Tom! You know what you're like though. If you think there's a sale in the offing, you lose all regard for your other commitments. You're quite likely to promise to see them at any old time!"

"You have my solemn promise. Your carriage will await you at 6.20 am prompt. Oh shit!"

"What? What is it? Have you agreed to do something else?"

"No, no! Of course I haven't. It's just that I had totally forgotten that we're having everybody round for a barbecue on Friday night. God knows what time we'll get to bed and we're off to the station at sparrow fart the next morning."

"Well, there's no way we can call it off and anyway it's our turn. You'll be able to catch up on your sleep during Saturday. After all I shan't be here to disturb you, shall I darling?"

"I guess you will be able to have a nap on the train . . ."

Tom was interrupted by the telephone ringing and as he moved to answer it, he thought it might be the callers from earlier who had realised that they had given him no contact details for the next day's appointment. Instead, it was the Mayor of Saint Val who, although she was by no means a remote person, had, to Tom's recollection, never previously contacted him at his home. Their several conversations in the past had mostly happened when he accompanied newly ar-rived Brits to the Mairie to introduce them to her or at other chance meetings. He had run into her the week before at an open forum of the Avallon Tourism Board where he had been invited to deliver a talk on the likely impact of British people settling in the area. He remembered that she had been amused when he pointed out that the British were referred to in their passports as 'subjects' whereas the French were 'citi-zens' and that this revealed much about the two societies. Dominique Bardot, the Maire of Saint Val, was popularly known as "Brigitte" after the voluptuous film star turned an-imal activist who shared her name and there was some irony in the soubriquet since she could not be, and probably never could have been, described as voluptuous. Moreover, as a farmer's wife, her attitude to animals was entirely utilitarian. Indeed, she was known to accompany her husband who was

President of the local hunting association on Sunday morning forays in the forests surrounding Saint Val. Certainly, the two Bardots, Brigitte and Dominique, would not have seen eye to eye on that issue.

She was ringing to ask him if he could spare half an hour to pop up to the Mairie and have a chat with her and Commissaire Renard who was in her office. Tom readily agreed although he was conscious that he needed to get on with preparing for the next day's house visits but it was easy for him to postpone that task as he was more irresistibly drawn to the Mairie by his curiosity and by his weakness, as Jenny saw it, for rubbing shoulders with the 'French Authorities'.

He left Jenny preparing soup for lunch and he undertook to be no longer than forty or fifty minutes.

He was obliged to knock at the door of the Mairie since it was not open to the public on Wednesdays. He was about to knock for a second time when the Mayor opened the door, proffered each cheek for the ritual greeting and led him into the inner office beyond the room to which the public usually had access. There he found Renard who rose and shook him by the hand.

"So we meet again, my dear Monsieur Fox," said the Commissaire inviting him with a gesture to sit next to him as the Maire was settling herself behind her desk.

"I must say it was a wonderful lunch we had yesterday with Charles. It was quite a surprise that he turns out to be your cousin. He has been very kind helping me to set up my business and if ever I need any legal pointers, I know I can call on him. I think very highly of him," Tom responded seeking in part to let the Maire know of his professional contacts.

"He has a good opinion of you too," Renard replied.

"Commissaire Renard came to see me about this terrible Guyard affair and I was glad to be able to confirm that if anybody in the village can tell him about the British who live here then that person is you. I explained that your compatriots do not mix very much with the local population and while I am on nodding terms with them, of course, I can't tell him very much beyond what we hold here in our files. The information we have is more, how can I put it, of a statistical nature—dates of birth, the taxes they pay, planning applications. That sort of thing."

'Brigitte' smiled at Renard to indicate that she was handing over to him and then she smiled at Tom too perhaps seeking to set him at his ease. But before Renard could pick up the baton, Tom, who was suddenly slightly apprehensive at what the Maire had said, intervened.

"I'm sorry. I don't understand. Are you saying that you think a Brit could be involved in this awful murder?"

He was really addressing his question to the policeman but it was 'Brigitte' who responded.

"Monsieur Fox, this is a small commune. There are fewer than one hundred souls in the village itself. So the ten or so Brits who live here form a significant minority. You don't need higher mathematics to tell you that there is a one in ten chance that one of them could be implicated."

"Well, yes, of course, that's true statistically. But, in reality, isn't it far more likely to be a wholly French incident? I just can't see how any of the Brits could be closely connected enough with poor Monsieur Guyard to wish to do him to death."

Tom hoped that he did not appear to be defending his compatriots simply out of jingoism since he genuinely could not imagine any of them being involved.

"You may be quite right of course," Renard took up. "Nevertheless, what Madame le Maire has said is true. Your countrymen represent a small but significant part of the population of Saint Val. Since this is the case, I do not see how I can conceivably leave them out of my investigations and that brings me to the reason why I asked the Maire to invite you to join us here."

Tom shifted on his chair.

"On two fronts," Renard continued, "you could be invaluable to me. Firstly, your command of French is exceptional.

My cousin confirms my initial opinion on that and now Madame le Maire has added her agreement to this view. My English is not bad but it is very rusty and I recognise that I shall not be able to question your countrymen without running the risk of missing an innuendo or even totally misinterpreting some of what they have to say. It would be possible, of course, for me to have an official interpreter attached to the case but he or she would not have the second of your advantages which is that you know your neighbours very well and, as you have heard from Madame le Maire, there is only information of a bureaucratic nature held here in her files. I feel that I need to be given a few pointers about what makes them tick, about how they interrelate, about their private lives so that I shall not be working in a vacuum."

Tom had suspected what Renard was going to say to him and his reaction was typically confused. On the one hand, he did have a penchant for rubbing shoulders with the authorities because it validated his need to feel worthy and to his credit he did recognise this tendency in himself. On the other, he was rather worried what the reaction of his countrymen would be in the face of what they may well consider to be 'grassing'.

"Although I have a large degree of autonomy, I have taken the precaution of running this proposal past my superiors and subject to a number of caveats, they are prepared to go along with the arrangement, at least for a trial period," Renard went on.

"Caveats, you say. Can you explain what these might be?" Tom asked.

"Willingly," Renard responded. "However, I am sure that we have taken up quite enough of Madame le Maire's time and we could run through the rules of engagement, as one might term them, elsewhere."

The Maire felt it necessary to underline her position and intervened.

"Please do not feel as though you have to dash away. I do indeed have other things which need my attention. However, this is a matter which has shocked the whole commune and if you are able in any way, Monsieur Fox, to help Commissaire Renard to a speedy resolution, then I am sure that this will earn the recognition and gratitude of La République Française."

Whether the Maire had just slipped into grandiose-speak from pure habit or whether she had been perspicacious enough to read Tom Fox's psychological map, it did the trick. Tom was hooked.

"Certainly if I can help the commune in any way, I shall be all too happy to do what I can."

"Then, my dear Monsieur Fox, could I suggest that we leave Madame le Maire to her other duties?"

They made their farewells and returned to their cars. Renard perched himself on the wing of his Citroen. Tom did not miss the fact that he was no longer using a marked police car and wondered if this was the usual way of things or whether there was a more clandestine purpose. Perhaps he had wished to keep the meeting at the Mairie secret and this thought only added to Tom's rapidly inflating sense of importance.

"We shall need to go somewhere to talk."

Tom looked at his watch and realised that he had comfortably overrun the estimate he had given to Jenny of the time he would be home.

"My wife is expecting me back for lunch. In fact, I'm rather later than I said I would be. What if I were to give her a ring and see if the soup she was making will stretch to the three of us, Monsieur le Commissaire?"

"Please. In view of the arrangements, I should be glad if you would call me Jean Luc and if you don't mind I will call you Tom. We ought to be more formal though when we are acting in an official capacity interviewing and so on."

"That I understand but please feel free to use my first name whenever you think the circumstances are appropriate."

To explore the extent of their new found bonding, Tom had tried out addressing him as 'tu' rather than 'vous' always a delicate and somewhat mysterious step for a Brit, even one with such good French as Tom and to his relief Jean Luc responded in like coinage.

"You were going to ring your wife?"

As it turned out, Jenny was unexpectedly calm at the prospect of Renard joining them for lunch.

CHAPTER . . .

8

' Il est plus honteux de se défier de ses
amis que d'en être trompé.'
(de la Rochefoucauld « Maximes » 1678)
(Author's translation : "It is more shameful not to
trust one's friends than to be deceived by them")

"If I had known that Tom was bringing you back for lunch, I would have made something a bit more special."

"Pas du tout! Not at all, Madame! Because I am away from my home base, I am obliged to go to a restaurant for my every meal. I cannot tell you how much I am looking forward to this opportunity to taste good home cooking for a change. This is exactly what I needed."

'This' was one of Jenny's wonderful soups decocted from the carcase of Sunday's chicken and flavoured with onions, potatoes and celery. After the soup, there would be cheese, including the last of the Cheddar that Nigel Barnes had brought them back from his last trip to England. Then there would be a scoop of home-made ginger ice cream to round off the meal.

Jenny observed the dark tufts of hair which protruded above Renard's unbuttoned collar. She thought the backs of his hands verged on the furry. It seemed to her as though the hirsuteness of his body was compensating for his receding hairline and she found herself wondering how simian he would look when naked.

"No doubt, your husband has told you about our lunch with my cousin yesterday. I can assure you, Madame, that if I had to suffer such excesses every day, I should not be long for this life."

"Wonderful as it was, the wine just about did for me," Tom added.

"I am afraid that my cousin Charles rather tends to show off both with the quality and the quantity of the wine he orders. Still I'm not complaining."

"Nor me," Tom agreed. "Are you absolutely sure that you are happy with just water to drink, Jean Luc?"

He had wondered if the reference to his cousin's wine ordering tendencies was not, in fact, a gentle suggestion that they should be having wine with their lunch. Unlike his English friends who would come straight out with a robust 'Don't be so bloody mean! Get some wine on the table!' it would be more in character, in Tom's experience, for a French person to be much more oblique in their request. In fact, this was a question which Tom had not been able to resolve in his love affair with all things French. How could they be so delicate, so careful not to offend in certain social circumstances and yet be, quite frankly, so downright rude in others? They displayed such refined courtesy when they were at one's house or when one was at theirs. Yet, if you came across them in the supermarket, it was as though you did not exist. They would happily stop to chat to acquaintances thus blocking the aisle with their two trolleys and when you indicated that you would like to get past, they would simply look at you and then turn back to their conversation, totally ignoring your presence. God help you if you dithered in the queue at the tills. Quicker than a rat up a drain pipe, they would scuttle in ahead of you. And the standard of their driving, a perilous mix of an apparently totally insouciant inability to concentrate on the task at hand and an instinctive imperative to overtake preferably in the most dangerous places, rendered Tom speechless with rage. He dragged his mind back to the question of what they were drinking and to spare Jean Luc the embarrassment of requesting wine, he added

"I think I could fancy a glass of Chablis. Not too heavy. What do you say Jean Luc?"

"Tiens, pourquoi pas! If you are sure you are having a glass then I shall be happy to accompany you—but only if Madame will be joining us."

"I'm sure she will," said Tom, thinking privately that he would not dare to try to stop her.

"I would love to," said Jenny, thinking privately that she would like to see them try to exclude her.

When the wine was poured and Jean Luc had gone through the formality of complimenting them on its quality, the policeman addressed himself to Jenny but at the same time he was taking the opportunity of spelling out to Tom just how he saw their cooperative efforts working.

"It seemed to me that I would need someone to help me out when I talk to your English neighbours. As I mentioned to your husband, I rather fear that the depth of my knowledge of your language is insufficient to allow me to be sure that I will absorb everything that is said. He made it clear from his initial reaction that he believes that the crime which has brought me to your charming village has nothing to do with your compatriots. It will probably emerge that he is correct. However, I am obliged, as you will understand, I am sure, to speak to everybody especially as at this stage of our enquiries, I have not been able to form any idea of who the murderer or murderers might be nor indeed why the crime was committed. Of course we know the where and the how of the killing. What I am saying is that just because I shall need to interrogate your friends, does not mean that I am trying to find a way of implicating them or still less of seeking to pass the guilt on to them. I should welcome help from both of you in preventing any feelings of victimisation taking root amongst them. It could be that as members of a minority group here some of them may feel they are being got at. That is not the case. If I appear to be giving them undue attention, they should be made aware that my number two, Captain Duvallon, along with other officers, is assiduously working his way through your French neighbours. Now what I am asking Tom to do is primarily to act as an interpreter. I have to admit that I am hopeful a secondary advantage of having him with me will be to put your friends at their ease. The other aspect of his involvement you may find a little delicate perhaps. The Maire feels that the English community is somewhat isolated and that you keep to yourselves. I need to ask you to tell me as much as you can about them. Whatever you feel able to divulge to me will remain our secret. That I can solemnly promise. By the same token, I have to insist that anything that Tom learns during this process must remain totally confidential. In fact that is the main caveat which I referred to earlier, Tom."

"What do you think about all this, Tom?" Jenny asked, giving herself the chance to take in what Renard had imparted.

"Well, above all, I think we have a duty to help as much as we can. That is part of living here."

"What worries me and I don't mind admitting it in front of you, Commissaire, is how our friends are going to take it. If they get it into their heads that Tom is somehow on the side of authority and against them, can you imagine how we could be ostracised. For me, Tom, our having a circle of friends is as you say 'part of living here' and a very important part it is too," was Jenny's rejoinder.

"Madame Fox, I understand what you are saying and I feel I have to remind you that a murder has taken place. Perhaps Guyard was old. Perhaps his life was coming to its close anyway. Perhaps he was only an old Frenchman but despite that I would hope that you could think of him as a friend. At the very least, he was your neighbour. The nature of the murder was horrifying. In total confidence, I have to tell you that the poor soul was tortured and that his death was long drawn out. There is someone vicious out there and that someone has to be arrested and quickly too. I shall do everything necessary to make sure that he is caught and, for me, that would include, if necessary, being disloyal to my friends and running the risk of losing that friendship. You see I wouldn't value any friendship which could not tolerate the actions I am asking of you."

The slight strabismus which afflicted Renard became more noticeable and added intensity to his gaze when he became animated.

They were both startled by the passion with which these words were delivered. In their previous conversations, Tom had only witnessed what he would have described as an almost languid urbanity in Renard. Perhaps they were now seeing a sign of what really drove him in his work and it was powerful enough, at least as far as Tom was concerned, to erase any worries about what their friends might think. In fact, their concerns seemed rather petty in the context of what had happened to Guyard, a man, after all, from whom they had bought their house and who had joined them in a glass of Champagne when they named the place "Les Chênes". He figured significantly in the events and memories of their time here. Renard was right. Guyard had been almost as much a friend and neighbour as the English who lived in Saint Val.

Tom had not missed the implication in what Renard had just said that they had been hesitant in going along with him in part because Guyard was French and, by inference therefore, that being French made a person less important than if he were English. It was not unreasonable that he should have made such a suggestion in the light of Jenny's reaction to his invitation. It was one, however, that was in disaccord with all that Tom liked to think he stood for. He wished to be at one with the French community.

"Jean Luc," said Tom "we are just voicing our worries. It would be particularly difficult for Jenny if she were suddenly to lose her circle of friends. She would become isolated. It is not because she has anything against our French neighbours. It is all about language skills. She finds it easier to converse in English and that's all there is to it. That's the only reason her friends are English and not French—for the most part anyway."

"It really doesn't matter what I say, Commissaire," Jenny continued. "If I know Tom there will be no stopping him now. But if it is any help I can assure you that I shall be fully behind him. I fully agree with you that it is a citizen's first duty to help to catch this murderer."

"I am most grateful to you both," Renard replied, returning to his urbane mode. "I shall be at pains to explain to your English that Tom has been enlisted purely to help me understand them. I shall also explain that you, Madame Fox, are not in any way involved with the enquiries and that you will not be party to whatever we discuss with them."

Jenny was not entirely thrilled at the prospect of not being privy to what emerged from the interviews. For his part, Renard had seen enough of her to be quite sure that she would extract from her husband whatever she wished to know. He had accepted when he first thought of recruiting Tom Fox that there could be problems surrounding confidentiality but that, on the whole, the advantages of having him on board probably outweighed such considerations. In any case, he had formed the impression that the couple might just about exercise sufficient discretion outside the marital home to justify the professional risk he was taking.

Jenny gave the men a cup of coffee.

"I ought to tell you that before I put this request to you to give me a helping hand, I had to ascertain that there was nothing reproachable in your background. So I apologise for having had to use the good offices of Europol to contact the police authorities in England and make enquiries about you. I am glad to say that you both came up with a clean bill of health which was, of course, not surprising to me. But nevertheless I am sorry that it was necessary to do this and I hope you will understand. Of course, in due course I shall be making similar enquiries about your compatriots who live here but I needed to get you cleared as a matter of urgency so that we can get on with the investigations."

"I came on here from Monsieur Casson's place," Renard continued as he liberally sweetened his coffee as the French are wont to do. "When I finally managed to get him to the door, I gather that you beat me to it and you went to see him before I got there. I thought it was your car I passed near his house."

Tom explained the arrangement for taking the old man to the shops each week and how Jenny had been worried by his behaviour when she had called to collect him.

"So, I—or rather 'we' I should say—thought it would be a good idea for me to pop round to check up on him and I'm glad I did. The old boy was petrified. He seems to have got to know the grisly details of the murder from the postman on Monday morning. For some reason he seems to think he is on the death list. I don't know exactly why he has come to that conclusion but from what he said it could have something to do with the time he and Guyard were in the Resistance together. I didn't get any details from him though. At least I was able to tell him to expect a visit from you and I tried to persuade him to be cooperative."

"I am grateful for that. I am not at all sure that he would even have answered the door if you hadn't softened him up first, so to speak. I'm very interested in what you are saying about their being in the Resistance together, him and Guyard. It's not something that came up when I was talking to him. Of course I don't know the old chap—well not yet anyway. I just wasn't able to decide whether his being so scared was his usual state of mind or whether this was something out of the usual. Now I think back to my conversation with him, I believe I may simply have assumed that he was suffering from some senile anxiety syndrome and that this had been aggravated into a state of terror by the news of the murder of a chap who was possibly his last remaining contemporary."

"Please don't take my word for it that the Resistance is in any way relevant. It could be that it's just that we English are fascinated by all of that."

"I won't take your word for it but it may be worth my while getting the Maire to point me in the direction of any local historians or any relevant archives she knows of."

"Forgive me for asking, Jean Luc, but when you came around here the first time with Capitaine Duvallon, you were asking whether we had come across any papers in English among the debris we had to clear out. We found that intriguing, didn't we Jenny? I don't suppose you could tell us why you asked us that, could you?"

"Well, yes, why not? I don't see the harm. Not now that you are part of the team so to speak. In any case, it will be a question I shall be putting to the other English as we do our rounds. When I first arrived at Guyard's place after the body was discovered, I didn't much fancy having more than a cursory look round. It may be that I am a bit too sensitive. But it was rather horrific I must say. Be that as it may, I don't think I have ever felt able in any of my investigations to make a proper search until the body has been removed. It has always seemed to me to be a bit intrusive to search through people's things when they are still there even though they are dead. For me, they have to be not only dead and gone but dead and gone away if you see what I mean."

Renard did not consider that it was appropriate to confess to them that he had found it nigh on impossible to remain in the same room as the mutilated remains that he had been presented with. The image of the butchered corpse, which in truth had not left him and which perhaps never would, returned to him so forcefully that he had to pause before continuing his explanation.

"Where was I? Oh yes. Then we did a deep search. The contents of all the drawers and of a suitcase which I guess must have usually been kept under the bed had been emptied out on to the floor. It seemed pretty obvious to me that whoever had killed Guyard was looking for something and it is more than likely that they found what they were after, of course. But we did come across something that seemed rather odd because of where we found it and it seemed out of place in a house belonging to an old French guy like Guyard bearing in mind what it consisted of."

Renard paused again and long enough for the Foxes both to wonder if he was going to leave them on the hook of half revealed information. To offer him encouragement, Jenny leaned forward on her elbows and stared steadily across the table at him. At length, he continued:

"You've been to Guyard's place, I suppose?"

"Yes, we've called in on him several times."

"Then you will remember the grandfather clock. The door of it was wide open so the murderer obviously looked inside it but didn't feel behind the clock. We found a plastic bag hanging from a hook which must have been screwed into the back of the casement especially for the purpose. Inside the bag was a collection of papers and what looked like newspaper clippings. As far as we could tell, they were all in English. We haven't been able to have a proper plough through them as yet because they are still with the technical boys for finger print tests and all the other whatnots they do these days. You can understand why I am curious about our find, can't you? He must have gone to some trouble to create that hiding place. Those huge old clocks weigh a ton and the chances are that he shifted it on his own so he could fix the hook in the back. That says to me that the contents of that bag were certainly important to him."

"Stuff in English? How very odd. And you were wondering if he had left similar items here!" Jenny added.

"Exactly so," Renard confirmed.

"Jenny, I've just had a thought. Do you remember our having that conversation about whether old Guyard had any knowledge of English?"

"Vaguely, I suppose. I don't remember why we should ever have imagined that he had more than just French though."

"It runs in my mind that Tony and Mandy arrived here once when Monsieur Guyard had come to call. I remember that he hung around quite a while, not saying anything, just listening. When he finally left, I think it was Mandy who said that he gave her the creeps and that she wouldn't be surprised if he could follow a lot more of what we were saying than we imagined. At the time I suppose I just thought it was Mandy being Mandy. Now, well, it's a thought, isn't it?"

"It is certainly something we can mention when we are talking to—what did you call them?" Renard asked, preparing to jot himself a reminder.

"Mandy. Tony and Mandy Parsons," Jenny volunteered. "They live at "Les Effraies" just behind the hill from here."

"We ought to agree when we can start to do the rounds of your English friends, Tom. I suppose we could begin with these Parsons?" Renard enquired.

"It's a bit of a nuisance really because I guess you would like to get on with things," Tom answered. "The drag is that I've had a call from some English people wanting to look at houses and they are going to be here tomorrow. That means I am going to have to make all the arrangements during the rest of today. I can't promise to be free tomorrow even later on either. You can just never predict how long the visits will take. I'm sorry, Jean Luc, I can't cancel because I don't know how to contact them. In any case, as you will understand, that's the way I make my money. I could set Friday aside though."

"Friday is not good for me. I already have a number of appointments set up and I shan't be sure to be through with them much before four. If you are not free tomorrow then no matter because I have plenty of things I need to do."

"Could I make a suggestion, gentlemen?" Jenny asked. "We are having a barbecue on Friday evening and all the English who live in Saint Val are coming. At least, we haven't had any cancellations so far. Why don't you join us, Commissaire? It will give you a chance to meet them all informally if that seems appropriate to you."

"That is very kind of you and it's a suggestion that I will think seriously about. Could I possibly let you know tomorrow?"

"Of course, Commissaire."

"We should tell you, I suppose, that Jenny is off to England for a few days at first light on Saturday morning. There's a new addition to the family. A granddaughter. That will mean that I can make myself available for the whole of the weekend if you want to start calling on the English then," Tom added. "But I do hope that you can be with us on Friday evening. You shouldn't miss a chance to observe the English at play."

"I will do my very best to be there. As I say, I will let you know tomorrow if that is alright with you both. At the same time, I can inform you whether it will be in order for Madame to leave the village, never mind the country, on Saturday."

Renard was gratified to see their sudden look of panic and prolonged their bewilderment for a few moments before bursting out laughing and saying

"It's just my little joke. Please forgive me."

Nevertheless, his 'little joke' had chilled them both to the core as, for the first time, they came face to face with the real power that he wielded and this was precisely the effect that Renard had wanted his 'little joke' to have.

CHAPTER...

9

*"Ask about your neighbours, then buy
the house." (Jewish Proverb)*

As a result of speaking to Lemaître and phoning round his neighbours, Tom had managed to assemble four properties to show to his prospective clients.

He had been particularly surprised, when trawling around his English friends, to discover that only one of the four couples had shown no interest whatsoever in selling. It had brought it home to him how transitory in reality was the social milieu in which one lived however permanent one assumed it to be. Mandy Parsons had been adamant that any thought of moving house was totally out of the question and had added, rather oddly to Tom's thinking, that they did not have any choice in the matter. Harry and Peggy Walker had indicated that while they were not in the market at the moment, they would not rule out selling up in a year or two. That left him with Nigel Barnes' rather splendid house which he had recently christened "Aux Abeilles" and Steve and Cheryl Brown's less grand but certainly habitable cottage. These along with a renovated longère which Tom already had on his books and the farmhouse he had picked from his notaire friend represented an acceptable portfolio of properties to show to his customers.

He had made an early start so that he could collect a bunch of keys from Lemaître in Avallon, discover the location of that property and still be back in the square in Saint Val in time for his appointment with his prospective buyers. A cursory look at the farmhouse from his car had done nothing to persuade him that it was anything other than a serious renovation project which was, in truth, exactly what Lemaître had said. Still, his clients had not given him any criteria to follow and they may well be looking for a cheap place to do up. At least, he felt, he had a range of properties to show to them and in any case he remained half convinced that they were not serious buyers. As he waited in the village square, he was even beginning to wonder if they would turn up at all as by his reckoning they were already fifteen minutes late.

He decided to get out of his car and smoke a cigarette. Another of Tom's pet theories was that when he lit up, it caused events to happen. Before the smoking ban it used to work unfailingly in restaurants when he felt he had been waiting too long for the next course to arrive. He would light a cigarette and lo and behold, almost before the first inhalation, the plate was being placed before him. It did not have such an absolutely immediate result on this occasion and Tom had almost finished the cigarette before a black Laguna drove slowly into the square. He wasn't exactly sure that this was the right car as he had been expecting an English vehicle and this one had French plates. The registration number was from another department though so it may well be a hired car and this was enough to encourage Tom to smile and give a restrained wave. In response the couple got out of the car and moved towards him. Tom noted that the man was smoking a cheroot which would give him licence to finish his cigarette rather than extinguish it.

The very first glance told Tom that these were not run of the mill customers. To start with he could not recall having had a chap with almost identical rings in both of his ear lobes. But what struck him most were the ornate tattoos which he wore on his forearms. He thought they might represent dragons but he was not quite sure as what would be the head part of the beast was concealed under the sleeve of his white T-shirt. His macho look extended to jeans and sturdy light brown boots. The woman whilst not unattractive had something rodent like about her. Tom decided that it was not so much her features which gave him this impression. It was more the mannerism she had of frequently wrinkling her nose as though she were testing the air and when she moved she seemed to be darting. This clearly differentiated her from her partner who moved stolidly. He was huge with hair worn in a pony tail whilst she was petite and wore her hair in a fashionably short cut. When he was describing them later to Jenny, they would be a bear and a weasel.

With some difficulty Tom averted his gaze from his fore-arms and her mobile nose and looked them in the eye as he introduced himself.

"Good morning, I'm Tom Fox. We spoke on the telephone yesterday I believe."

"That's right," the woman replied. "This is Ted and I'm called Wendy."

'Teddy Bear' and 'Wendy the Weasel' was Tom's imme-diate reaction. What with him being called 'Fox', between them they were on their way to populating the wild wood. He thought that it would not be a good move to share this thought with the pair. They had only just met and he had learned that people did not always share his sense of humour. In any case, it may have been something in their eyes or sim-ply the man's earrings, tattoos and boots that persuaded Tom that these were a pair to be wary of.

"What you got for us then?" the weasel continued.

"I've got four places to show you. I could show you a lot more if you are prepared to look beyond Saint Val. I've got some interesting propositions not too far away . . ."

"No. It's got to be here, hasn't it Ted?"

"Yeah," the bear replied.

"Is there any particular reason why you're interested in Saint Val?"

"No. Not really," Wendy responded with a sideways glance at Ted.

"How did you come to hear about the village if you don't mind me asking?"

"From a mate, wasn't it Ted?"

"Yeah," Ted confirmed.

"I wonder if I might know your friend in that case . . ."

"Doubt it," was Wendy's reply, curt enough to clearly indi-cate that this avenue would not be explored any further.

Tom explained that they could either all travel in his car or if they preferred they could follow him in their own vehicle.

"We'll follow you."

"If you're sure . . . Some people like to be able to take in the scenery and prefer to be driven."

"No. Like I said we'll follow you. We got our gear and stuff in the motor."

Tom was about to explain that there was almost no crime around this area and to boast that most folks didn't even bother to lock their cars. The fact of the murder caused him to pause however. One certainly couldn't claim Saint Val was crime free any longer. He wondered at what point he should tell his clients about the murder or whether indeed he should tell them at all. Tom decided to take the scenic route to his first property which was the longère he had on his books already. In that way, he hoped the beauty of the countryside would distract them from the house itself. The owners had rendered what was once a traditional granite long house thoroughly and unsympathetically into an unappealing modern looking bungalow. 'Rendered' was the appropriate word since every square centimetre of stone had been covered over. The owners were mystified that their 'lovely' house had not sold during the two years it had been on the market and Tom did not have the heart to explain the problem. As they drew up in front of the property, he determined to concentrate on the advantages of acquiring a place that was ready to move into. He would also talk up the beautiful views from the back garden. That had ever been his routine with this property. It had never worked.

"I'll just go ahead and open up," said Tom. "I'll need to open the shutters because the owners have had the electricity disconnected. Otherwise, we'll be stumbling around in the dark."

He left them in the front garden and saw with a glimmer of optimism that they seemed to be appreciating the fine view.

"Lovely view, isn't it? It's even better from the back garden. That lime tree doesn't block out the valley so much from there," Tom called out from the front door.

When he had opened the shutters they joined him in the house. They made the tour of the interior and Tom's commentary on its various qualities elicited no response from the pair. At length, they found themselves in the back garden which was becoming rather overgrown.

"Well, there you are. What do you think? As far as I am concerned, there's no major work needed. It has a great location. I don't think it's overpriced either. They are asking one ninety thousand euros but between you and me they'll probably accept twenty or even twenty five thousand less than that. What do you think?"

"Who owns it then?"

"An elderly French couple who wanted to move to Auxerre to be nearer to their children."

"We need to see the others. We'll tell you then," Wendy replied and the pair made their way back to their car.

Their visit to the dilapidated farmhouse Lemaître had passed on to Tom was even briefer and afterwards, Tom could only recall one remark which, for a change, had come from Ted.

"Christ! It's a shit heap. If they want to sell why don't they clear the mess up."

It did not seem that they would be buying this property and, because he was not at all sure how serious either Nigel Barnes or, in her husband's absence, Cheryl Brown was likely to be, he was beginning to feel that his misgivings of the previous day had been well founded. He could well end up having wasted the whole day.

He determined to press on, however, mainly because having made the arrangements he did not want his neighbours to think that he was letting them down. He led them first to "Aux Abeilles", the house owned by Nigel Barnes and which he shared with his partner, Tim Foulkes.

The pair met them at the front door and Tom made the introductions.

"Please do come in, my dears," said Nigel with a theatrical bow and a grand sweep of his arm.

Tom guessed at once that Nigel was in his highly animated mode and this was confirmed when he glanced at Tim by the latter raising his eyebrows. Tom was not at all sure which of Nigel's moods he could most abide. He most definitely found him very difficult when he was in what he himself termed his 'blubbing and hymn singing' bouts of depression. He supposed that he enjoyed most his wickedly acerbic persona which he often revealed at social gatherings especially when the wine was flowing but that was because Tom was never the victim of his acid witticisms. For some reason, Nigel reserved his barbs for his other neighbours. He could put up with his present manifestation as much as any of the others he displayed since, however outrageous Nigel could be, Tom found his behaviour amused him at least some of the time. He was aware, however, that Tim found this mood hard to bear since it expressed itself in exaggerated effeminacy and, no matter how inappropriate the circumstance, in flirtatiousness.

They went into the spacious living room which as ever looked as though it had been set up for a 'Home and Gardens' photo shoot. There were fresh flowers everywhere. Tom did not imagine that Ted and Wendy would be sensitive to the attractions of the room and was surprised to hear the latter exclaim:

"Now that is what I call a lounge. It's just huge. You got to have space I always say. And all them lovely pictures on the walls. It's great. Innit, Ted?"

"Yeah," Ted responded.

"How very sweet of you. I simply adore my paintings I have to confess though I say it myself. I just couldn't survive without flowers and there would be no point in living if one couldn't surround oneself with 'all that is most beauteous' as Wordsworth wrote," Nigel twittered.

"To be honest," Tom intervened, "if it is all the same to you, Nigel, it would be better if you showed our friends around the house rather than me. After all you know much more about it than I do."

"Wild horses couldn't stop me, Tom. It's been ages since I showed a stranger round my bedroom—and as for a man with tattoos . . ."

This was more than enough for Tim who headed out into the garden with a muttered 'Christ' of exasperation.

"So you just trot outside as well, Tom. Knowing you, you're just gasping for a faggy-poo anyway. Come along, my loves, we'll start upstairs, shall we?"

Tom watched them climb the superb oak staircase and noted that Nigel had laid a soft hand gently on the tattooed arm of the male house hunter. As he made his way to the door, he heard Nigel declare:

"I've always had a soft spot for Estuarines—and when they come with tattoos, there's no holding me. The times I've had in Chelmsford! I've still got the love bites to prove it."

Tom paused on the front terrace to light his cigarette, wondering seriously if Nigel wasn't in danger of being smacked about by Ted who, in his judgement, was not the type to mess with. He crossed over to the already immaculate flower bed where Tim was on his knees removing scarcely emerged weeds.

"Christ, Tom. I just can't stand it when he's like this. He thinks it makes me jealous, you know."

"Well, I don't know, not really," Tom replied lamely.

"It's bad enough when he takes the piss out of me, thinking he's being funny. But all this queening it up is just too much to take. I should just push off out of here."

"You're not being serious, Tim. Anyway, you know Nigel. He takes the piss out of everybody. This Mae West business is just an act. These are the ways he tries to be funny. Underneath it all, he's a very likeable man or at least I find him so," Tom said loyally.

"Well he is not bloody funny. Not any more he isn't. I'm not kidding. Don't be surprised if I get out."

Tom, recognising that he had fallen from the frying pan of Nigel's diva dramatics into the fire of Tim's exasperated rancour, decided to beat a retreat across the lawn and finish his cigarette in peace taking in the view over the valley. There in the distance, he could make out Guyard's farmhouse. He hadn't realised that you could see it from here. It was probably his imagination but the house looked so very sad and abandoned.

It was not very long before Nigel appeared around the corner of his home. They must have exited through the back door to look over the grounds which like the interior of the property itself were impeccably maintained. As they approached, Tim strode off into the house.

When finally Tom was able to prise his clients away, Nigel's parting remark was to the effect that he would give him a ring during the evening or next morning. Tom hoped that Tim was not watching from the window because he would have been appalled to see Nigel blowing kisses in the direction of the departing cars.

By the time they reached the Browns' house, it was lunchtime, but Tom determined not to take a break to eat as was his normal routine when he was showing customers around. He really didn't think it would be useful spending the time that lunching together would afford as nothing had happened to convince him that Ted and Wendy were serious buyers. Besides, he really didn't think he would enjoy their company.

Tom found the gates locked and was obliged to ring the bell. They didn't usually lock up like this but Tom was aware that Steve Brown didn't commute back from London until Thursday evening and as the two boys were at school, Cheryl would be alone. Even so it was no doubt Guyard's death which had brought about this unusual concern for security.

Tom was about to ring a second time when Cheryl shouted

"Hang on. I'll just get the key. I won't be a minute."

After Tom's cheek had been pecked and the strangers' hands shaken, Cheryl launched into an extended apology for the state of the house which she confessed was neither tidy nor by any means fully renovated although she added breathlessly that most things had been done and just needed finishing off. As Tom recalled she was speaking the truth although it was not good business sense to kick off by drawing attention to the imperfections. But at least her apologia convinced Tom that she really was keen on selling.

The state of the garden contrasted with the perfection they had just seen chez Nigel. Cheryl and Steve's two boys with their endless football had done a thorough demolition job on what had, in truth, never been much of a grassed area and the parents had clearly given up on the flower beds which were being rapidly trampled into a mere extension of the bare earth that had once passed for their lawn. Tom felt as though he had leapt directly from Kew to the sort of council estate where he had spent his early years.

He and Cheryl showed the visitors around the house, she preceding them, scooping up discarded items of clothing and apologising for each imperfection in the renovation work of which there were more than a few. The plasterboard behind the bath had not been covered with tiles yet, although there were boxes of them already stacked in the bathroom. It looked as though regular and thorough soaking would mean that the work would have to be started again from scratch. Decoration of the bedrooms seemed to have been begun and then abandoned in mid wall. Tom, to his shame, heard himself, just like a real Estate Agent, banging on about the opportunities offered by a blank canvas and that the basic work had all been done. Even he, however, was pretty sure that the basics themselves had been carried out in a less than professional manner. He could understand that Steve was away from Monday to late Thursday. He could accept that Cheryl was worn out by the two boys and then by running around after her husband all week-end. What he could not comprehend was why they didn't get some outside builders in. After all Steve must be earning a fair income or why else trek back and forth to London each week. Failing that, Tom asked himself with growing indignation, why didn't Steve get up off his backside when he was there at week-end. In passing, he wondered why Tim did not seem to be coming over to the house any longer to get the garden in shape. Perhaps he had felt obliged to give up his attempts, beaten by the trampling of Cheryl's two sons.

After they had seen the house and he had elected not to show them around the grounds, Tom asked the clients if they had any questions they would like to put to the owner since they had been remarkably taciturn thus far.

"Yeah," Wendy began,"Where you from back in England, then, if you don't mind me asking?"

"Well," Cheryl replied, "I'm from Exeter originally. Alphington to be more precise. Steve's from Worthing. Our last house before we came over here though was in West London. We just had to get out though."

"Oh really. Why was that then? Why did you have to get out?"

"We just felt we couldn't breathe. It was no place to bring up the boys either. We took one look at the school they would have been going on to and that did it."

"Tom here was telling us your old man goes back to London to work every week. What's he do then?"

Tom felt he should intervene.

"What I actually meant Wendy was have you any questions about the property."

"Right then. No. I don't think I have really. We was just curious about what her husband does in London. That's all."

"He's sales manager for a packaging company. There's no harm in telling them that, Tom."

"Fair enough, Cheryl." Tom then addressed himself to his clients. "You don't want to know the price of this place? Or of Nigel's house? Usually it's the first thing people want to know."

"Yeah, well, we're not like that. If we like the look of a place, the price can always get sorted out later, can't it?"

"Well, if you are sure there is nothing you want to ask about the house then I think we ought to leave Mrs Brown to get on. I know Thursdays are busy for her. She has the boys to collect and then she has to pick up her husband from the station in Montbard."

Tom thanked Cheryl, promising to give her some feedback and led the two out to the cars.

"I'm sorry if Nigel was a bit over the top this morning. He can be like that from time to time."

"No problem," Wendy replied. "Ted's cousin is a bit like that. He's a poofter as well, ain't he Ted?"

"Yeah," Ted smiled.

"Shall I run through the properties with you? Shall we see where we are at? Have you any more questions, for example?"

"Yeah. There is one thing. We know there's you. We know there's that Cheryl and her old man. We've seen Nigella and his boy friend. What I want to know is what other Brits live here in this village?"

Although Tom thought this was a little adjacent, he guessed that people might want to know about their potential neighbours before they decided to buy and so he felt obliged to respond.

"There are just two other couples. The Walkers and the Parsons."

"How old are they then? Where are they from back home?"

"Well let me see. Harry Walker would be about my age and his wife Peggy is a year or two younger than him perhaps. The Parsons are a bit younger. Round about forty, I would say."

"Right. So these lot, Parsons did you call them? Where are they from then?"

"To tell you the truth, I'm not exactly sure," Tom answered although he could remember from the details on the deeds of their house, the sale of which he had handled, precisely where they were from.

"All I can tell you," he continued, "is that from their accents, I should say they are from the London area."

"That's useful to know, aint it, Ted?"

"Yeah," said Ted.

"Now, how would you like to proceed from here, Wendy? Do you want to sit down and go through some figures? I can give you the legal costs and all that sort of thing."

"No. To be fair, I think me and Ted have got a bit of thinking to do. What about if we sleep on all this and get in touch with you in the morning?"

"Why don't I give you a ring? It might be easier that way?' Tom asked thinking that contact would at least be made if he arranged to call them rather than the other way round.

"Er, I'm not sure. It's just that my mobile's out of battery."

"I could give you a call at your hotel."

"That's a bit of a pain for you really."

"No problem! It is what I get paid for after all. Where are you staying?"

"Let me think. Same as last night, I suppose. Where was it? Camomile or something."

"Do you mean the Campanile? Just outside Avallon?"

"Yeah! That's it."

"OK, then" Tom said, eager now to see the back of the pair, "I'll give you a call at ten o'clock in the morning. Will that suit you?"

Tom watched them drive off towards the centre of the village and he suddenly felt in need of food. He had gone well past his usual lunch time but at least he had avoided having to take them to a restaurant. He promised himself a runny omelette with herbs fresh from the garden and, why the hell not, a glass or two of Côtes du Rhône Villages to flush it down. When he got home he found that Jenny had left him a note on the kitchen table. She informed him that she had gone to the supermarket to make a start on the shopping for Friday night and to buy her wine for the trip to England. From past experience, Tom reckoned that she spent as much on the wine she took with her as on the cross channel ferry ticket itself. Her counter argument was that it was her way of recompensing the friends who put her up since she could not overnight with her daughter whose flat was too small. There was a scribbled addendum to the foot of the note to the effect that Renard had rung to say that he would be glad to join them at their Friday soirée and to ask whether it would be in order to bring along his assistant, Duvallon.

This news went some way to relieving Tom's disgruntlement at having, in all likelihood, wasted the day so far on the strange pair of Brits. He found himself looking forward to presenting his new found French friend and colleague to the assembled Brits. It would be fun watching their reactions both to Renard, a senior French policeman, and to himself as his newly appointed English aide. He was aware of just how uneasy his wife, Jenny, was at the way Friday evening was going to work out and, in the longer term, how their relations with their British neighbours would be affected. He was getting used to the idea of becoming Renard's helper and was growing more confident that their neighbours would be understanding about the necessity of his new role.

CHAPTER . . .

10

"There never was a merry world since the fairies
left off dancing, and the Parson left conjuring"
(John Selden "Table Talk" 1689)

Unusually for him, Tom did not wake up until almost nine
o'clock. He remembered that he had said that he would contact his visitors of the previous day at ten and, hearing that
Jenny was in the shower, he decided to hasten his morning
into life by using the downstairs bathroom. As this was situated next to the kitchen, he decided to make himself a coffee
and take Jenny a cup of tea first. He brought down an arm-
ful of clothes from the bedroom, gulped his coffee and had
made himself presentable all in less than fifteen minutes. He
would not fail to point this out to Jenny who inevitably adopted a languorous approach to her toilette.

After a second cup of coffee which he drank less hur-
riedly than the first, he made for the telephone. Next to it he
located Renard's visiting card and called his mobile number.
One of Tom's habits was to count along inwardly to whatever
he was doing. He knew it took him one hundred and twenty
five paces to reach their gate. When he was swimming in
their pool, he counted not only the lengths he completed but
also the strokes per length and purely from an involuntary
calculation he was aware of the total number of strokes he
had done. He also had an almost total recall of numbers and
his head was full of strings of the ten digits which make up
French telephone numbers, of five digit French post codes
and of car registration numbers. Because of these particu-
larities he would recall that it was after six rings exactly that
Renard's mobile switched to message mode. Tom left a brief
message to let him know that it was fine to bring his col-

league, Duvallon, along and to ask them to arrive around eight in the evening. He did a quick mental check that he had accurately registered Renard's number in his head and having passed the test, he put the visiting card away in the telephone drawer.

It was still well short of ten o'clock and Tom decided to call the Browns and then Nigel to give them feedback on the previous day's visits. He rather thought that the shorter of the conversations was likely to be with the Browns and he started with them, plucking their number from somewhere inside his brain. It was Cheryl who answered and, when he had announced himself, asked:

"Could you just hang on a sec, Tom?"

After a brief delay, she continued:

"OK, Tom. What can I do for you?"

Tom imagined that she had taken the handset out into the garden because her voice was much more fuzzy now and there was a fair bit of interference.

"It's just a quick call, Cheryl. I just wanted to let you have some feedback from yesterday. Hello, hello. Can you still hear me?"

"Just about . . . crackle . . . crackle . . . want him to know . . . visit."

"Look! I can't hear you properly. What did you just say, Cheryl?"

"Don't tell Steve, Tom. I haven't . . . crackle . . . crackle . . . get angry."

"I won't say a thing. We can talk tonight at our barbecue. Eight o'clock start. Okay?"

"Fine. Will it be alright . . . crackle . . . crackle . . . the kids?"

"I'll dig out some DVDs for them. They seem to like that sort of thing," Tom responded, trusting that he had interpreted correctly that they would be bringing their two boys with them.

"See you ton . . ."

At which the telephone cut off completely. The granite highlands of the Morvan and the sixty centimetre thick walls of its houses were unforgiving to mobiles and to handsets that were taken too far from their base. As Nigel had described it, the Morvan was 'a Black Hole brought to Earth'.

So what was going on at the Brown household Tom asked himself? If he had understood the fractured conversation he had just had with Cheryl, it seemed that Steve was not in the picture about the potential sale of their house. This could quite simply be because they hadn't had chance to discuss the matter together given Steve's absence in London from Monday to Thursday each week. But still to Tom's mind it was odd since he had always assumed that it was Steve who made all the significant decisions whilst the style of their marriage restricted her to day to day domestic responsibilities. Perhaps, now that her two sons were at school and the house was, if far from being fully done up, at least satisfactorily functional, she was beginning to feel the need to emerge from below stairs. It was something which Tom would discuss with Jenny. She may have picked up murmurs of discontent from Cheryl.

Next, Tom called Nigel. At least with his household, it was absolutely clear that it was Nigel alone who would decide the major issues. He had always been most explicit to whomsoever would listen that "Aux Abeilles" and all that was contained within it belonged to him and to him exclusively. He did not hesitate to proclaim this fact even when Tim was present. Tom had always believed that Nigel must have inherited his money and perhaps also some of the more expensive furniture and artefacts which adorned his house from a former wealthy lover. He based this uncorroborated opinion upon having picked up from Nigel's accounts of his past no discernable evidence of his having had a financially rewarding career and yet there had been hints of his having enjoyed the high life in London. In addition, to Tom's sure knowledge, he had had no problem at all in stumping up the cash for his house in Saint Val which when he bought it had been Tom's most expensive house sale. For sure, also, he had poured a fair additional amount into the property. The garden plants alone must have cost a small coffer of euros, Tom imagined.

His call was finally answered after several rings and just as he was about to hang up.

"Aux Abeilles. Nigel speaking."

"Hello, Nigel, it's Tom here. I just wanted to give you some feedback on yesterday's visit."

"Rum sort of couple if you ask me. They didn't seem the types to have enough cash to afford a place like mine."

"We never got the chance to talk prices, did we?"

"You're the Estate Agent, Tom. What do you think I should ask?"

"I can give you a basic market price. But it's very much up to you to set a figure."

Tom was hedging. To Tom, giving an initial valuation was the least favourite part of the whole selling process. Vendors always seemed to want more than his estimations and this was only natural Tom supposed. There was always the danger that they would be upset if he proposed too low a sum and this could easily sour their relations. There was an equal danger that they would price themselves out of the market. Tom was quite sure that these two dangers would be present with this particular transaction. Nigel, he was sure, was likely to be touchy if he went too low. Left to his own judgement, Nigel was equally likely to push the asking price through the ceiling of acceptability. To resolve the dilemma, he decided to suggest a figure rather higher than he might otherwise have done.

"I only want to sell if I get a good return on my investment. You'll understand that, Tom, I'm sure."

"Absolutely. I was thinking of somewhere in the region of five hundred thousand euros give or take. But as I say, it's very much in your hands. What I would suggest is that we wait and see if our two friends from yesterday actually make an offer. I have my doubts that they are serious buyers. In the meantime, you can think about price and we can talk it through at length. What do you think?"

"That suits me."

"Could I just remind you about the barbecue tonight? We thought around eight o'clock."

"Wonderful. I have to say though that I am not sure whether Tim will be joining us."

"Is there a problem then?"

"He's been in a ferociously foul mood with me. He's said some very cruel things which I won't repeat. Suffice to say that I am very upset and we're not speaking. I don't know what's got into him. He seems to have changed completely from the happy, sunny Tim I thought I knew."

Tom was conscious that it was now after ten and he needed to ring the hotel to speak to yesterday's house hunters. He was also very sure that Nigel would have more than matched whatever 'cruel things' Tim might have said. Tom certainly did not want to be drawn into the intimacies of a type of relationship with which, despite his claim to open mindedness, he could not, in his heart of hearts, easily empathise.

"I'm very sorry to hear that, Nigel. Life is rarely smooth, is it? Please don't think that I don't want to listen to your problems but it's just that I promised to ring our punters at ten and I really don't want to miss them"

"Of course you don't want to miss them and you don't want to hear me wittering about my love life. I forgive you though. Abandon me for others if you will. See you tonight, my dear."

Tom found the telephone number of the Campanile Hotel in the Yellow Pages, rang and, as he waited, was treated to a rendition of the William Tell Overture which from time to time was interrupted by a recording of a sexy lady inviting him to be patient. He was patient and was rewarded after a couple of minutes with a live response.

"Good morning. Campanile Hotel. How can I help you?"

"Good morning. I should like to speak to someone who is staying with you. Well, in fact, there are two of them. An English couple."

"Certainly. Could you tell me their names, please?"

To his dismay, Tom realised that he had not got a surname for either of them. He was usually most punctilious in noting down as many personal details of house hunters as the bounds of politeness allowed. Perhaps he had been slack on this occasion because he had convinced himself that the pair had not been serious house hunters.

"I am afraid I only have their first names. The man is called Ted and the woman is Wendy."

"How long have they been here? Is it one night or two or longer?"

"From what they said they were with you certainly on Wednesday night and they told me they were going to stay again last night."

"Just one moment please. I need to check the register."

"Of course. I'm sorry I don't have their full names . . ." Tom began and then realised he was talking to himself.

After what seemed rather a long wait the receptionist returned to the telephone.

"I'm very sorry, sir. According to our records we have only had one set of English guests in the last two days. A couple with their two young children and they left yesterday morning, in fact. According to the register their names were not those you gave me."

"That's very strange but if you're sure. I'm so sorry to have troubled you. Many thanks."

"It's no trouble, sir. Have a nice day."

"I bloody-well knew it. Couple of time wasters" Tom said to the dogs who had not yet had their morning snack.

As he put a handful of biscuits, which he had always referred to as pheromone drops so powerfully attractive were they to canines and so stinkingly repulsive to humans, in the dogs' two bowls, he thought of Ted and Wendy and sought to categorise them so that he could file them away in his bulging drawer of lost causes. He realised that he could not find a category under which they could be filed. Most 'lost causes' could be loosely termed as 'dreamers'. Others had their feet a little more firmly on the ground but were not able to raise the amount of money they needed to buy the sort of place they wanted. Others were just using him to fill in a day of their annual holiday. Ted and Wendy did not fit any of these types. He needed to talk it through with Jenny. Together they would come up with a file that would accommodate the unusual pair. Nevertheless, he wondered why they had been untruthful about where they were staying. They hadn't been sure of the name of the hotel though. Perhaps they had just made a mistake. Perhaps they would get in touch with him. Perhaps—but he doubted it.

With that thought in mind, he turned his attention towards what he and Jenny needed to do to prepare for the evening's festivities. He would have to wait for her to return from her second trip to the shops in two days before starting on food prepping and so he thought he might begin to clean up around the barbecue area and start to set the plates and cutlery on the outside tables. The same old crowd would be coming, of course, which he would normally have grumbled about to Jenny. But this time there would be Renard and his sidekick as well. Tom recognised that he would perforce be centre stage in the evening's performance. His role was key. He also recognised, without too great a burden of shame, that he was looking forward to what could be a very satisfying evening in the spotlight.

Others in Saint Val were feeling less smug. One was consumed with growing grief; another with a strong sense of guilt and yet another, not unreasonably, was absolutely terrified.

11

*"An Englishman thinks he is moral
when he is only uncomfortable"
(George Bernard Shaw—"Man and Superman")*

Tom and Jenny surveyed their handiwork. Both barbecues had been lit. The meats were marinading in dishes which they had placed atop the high wall beside the terrace so that the dogs could not reach them. Salads, bread, cheeses, plates and cutlery were set out on one long table. Glasses and red wine boxes sat alongside two cool boxes which held white wine, beer and fizzy drinks on another table. Tom remembered at the last minute to make sure there was a good supply of mineral water for Steve Brown who never touched alcohol. They had put out chairs here and there on the terrace and beside the pool. They had turned on the pool lights so that as darkness fell their guests would not fail to be impressed. This would be one more occasion which would help them to justify the amount of money they had spent on their pool.

"Shall I get us a drink before the storm breaks, Jen?"

"But the weather's wonderful. . . . Oh, I see. You mean before they start to arrive. Go on then! Let's have a gin and tonic then we can shut the spirits away. We'll light the candles when the first people arrive, shall we?"

They had decided that they would not offer spirits mainly as an economy measure but, in the back of their minds, they had thought its absence might delay the on-set of 'inappropriate behaviour', a euphemism which they had addressed to their children during their teenage years. These days the children, now grown up, got back at their parents by turning the expression back on them.

"Mummy, Daddy's doing 'inappropriate behaviour'. Tell him to stop!"

Thus the phrase had passed into the Fox family's lexicon.

"Jen what do you think about the Browns putting their house up for sale? Bit of a surprise, isn't it? Or perhaps you had picked up something from Cheryl?"

"No. Nothing at all. You'll have to ask Steve about it tonight."

"Well that's a problem. You see Cheryl has asked me not to say anything. Well, at least I think that is what she was asking. It was such a lousy connection. I don't think Steve even knows that she's had people looking at the place. So we'd better not say anything until one or other of us has had chance to chat to Cheryl privately."

"I must say that doesn't seem to be in character at all. I really thought she left all the decisions to him. You showed the people round Nigel's house too, didn't you? I don't suppose you were daft enough to tell him that you were handling the Browns' place as well, did you?"

"Oh shit! Did I? I'm sure I didn't. If I did the news will be everywhere by now. No. No. I'm sure I didn't mention it either when we were visiting the house or when we spoke on the phone this morning. No. I'm sure. Phew!"

"Well I certainly hope not because tonight is going to be tricky enough as it is already what with you and Hercule Poirot sniffing around everybody."

"Thank you for your warm support, Jenny. Perhaps I ought to warn you that Nigel is in a bit of a state. Things are running far from smoothly between him and Tim and you know what he can be like when he's in the dumps—especially if he starts to hit the bottle."

"Lots of potential for inappropriate behaviour then! Oh this is going to be fun, I don't think. It could turn out to be the most uncomfortable evening we've ever had here."

"I'm sure we'll cope. We always do. In any case, it is bound to be a bit of a different sort of evening. As for helping Commissaire Renard out, well, even if it causes a few difficulties with our friends, even if it is 'uncomfortable' as you put it, I don't believe we have any choice in the matter. We have a duty to help Renard. We have a duty to old Guyard, let's not ignore that either. That's what I believe anyway. In any case they'll get used to the idea. I think I'll just check that everything's in place around the pool area."

Jenny was quite aware that he was escaping for a smoke. She was also aware that underpinning the noble sentiments he had just expressed was a need in Tom to strut in the lime-light and that it was as much a psychological as a moral imperative that was motivating him.

She sighed and went into the kitchen from the terrace to rinse out their glasses. When she re-emerged, she could hear Tom greeting the first arrivals. They must have parked on the gravelled area next to the pool and this suggested that it was Nigel and Tim because that is where Nigel always insisted on leaving his car. His identity was confirmed when she heard his voice booming up the brick path which led from the pool to the terrace.

"I wasn't at all sure whether I should come along or not. I am in such a wretched state. But noblesse oblige and all that. I've been singing "Abide with me" at the top of my voice all the way here. It was either that or tears."

Although she couldn't catch his words, Tom must have replied because Nigel continued to resound.

"I'm just at the end of my tether. The little shit is being absolutely beastly to me. I just don't know what's got into him. He's been like this for days. If anything, it's getting worse. Today I made him such a lovely lunch. I put all my heart into it and he wouldn't even touch it. He just stormed out of the house and I haven't seen him since. I left him a note telling him that I was coming over here but I don't suppose he will turn up. That's what he's like. He's just fucking rude. Mummy always taught me that if you were invited somewhere, you had to do your level best to turn up however dismal you were feeling. Not him though; not our Tim. Anyway, if he does decide to come, he'll have to walk here. He can't even bike over because the tyre is punctured. I told him to mend it over a week ago. But did he do it? Of course he didn't, the little turd."

Jenny sighed once more. Nigel with the mopes could cast a cloud over the whole evening. Thank God at least that they had removed the gin. With wine, he would take longer to slide totally into the Slough of Despond. She saw Tom escorting Nigel up the path from the pool and was just steeling herself to cope with his gloom when she heard someone arriving at the front door of the house. Blowing a kiss in Nigel's direction, she made off to greet the new comers. To her relief it was Harry and Peggy Walker. Peggy was always good in an awkward atmosphere as nothing seemed to divert her from her meandering monologues and these worked like bicarb in any dyspeptic social situation.

As they emerged on to the terrace to join Nigel and Tom, Peggy was already in full flow

"I thought you were off to England, Jenny," she went on.

"Well yes I am. First thing tomorrow in fact. That's if we manage to wake up after tonight's bash that is. You know how wretchedly early the train is."

"I know. I had to drive myself last time. Harry just wouldn't get up and take me there."

"I'm only going to see the new baby—really I would much prefer to stay here."

"You'll love it once you're there. You won't be able to put the baby down if I know you."

Without pausing, she turned her attention to Nigel

"Where's dear Tim, Nigel? I wanted to ask him about the azalea we planted. It's not doing very well at all."

"T'were better you did not ask about him. We are having a spat and I don't think he will be coming. As I was saying to Tom, I think it's very rude of him not to turn up. Goodness knows I am feeling very low myself and I could have stayed at home to mope. But I am not so uncivil and, in any case, I much prefer moping in public. It's so much more rewarding. I say Tom, to save you asking, I would love a large glass

of red—so long as it is decent and not like the stuff someone who shall be nameless but who is standing not a million
miles from me at this moment serves up. I shall let you have
my opinion after I have tasted it and if it is not up to scratch,
I shall beg gin from you. The thought of taking myself off to
a dark corner of your terrace with a bottle of gin and some
tonics has its appeal. But red it shall be for now always providing that you are not expecting me to sup from a wine
box. Why don't we secrete a decent bottle somewhere in the
kitchen and then I can just keep helping myself?"

"Well I don't see why not. I was going to open some reasonable stuff when our French guests arrive anyway," Tom
responded so that Nigel would not feel that compliance to
his demands had been given too readily.

"French friends? Do we know them, Tom?" Peggy intervened.

"They are not exactly friends are they Tom? You had better
explain who they are," Jenny said to Tom as he re-emerged
from the kitchen with Nigel's wine.

"Well I shall be introducing them when everyone is here,
of course. But if you wish to know, it's come about because
of poor old Guyard's death. I have been approached by the
investigating officer. He has asked me to help him out with
the language when he speaks to the English who live in Saint
Val. I thought it would be a good idea if he and his sidekick
met you all for the first time socially rather than during a
formal interview."

"Fucking typical! Christ!" Harry muttered just loudly
enough for the others to hear.

"We're all very sorry about Guyard, of course. It's just
horrible. He is one of our neighbours after all. But why on
earth would the police be interested in talking to us Brits for
God's sake?" Peggy added.

"I think you have just said why, Peggy. Neighbours. It's
because we are his neighbours—or were I should say. Besides, as was pointed out to me by our Maire, we make up a
significant portion of the inhabitants of Saint Val. It would
be very surprising if they didn't want to talk to us."

"My dear Tom," Nigel cut in, "it's one thing to have to talk to them as part of their enquiries but it's quite another inviting them to quaff with us. But then it is your party I suppose. I for one though would have liked to have been forewarned."

"Too bloody true," Harry joined in. "At least I would have had the choice of staying at home. It's not my idea of how to spend a Friday night rubbing shoulders with coppers."

"Look! All I was trying to do seeing as I had been asked to help was to start things off on an informal footing. I thought if everyone had met Renard—that's the Commissioner of Police by the way—in a social setting it would make any formal interview that may or may not take place afterwards less intimidating for you."

"Tom thinks that we have to face up to our civic responsibilities especially under these dreadful, ghastly circumstances. We have to be seen to be helping. He believes that we need to do this sort of thing if we wish to be accepted by the locals." Jenny added in a loyal attempt to back Tom up although she felt that her previous misgivings were being confirmed.

It was at that moment that the bell at the front of the house rang and, relieved at being able to escape, Jenny went off to meet the latest arrivals. Tom too took temporary refuge from what had certainly been building up into confrontation by finding some pretext to disappear off to the kitchen. Peggy and Harry went away to the far reaches of the terrace and were engaged in whispered but extremely animated discussion. Nigel, finding himself alone, seemed suddenly to crumple. All his social exuberance had flown and if anyone had been close enough they would have seen that fat tears were running down his cheeks. They would also have been struck by how much older, in a matter of seconds, he looked.

Jenny returned with Tony and Mandy Parsons in tow. Tom re-emerged from the kitchen. Nigel loudly blew his nose, dabbed at his eyes and turned to meet the others. The Walkers interrupted their tête à tête and came forward to join in the general pecking of cheeks and handshakes. During these rituals, the bell rang once more and Jenny with a twitch of her head signalled to Tom that he should accompany her to the door.

When they were out of earshot, she hissed at her husband.

"I just knew this was going to happen. They will all turn against us, you know!"

"Jen we'll just have to ride it through. They'll come round once they see the sense in what we are doing. They'll get used to the idea. In any case, Renard will charm them, just you see."

Tom's scowl and Jenny's anxious expression both transformed into beaming smiles as, standing at the open door surrounded by wagging dogs, they saw all five of their other expected guests as well as the two Brown children. Tom noted that Steve and Cheryl Brown, who were evidently introducing themselves to the two policemen as they were in the process of shaking hands, must have brought Tim Foulkes along with them.

"'Hello, Tim" said Jenny. "I didn't think you were going to be able to make it tonight."

"Well not according to Nigel anyway," Tom added.

"He's here then, is he?" Tim answered. "I thought he would turn up and I need to be here so that he doesn't have the stage entirely to himself. If he decides to reveal all, I need to put in my perspective on the break up."

The other four English adults registered the last phrase.

"So it's as bad as that is it?" they were all asking themselves.

"Well come on in everybody, please. Tom, will you look after our French friends? Tim, we can have a quiet chat later if you want—but only if you want," Jenny whispered before she shepherded the two boys towards the sitting room and dug out a selection of suitable DVDs for them.

Tom stepped towards Jean Luc Renard and his colleague, Jérôme Duvallon, and taking them each by the elbow followed the others across the hall and through the kitchen to the terrace.

"It's good to see you both," Tom said as they were making their way towards the rest of the guests. "I think I or we or you ought to say something to break the ice. As Jenny and I suspected they are a bit unhappy at being under the eye of the police. I suppose I should have warned them that you would be here."

"I should tell you that my colleague is not entirely charmed by the idea of this evening either," Renard answered.

"I was just expressing my opinion to my boss, that's all, Monsieur Fox. I'm not convinced that it is such a good idea to try to mix police business with social pleasure," Duvallon explained, expressing an opinion which coming from him would later seem ironic in the extreme.

"Let's just see how it goes, shall we? As for your suggestion, I think it may be a good idea if I said a few words to your guests to try to make them relax. After all we will get nowhere if everyone is on edge. It will give us the chance too to demonstrate that your role is purely to translate. May I suggest, my dear Tom, that if you feel that we are in the way, you should just give me a nod and we will make our excuses and leave?"

"That's very thoughtful of you. Just let me check that everyone has a full glass first and then I'll introduce you. What do you want to drink? If you want red wine, I have a decent bottle or two open in the kitchen."

"That sounds good to me. You too Jérôme? Yes? Then two reds it is please, Tom."

As he went to the kitchen to supply their needs, he rehearsed what he was going to say. He decided it would be a good move to utter a few words of apology and reassurance. At least that would please Jenny. Then he would give the briefest of introductions and simply translate whatever Renard had to say.

It was apparent to Tom that his English guests were discussing the presence of the police in whispering huddles. Only Nigel stood a little apart staring at Tim who was in a group consisting of the Parsons and the Walkers. The latter were doing most of the talking. Tim was studiously ignoring Nigel.

Jenny was listening to Steve Brown who was explaining how to get to the tube trains from the St Pancras terminal. Cheryl was looking rather apprehensive and Tom guessed that she still had not told her husband, Steve, that she had unilaterally put their house on the market. After checking with Jean Luc Renard that he was ready to talk to the guests, Tom cleared his throat, banged a spoon against his glass and began:

"If I could have your undivided for a moment or two, I'd like to introduce Commissaire Renard and his colleague Captain Duvallon to you all. But first, if I may, I should like to apologise for not telling you all in advance that they would be here. I ask you please not to worry. Please if you can, enjoy yourselves because you are our friends and you are all very welcome. And now I will hand you over to Commissaire Renard—and from time to time he will pause so that I can translate what he is saying to you. First I will tell him in French what I have just said to you and then over to him."

After a quick muttered exchange in French, Renard looked around at the assembled English and then he smiled and said:

"Messieurs, Mesdames, I am very honoured that you are letting us share in your delightful soirée. I and my colleague are here to make your acquaintance and that is all. As Monsieur Fox has said please do not let our presence stop you enjoying yourselves. I certainly hope to do so myself. I should first explain that I have had permission from my superiors to enlist Tom Fox's help as a translator when we are talking to you. Other than that he has no official status. This being France he will not be receiving any reward for his efforts. I'm sorry about that Tom."

This brought a smile and even a titter from those who had been able more or less to understand the last two sentences. Renard extended his hand, palm upwards, towards Tom to signal that he should translate. When he had done this, there was a perceptible détente. When Renard's quizzically raised eyebrows had been answered by a nod from Tom, the Commissaire continued:

"But—and it is a big but, Messieurs, Mesdames, I am obliged to remind you that we are dealing here with the murder of an elderly neighbour of yours. I am afraid I can give you no details of the murder at this stage of the investigation. In fact even if I could I would not be happy to describe the murder scene. It is enough perhaps to tell you that Monsieur Guyard suffered a vicious and prolonged death. I wish to assure you that I and my colleagues are totally committed to finding the person or persons responsible for this hideous crime. If, when I call at your homes to talk to each of you, I am less than polite or if I appear insensitive, my only apology will be that I am very likely to become single minded in my quest to find the killer or killers. Perhaps if you have any questions, now would be the time to ask them. Please, Tom, could you translate?"

When he had finished, there was silence and serious expressions had replaced the smiles. After a moment or two, Steve Brown raised his hand just as though he were still a schoolboy.

"Yes, Monsieur, how can I help you?" Renard asked with a kind smile just as though he were a schoolmaster encouraging a nervous pupil.

"I'd like to ask you about security. You see I travel to England on a weekly basis. I'm away from Monday to Thursday. Cheryl and the boys will be here on their own and I was wondering whether they will be safe."

"We are still in the dark as to the motive for the killing so I am afraid I can't be sure about who is and who isn't in danger. Of course, there is a murderer or murderers out there somewhere but the main thing is not to panic. I can only recommend that you go about your lives as normally as possible. Perhaps you should be doubly careful about locking your doors and closing your shutters. Perhaps, if you are nervous you could arrange to speak on the telephone at predetermined times to people whom you trust. If it helps to set your mind at ease a little, Monsieur, I can tell you that this crime was not sexually motivated."

Tom translated and recognised that the sage nodding of heads showed the Brits were beginning to accept that Renard was probably no fool. The Commissaire raised his hand to interrupt the conversations which were developing.

"Your question raises another matter, Monsieur. As I have explained to Madame Fox in connection with her trip to England tomorrow, there is no problem at all in your leaving this area at least on a temporary basis. What I would insist on, however, is that I or Capitaine Duvallon be kept fully informed of your plans."

Harry Walker raised his hand and asked

"Tom would you ask him something for me? I noticed he kept on saying 'killer or killers' and 'murderer or murderers'. Does this mean that he thinks there's more than one of them out there somewhere or what?"

When Tom had passed on Harry's question, the Commissaire gave a Gallic shrug of the shoulders and replied

"You should infer, Monsieur, only that our minds are open to the possibility that more than one killer was involved. More than that I cannot say. And now if there are no more questions, I notice that my glass is empty as are several of yours. It also seems to me Tom that your barbecues are almost ready to do their work. So let us continue with our evening and if you permit I should like to have a friendly chat as I pass amongst you. A final remark just to set you at ease if you don't mind. Let me say that I shall be staggered if any of you such charming people turns out to be our criminal."

It escaped none of them however that Renard had in no way ruled out that possibility. So his closing remark fell far short of setting them totally at ease and it occurred to Tom as he was translating that this had been done quite deliberately.

12

*"The wine urges me on, the bewitching wine, which
sets even a wise man to singing and to laughing
gently and rouses him up to dance and brings
forth words which were better unspoken."*
(Homer—"The Odyssey")

As Tom felt that he had to stay by Renard's side to exercise his appointed role, it fell to Jenny to take charge of the barbecues and the distribution of the rest of the food. Her job was made easier by Tim and Cheryl who, without being asked, came to her aid, he doing most of the grilling and she serving out the Toulouse sausages and spiced chicken when they were deemed to be ready. This allowed Jenny to keep an eye on everything else. It was not very long before she realized that the drink was disappearing fast, even faster than was usual on such occasions. She spotted that Nigel was standing glumly on the periphery. Duvallon also seemed to be a bit out of things. She therefore decided, despite the fact that Tom would be horrified, to ask these two to go down to the cellar and bring up fresh supplies.

"Nigel darling, would you be an absolute sweetheart and fetch some more bottles from the cellar? The key is in the door I'm sure."

"But my dear lady, are you absolutely sure about this. I mean you know Tom. He guards his bottles as though they were Inverness virgins and we all know what state they were in after the ball."

"I don't want to interrupt Tom. He's up to his neck playing a bilingual Captain Hastings to our very own Poirot. Most people seem to be on red wine. So if you could bring mostly that. . . . Anyway you know your wines, Nigel, and I know that you can be trusted to leave the very best stuff alone. From the way things are going, we need a plentiful supply of decent quaffing wine."

Turning to Duvallon, whom she addressed in reasonably accurate French, she asked:

"Capitaine, I wonder if you would be kind enough to help Nigel to fetch up some more wine from the cellar? Above all as I have said to Nigel we need red wine, I believe. Is that okay?"

To her surprise, he replied in heavily accented, slightly hesitant but nevertheless correct English.

"It will be a pleasure, Madame. I will go with Monsieur Nigel to your cellar. He can tell me what I must do and I will do it."

Nigel adopted a mock coy expression and laying his hand on the young man's sleeve said

"Oh, you foolish young thing, you don't know how I would love to take you up on your offer!"

"Steady, Nigel. It's probably not a good idea to flirt with the law," Jenny said with a chuckle.

"You never know. It may be worth the risk. He is a pretty young creature, isn't he?"

"That's certainly true. But just make sure that, if the wine you have consumed has made you foolish enough to tell him so, you use the word 'beau' and not 'joli'. Best to be on the safe side!"

Jenny noticed that Duvallon was smiling along with them and thought that he had probably not followed their exchange. Happily, if he had caught their drift, he had a pretty tolerant sense of humour.

"Go on with you. Get us some wine quick. Harry is almost empty and he'll not be happy if the well runs dry!"

"Certainly ma'am! Come, my dear young thing, let's away to the cellars!"

Jenny turned towards the barbecue area and realized that only Tim and Cheryl had remained on the terrace. All the others had drifted down to the pool area. She was about to take a surviving bottle and do the rounds by the poolside when she changed her mind and instead strolled across to chat with Tim and Cheryl. They were standing rather close to each other and she saw Cheryl hold her hand to Tim's cheek. It was apparent to her that they were having a heart to heart exchange and this was more than her curiosity could resist. She was desperate to discover whether Tim was being serious when he had said there had been a 'break up' between him and Nigel.

"Hello, you two. Thanks for all your help with the cooking. It looks like everybody has got what they want to eat. There are bits and pieces on the table so if they do want anything else they can serve themselves. Not joining the rest by the pool then?"

"No. Later perhaps. We needed to talk in private. Tim's been with us at 'Le Bois Burot' all day but Steve has been hanging around so we haven't been able to talk properly."

"Oh, if I'm in the way, just say so and I'll clear off and leave you in peace. I just wanted to see, assuming that the 'break up' is genuine, if there was anything I could do to help," said Jenny trying to keep the pique she felt out of her voice.

"Don't be daft, Jenny. Of course you are not in the way!" Cheryl continued. "In any event Tim is going to be staying with us for a little while so we are going to have time to talk. At least until things have calmed down chez Nigel that is."

"So it's that serious then Tim?" Jenny probed.

"I am not going back to Nigel or to his place in any circumstances. As far as I am concerned, it's all over. There would have to be a total change in . . . No. It's too complicated. I just can't explain everything, not yet anyway."

Jenny failed to catch his eye because he was looking fixedly at Cheryl as he spoke. She was returning his gaze and Jenny noticed that she was giving him a supportive smile and nods of agreement. Jenny felt decidedly that three was a crowd and, in any case, Nigel and Duvallon were arriving back laden with bottles.

"I'll leave you two . . . in peace then," she finished lamely as she had been about to say 'you two lovebirds' and that, given his orientation and her domestic situation, would merely have been gratuitous bitchiness.

She felt equally supernumerary when she got over to Nigel and the young detective. They seemed to be getting on famously in a strange mix of French and English. She did pick up the fact that Nigel was addressing Duvallon as 'Dear Jérôme' whilst the latter was happily calling him 'Neejell'. As she swept up a couple of bottles, left them and wandered down to the pool, she suspected she heard them teaching each other vocabulary of an extremely dubious nature.

In the meantime, Renard, aided by Tom, had been talking to Tony and Mandy Parsons. Tom realized with admiration that, without appearing to be interrogating them, Renard had elicited information which even he himself had not previously known. Certainly some of it was fairly generalized but Tom had no doubts that over time even the fine details of the Parsons' lives would be laid bare.

"Alors, you were in Spain before you came here to Saint Val, you say?"

"Yeah, that's right. We had a few years down there, didn't we Mandy?"

Mandy was showing some signs of beginning to lose the thread. Tom imagined she might have had a drink or two before they even arrived. She did not respond to her husband, Tony, but rather stared off into the middle distance. Tom took an executive translatorial decision to ignore any further examples of Tony seeking corroboration from his wife. In that way, he hoped to partially conceal Mandy's increasing befuddlement from Renard.

"You are still a young man, Monsieur Parsons. You are much too young to be retired. You must have been working when you were in Spain?"

"Yeah, that's right."

"What did you do there, if I may ask?"

"I had a bar. Fish and chips. Pizzas. That sort of thing."

"So what made you sell up and come here? From the Costa to the Morvan. It must have been a total change for you both."

"Well, you can have enough of a good thing, can't you? I'd made a bob or two. I sold for a good price. So here we are."

"So now you are retired? But you are only 42 years old as I understand it."

"You jealous, then? In any case, don't go thinking I sit on my arse all day. I do bits and pieces. I turn over a nice profit sending the odd antique or three over to London and flogging them to some dealer pals of mine."

Suddenly, Mandy seemed to come back into a semblance of focus and joined in.

"I'm not going to pretend that I have any intention of working any more. I've put my graft in, I have. From now on in I'm going to put all my efforts into being a lady of leisure and pleasure."

"She's bloody good at it too. Believe me!" Tony added by way of annotation to her text.

"Listen, smarty! Aren't you supposed to let the Inspector know if you're going away anywhere. Because you are, aren't you?"

"Alright, alright! I was getting round to it. I don't suppose there will be any problem will there? I'm off to Magny-Cours for the motor racing tomorrow. I'll be down there for the week end."

"Your wife will have your contact details, I expect, and so I do not see any problem. It's not generally very popular with us French that Mitterand pushed through the siting of our Formula One venue down in the backwoods beyond Nevers. There's no convenient airport; there's no rail link. But he kept on getting re-elected. So as far as he is concerned long live Magny-Cours, I suppose."

Both Renard and Tom had noticed that Mandy had called the Commissaire 'Inspector' but neither thought it useful to pick her up on it. Tom suggested in an aside to Renard that, as she watched so many detective series on television, all policemen were 'Inspectors' to her because that is what it must seem like to judge from such shows with their Morses, Alleyns, Lynleys, Pascoe, Wexford and the like.

"Anyone for a top up?" Jenny sang out as she arrived by the pool.

"I thought you would never ask, darling," said Tony taking a step towards Jenny. "Mandy probably doesn't need any more but there's no point trying to turn her tap off now."

"What did I tell you?", he added as his wife, glass held out, veered towards Jenny in a scarcely controlled ellipse.

Renard with Tom ever at his shoulder took this opportunity to move away from the Parsons and head with a disarming smile towards the Walkers and Steve Brown who were sitting on the low wall at the far end of the pool. The men were both wearing white shirts and Peggy was in her habitual white cotton dress. The fluttering bluish light from the pool was reflected against the whiteness of their garments and it was difficult to read their facial expressions in the contrasting semi-shadow. This proved to be no disadvantage since Harry revealed what he at least felt about their approach. He made no effort to conceal his remark delivered in a slurred growl.

"Watch out! Here they come, the French filth and his fucking sidekick."

Tom had not drunk much but he had had just enough to express his anger to Harry.

"That's a brilliant piece of alliteration, Harry! Not that you will understand what the hell I'm talking about. I think it would be good idea, Peggy, if he's too pissed and too uncouth to recognize that he is way out of order, for you to take him on one side and explain the rules of civilized behavior to him."

The Commissaire must have picked up enough of what was going on to feel that he should intervene.

"Tom, if you would be so kind, would you explain that I wish to ask Monsieur Brown for his suggestions about the best way to travel to London as I understand he commutes there each week? As for you Monsieur Walker, I have already decided that there would be no point in trying to talk to you in a sociable way this evening. I shall therefore be calling on you at your home in the next couple of days and, if that is not convenient to you, I can always invite you to my local headquarters in Auxerre. Now, Monsieur Brown could I drag you away for a moment or two?"

As Renard moved away with Steve, Tom saw that they were shaking hands and with a final remark fired at Peggy, he too turned on his heel.

"For God's sake, Peggy, does he have to be such a prat? What is there for him to be scared about because that's what it seems like to me? Please talk some sense into him, will you?"

As he rejoined Steve and Jean Luc Renard, he looked back over his shoulder and saw that Peggy was indeed giving Harry a good talking to. He was anxious to know why Jean Luc wanted to find out about travelling to London. He suspected that it may just be a ploy to set Steve at ease but, on the other hand, if he really was going there, he wondered if this meant that he did seriously suspect that one of the Saint Val Brits was involved and that he was going to do some serious checking up. Tom looked around at his assembled neighbours and found it difficult to accept that any of them might be capable of murder. If he was wrong, however, it was a chilling thought that he was entertaining a killer. A further and entirely mercenary thought presented itself to Tom. If the Commissaire really was planning to cross the Channel, then surely he would want Tom to accompany him and the thought of a free trip was not disagreable.

As Jean Luc and Steve had been joined by Jenny with her basic French, the policeman suggested to Tom that he should have a break from interpreting and that he should go and chat to his other guests so that they did not feel neglected. Tom had a slight sense of being rebuffed but recognized that this derived from his thwarted curiosity and, after the exchange with Harry, he felt he could do with a good scoop or two of wine not to mention a nibble of cheese as he had not had much to eat earlier. He could always ask Jean Luc about London later.

As he walked up to the terrace, Nigel boomed out a greeting in a cod French accent.

" 'Ere 'e eez, our famous Eenglish detective. Leetle does 'e know zat we 'ave been despoiling 'eez cellars."

"What do you mean, Nigel?"

"I mean that, at the behest of Madame Fox, my dear new friend, Jérôme, and I have been to fetch fresh supplies of wine from your now rather ravaged cellar. We were having a serious liquidity crisis. Don't worry though! We didn't touch your special stuff, alluring though the prospect was. I would like, with your permission, to bring you over a few bottles to make good some of the damage."

"That would be very kind of you but it's not necessary, really it's not," Tom responded, since, in truth, he was strangely unconcerned by the raid on his stocks. He was still mulling over his exchange with Harry Walker. He realized that, suddenly, he was tired and he began to want people to go home.

It was the Parsons who began the exodus but not before Mandy had wrung out of Tom a promise to have dinner with her and Cheryl the following evening. If he understood her mumbled words correctly he would be standing in for Jenny at what had been planned as a girls' dinner together and of course she would be in England by then. The rest gradually made their farewells. Tom was intrigued to note that Tim went off with Steve and Cheryl Brown while Nigel, claiming a total aversion to driving in the dark and it was true that normally he would have been chauffeured by Tim, cajoled his new found friend Duvallon into driving him home in the Barnes' Mercedes. Tom registered with some satisfaction that Harry and Peggy seemed a little shame faced as they made a rather muted departure. He told Jenny to go to bed as she was looking worn out and they had a very early start to face. Tom overcame her feeble protests by promising to do all the clearing up when he got back from the station the next day.

The last to leave was Jean Luc Renard.

"I am very grateful to you and Madame Fox. It has been very interesting to make a first contact with your compatriots. I have not learned very much I must admit but at the same time the evening has done nothing to remove my gut instinct that somewhere there is an English connection."

"Really? What's this London trip all about, Jean Luc?"

"Oh it may or may not happen. I don't know yet. Could I give you a call tomorrow morning? I think I need to share a few things with you."

"With pleasure. Could you make it late morning to give me chance to get back from the railway station and do a bit of clearing up?"

"Do you want me to give you a hand now, Tom?"

"It's very kind. You must be very tired though. I know I am. Shall we call it a day for now?"

So they did.

Tom had a final cigarette followed by a long drink of fizzy water, discovered that the dogs had gone off to their beds of their own accord and, gratefully, did the same himself.

CHAPTER . . .

13

'Un jour sans vin est comme un jour sans soleil'
(Translation: "A day with no wine is
like a day with no sunshine")
French Proverb

Tom got Jenny to her train just as it was drawing into the station after a drive during which neither of them had said a lot. They were both still in bilious shock after too short a sleep, too early and rushed a departure and with too strong a reminder in their bodies of the excesses of the previous night. Beneath these symptoms of a hangover, however, Jenny was thrilled at the prospect of seeing her latest granddaughter for the first time.

They only had time for a quick embrace and a perfunctory exchange of

"Have a good trip, love! Give the new baby a kiss from me, will you?"

and

"Of course I will. Behave yourself! I'll give you a ring when I get there."

before the TGV accelerated out of Montbard on its breakneck way to Lille where Jenny would pick up the Eurostar from Brussels.

Tom made his way back to the car already desperate for a life restoring coffee which he would enjoy before starting to clear up the debris of the night before. Two hours later the dishwasher was half way through its second run and he had finished cleaning up and putting away the empty bottles and large dishes. He would take the mountain of empties to the bottle bank another time. He couldn't face it now. He had just printed himself off the Guardian Prize Crossword, this being Saturday, and made his sixth cup of coffee in preparation for at last making the most of being home alone—a circumstance to which he was not too averse from time to time. He hadn't even had time to look at the first clue when the telephone rang.

"Hello, this is Mandy here. I thought I should give you a ring to remind you about this evening. You hadn't forgotten had you?"

"Hello Mandy. No," he said, though he had rather been hoping that it had slipped her mind, "I hadn't forgotten. What time would you like me to come round?"

"Shall we say half past seven? Will that be alright?"

"That will be fine. You know it's the first girls' night out I've ever been invited to. I'm looking forward to it."

"See you later then. Bye."

As he hung up, the 'phone rang once more. He was tempted to let it ring but habit and his conscience got the better of him. It was Renard. Tom realised he had forgotten that they had planned to have a get together towards the end of the morning. As they spoke, he was wondering if he should be worried at this alcohol induced short term memory loss. At the Commissaire's suggestion, they decided to meet for lunch at 'La Vieille Auberge' in Saint Agnan. If truth be told, he had no desire at all to go out to eat especially in view of Mandy's invitation for later on. But if it was to be, then he could think of no better place to visit. He realised he was after all hungry and he would be able to do justice to Jacques' 'Trilogie' of exquisitely presented dishes served by the ever welcoming Annick.

He would have to leave in half an hour or so which would just give him time to sit outside on the terrace, finish his coffee, smoke a cigarette or perhaps even two and have a first stab at Araucaria's crossword. This prospect of bliss was interrupted by yet another telephone call. This one was from Jenny to let him know she had got to London. It never ceased to stagger him how rapid the journey was. He complained about Mandy's invitation and asked if she had remembered about it.

"Of course I did. Why do you think I told you to behave when you dropped me at the station?"

"No need to worry on that score. I'd far rather be staying here with a bit of television and an early night."

He explained that he was going out for lunch with Jean Luc to which Jenny's response was

"Quite the bachelor gay, aren't we. Talking of 'gay', try and find out what's happening with Nigel and Tim, will you?"

When they had finished talking, Tom realised that time was pressing and he would have to set off to meet Renard at once.

Jean Luc was already at their table when Tom got to the restaurant and to the latter's admiration was half way through a glass of pastis. The man had staying power. He turned down the offer of the same thing, preferring the somewhat gentler prospect of a beer. After Jean Luc assured Tom that the cost of the meal would be put on his expense sheet, they ordered their food and, despite Tom's protestations, he went on to order a bottle of Meursault to be followed by a Monthélie.

The Commissaire wasted no time in cutting to the chase.

"Tom, what is the expression? Something like 'There is no such thing as a free lunch', I believe?"

"Something along those lines," Tom agreed warily.

"You see this will have to be a working lunch. I need to ask you a few things, if you don't mind. I cannot get out of my head the suspicion that there really is some link between Guyard's murder and one or more of the Brits who live in Saint Val. I would like to explore this with you."

"By all means. I'll be as helpful as I can. But you know what my feeling is and this is largely based on what old Casson said to me the other day as well as the way he has locked himself away in his house ever since he learned of the murder. For me, all this has something to do with those grim days when the two old boys were in the Resistance together."

"We are not ignoring that possibility, of course. But for me I have to find an answer to a fundamental question. If it is to do with the Occupation or perhaps the early days of the Liberation, why should this crime have been committed now sixty years or so on. Why not earlier? Why not at some point during these many, many years? If there is a connection, I shall need to discover what it is that triggered off the murder at this particular time. I have in mind to pay a visit to Monsieur Casson on Monday. I would like you to accompany me if you are free. I just think that he may be more forthcoming if someone is there that he knows and for whom, I am quite sure, he has a high regard."

"Of course. If you think it well help I should be glad to be there. I'm not implying that he is the murderer by the way. I wouldn't want you to think that is what I mean by bringing up the possibility of there being some link between the killing and the Resistance days. I want to be clear on that."

"That is understood. In my opinion, it is highly unlikely that he could be our killer. I certainly don't see, because of the way the murder was inflicted, that he could have done it without help from another person and that person would have to be in pretty good physical shape too."

"It must have been very violent."

"That would be a mild way of describing it. If you really want to know what we are up against, I have got the scene of crime photographs back from the lab. I have them in my car. Have a look afterwards. It wouldn't be a good idea to look at them before we eat."

"Thank you for that. For having confidence in me, I mean."

"I don't think you will thank me after you have seen them. At least they are in black and white so you won't get the full effect. They are still upsetting though—to say the least."

Emboldened by the feeling that Jean Luc seemed prepared to be more open with him about the case, Tom ventured to ask

"Can you tell me what, if there is anything specific you can put your finger on, makes you feel there could be an English connection?"

"You would have had to have seen Guyard's house after the murder. It was quite obvious that whoever was there was very interested indeed in finding something. To start with there is no doubt, as I think I said to you previously, that the poor old boy was tortured before he died and why do that unless you are after information—always assuming of course that we are not simply dealing with some sick in the head sadist with no other motive than the pure pleasure of the kill? The murderers were sick and certainly they were sadists but there were signs that a thorough search had been carried out. All the drawers had been tipped out; a suitcase he probably kept under his bed had been ransacked. So it's hard not to conclude, as I say, that the purpose behind the crime was first and foremost to discover some object or more likely perhaps some document which either had some value in itself or which contained information desperately important to the perpetrator. Now, that in itself, I hear you say, does not point to an English connection. But you will perhaps remember what I asked you when I first called on you at your house—you call it 'Les Chênes' if I remember correctly—on Tuesday morning, I think. Mon Dieu, was it only five days ago, it feels likes weeks."

"Doesn't it just! And you asked if we had come across any papers or documents in English when we were clearing out the house to move in. I remember. It seemed such a strange thing to ask at the time."

"I think when you kindly gave me lunch the other day I also mentioned that we had come across a package of assorted papers, clippings from newspapers, that sort of thing. You will recall I told you that we found them hidden in a plastic bag secreted behind his huge grandfather clock."

"So you put two and two together and came up with a link to the Saint Val English contingent. I should have seen that for myself. I was being dim as usual, I suppose."

Renard did not contradict him, Tom noticed.

"Unfortunately the bag of papers is still with the Lab boys. I'm desperate to make a proper examination of the contents.

I only had chance for a perfunctory glance when we first found them. Didn't want to risk contaminating what may turn out to be valuable evidence. They have promised I can have them on Monday and if they are not finished with them by then, they can damn well give me photocopies."

"I expect you are hoping that the papers will point you in the direction of particular English residents."

"Precisely so. I need to make some progress. Guyard was killed a week ago today or at latest during the early part of Sunday and at the moment I just don't feel as if I know any more than I did when I was first called in last Monday. A whole week! It's just not good enough. I have had to give Duvallon the day off today to recover from last night and that doesn't help. I don't expect I'll see much of him tomorrow either, it being Sunday."

"I'm terribly sorry. I hope you don't think that we were forcing drink on him."

"No. Not at all, my dear Tom. I noticed that people were free to help themselves. There was no compulsion involved. Not unless it was their own inner compulsion driving them to over-indulge."

"I'm afraid that is the latest 'maladie anglaise'. It's particularly rampant among the young who just seem to aim to get as drunk as they can as quick as they can and I regret that the older generations, as you were able to observe last night, are not immune to the maladie either."

"Interesting. 'La Maladie Anglaise.' That's what we call syphilis."

"It's been used to refer to many things over the years including the rampant Trade Unionism of the Seventies. We used to call syphilis 'The French Disease' by the way. I suppose there was an increased risk of contracting it if you had taken 'French Leave' and neglected to wear a 'French Letter."

"Now that says much about the relations between our two nations. We French would say one could catch 'la maladie anglaise' if you had decided to 'filer à l'anglaise' and did not use ' une capote anglaise."

"Exactly so. I think the expression 'The English have disembarked, Les Anglais ont débarqué', referring as it does to the soldiers' uniforms is, historically, a most evocative way of describing the onset of menstruation," Tom added by way of illustrating the breadth of his knowledge of French usage.

"My sisters were less jingoistic but perhaps more irreligious. They used the expression 'There's a letter from Rome'—'Il y a un courrier de Rome," Renard added.

"In both instances referring to the red of the clothes that were worn and in the instance of your sisters' expression, there is a reference to cardinals, of course."

They paused until Annick served their eye pleasing puddings and was out of earshot. Then Renard continued

"Well indeed that is all very interesting, Tom. However, I should like to lay out an agenda of my priorities."

"Fire away, boss," replied Tom who was conscious he was once more becoming the worse for wear.

"I need to pursue the question of whether Guyard was competent in English. I need to try to find out if anyone is aware if he ever went to England. We'll try that one on Casson and the English people. We need to run through together the papers that were found at Guyard's place. We really must have searching chats with all of these people. In addition, since you are so convinced there is a connection, I must pursue the matter of events at the close of the war. I'll see if I can find an expert. Otherwise we may find ourselves having to rely on Casson and he may be too closely involved to give us an unabridged version. So, yes, dear Tom I have not dismissed your preferred option. We might just find some illumination there. I must also see how the hounds I have let loose on tracking down any surviving members of Guyard's family are getting on. My request for background information on all you English from your authorities met with a very cursory response. I need to enlist some high ranking help in getting more out of your powers that be. All of which inclines me to think that I shall take tomorrow off so that I can do some brainwork and hopefully rest for the week ahead. You look as though you need to have a rest too, Tom."

"Some hope! I have to go to dinner at Mandy Parson's house this evening."

"As I recall, the cat is away, n'est-ce pas?. Take care, Tom!"

"Oh you need not worry on my behalf. In any case there will be a chaperone. Cheryl Brown will be there as well."

"Two ladies eh? Now that could be very interesting. Never mind Tom! If you are really not interested in flirtationary activities you can always play the detective."

Renard settled the bill and as promised allowed Tom to view the photographs he had spoken of. Tom found them so horrific that he handed them back to Renard almost at once. He started to weep silently for the old man, appalled at what he had gone through.

His growing loyalty to Renard's cause was immediately girded with as fierce a resolve to find the killer as drove the Commissaire himself. This was just the reaction that Renard had been seeking by showing him the photographs.

As Tom prepared to drive away, Jean Luc shouted across to him

"Don't feel personally guilty about Duvallon being the worse for drink, by the way. It appears that he launched into a very fine bottle of Cognac at Monsieur Nigel Barnes' house when he took him back home last night. So much so in fact that he was obliged to spend the night there. I just hope he didn't fall victim to that other well known English Disease!"

14

'Il est grand temps de rallumer les étoiles'
Apollinaire 'Les Mamelles de Tirésias'
(Author's translation 'It is high time
the stars were lit up again.')

An afternoon spent dozing in the chair in front of the television followed by a short walk with the dogs and then a long shower had done much to reinvigorate Tom. He had been, he had to admit, close to collapse after lunching with Renard so rapidly had the wine they had supped topped him up from the previous night. But now, as he drew up in front of the Parsons' house, 'les Effraies,' he was surprised to find that not only had he overcome his earlier aversion to the evening ahead but that he was almost looking forward to the experience.

"Anyone at home?" Tom shouted as he approached the front door clutching his contributory bottle of Crozes-Hermitages.

"Come on in, Tom," was Mandy's response from the kitchen. "We're in here, come on through!"

He found her and Cheryl Brown sitting at the kitchen table. They appeared to have almost emptied a bottle of Crémant together and this he surmised might account for the charming pinkness of their cheeks which when proffered he touched with his lips by way of greeting. As he did so, he breathed in the waft of their perfumes which did nothing to diminish his growing sense of flirtatiousness.

"Where are Steve and the boys, Cheryl?"

"This was going to be a girl's night in together until we realised that Jenny was off to England. So, for once, Steve is at home minding Richard and John. In any case, he couldn't really object too much to me going out on my own for once because I know what he is planning for this evening. There's some damned football match he just can't miss on television. Anyway he's got Tim to keep him company. After the match I expect they will all end up watching some horrendous macho film together. They'll enjoy that. Apart from Tim, they probably won't even notice I'm not there. Not until they need something to eat, that is!"

"Perhaps I should not have come either. I mean, if you really want to have a girls' heart to heart, I don't want to be in the way."

"Don't be silly, Tom! I told Cheryl that I had insisted on your standing in for Jenny," Mandy chipped in.

"Well, if you're sure."

"I'm sure. We're both sure, aren't we?" Mandy asked Cheryl who nodded, smiled in agreement and added, a trifle darkly,

"At least you won't keep on about how much I have to drink. My precious husband is always banging on about how much we all put back—and me in particular naturally."

It was on the tip of both Mandy and Tom's tongues to ask why Steve was a non-drinker. However, Tom, with his theory of people's hidden pasts and the suspicion that Steve could well be a reformed alcoholic and Mandy, despite her own conspicuous consumption, who secretly agreed with Cheryl's husband that the Saint Val Brits drank far, far more than was wise, opted not to be inquisitive. Instead, Tom joked,

"I could have always worn my royal purple party frock, you know."

"Well that would have been something wouldn't it Mandy?"

"I expect you were going to borrow it from Nigel, were you Tom? I expect he's got an exotic secret wardrobe. You ought to ask Tim about that, Cheryl, while you've got him at your place" was Mandy's reply.

"I really don't think that Tim wants to be reminded of Nigel at the moment. He just needs to put all that behind him for now."

Tom was interested that Cheryl's reaction had been almost frosty and this made it clear to him that she was very much on Tim's side in the dissolution of the relationship, if that is what was actually happening rather than just the serious lovers' tiff he had first imagined it to be. He thought it was more than likely that she had become totally privy to Tim's intentions in the matter. They could even have become close in earlier days when Tim used to do the Browns' garden. If the split was irrevocable then it must have been brewing up for some time and for Tom it was becoming clear that Nigel's interest in selling up may be more than just a whim. He determined to talk to Nigel about formalising the decision to sell and get a Mandat de Vente from him so that he could promote the property legally. Asking people to sign a legally binding document was usually a good litmus test of their serious intent to proceed with a sale.

When Mandy went out to her car to fetch the baguettes she had forgotten to bring into the house, Tom took the opportunity to ask Cheryl if she had spoken to her husband, Steve, about selling their place and whether, in fact, Mandy knew that he had shown people around the house already. She indicated that Mandy was fully in the picture and went on.

"You know Steve! If he thinks we can make a profit by selling he'll be for it. Anyway, I think it should be as much my decision as his. I've done all the renovating either myself or by overseeing the contractors. I do the garden on my own now—such as it is. I've brought up the boys with very little help. God, I even have to sort out car repairs on my own. His mind seems to be back in London all the time these days. Oh, he was keen in the beginning what with the land we have and all that. All he does now is sit on his backside. Tim has been more help in the few days he has been staying at 'Le Bois Burot' than Steve has been for the last year."

Tom was rather taken aback at the vehemence in the tone of her reply and thought to himself that he would probably be preparing two Mandats de Vente by the sound of it. He did not know how to respond but was saved by Mandy re-appearing clutching a couple of baguettes.

"Now that we have got you on your own, Tom," she launched in, "you must tell us more about this murder. Poor old man. You remember me telling you that we—well Tony really, it didn't much bother me actually—had this problem with him lurking in the trees beyond the back garden watching us. Tony thought he was trying to catch a full frontal of me sun bathing. It used to happen quite often and a couple of times Tony shouted at him to push off. It's awful though what's happened to him. I feel really sorry now that we acted like that. He wasn't doing any harm actually. Anyway Tom, you've got to realise that we know next to nothing about what's going on, what the police are up to and so on. So tell us more!"

Tom should have expected to be asked for information of this sort and he should have worked out in advance what it would be politic to pass on to them. But since he himself, when he thought about it, knew precious little apart from conjecture, he reckoned he would not risk irking Renard if he told them pretty much all he was aware of.

"And while you're doing that, Tom, would you open us a couple of bottles and then we can start to eat. A red and a white would be good, if you don't mind."

As they made their way through a bought in three fish terrine starter and a very passable coq au vin, Tom recounted all that he could about the murder case. What seemed to interest them greatly and not unnaturally was the connection to the English that Renard seemed so keen on. However, this was firmly put to one side when he had to admit that he did not know who was looking after Guyard's dog. The true English animal lover in them came shrieking out so that Tom eventually had to relent to their demands and telephone Renard to find out about the animal. He took the opportunity, as he was disturbing Jean Luc anyway, to ask about something which had been bothering him.

"Jean Luc, is that you? This is Tom. I'm ringing from the Parsons' place. Look I'm sorry to disturb you on a Saturday evening at this hour especially," as to his dismay he realised it was after ten o'clock. "I just wanted to put something to you and then ask a quick question on behalf of my neighbours—if you have a moment that is."

"It's good to hear from you. You are not disturbing me at all. Fire away!"

"Well, first, you know that you were telling me that whoever did the killing was obviously looking for something? Then, when you came across the bits and pieces in English hidden behind the clock, you thought that was maybe what the killer was looking for? Yes? Forgive me. I know you are the detective not me. But I was wondering why the killer couldn't just have been looking for money. I was wondering if the stuff behind the clock has nothing to do with the crime."

"You are quite right. You are not a detective but I very much appreciate your desire to be helpful. Because you are not a detective and partly also because I have not filled you in on everything I have discovered, which maybe I should apologise for, you could not know that we too suspected that robbery was the motive. It's a sort of frame of mind with us. It would always be the first question we ask ourselves. However, we know from the lady who lives next to the Post Office, Madame Leroy I think she is called—you may know her—that when she took Guyard to the shops on the first Tuesday of every month, he would pop into the Crédit Agricole and draw out two hundred and fifty euros. It was never more and never less. So there can't have been much cash hanging around. I have confirmed this habitual behaviour with the bank of course and just in case there was a cheque book missing, they have put a stop on the account."

"I see. But even so I have heard of people being killed for piddling amounts of money."

"I agree. There is no understanding the baseness of some murders. However, the scene of crime officers' report, which, coincidentally, I have been looking through again this evening, indicates that Guyard had well over two hundred euros in his hip pocket. The healthy balance in his bank account—and that is all the bank is prepared to tell me at this stage—would seem to indicate that Guyard was not like many country people around here who keep large amounts of readies hidden away at home far from the eyes of the authorities. You should have been around when France moved from the franc to the euro. Talk about panic as the changeover day drew close. In the end the government felt obliged to declare an amnesty. Now that we are well into the euro period, I expect that the buggers are at it again, stashing away cash under beds, on top of wardrobes. But to get back to the point, obviously we had to conclude that robbery could not have been the motive. I think you will agree that it is intriguing that a man like Guyard should have secreted away the English paperwork that we found. As soon as I can get my hands back on them, I think we need to run through them together if you wouldn't mind. Until we can do that and until I am persuaded that the papers have no significance, I cannot ignore the possibility of an English connection however vague that may sound."

"Yes. I see. I do begin to understand now."

"And the question from your neighbours?"

"Oh yes. It's just that they are a bit worried. They want to know who is taking care of Guyard's dog."

"The dog has been taken care of. Permanently. Guyard's killer did for the animal as well. Smashed its skull in. Perhaps it was too good a guard dog to be left alive."

"Oh Lord. How am I going to explain that gently?"

"I'm sure that you will find a way to put Madame Parsons' and Madame Brown's minds at rest."

"But how the hell did you know who else was . . .?" Tom blurted out, quite sure that he had not mentioned to Renard who his fellow guest was to be. Perhaps Jenny or one of these two women had told him at the barbecue. Perhaps it was another example of his own alcohol induced short term memory fallibility.

"Don't let it worry you, my dear Tom. We are simply keeping a discreet eye on the village. I've got a couple of officers spelling each other on round the clock surveillance so naturally I know who is where."

"Yes. Of course. Obviously. Well, good night and I'm sorry to have disturbed you."

Tom found it rather chilling that Renard knew where everybody was at each hour of the day and night. It brought it home forcibly to him that the Brit community really was under the spotlight and he did not like it one little bit.

It seemed possible to Tom that the news of the death of Guyard's dog upset the two women more than the demise of its owner himself. This did not overly surprise him since he had always believed that the English, particularly English females, were more readily moved by animal suffering than by human disaster. When his daughters were small and they were watching films together, he chaffed them for thinking that the death of Bambi's mother was a far greater tragedy than the loss of the Titanic. Later, he accused them of reversing this opinion when they saw the remake of the Titanic movie and then only because of their passion for the young Mr Di Caprio. All along though, he had been aware that the female of the species is a complex being and that if they were so openly moved by the fate of animals, it was that this was some emotional release mechanism, some manageable sorrow which permitted them the huge strength needed to cope with the loss of people and, in even more personal circumstances, the death of loved ones.

None of them was interested in cheese and they passed on to the pudding which was one of Mandy's justly famous, highly alcoholic trifles. To accompany it, Tom was asked to open a bottle of Monbazillac, which in his view was an excellent alternative to over-priced Sauternes, and this, on top of the wine they had already drunk, along with the fiendish trifle which Mandy happily admitted to liberally lacing with Cointreau, released them into mellow indiscretion.

The two women began to talk about their husbands and it was as though they had forgotten that Tom was present.

"They say that absence makes the heart grow fonder. That's just a load of codswallop, I think. Since we've been in France—What is it now? Almost two years, I suppose—and Steve has been away all week, I've really started to appreciate being on my own, having my own space. Oh I know I have the two boys but they are both at school now and these days I feel as though I'm the one who is in charge. I can't describe how it grates on me when he comes home and starts telling us all what to do. The boys are bound to start to copy him as well."

Tom was clear in his mind that the boys needed no role model and he had often remarked to Jenny when they had spent some time in their presence how appallingly rude and hectoring to their mother they were. So much so that he sought to avoid their company unless he could find no excuse.

"I know what you mean," Mandy replied. "Tony's just the same. If he had been here tonight instead of going off to his precious motor racing, it would have been totally different for me. It would have been as though I were a domestic while he was some sort of duke prattling on about boring old stuff. I'd have been up and down from the table, in and out of the kitchen and there his Lordship would be at the head of the table, holding forth and boring the tits off everybody."

Tom began to wonder if this was what girls' get-togethers were about and, if they were, what on earth would Jenny have said about him. It fell to Cheryl to pursue the excoriation.

"I just feel as though we have nothing in common any more. You're so right Mandy. I am not interested in anything he has to say and therefore it is so, so boring. I used to pretend to be interested and I guess to be fair we used to talk about the kids an awful lot so it was my job, in a way, to be interested. But now even that pisses me off. When I think of the years we have ahead of us, I just don't know how I shall survive."

"Can you imagine what it's like if you don't have any kids like me? I just don't know how much longer I can carry on pretending to be fascinated by which engine is best in which car. As for stuff like 'torque', what the hell is it, that's what I want to know—or don't want to know would be more accurate, thank you very much! Do you know who his hero is? He thinks the sun shines out of that gobby, superannuated schoolboy from that television programme about motor cars. He even records those so he can watch them over and over again. It's fucking subnormal that's what it is!"

At one time Tom would have been shocked to hear a woman using trooper language but it seemed almost acceptable these days and in any case with him along with inebriation came tolerance.

"You're quiet, Tom. What would you do, if you were me?" Mandy asked

"Oh. Sorry. I'm not sure I am qualified to give marriage guidance. I'm sure Jenny is better than me at this sort of thing."

"Go on Tom. All the girls think you're a smashing, sensitive bloke. Don't they, Cheryl?"

"They do," Cheryl confirmed.

The warm glow he felt from the wines and Mandy's trifle went up several degrees as Tom absorbed this piece of coquettish flattery. He felt constrained to respond.

"Well if I were forced to comment it would be to say that, as you get on in life and in a marriage, you simply have to have friendship. Every married person, I'm sure, goes through stages when his or her partner seems like a stranger. The only way through that is deep, abiding friendship, I think. If there is magic as well then you are bloody lucky and you can't ask for more than that."

"'So what you are saying, Tom, is that it's all about your partner being your best friend with whom you also happen to go to bed? Well what do you do then if he is a total stranger to you and when you go to bed with him it is to sleep—and that's all!" Cheryl responded, discretion quite evidently no longer of any concern to her.

"That's what I'm talking about as well. That's what Tony is. A total stranger."

"Do you know when I first heard about the murder I wondered whether Steve was capable of doing such a thing. I accept that it sounds awful thinking like that. What is even worse though is that he has become such an alien being to me that I just don't know whether he could or could not have done it."

"God, that's scary Cheryl!" Mandy said with her hand to her mouth, doubtless weighing up whether Tony was capable of such a crime.

Tom thought it was time to step in and to try to bring the women back from beyond the bounds of dark disloyalty.

"You mustn't think like that, Cheryl. I've seen the photos of the body and believe me whoever did the killing must be some sort of monster. Steve is no monster," Tom felt obliged to say although of course many convicted hideous murderers had somehow managed to lead apparently normal family lives.

"But you see I don't have the same doubts about Tim."

"But then, as Tony would say, 'He sits down to pee' if you see what I mean," Mandy countered.

"There is more to him than meets the eye. It's not as straightforward as you may think, Mandy. You don't know him like I do. In any case, talking about Tim, I really should get home to see if he's alright and cheer him up before he goes to bed."

Tom decided to leave at the same time as Cheryl and turned down Mandy's invitation to stay for a coffee and brandy. As they stood together at the door watching to see that Cheryl got away safely, Mandy remarked on the multitude of stars there were. Tom leant to give her a farewell peck on the cheek only to be met by her moist and eager lips. As their mouths parted she whispered

"That's what I need Tom. I need someone to light up my stars again. Won't you stay?"

Tom was sorely tempted for he had always thought Mandy an attractive woman. There was no denying that she kept herself trim and although it passed him by, Jenny could have told him that Mandy was adept at using just sufficient cosmetic aids to enhance her olive skinned, dark eyed good looks and yet still retain a natural allure. Given that he was some twenty years older than her, Tom could not help feeling flattered too.

"That is the most wonderful offer I've had for a long time. I would dearly love to stay but I must not. We have both had too much to drink and, along with all the rest of what goes on in our marriage, Jenny really is my best friend in all the world as well."

Thus, with not a little regret, he made his way home not realising that his gentlemanly refusal, far from deterring Mandy in her little game, had made her more convinced than she already had been that, if it actually came to it, Tom might well be worth lighting up a few constellations with.

"Fuck you and your torques and for leaving me on my own, Tony!" she muttered as she wove her way to bed alone.

From the vantage point of his car concealed in the farm lane higher up the road, Renard's man had a clear view of the Parsons' front door. He dutifully recorded the time the guests left and for the sake of ensuring that his notes were comprehensive, he made an entry which read 'Passionate (?) embrace between Madame Parsons and Monsieur Fox.'

CHAPTER . . .

15

"Only the deep sense of some deathless shame."
(John Webster "The White Devil" 1612)

Despite the fact that it was some years now since Tom had had a regular job, he still enjoyed waking up on Sunday mornings more than on any other day of the week. Habitual behaviour is reluctant to disperse. He saw with added joy that the skies were cloudless and, as, at this time of the year, the surrounding woods and fields were free from hunters, he decided to take the dogs for a walk. Doing his duty by them would allow him to feel righteous and he could do with a touch of soul cleansing, he thought, after the close run temptations that Mandy had dangled before him the previous evening. A few lingering regrets were still gently knocking at the edges of his libido although he was glad that he had been loyal to Jenny and that he did not have to face the complications which would surely, he thought, have been the inevitable aftermath of submission.

As he walked past his lake wondering which route to take, the dogs no doubt scenting a deer or perhaps a fox or a badger hurtled off into the undergrowth. More exactly, the Spaniel hurtled and the two Briards clumped. He decided that it would be a good move to call in on old Jean François Casson as he had not seen him since his rather forced entry of the previous week and fulfilling a neighbourly duty would offer him a further opportunity to shrive himself. Besides the walk through the woods and over the hill to Casson's place avoided all roads and on such a day as this would be a glorious experience. In any case that was the direction in which the dogs were headed.

Most of all though, he would welcome the opportunity to try to winkle out of the old man anything which might support his suspicion that the murder was related in some way to the murky past of the village, dim and distant though it may now be.

As he got to Casson's front yard, the dogs, sensing that they had reached some sort of destination, reassembled at his side before spotting a couple of Casson's horde of semi-feral cats sunning themselves in front of the open barn. Barking loudly, the three dogs made for the cats but this did not worry Tom as he knew from previous experience that the cats would languidly jump up on top of the piles of clutter which filled the barn and stare unperturbed down on the dogs. Compared with the defter dangers of the wild woods which surrounded the old farm and with which they instinctively coped, such a naive direct attack was no threat at all to these cats. The hue and cry served to warn Casson of their presence and perhaps recognising the dogs from their barking, reassured further by Tom announcing his arrival in a loud voice, he was, on this occasion, quicker to open his front door.

"Good morning, Jean François. What a lovely day it is! Sorry about the racket. I thought I would drop in to see how you are and to find out if there is anything you need."

"That is very kind. Please, please come in, will you?" and with a nervous glance around the farmyard and its surrounds, Casson asked if the dogs would be alright outside or whether Tom wanted to bring them into the house.

"Perhaps if you don't mind, the Spaniel could come in with us. Without her egging them on, the Briards are more likely to settle down and give us a bit of peace."

Tom was in no doubt that the two larger dogs would take up their posts as close to the front door as they could, waiting for him to re-emerge. It was in their nature to herd and to guard rather than to chase and hunt like the Spaniel and without her lead, they would revert to type. Besides, Tom was well aware that Casson was particularly fond of the Spaniel and, since he did not think he should have a dog of his own any more now that he had become so aged, it would give him pleasure to do a bit of bonding and it might release the old boy from his apprehensions to the extent that he could well be more receptive to the sleuthing that Tom fully intended to carry out.

Tom took a seat at the kitchen table while Casson without enquiry shuffled off to the back pantry to fetch white wine chatting to the dog as he did so as though it were a favoured grandchild. The dog followed him to the pantry and back and then, as the old man sat opposite Tom, lay down across his feet. Casson's affection for the dog was adoringly reciprocated as Tom well knew.

Again without asking, Casson poured them both some white wine in glasses that were far from sparkling clean. Tom liked the lack of discussion about what they should drink. That was the way among country people. Until lunchtime the men drank white wine and that was that. In fact, Tom was feeling so right with the world that he did not even mind his grubby glass.

"So, Jean François, how have you been since I saw you last? Are you feeling less worried now?"

"So far so good, I suppose. At least I am still alive and kicking. But maybe that is because I am being very careful."

"Have you been out at all?"

"Not actually out. I have opened the door once or twice to throw some scraps out for the cats. I haven't been getting the chickens in at night. That would have been too risky. I just hope they have had the sense to roost up in the rafters in the barn. Otherwise the foxes will have had them by now. Better them being attacked than me though."

Tom thought that he seemed far more prepared to chat than had been the case during his previous visit and he began to hope that he would be able to get out of the old man just what it was that was filling him with such terror.

"Actually, you could do me a favour and check on the chickens a bit later. There were fourteen of them at the last count. I reckon there should be a few eggs at this time of year. Would you mind having a good look around because it's quite likely that they will have been laying anywhere that takes their fancy? You must take half of what you find for you and Madame. The rest will keep me going for a while."

"That's no problem at all. I take it that the plastic bags in the corner there have to be taken up to the road and put in the bins. Yes? I'll take those for you before I go."

"I've got a list of bits and pieces of shopping I need. Would it be possible . . .?"

"No problem."

"Don't ask me to come to the shops with you though. If you could just bring them here for me I would be very grateful to you. I'll give you a signed cheque and my identity card to pay the bill."

"You needn't bother about the payment. We can sort that out later. But, you know, you would not be in any danger taking a trip to the supermarket especially if you were with someone else. I would stick with you all the time, you know."

"But then you would be at risk as well and I couldn't expose you to that. So I would rather stay here—and I would also prefer you to take a cheque. I don't want to have debts."

Tom knew better than to argue either point. It was clear that Casson was determined to stay put at all costs. From his dealings with elderly country people whose houses he had sold, he recognised in Casson the same unfamiliarity and therefore reluctance to deal with such new-fangled inventions as bank cards and credit; among his house vendors he saw a similar obsession with being financially correct, neither generous nor mean, simply correct. So rather than trying to persuade him to change his mind, he decided to start to steer Casson back towards the past. Merely having been shut up on his own for the best part of a week might mean that he would want to open up a little. If Tom did manage to get him chatting, if not freely then at least with a measure of willingness, this would offer him as good a chance as any for a spot of delving. Certainly the fact that his neighbour was pouring them a second glass was propitious.

"It has crossed my mind, mon vieux, that if you have any relatives—and I must apologise that I have never asked about your family circumstances so I am not sure what the situation is—it might be a good idea to get someone to come and stay with you, at least until this affair has been cleared up. I know that if the need arose for Jenny or me to have support, one or other of the kids would be over from England like a shot."

"There is no family. Not any longer. My wife died twenty years ago. She had never been strong and we didn't spot the onset of cancer until it was too late. We had a son, Michel. But working on the land wasn't for him so he went off to college and after that he got a job in a bank in Montpellier. He didn't really come back here much at all after he left for his studies. That might have been my fault, I suppose. At least, that's what my wife used to say to me. She reckoned I used to go on at him for being a townie, criticising the way he dressed, suits and ties and shiny shoes. On the few occasions he came here in the early days, he seemed to spend most of his time cleaning the shit off those shoes. Well, farmyards and shit go together and that didn't suit him at all."

"Where is he now? You have kept in touch with him at least, haven't you?"

"It was his job to keep in touch. After all, he was the child not me. Well anyway he's dead too. It was the local police here who came with the news. He was killed in a pile up on the A9 between Nîmes and Montpellier and by the time we were told, the funeral and all that was over. His mother went down south to see the grave. I couldn't go because of the animals. I have always thought that her real decline started from the time of the boy's death and I probably blamed him for that. Not that he could help being killed in a road accident of course. But I guess I had to blame somebody for her deterioration and death."

Tom did not know how to respond. He had supposed that enquiring about Casson's family might naturally lead on to a wider discussion of the past but he had not reckoned on this sad account of a little family withering away. He was also struck by how tight lipped the old man had been until this moment about his family losses. He felt sure that he himself in similar circumstances would have felt driven to share his sense of loss with others and thereby hope bit by bit to learn to bear the pain. He was reminded that Casson had told him that openness was not their way here in the Morvan and his previous silence about his losses was a clear example of that inbred reticence. But at least he had shared the information with him now and this might mean that he had developed enough trust in Tom to make other revelations about those matters to which he had darkly alluded when they had last met the previous week.

They sat opposite each other at the kitchen table for several minutes without speaking until at last Casson picked up the wine bottle and by raising his eyebrows to Tom silently enquired if he would like a top up.

"Why not! Why not, mon vieil ami!" Tom answered, aware that as long as he could totter his way home with the dogs he had no other demands on his Sunday and, despite the unease he felt at having occasioned Casson's revelations of his sorrowful domestic history, he was determined to press on with his wish to get the old man to talk about the past

"I'm very sorry to hear of your losses. Is there no other family? No old friends around?"

"My wife had cousins down in the south where she came from. I don't think I met them ever again after our wedding day though. For all I know they are dead and buried too. If they had any children, I don't know about them and there is no reason why they should even be aware of my existence. As for friends, I have never been one to spend time at the café or at other folks' houses. Naturally, I would run into people from the village from time to time in the lanes or at the market maybe. We would pass the time of day, remark on the weather, the crops, make mention of those who had died or moved away from the village. But I would call these passing acquaintances rather than friends. In any case, I've outlived all of my generation now that Guyard . . ."

Casson looked past Tom's right shoulder in the rough direction of Guyard's house and fell silent briefly. Rather than allow the old man to settle into private reverie however, Tom dived in:

"Guyard. Yes, you're right. I suppose he must have been the last of your contemporaries. That must make you the oldest person in the village although I could readily understand if you find that a dubious honour."

"No," Casson interjected. "You can't saddle me with that. At least I don't think you can. The last I heard Marie-Louise Bertrand was still alive. She had already left the village school when I started there so she must be over a hundred now. Of course, she's been in a home in Avallon for years now. The postman told me she's lost her marbles. Probably messing herself as well, I shouldn't be surprised."

"Nevertheless, mon vieux, there are things in the history of this village that only you know about and—forgive me for saying this—which will disappear forever when your turn comes. As far as I am concerned that would be a great shame."

Tom felt like telling him to get on with it and begin to unlock his memories of the past. Instead, he remained patient and as he waited for the old man to respond, in his mind's eye, he had a sepia coloured image of a very young Casson in shorts, books contained by a belt which was slung over the child's shoulder, at the gate of the village school. In the yard, were a dozen or so other boys and girls all motionless as in a post card and all, except Casson, had now become ghosts.

All of a sudden, Casson began to speak, so softly that Tom had to lean forward and strain to hear. The old man's eyes did not leave his glass which he was rotating to stir the wine. He seemed, as he spoke, to be seeing his memories pictured in the reflections in the amber liquid.

"I don't share your fascination for the past. It really is a fascination for you. I can see that. Perhaps I don't have that feeling because I have that past here in my head, in my memories. But when you think of death—and, obviously, such thoughts have not been far from me for some time and have become even more immediate with recent events and, if I may say so, with our conversation the other day—you have to accept that there will be no more 'me' when it happens. No other person will have anything resembling the volumes of my stored up recollections. My uniqueness will die along with me. But we are all human beings and we are therefore all prone to vanity. I have tried to suppress vanity in myself. Perhaps that is the legacy left by the priests who instructed me in my childhood when I still believed. But their admonitions and my own attempts must have failed for I discover in myself a need for my bundle of memories, my life, in short, not to totally disappear with me. That must be vanity and must also be a useless ambition as well because one can only give a crude outline of what it has meant to be 'Casson'. In any case, there are things which it is not proper to share, such as the often nasty, very private events of nascent adolescent sexuality for example. I'd rather leave that sort of thing to you English with your cursed need for 'openness'. What I am able to do though is give you some feeling of what it was like to be here during the war and its immediate aftermath. After all, that is what seems to intrigue you most of all. My friend, would you fetch another bottle from the back kitchen—it's on the draining board—while I gather my thoughts together?"

"But don't do too much editing!" Tom thought to himself as he went to fetch the replacement bottle.

He hastened back to his chair for fear that if he delayed too long Casson would lose any enthusiasm, however grudging it already was, for revealing the past.

He need not have worried however for the old man began to speak even before Tom had settled himself into his chair and replenished their glasses.

"I was thinking about the people who lived in Saint Val when I was a child and of the many families who have left the area or, simply died out because the children never married and so had no children in their turn. It was a hard place to live in those days. Most people were peasant farmers and the Morvan land is not bountiful. A particularly hard winter was all it needed to make life itself hazardous. Just imagine, we were only just emerging from the days when grown up daughters were sent off to Paris as wet nurses to well to do families, leaving their sisters to look after their own child. Moving around the Morvan was a question of walking or, if you were lucky, getting a ride on the back of an ox cart. In any case, the demands of working the land and tending the animals didn't allow us the luxury of free time so we couldn't have gone far from home anyway. When it came to start looking around for a potential marriage partner, you had to make do with what girls there were in the village or not too far away from Saint Val. The great attraction of church for young people was less that we were devoted to our faith but that it was there that we were likely to meet the opposite sex. The village markets, too, were central to our lives for all sorts of reasons. Of course, there was the trading of beasts and produce that went on; the grown-ups caught up on all the news and gossip; we teenagers promenaded, looking at the girls who were looking at us too and one fine day you found you had left the group of young lads and were walking alongside a girl, just the two of you. That's when the parents really began to take notice, I can tell you! You might as well have signed the marriage contract there and then!"

Casson paused to take a drink, smacked his lips and asked Tom:

"Not a bad drop of stuff this, is it? It's Chablis, you know. Unlabelled of course and I get hold of it from a chap who is able to access what is left when the winegrowers have used up their permitted quotas. It's all on the black, it goes without saying. But if you like it, I could maybe get hold of a few bottles for you."

"That would be very kind. It is a very good drink and reasonably priced too, I expect?"

"Less than two euros a bottle, my friend!" Casson exclaimed with the proud smirk of a successful bargain hunter.

To bring the old chap back to his recollections, Tom asked:

"Is that where you met your wife, then, at the market?"

He realised how crude this may sound with its association with 'cattle market', but Casson did not seem deterred.

"No. I met her while I was doing my military service. She was the sister of a pal of mine in the same billet when we were stationed in Arles. That was her home town. We got married there and she came back here with me when I had finished my service. My parents were a bit upset that I hadn't married locally and they never really seemed to accept her what with her accent and everything. She never got used to the Morvan. I should have known better than to uproot her from her warm soil and bring her to this god forsaken place. You can't grow tender plants here. Well as I said she died and our son must have felt he belonged down south more than here because that's where he'd gone when . . ."

Casson paused and stared into his glass. It was difficult to be sure since the old man's eyes were naturally rheumy but Tom suspected that he was shedding a silent tear. Despite this, Tom pressed on implacably.

"And Guyard? Was he ever married? Did he have any family?"

Casson did not respond for several moments and Tom's question hung heavily in the air. At length, he cleared his throat and continued:

"He never was what most of us would understand as father to a child. But yes, in a way, he was married. It is not easy for me to talk about this because I had a hand in the end of that marriage."

He paused again and Tom wondered at the strangely worded phrase he had used in answer to his question about Guyard having any family. Was he about to be let in on some tale of rural infidelity involving Casson and Guyard's wife?

Sure enough, as he was to learn, there was infidelity but Casson was far from being the cuckolder. In a way, his role was even more decisive.

"He too brought a wife back with him when he returned from his military service. It was pretty plain to see that he had found her in some bar or other. He admitted as much to me later before we stopped talking to each other. I always knew she wasn't going to fit in here. Well I suppose they got on reasonably until the day we got our letters. The Germans had overrun France so quickly that, although we were both on the reserve list for call-up, we never got chance to go to the army. So here we were in the Morvan trying to carry on as normally as we could. Trying to farm with no fertilizers, no petrol and the boches even requisitioned all the decent horses. Then, after eighteen months or so it would have been, in the spring of 1943 because that's when that bastard Laval brought in his Service du Travail Obligatoire and both of us on the very same day if you can believe it, we got those putain de lettres, fucking letters, telling us to report to Auxerre railway station the following Monday for transportation to Germany. We knew what it was for. Forced labour. Toiling for the German war effort. I can tell you those letters were the best recruitment drive to join the Resistance you could have dreamed up. Like many others before us we legged it. Everybody around here had a good idea that a guy who worked at the saw mills was a contact for the local maquis cells. He told us to go home, say nothing, pack a few things and bring a gun and ammunition with us. We would be summoned probably during the night but certainly before we were due to go to Auxerre. I got my rifle which I had wrapped in oiled cloth and buried under the earth floor of the stables and waited. Nobody had handed in their guns as they had been ordered to do. To be accurate, one or two people who had several guns might have handed over some ancient rusty old piece or other to the authorities. Well, very early on Sunday morning, a chap from the village who had taken to the woods a few months before collected us both.

I'd made sure that my wife could get help from some old neighbours if she needed it and I promised her that when I could and if it didn't put her in danger, I would slip back from time to time. I think some of the guys actually enjoyed being outlaws—because that is what we were—but I never did. I guess I had too many responsibilities back here on the farm. We spent most of our time moving on from place to place. We'd sleep in barns mostly. Sometimes, when we were lucky, we'd be taken in overnight in some remote farmhouse. That was real luxury! When the coast was clear we even used to have Sunday lunch sat round a trestle table in a barn belonging to friendly farmers. There was no way the Germans could patrol the whole of the Morvan. In fact, people who lived in villages were in more danger than us because of the reprisals which followed on from our activities. There were some terrible things happened. You'll have heard about the massacre at Dun les Places where they shot twenty or so villagers including the maire and the headmaster of the school and chucked the priest off the church tower to hang. They burned a dozen buildings as well. Such events would have caused me to stop our attacks but we were led by men who were, call it what you will, more patriotic or more fanatical than me. As time went on we became more and more organised. We had British liaison officers and when they arrived we began to get more supplies on a regular basis. In fact, Guyard was attached to one such officer, a lieutenant I think he was or he could have been a captain maybe, and when we came across each other he couldn't help showing off the English he was picking up. I remember thinking that English must be bloody easy because he had been no brain box when we were at school in Saint Val. But something happened that took the wind right out of his sails. Very soon after we went to the woods, he slipped back home one night. His wife wasn't there. It turned out that she had picked up with a German soldier that she'd met at the café in Saint Val. We found out that when this Fritz had been posted to Cissey les Champs to be part of the guard post at the railway station, she had gone with him. She went to live with him in a house that had been requisitioned by the boches. It changed Guyard that did and not surprisingly either. He became withdrawn, sullen, always ready to get into a fight if he suspected someone was laughing at him. He started to volunteer to go on the most dangerous missions and he never missed an opportunity to kill Germans. He seemed to enjoy that part the most. Anyway, whether it was because of this ferocity in him or whether it was because he was close to the English who were important because they were our suppliers and did a lot of organising especially as the end drew near, he got promoted up the ranks. We were doing a lot more blowing up of railways and bridges in anticipation of the Allied landings in the north so as to stop German troops flooding up from the south. We were supposed to wait for the signal before we openly attacked the Germans. But because we had leaders who were just as impetuous and as bitter as Guyard, we jumped the gun. Our group, probably influenced by Guyard, decided to take over the railway station at Cissey. I should have seen what was coming. I probably did, in fact, but kept quiet. When we got there the Germans were just packing up to leave. There were only six or seven of them including, as I later discovered, the one who had cuckolded Guyard and we fell upon them like wolves from the forests. We slaughtered them—even the one or two who had raised their hands in surrender. I found this sickening but there was worse to come. There were four young women—no more than girls really—cowering in the houses opposite the station. I can't say for certain sure if it was Guyard alone who gave the orders. Whether it was the two or three old women who had emerged from other houses cawing for revenge or whether we were carried away by the bloodletting which had just gone on, I just don't know but before we knew what was happening the young women had been dragged out into the station yard. The old women supplied scissors and helped a couple of our guys to shear their hair. I don't know who had the idea but four of our chaps, including Guyard—and of that I am sure—took a vote and decided they should be put on trial for treason because they had aided and abetted the enemies of France. Of course, in a matter of minutes they were found guilty. The same four men selected the firing squad of six. I was one of the six. Guyard's wife was one of the four women we shot. I shut my eyes when I fired. But fire I did."

Casson fell silent and Tom was too stunned to speak. Instead he filled their two glasses once more.

After the old man had taken a deep drink and wiped the back of his hand across his eyes, he continued.

"After that Guyard and I never had anything to do with each other. I knew I was no good anymore for direct action, for killing and the guys in charge must have realised it because I was put on messenger duties. I fetched up down in the Beaune area. I was there when the town was liberated early in September. That was one of the very few good memories of those dark times, what with all the drinking and the singing and the flag waving. For me, the joy didn't last beyond that day though. I couldn't get the images of the slaughtering in Cissey station yard out of my head. You wouldn't get me to go back there even now. I only returned there the once just after the killings. I was torn apart with shame for what I had done. You can imagine how often I have asked myself why I didn't refuse to take part, why I didn't speak out against the atrocity. The only way I have found of easing my conscience has been to say to myself that it would have still happened whatever I had done. But that doesn't take away my feeling of guilt for very long. I had a deep anger towards Guyard for what he had brought about. I suppose from that terrible day I hated him. As for him, he must have felt some remorse. He must have done, surely. He may even have blamed me, in his own mind, just so as to take away some of the guilt from himself. No doubt, he grew to hate me too. We have been bound together all these years by this hideous secret we shared and yet separated by our loathing for each other. I have never spoken to anyone about this before. I didn't even tell my wife though she knew something had happened to change me. You know that I didn't want to lay the burden on you. But perhaps it is right, now that Guyard is dead, that the secret should be shared. I'm just sorry that it had to be you."

"Please don't let that worry you. I'm honoured that you feel you could take me into your confidence in this way," Tom said, aware of how facile his response sounded.

Casson was silent, no doubt reliving for the millionth time the events in which he had been involved. To fill the silence Tom remarked:

"Well, at least there were no children."

"I didn't say that, Tom. There was a child but, although he was the biological father, Guyard never even saw it let alone looked after it. It was a little girl, the daughter of Cécile—that was what Guyard's wife was called. The German soldier took over the role of the child's father."

"Good God! What on earth happened to her, to the child?"

"I did go back to Cissey as I said just that one time three days after the killings. I don't know why exactly. I just felt that I had to. At least the bodies had been taken away. I didn't enquire what they had done with them. I didn't dare. But I did come across one of the old hags who had been screaming at us. Now, she seemed just a harmless old lady. Perhaps she was salving her conscience, I don't know, but she told me she had gone to the Mairie with the baby and that somehow they had managed to find some relatives of the mother, her parents or cousins she thought, back where she came from. They agreed to take the child in."

"Do you think Guyard knew about the child?"

"The baby was born after we left for the woods but I don't see how he could not have known. He knew all about Cécile and her German after all. For my part, I have always been convinced that he knew and I have always been sure that the fact there was a child only fuelled his rage."

"In a way that just makes it all the more terrible."

Tom was aware that the revelation of his tragic secret had tired Casson. In addition he thought that the old chap had probably drunk far more than usual. So it was convenient that one of the Briards decided at that moment that she had had enough waiting around outside Casson's house and began to scratch at the door. This set the Spaniel off barking and Tom was able to make his excuses.

"Look. I think the dogs are telling me I had better be making my way home. You look as though you could do with a little rest as well. If you're sure you are going to be alright on your own, I'll take your shopping list and get on my way. Would you mind if I just collect the eggs for the moment? I'll pop back to check on the chickens' water and feed later."

This met with no objection from the old man. In fact he seemed to want to be alone now that he had spoken out and so Tom, slightly unsteady on his feet, set off over the hill.

He had much to think about and when he had unravelled the implications of Casson's account, he had a suspicion that he would find that he had been privy to some very significant information.

16

'Tout le monde se plaint de sa mémoire et
personne ne se plaint de son jugement.'
La Rochefoucault
(Author's translation : "We all complain
about our poor memory but we never
complain about our poor judgement.")

When Tom got home he first made sure the dogs had plenty of water to drink. Then he thought he had better check for messages on the house telephone, a feat which he had taken a while to master. His mobile was still very largely an instrument of mystery to him and he only used it to send and to receive calls. In fact, he often deliberately left it behind when he set off somewhere.

He discovered that there were brief messages all of which asked him to ring the callers back. They were from Jenny, which he had expected as he had been remiss in not calling her earlier, from Mandy, from Nigel who had called three times and from Jean Luc Renard. He realised that he was exhausted by the wine he had consumed and by the stiff walk back home with the dogs. He also had a jumble of thoughts in his mind and he was convinced that he needed to have a nap so that he would be refreshed enough to sort these out before he answered any of the calls. He turned off his mobile phone and took the house telephone off the hook so that he would not be disturbed since from past experience Nigel was quite likely to keep on ringing him until he got through. He really couldn't face him and his problems, especially now when his mind was filled with what he had heard that morning and which seemed so much more weighty. He took himself off to the sitting room, turned on the television, slumped in his armchair and was asleep in seconds.

He awoke with a dry mouth which a glass of fizzy water temporarily cured. He was surprised to see from the kitchen clock that it was after four but as he had not noted what time he had got back home, he had no sense of how long he had been asleep. One thing was evident and this was that the dogs had been tired too for they were all still out to the world. All he got as he passed their prone bodies was a single, languid wag of the tail.

Armed with a cup of coffee, he sat at the kitchen table with pen and paper and started to make some jottings of what he had learned from Casson. He felt confident that, during his rest, his brain had been sifting and sorting the information he had been given. On several occasions previously, he had awoken in the middle of the night with the answer to a crossword clue which had earlier seemed unsolvable and if sleep could unravel such a conundrum, it would surely have helped him to abstract what was significant in Casson's account.

First he wrote out 'New information about Guyard', underlined this and below he made the following entries.

1. G was married to Cécile
2. When G joined the Maquis C left to live with a German soldier
3. She and her lover were tracked down (by G?)
4. They were shot in Cissey (did G orchestrate this?)
5. G knew about the child Cécile had had (or so Casson believes!)
6. G resentful his child being brought up by German soldier?
7. In different times, G might have been accused (guilty?) of murder/manslaughter.

Tom then squeezed in after 'New information' the words 'and questions.' He then added

8. G hated Casson?

After this he did the same for Casson and his list read:

1. Casson. was married. Wife dead. (Name?)
2. He had a son Michel also dead in a car crash.
3. He joined the maquis the same day as G.
4. Casson was a member of the firing squad in Cissey
5. Casson found out about the child
6. Casson hated Guyard

Next he drew up a section consisting of no more than a simple list entitled 'New personalities.'

1. Madame Casson
2. Michel Casson
3. Cécile Guyard
4. Cécile's baby
5. German soldier

This led him to the most important section which he would be happy to limit at this stage to a few random thoughts and questions.

He was about to launch into this when he realized it may occupy him for quite a long time and he really ought to answer those telephone calls. At least, he should ring Jenny and Renard for certain. Perhaps he could leave the other two for later.

Out of husbandly duty he called Jenny first.

"Hello, darling. How are you? I'm sorry I didn't ring you sooner but I've been out with the dogs," Tom said when she picked up, neglecting, for reasons which were not clear to him, to say that he had been with Casson.

"'It must have been a very long walk, my precious. I expect you are all worn out. But no matter, it's good to hear from you. How was your hen party last night?"

"It was fascinating and shocking too, I have to say. I simply hadn't realized how intimately women discuss their menfolk. It was as though I wasn't there. I hope you don't talk about me like that."

"Of course not. What could I possibly find to say about you to my girl friends?"

"'I don't know whether you are trying to be flattering or whether you are having a go at me."

"Don't worry, my poor Tom. I'm just pulling your leg. I find it entirely charming that you were shocked by Mandy who can be very frank to say the least. Usually Cheryl is far less forthcoming although she does seem to be coming out of her shell lately. It sounds as though you were a bit out of your depth and that does you nothing but credit. Anyway, the reason I rang earlier was to find out if you would have any problems if I were to stay on here until Wednesday. It's just that Caroline has arranged a girls' night out to see a show in town on Tuesday evening."

"No, not at all. You do that. Is there anything I need to take care of at this end? You haven't got any appointments or anything like that have you?"

"Not that I can recall. You might need to get some shopping. Just check on the dog food would you? I'll be on the usual train on Wednesday evening at Montbard so keep the evening clear, won't you sweetheart?"

"If I can fit it in around all my girls' get-togethers."

"'In your dreams. Anyway, I must fly. I'll see you at the station on Wednesday but we'll speak on the 'phone before then of course. Lots of love!"

"Bye! Lots of love to you as well."

Tom was not at all disconsolate at the thought of an extra day on his own. In any case, he rather imagined that things would begin to hot up on the investigation front and it would be much easier with Jenny away to make himself available if Renard had need of his services.

It was to the Commissaire that he addressed his next call and as he was waiting for him to answer, he took the decision not to share what he had learned from Casson at least until he had chance to sleep on it. It would be wise all the same to let him know that he had visited him for, no doubt, the watchdog he had left in Saint Val would have already reported his movements to his boss.

"Ah, Jean Luc, I think you rang me earlier. What can I do for you, my friend?"

"It was nothing terribly important and you seem to have been having such a busy time this weekend, I thought I would try to get you later. It is only to ask if I could call on you at around ten o'clock tomorrow morning so that we can sketch out our plans for the first part of the week. It's been seven days now since the murder and I really feel as if I should have made more progress."

"I'm sure that things will move rapidly. Something is bound to come up to open a few doors," Tom said, thinking of how much he had learned from Casson.

"Thanks for your optimism. I hope you are right. So shall we say ten at your place then?"

"The coffee will be waiting. See you tomorrow Jean Luc."

"See you then. Just imagine snogging in doorways at your age!" Renard threw in as he put down the telephone.

Tom thanked providence and his own good sense that it had not been more than a brief 'snog' as Renard had put it. Nevertheless, he felt himself blushing which for him was a most unusual occurrence.

He settled down at the kitchen table with a second cup of coffee with the intention of adding to his previous list. What he recognized most of all was that his earlier intuitions that Guyard's murder was in some way connected to events which had happened during and at the end of the war had certainly not been shown to be completely misguided by what Casson had revealed to him. In his judgement it was quite the reverse since it seemed that he had been given motives aplenty and, in addition, surely the passions involved could well be the stuff of murder. Much as he thought of Casson as an old friend, it was not possible to eliminate him from any list of potential suspects. After all he had freely admitted that he hated Guyard for what he felt he had forced him into doing all those years ago. Therein, however, lay a problem because the hatred had been lit 'all those years ago.' So why, if he was the guilty party, had he not acted much earlier? Hadn't Renard also said that there could have been more than one killer? Tom couldn't see Casson having the physical strength to carry out the murder in the way he now knew it had been committed. Not on his own in any case and Tom, for the life in him, couldn't think who could possibly have acted as his accomplice. Casson was a self avowed loner and unless this was just a pose and there was someone close to him in the background that Tom knew nothing about, there simply was no-one who came to mind. A sudden thought struck him. What if Casson's son did not die in a car crash. He had only the old man's word that his son was dead. As this thought was conceived, another was telling him that this was all wildly speculative, unlikely and above all disloyal to the old boy. Despite this, he jotted down 'Could Casson be the murderer? If so, why now instead of years ago and who could his accomplice be?'

There was Cécile's child, of course. Tom wondered if it could be that the little girl or a person or persons close to her had been responsible. At once he rejected this theory as being simply too wild. He recognized that he should stop thinking of her as a little girl. Sixty years or so had passed by. Tom realized with a jolt that she would be roughly the same age as himself. There was no way, in any case, he could pursue this unlikely avenue any further without more information about the girl. He would have to put his thoughts to Renard and hope they were convincing enough to persuade him to do some digging around. Tom thought that it would be useful to find the girl for more than one reason. Despite his misgivings, it was just about possible she could be directly or, more likely, indirectly involved with the killing and, of course, if she were still alive and they managed to locate her, she would probably be Guyard's inheritrix. Tom's imagination fleetingly took over from rational considerations.

What a powerful motive that would be! The marriage of vengeance and financial gain! He contented himself, however, with merely writing down 'Find out if Renard is prepared to look for the girl.' As an afterthought, he added 'She could be involved somehow (????)'

There was something niggling away in the back of his mind. Something which Casson had said and which Tom had thought would be of interest to Renard. He cursed his poor memory. It had to be something he had learned about Casson or Guyard. He searched in vain and had to content himself with a brief note reminding himself that there was something he had to pass on to the Commissaire. He was sure that whatever it was, it would pop up to the surface with the appropriate stimulation and this would be bound to occur, he thought, during his conversation with Renard the next day if not before.

The dogs were beginning to stir themselves and reminded Tom that it was time for them to be fed by staring at him balefully and by gathering at the door to the utility area where their food and bowls were kept and where they ate. He had just finished filling their bowls with more meat and biscuits than Jenny would have approved of and set them sufficiently far away from each other to ensure they would get on and eat rather than standing over their food growling jealously at each other, when the telephone rang.

"Allo, oui, Tom Fox," he sang out.

"Hello Tom! It's Nigel. I rang you earlier. I don't know whether you picked up my message."

"Yes, I did. I was going to ring you back but I hadn't got round to it yet. My apologies but it's a bit busy what with Jenny not being here to share the chores," was the excuse which tripped readily from his tongue.

"Of course. I understand all too well seeing that Tim is not here any longer and it falls to me to try to keep up to all the work in the garden as well as the cooking and cleaning."

"So there is no change between you and him yet, then."

"No, my dear old thing, there isn't. That's partly why I am ringing you, Tom. I am enlisting your help in bringing things to a head. I suppose you know he has holed up at the Brown's house. I expect that earth mother Cheryl is clucking all over him. I wondered if you could contact him for me and tell him that if he isn't back here by tomorrow at five o'clock, I shall be putting the rest of his things in a pile outside the gates and that, as far as I am concerned, will be that."

Tom's first reaction was one of dismay. He had no wish whatsoever to be caught in the middle of a spat which, if he was brutally honest, he felt was not his concern. It irritated him that Nigel had thought fit to seek to employ him in this way. Besides, he wished his attentions to remain focused on the Guyard case and he resented any distraction from that.

"I'm not sure I'm the right person to do that, Nigel," he replied rather weakly he felt.

"I'm sorry to ask you to do this, Tom. But I can't think of anyone else I can approach. The matter really does need to be resolved and if it does turn out that he's not coming back then I shall most definitely be putting the house on the market with all the stops out. Of course, I shall be asking you to handle the sale and I would be prepared, at least for an initial period, to let you have exclusive selling rights."

Tom bridled at this obvious piece of attempted bribery and even more at the implied threat that if he did not comply, Nigel would be giving the house to another agent. Despite his irritation, however, he could not readily see an escape route. Perhaps there was a way it could be done. Perhaps he could ring Cheryl and get her to deliver the ultimatum. After all she was apparently all too happy to look after and guard over Tim.

"Nigel, I have to say that the sale of your house has nothing to do with it and I'm agreeing to help not because of that at all," Tom replied in an attempt to make it plain that he had recognized Nigel's ploy and was unmoved by pecuniary considerations. "I am not at all happy at the idea. However," he continued, "leave it with me and I'll see what can be done."

"Thank you, Tom. That is most accommodating of you. It would be simply wonderful if you could give him the message this evening by the way."

"I'd rather assumed that would be the case given that you have set a deadline of five o'clock tomorrow. By the way, talking about selling your house, I still haven't heard anything from the clients I brought over to you on Thursday. I'm sure my first instincts were right and they are simply time wasters."

"I'm not at all sure I would have liked the thought of them living in my house anyway. They were a bit rough weren't they? They were a bit scary as well. Still I have never been one to turn down a bit of rough and a hint of scariness can add a little piquancy too in my experience. That aside though, I ended up being convinced that they weren't here to buy on their own behalf. They were more the types to be looking at the Costa Plenty in Spain if they had been house-hunting for themselves."

"You could be right. Anyway I've got some notes to write up for Commissaire Renard before I see him tomorrow morning and if I'm going to make your phone call for you, I'd better hang up."

"Oh my dearest Tom, if you're writing anything about me, do keep it clean. I don't expect you'll need to talk about my orientation. I have a teeny weeny suspicion that your French friend may have worked that out for himself. In any case, if he hasn't, I'm sure dear, sweet Jérôme will fill him in—if you'll pardon the expression. To save you from wondering, Jay-day—that's what I call him and have you ever heard such sexy French initials in your whole life—has just gone off home. He will be coming back for dinner a little later though. I love his accent when he speaks English. Shades of a 'Fish called Wanda'. It goes straight to my nethers when he talks."

"Christ, Nigel! Do be careful. He is a policeman after all."

"Don't worry, Tom. The skirmishes have been entirely preliminary so far and in any event I am no stranger to Policemen's Balls, you know. I'll keep you posted. Bye bye, sweetie!"

Tom was at a loss to know what to make of Nigel's present state of mind. Surely, he couldn't be recovering from Tim's apparent departure so quickly. Surely, he couldn't actually be in the process of seducing Duvallon.

Bemused, he found himself telephoning the Browns' house before he knew what he was doing. Fortunately it was Cheryl who picked up the call and when Tom had passed on Nigel's message to her she replied:

"Silly old fool. Doesn't he realize that there is no way on earth that Tim is moving back in with him. It's over. I can assure you of that."

"Well, actually, Cheryl, it's not me that needs the assuring. It's Nigel."

"Well, we are not doing anything about it this evening. I'm just about to drop Steve at the station. Nigel will just have to find out the truth when I drive Tim round to his house to pick up his things at five tomorrow!"

"As you wish. I've done what I promised Nigel I would do. I won't keep you, Cheryl. Drive carefully. Bye."

"Bye, Tom. Sorry if I sound a bit shrewish and, by the way, if your policeman friend needs to get hold of Tim, you can tell him he'll be staying here for the time being. Bye."

Tom was beginning to feel that he had enough of other people's lives, of their intimacies and, above all, of their revelations for one day, when the telephone rang yet again.

"Tom. It's Mandy. I really need to speak to you. Do you want to pop round for a drink in half an hour or so? Or I could come to your place."

"I've had a terribly busy day, Mandy. Couldn't it wait for tomorrow?"

"It's very important, Tom."

Tom found himself reluctantly agreeing that she could come over to his house. When he put the phone down he reckoned he had made tactical errors both in agreeing to see her at all and also, he realized, in not going to her house instead of her coming to his. From her house he could at least have made his getaway when it suited him.

What, he wondered, would Renard's sentry make of this?

CHAPTER...

17

*"A gentleman knows how to play the
accordion, but doesn't."
(Attributed to Al Cohn, an American saxophonist.)*

When Mandy drew up in front of the house some twenty minutes later, Tom had made sure that the dogs had been outside to do the necessary and he had done a swift bit of rudimentary tidying up.

He was intrigued to such a degree by her insistence that there was something 'important' she needed to talk to him about, that he now felt less irked than when he had been feebly trying to put her off during their telephone conversation. The annoyance at his failure to discourage her had almost abated. He realized that, being, as he now felt he truly was, a part of the Guyard investigation, his usual and natural curiosity had been sharpened and somehow legitimized.

He met her at the door and was careful to draw her inside before offering a welcoming embrace lest the twin pecks on her cheeks be manoeuvred into what Renard had referred to as a 'snog'. He even peered up the drive and across their field to the road to see if he could spot the police look-out before he closed the door behind them.

"Here you are, Tom. I've brought you a bottle of red. I hope it's alright because to be honest I don't know one bottle from another. It should be pretty good though because I pinched it from Tony's reserve supply in the cellar."

Tom examined the label.

"This is a seven year old Monthélie, Mandy. It should be more than 'pretty good'. Are you sure though? Won't Tony be a bit put out when he finds that one of his prize bottles has disappeared?"

"Well, if you don't tell him, I shan't. He'll probably never realize it's gone."

She had at once taken the opportunity to draw him into a private plot which excluded her husband, he noticed. Whilst the concealment of a missing bottle of wine was of no great import, Tom saw it nevertheless as symptomatic of her potential for uxorial disaffection and, indeed, for more than that if her blandishments of the previous evening were anything to go by. It served to reinforce his determination to stay on his guard.

"So, shall I open the Monthélie or would you prefer something else perhaps?"

"It depends what's on offer, Tom," she purred with a feline squirm of her shoulders.

"Drink, Mandy! I meant what do you want to drink!"

"Of course, Tom. Whatever else did you think I could have been meaning?"

She had deftly wrong footed him so that it seemed as if, of the two of them, it was he who was harbouring lascivious thoughts. He found himself wondering if her suggestiveness was merely the usual persona she adopted when she was in the company of any man. Unless, however, he had badly misread her behaviour as he was making his farewells the evening before, she had been very specific in her intentions. He was inclined to believe he was not just 'any man' as far as Mandy was concerned. He felt much more of a target than that.

"I'll tell you what, Tom. I could really enjoy a gin and tonic. You go ahead and open the red though. I know that is your favourite tipple. No doubt, I'll join you later."

As he was finding lemon and ice from the fridge in the utility room he called out to her:

"You said you needed to talk about something important.'

"Well it may be nothing. It's probably me just worrying unduly. It all seems so different now that I am here with you. It may not even be worth mentioning at all."

Tom emerged with her drink, still feeling that he should be annoyed at how she had inveigled herself upon him but at the same time recognizing that, so much did he find her modus operandi intriguing, he was actually enjoying this encounter with her. He was not unaware, either, that being alone with an attractive and, possibly, more than compliant woman was in itself a rare and pleasurable experience however firmly he was determined that it would lead to nothing more compromising than a playful verbal exchange.

"Mmm. That's lovely. Thank you, Tom. Just what the doctor ordered."

"I still think that if you were worried enough by whatever it is that is on your mind to ring me and to come here, you should perhaps tell me about it. It may help just to talk, you know. That's what they say, isn't it?"

"You're such a darling, Tom. You don't know how rare it is to come across such a considerate man."

Tom thought to himself:

"Bugger being considerate! I'm just being curious. No. More than that! I'm being plain bloody nosey!"

"But I don't know about telling you what was worrying me. You might think it is just something and nothing and I couldn't bear it if you thought I was being silly."

Tom had opened Tony's bottle of wine, had poured himself a taster measure, held it to the light and taken a sample sip.

"Now that is divine. Many thanks, Mandy. Cheers," said Tom chinking glasses.

"I hope you are going to leave me a drop. After all, this little lady has thieved for you and she needs some reward for her devotion. I'll think about it. Telling you what's on my mind, I mean."

"Do what you think you want to do."

"Oh, I will, Tom. Have no fear," she responded with a meaningful chuckle.

She finished her gin and tonic and Tom passed her a glass of the Monthélie.

"Thank you, Tom. Oh it is very good, isn't it? I suppose we should thank Tony as well. Thanks, Tony!" she said rais-

ing her glass into the air. "You know what has struck me
though? Of the five households in Saint Val only Peggy and
Harry are both together at home tonight. There's you with
Jenny in England. There's me with Tony off at his bloody
motor racing. There's Cheryl who will be packing Steve off
at the station just about now. Not forgetting poor old Lady
Nigel all on his lonesome now that Tim has upped sticks.
Quite a thought isn't it?"

"I'll tell you something else as well! Trust me because
I've got a bit of a nose for that sort of thing," she continued,
giving Tom, who had adopted the defensive ploy of placing
himself at the opposite side of the table from Mandy, a generous view of her cleavage as she leaned forward conspirato-
rially and leaned her bosom on her arms. "I've got a shrewd
suspicion that there's more going on between those two than
meets the eye."

For a brief second Tom thought she was referring to her
breasts for that was where his thoughts and eyes were as
she was speaking. He found himself wondering if she had
had an enhancement performed. His brief misunderstanding
obliged him to avert his gaze and look her in the eye instead.
He realized with a flash of schoolboy guilt that she was quite
aware that he had been ogling. She was, however, smiling
at him as if to grant him licence to stare. Pulling himself
together, Tom asked:

"I'm sorry. Who do you mean 'those two'? I'm not with
you."

"Cheryl and Tim, of course. Who did you think I meant?"

"Surely not. You can't be serious, Mandy. Tim's not—
um . . . He's gay."

"That's one of the things I adore about you, Tom. You're
such an innocent. You're so straight and uncomplicated yourself that you simply can't contemplate that things may possibly, just possibly be a little ambiguous."

Tom was not at all sure that he appreciated her assessment
of him. He was not, in his own opinion, in any way naïve. On
the contrary, if anyone had called him a man of the world, he
would have more happily agreed with them.

"I suppose anything is possible but . . .," he tailed off lamely.

"It's more common than you might think. Quite a lot of men are ambidextrous as far as I can see. I never thought of Tim as being the feminine half of the partnership with Nigel, did you?"

"Well no, of course not. But that's only judging from the way they behave, especially with Nigel queening it up all the time," Tom answered, although in truth he had never been too keen on analyzing their relationship too precisely.

"Besides, ask yourself this. How did Tim know that he would be welcomed in at the Browns' place, if he and Cheryl hadn't already arranged it all in advance? He would hardly have negotiated with Steve about moving in with them, would he now?"

"You never know. As you said a lot of men may be ambidextrous."

"Not Steve though. Trust me I would know. Besides just think how closely Cheryl and Tim have stuck together since he left Nigel. Did you see them more than a foot apart during the whole evening at your barbecue? Did you spot her stroking Tim's face? It didn't strike me that she was just being sympathetic. It seemed much more like the spontaneous gesture of a lover."

"I suppose there may be something in what you say," Tom admitted grudgingly.

"Do you remember how defensive she was about Tim when we were talking about him at my place?"

Tom recalled that he had been a trifle surprised at Cheryl's championing Tim's cause that evening and, of course, he had had the telephone conversation with her subsequently. It certainly seemed to him in this new light that she had been confident speaking on Tim's behalf about the ultimatum from Nigel. As he considered it, Tom had to acknowledge that Cheryl had spoken with the self assurance of one half of an established couple who felt no need to consult the other before making a pronouncement which concerned them both.

Perhaps, he began to believe, Mandy was not so far wide of the mark after all.

However, all he was prepared to concede was that he had an open mind on the matter.

"There could be something in it, I suppose. But whether it's got as far as being a full-on affair, I have my doubts."

"Don't forget they are going to be alone together in the house now that Steve has gone off to work until Thursday evening so I don't expect we'll be kept in doubt for very long!"

"Yes but the boys are going to be there. Surely they won't get up to anything in front of them."

"And when they are at school? Don't try to tell me, Tom Fox, that people don't shag during daylight hours because they do!"

Mandy had not revealed her feelings about Cheryl and Tim simply to make idle chitchat, merely to gossip. Her hidden agenda, of which she herself was fully aware, had been to establish an ambience between her and Tom in which infidelity was recognized as being possible and, more than that, was actually being practised in Saint Val. In such an atmosphere her ambitions would be more easily attained or so her intuitions were telling her.

Tom refilled their glasses and, excusing himself, disappeared into the pantry to knock up a cheese board. It had suddenly occurred to him that he had not eaten much all day and, with the thought, came pangs of hunger. During his brief absence, Mandy determined after all to broach the matter which she had described as 'important' when they were speaking on the telephone.

As they started to attack the cheese and biscuits, she began by asking a question.

"Could I ask you, Tom, if you think the police here will delve into our lives in the U.K?"

"I am absolutely sure they will. In fact, I've already been given the once over. They had to be sure that there was nothing too horrendous in my background before I was asked to be Renard's interpreter. As I understand it the Commissaire is waiting for responses to his request for information from the authorities about all the Brits in Saint Val."

"'That's what I told Tony."

"I don't think there is any reason to panic," Tom went on. "It's a pet theory of mine that most of us Brits are over here because, in some sort of way, we are all keen to put certain things from our pasts behind us. That and, of course, the fact that this is such a wonderful place to live anyway. They will only be interested if they turn up something which they can link directly to Guyard's murder. Nobody is so pure and innocent that an investigation of their lives will not throw up something they would rather keep under the carpet."

Faced with her silence, as she sipped her wine, Tom continued:

"I can't think there is anything to worry about. I mean I'm sure nobody among us has a record as brutal murderers."

"No, of course not. But there are things, as you say, that we would rather keep to ourselves. Some of us have more to hide than you, for example, probably have. You had a professional career according to Jenny. Well, people like me and Tony weren't so lucky. Maybe we were too dim. I don't know. But we've had to come up the hard way and if there were corners that could be cut, then, sure as hell, we cut them. You're probably thinking that means we were ready to step outside the law when we needed to. To be fair, you wouldn't be far from the truth either."

Tom wondered whether she would be more forthcoming and, after a short pause during which she was presumably weighing up how much to reveal, she obliged.

"I'm not saying that I, personally, have got any sort of police record. I might have had though. When I was a kid, I was pretty good looking. The blokes seem to think so anyway. So it was never difficult for me to get jobs in one of the clubs or other. You would have to have been blind or stupid not to notice some of the things that were going on. There were some real villains around, I can tell you. You didn't need to get your hair permed. What I heard sometimes made it curl all on its own."

Mandy fell silent and Tom felt obliged to say something encouraging in response to her revelations.

"If you were good looking as a young woman, then time has certainly been kind because you still are a very attractive woman."

"Christ, Tom, I'm not that ancient. But thank you, kind Sir, for the compliment anyway."

"Is that where you met Tony? At one of the clubs you worked in?" Tom enquired and added, in an attempt to recover from his implication that her young days had passed her by, "He's a very lucky man in my opinion."

"That's what I keep telling him. Since you ask I did meet him at the club. We recognized each other straight away. We'd been at school together you see. And here we are still together. Just about anyway."

Tom couldn't bring himself to enquire too directly about Tony's past which he assumed could have been more dubious than Mandy's. She added of her own accord, however, that he had never been what she termed 'a real villain' but that he had been a bit handy with his fists.

"That's what worried me, you see, those times when that old geezer, Guyard, used to come round and stare at me when I was sunbathing round the back of the house. It didn't bother me too much in the beginning. I mean if it gave him a cheap thrill then why not is my philosophy. I suppose, if I'm honest though, it did give me the creeps a bit after a while. He'd be out there sort of watching us for what seemed like hours on end and not just if I was taking in the rays either. I never mentioned how I was feeling to Tony though. I was scared he would turn a bit nasty with the old chap and it didn't warrant that."

It did not escape Tom that this was another sound reason for avoiding a dalliance with Mandy. He was not anxious to put Tony's understanding nature to the test, nor, even less, to evaluate the efficacy of his right hook, let alone a knee in the groin or whatever other punishment he might choose to mete out.

For her part, Mandy seemed to recognize that the atmosphere had changed and she prepared to make her departure but not without being able to resist a final come on remark.

"I suppose I should go in case Tony rings me. It's very odd that he hasn't telephoned already in fact. It's most unlike him. But while he's away, this little mouse can play. I'm still waiting for my chosen playmate to join in though."

When she had left, Tom had the same mixture of regret and relief that he had previously experienced. At least this time, he had not had the tantalizing farewell kiss to further eat away at his resolve.

There was much to impart to Renard the following morning and, after hearing what Mandy had half revealed, his appetite was wetted for the series of interviews with his compatriots which, he was sure, the policeman would be fixing up at their next meeting.

CHAPTER . . .

18

"Expatiate free o'er all this scene of man;
A mighty maze! But not without a plan".
(Pope "An Essay on Man")

Tom had risen early and had drunk so many cups of strong coffee that he felt he could have run a marathon while simultaneously speed-reading the complete works of Shakespeare. So it was with gathering impatience that he noted Renard was already late. It was twenty minutes past the appointed hour for their rendezvous in fact and, in his present caffeine induced state of high alert and low tolerance, he was finding it hard to be patient. Years of living in France however should have taught him that when an appointment is fixed for a certain hour, it should be taken to mean that the meeting would take place not before that hour but some time thereafter. He had also learned to expect a more or less acceptable excuse for the tardiness.

At half past the hour, Tom finally heard a car making its way along the drive and he went out to meet it.

"Salut, Tom! I'm so sorry to keep you waiting like this," Renard cried as he crossed from his car to shake hands with Tom.

"Don't mention it. I was here anyway and I wasn't about to go anywhere else," he responded with a forced smile, thinking to himself that the excuse would be sure to come next. As indeed it did.

"I had to see the juge d'instruction before I came on here. He had insisted I bring him up to speed with the investigation. As it turned out, it was a rather embarrassing encounter. I didn't really have very much to report and certainly I couldn't begin to deliver up the names of any strong suspects and that tends to get their backs up. They like to get the paperwork drawn up and the case logged into the schedules as soon as they can."

Tom didn't really follow what Renard was saying and he put this down to his not being at all clear what a juge d'instruction actually was. He decided not to ask, thereby revealing his ignorance, but rather to find out for himself later testing out his shaky lack of confidence with his computer by referring to an appropriate website.

"Come inside, Jean Luc. Can I get you a coffee?"

"That would be very welcome. I don't suppose you have got any of those wonderful English ginger biscuits, have you? Forgive me for being so bold!"

"I think I can oblige. We generally bring a few packets over when we go to the UK."

"Don't let me take the last ones, will you!"

"Jenny will be bringing more stock this trip I'm sure, so don't worry. I should let you know, by the way, that I spoke to her over the weekend and, assuming it's alright by you, of course, she will be staying on an extra day in England. So she won't be back until Wednesday evening."

"That is absolutely no problem, mon vieux. But thank you for keeping me informed all the same."

Renard dunked each of the three biscuits he had allowed himself in his coffee. When he had eaten them with gratifying grunts of enjoyment and drained his coffee, so as not to miss the mush which had been detached from the biscuits, he set assiduously about the dregs with his spoon.

Tom remained quiet, content to witness the policeman's performance. When he seemed to have finally finished, Tom felt like applauding but instead contented himself with saying:

"You really do like your ginger biscuits, don't you, Jean Luc? Look, why don't you take the rest of the packet?"

"That would be most kind . . . Ah, I see! Am I detecting an example of the famous English irony perhaps? I think I understand the nuance! I was perhaps a little, shall we say, over exuberant when I was attacking the biscuits and you gave me a gentle rebuke. You see I am beginning to understand the subtleties of your culture."

This enlightenment had not prevented him, however, from taking Tom up on his offer and as he had been speaking he had taken some blank sheets of paper from his briefcase and stuffed the biscuits into it in their place.

"So, my dear Tom, I think it would be useful if I outlined to you what has emerged from our digging around last week."

"That would be interesting. Thank you. I have one or two thoughts too which I believe may be of some interest. So if you wish I could share those with you."

"By all means. I rather thought you may have come up with something. After all, I have been reliably informed that you have had a socially busy weekend. Dare I say it, the sooner your wife comes back the better. Although I have to say that I feel a little jealous of your conquest."

"I wouldn't call it a conquest exactly. But I suspect that the possibility is there—if I were foolish enough to take the lady up on her apparent offer. I hope you don't mind my asking. Is there a Madame Renard?"

"There are—or were, to be more accurate—two. It seems that my job and married life don't sit easily together. I am afraid neither marriage survived my prolonged and irregular absences from the family hearth. I've resigned myself to bachelordom these days. It seems a wiser course to be satisfied with the occasional dalliance although as I get older the thought of having a wife to go home to seems to get more appealing."

"Life can be rather complicated, can't it?"

"Yes indeed. I gather you have had your share of domestic turmoil in the past. Your present wife is your second partner as I understand it."

"Yes. I suppose you must have picked up quite a lot about my past when you were checking up on me."

"I am sorry. Please think of it as being something I had to do rather than simple prying on my part."

"Please. I do understand. I assure you."

"Well now. Enough of this idle chatter. What would it be useful for me to tell you?"

Tom was burning to pass on what he had learned from his encounters over the weekend but thought it more appropriate to let Renard have his say first.

"As you know, I am inclined not to dismiss the possibility of someone English being involved and I've told you why I feel this. Finding the collection of English language papers behind Guyard's grandfather clock, if you remember, is for me somehow significant although I don't know in what way. Despite this, it would have been very foolish to concentrate purely on the English people here in Saint Val. So, my officers have been carrying out a very comprehensive door to door of all the natives—if I can call them that. It's very much been a first sweep round and I wasn't expecting any more than an inkling of something or other significant enough to justify a second more in depth visit. As I feared though, they are a pretty tight mouthed bunch. They are typical country folk. Say as little as possible to outsiders and especially to outsiders who represent the authorities. I was counting on the received opinion that they are all jealous of each other and spend their time keeping a close eye on each other to at least discover some lead or other. However, when I come to analyse the accounts of all the interviews, all they tell me is what I probably knew already. In brief, there is common accord that Guyard kept himself very much to himself. Nobody seems to have been on more than nodding acquaintance with him and can't—or won't possibly—identify anyone who might have it in for him. I had higher expectations of the woman who used to clean for him. After all, there is the general assumption that besides doing a bit of cooking and washing for him, she was more than likely providing him with whatever sexual gratification he needed. You would have thought she would have been able to tell us more about him. The little we did get was like drawing teeth. Until we assured her we weren't going to tell the tax people, she wouldn't even tell us how much Guyard paid her. I'm not sure even now if the figure she gave us was not much less than she really received. If it wasn't then Guyard was a tight wad alright considering that he got all the domestic help he required and a shag when he needed it into the bargain. Mind you, I expect that side of things was very much a functional, farmyardy sort of process. You know the woman I'm talking about? There is no way I could fancy her, I'm absolutely sure about that."

"Yes, I know who you mean. You would have to be desperate indeed or in your nineties like Guyard—not that I want to be unfair to the old girl. I must confess that I had always been convinced that she had a few keys missing off her piano. Whenever I called on Guyard and she happened to be there, I can't honestly remember her saying a single word although people tell me that if you come across her walking the lanes around here, she's always talking nineteen to the dozen to herself."

"I'm still not sure whether we got so little information out of her because she was being cunning or because she is just simple minded. Anyway, that is about it. Of course, we asked everybody to account for their whereabouts from Saturday evening up to Sunday lunchtime. There were a few unsatisfactory answers. So as well as the old girl, they'll be getting further visits from us. Two people think they may have seen a car near Guyard's place late on Saturday. One of them is not sure if she has even got the right date. The description we have been given would fit half the cars on the roads of France. All we know is that they think it was 'probably dark coloured and it could have been newish'. No clue about the model and, it goes without saying, of course, no licence number—not even part of it. We'll be going to call on them again, as well, to see if we can sharpen up their memories a bit. It doesn't look promising though—any of it. The one guy in the area with a bit of form—the local lads picked him up for a bit of grievous on a couple of occasions– seems to have a cast iron alibi but as, for part of the time in question, he claims to have been with a married woman, we agreed to wait until her old man is out of the way at work before we check up with her. You see, Tom, we can exercise a bit of delicacy occasionally! So, as I say, that's all we've got at this stage. A few loose ends to tie up and that's all. None of those are promising either."

"Have you got any results back from your technical people?" Tom ventured to ask.

"Frédo—he was the attending medic—has confirmed the time of death as being between eleven on Saturday evening and six on Sunday morning. He doesn't want to narrow it down any more precisely than that. The autopsy, he tells me, indicates that Guyard died from heart failure to put it in layman's terms. He can't be categorical about the precise moment during the attack on him, that the old man actually died. He is pretty sure that he was still alive when the nails were hammered into his hands but he reckons he was gone before his throat was cut. He has promised to give me his best guess about the order in which the various wounds were inflicted. What else was there? Oh yes, I remember. The forensic boys reckon they have up to five unidentified sets of fingerprints after eliminating those belonging to Guyard and to his woman, of course."

"You will probably find my prints among those. I was at Guyard's place a few days before the murder." Renard nodded as Tom continued "I expect you'll want to take all our prints. I've certainly no problem with that at all. What about those papers you found behind the clock? Have you got those back yet? I recall you said you wanted to go through them with me."

"The sad bastards in the labs are still farting about with them. I've told them I want photocopies by five o'clock today at the latest."

"That would make two ultimata for five o'clock," Tom mused and, as it seemed that the Commissaire had reached the end of what he had to share with him, he decided that his moment to step forward on to centre stage had at last arrived. He cleared his throat and then wished he hadn't for fear that

Renard would think him a trifle over concerned with his own importance.

"Well, for my part, as you so kindly pointed out, I have had a rather busy weekend. Actually, I rather think I may have stumbled across one or two items which could be very pertinent. However, I think that I should ask you to treat whatever I say to you with the utmost confidence. I hasten to add that I ask this not because I am afraid of upsetting people if they know that I have been frank in passing information on to you but rather that if they do realize that this is the case, they are likely to become less open and revelatory with me. There would, in my opinion, be a grave risk of my usefulness to you being seriously diminished."

Tom recognized that his pompous opening remarks sounded as though they had been well rehearsed. That should not have been very surprising since that was exactly the case.

"I had rather assumed, Tom, that as colleagues, so to speak, whatever we share between us will be treated as confidential and indeed as a matter of professional and personal discretion."

"I never doubted that. But I am sure that you get my drift. It would be more advantageous if I remained on the inside of the English clique rather than becoming an outsider."

"Yes of course but I imagine there may be occasions when the demands of the investigation override such a consideration."

Tom wasn't exactly sure what these 'occasions' might be but Renard's assurances were sufficient for him to feel that he could risk speaking freely.

"Well here goes then. Where can I start, I wonder? Perhaps it would be good to deal with what may seem to you to be tittle-tattle and to get that out of the way."

Tom was encouraged by Renard nodding in agreement and taking up his pen, preparing to make notes on his sheaf of papers.

"I'm not sure whether this will have any bearing on the case but it may be useful for you to know that there seems to have been a serious break up between Nigel Barnes and his erstwhile partner Tim Foulkes. So much so, in fact, that Tim has left the marital home, if that is the right expression, and is currently staying at the Browns' house. I am telling you this partly because you need to know where people are when it comes to interviews. For what it is worth, my neighbour, Mandy Parsons, is convinced that, whatever previous sexual form might seem to indicate, Tim and Cheryl—Mrs Brown that is—are having a relationship. She believes that the absence of Steve Brown who, as you will recall, works in London from Monday to Thursday evening each week, will allow this relationship to flourish. I am not sure myself if Mandy is not leaping to conclusions because that is the way her mind seems to operate. But if she is right, then at least it shows that Cheryl and Tim are dark horses and, as such, may be worth keeping an eye on. What may be of more concern to you is that your associate, Capitaine Duvallon, according to Nigel has more or less spent the weekend at his place."

"That is a matter of considerable concern to me. The officer I left patrolling the village has already indicated that Duvallon was there for most of the weekend. I was inclined to think that the officer had got it wrong somehow. But what you have just said seems to confirm it. I didn't imagine that Duvallon could be so stupid as to consort with a potential witness. Good God, Monsieur Barnes could even turn out to be a suspect. It wouldn't surprise me at all if Duvallon is of that orientation but he should know better. I shall be having a very strong word with him. I may even have to take the young fool off the case."

The Commissaire was as angry as Tom had seen him. He had become accustomed to the policeman's usually controlled urbane manner. He had seemed calm even when he was dressing down Harry Walker at Tom and Jenny's barbecue evening. But calm he most certainly was not as he wrote in heavy capitals a reminder to haul in his colleague urgently.

Tom thought that it may not be a bad idea for him to warn Nigel off although whether he would heed a gentle piece of advice of this nature, Tom had his doubts.

"I'm sorry about that. But I think it needed saying. To go back to Mandy Parsons, if I may. Her husband, Tony, is away at Magny Cours for the motor racing as you know and she seems to have used his absence and Jenny's being in England to see quite a lot of me, for some reason or other."

Renard's quizzically raised eyebrow indicated that he had his suspicions about her motives and he asked quite bluntly:

"So did you, old chap?"

"Did I do what?' Tom asked with as much innocence as he could muster.

"Don't be coy, Tom. Did you take her to bed?"

"No, of course I didn't!" he spluttered and then added with an all chaps together leer "Not that I wasn't tempted though. She's a good looking woman and it is very flattering."

"I can imagine. I kept my eye on her at your party for purely unprofessional reasons. I just hope Duvallon exercised the same restraint as you claim you did. It would be too much if my two right hand men had been busy screwing witnesses all weekend."

"You'll just have to accept that I was a good boy. At first, I suppose it was just loyalty to Jenny that kept me on the straight and narrow. But as we talked and she opened up about her past, it became clear that it would have been rather a foolhardy thing to do."

"In what way?"

"Well, first of all, she gave me to understand that her husband might have had a criminal past—or at least that's what I thought she was saying. But she did make it absolutely clear that her Tony, whether it actually got as far as the courts or not, had a record of violence, certainly when he was younger, and I make no pretence to be anything other than a physical coward. For me a good thumping for a bit of sex on the side is not an acceptable quid pro quo. I had a pal at school who thought that phrase meant 'a pound for a whore what'."

Tom regretted his unfunny schoolboy joke as he was obliged to explain it to Renard. The explanation made it even less funny as the play on words simply didn't work in French.

"A strange school you went to, Tom! But what you say about Parsons is interesting especially as I have got nothing whatsoever back in response to my enquiries about either of the Parsons. So our Monsieur Tony could have a record and he has a history of violence, does he? Were you able to assess whether he was violent enough to have done for Guyard in that terrible way?"

"No, I couldn't really say that. It's impossible to imagine anyone being capable of that degree of brutality. So I shouldn't have thought so. It only came up when she was talking about his getting annoyed when Guyard used to hang around their place. He thought the old boy was ogling Mandy when she was sunbathing and she was afraid he might get a bit physical with him. She didn't seem to mind Guyard loitering around too much though. She claimed he was there an awful lot and I think she implied he seemed to be spying on them just as though he were fascinated by them."

"In total confidence, Tom, I am quite interested in the Parsons. As a matter of routine, I have asked for transcripts of the records of all the Brits in Saint Val from the U.K. Criminal Records people and banking and medical histories as well, although the latter take a little longer to come through so I'm still waiting for those. As I have just told you I have had nothing back from Records about the Parsons. I find that most intriguing. I've had some interesting bits and bobs about the rest of you but they say they can't even trace a Tony or a Mandy Parsons. Now that becomes even odder in the light of what you have just been telling me."

"Very odd I should think although you know more about that sort of thing than I do. It's probably stupid of me to ask but you do realize, I expect, that 'Tony' is short for 'Anthony' and the proper form of 'Mandy' is 'Amanda'."

"I didn't actually but I'm pretty sure that my British colleagues would have checked that out as a matter of course. It's particularly strange because I didn't get a nil return, as I did, for example in your case. I got a message to the effect that no records in those names even existed. I will have to put in a repeat priority request and see what that turns up. It could simply be that some clerk or other over there couldn't be arsed to do the searches thoroughly."

"I expect that you will want to talk to them in any case so you might be able to clear up the mystery then. It's not for me to say but there may be some very simple explanation, couldn't there?"

"It's very likely. I prefer to have a bit of background information about people before I interview them properly though. It can be very useful to be able to suddenly pull a skeleton or two out of the cupboard. In any event, I shall want to see them at the same time and I don't suppose he's back from his trip yet. You must know more than me on that score, Tom, seeing that you are so involved with the wife. Has he got back yet, do you know?"

"I will ignore your insinuation. As of last night, he was still away according to Mandy."

"As of last night at what time? Would that be before or after midnight?"

"Do leave off! She left here no later than half past eight or nine o'clock. It was still light and, as you apparently believe that the English don't allow themselves to have sex until dark, no hanky-panky could possibly have gone on, could it?"

"Forgive me Tom. I can't resist having my little jokes."

"I expect that you are just jealous."

"That is most certainly true. Touché!"

"One thing she did say however was that she hadn't heard from him and she claimed that wasn't at all usual."

Tom didn't think he needed to reveal that Mandy had worked in clubs in London nor that she had come across what she had referred to as 'villains'. He would rather not risk exposing himself to further ribbing at this stage. He could just imagine what Renard would be able to make out of 'consorting with professional women' and so on. In addition, he was convinced that what he had learned from old Casson was of more pertinence to the case. He believed he had discovered items of some importance from his conversations with him. What was more he was very sure that what he had to reveal would come as news to Renard and might even shake his conviction that the Brits were involved. His certainty that he was holding crucial and fresh information made him impatient to move on from the Parsons to the old man.

"I spent an interesting couple of hours with Casson yesterday," he began and he remembered as he did so that he had promised to get him one or two things from the shops. "I believe he was as forthcoming as I have ever known him. He spoke mostly about the times when he and Guyard were in the Resistance together. What an amazing tale it was too. It is pretty obvious to me now why he feels so threatened. I am sure that he has never spoken about what he revealed to anybody ever before. It seems that when he and Guyard made off to join the Maquis they both left young wives behind on their farms."

Tom went on to relay Casson's story to Renard laying particular emphasis on the infidelity and subsequent cruel fate of Guyard's young wife, Cécile. He sought to explain Casson's lifelong sense of guilt and fear of retribution by describing his role in the death of the young woman.

When his account was completed, he saw with satisfaction that the policeman was as disturbed as he had been even though he was hearing it only second hand. A few minutes went by with only the sound of Renard's pen disturbing the silence as he wrote up notes of what he had just learned.

At length, he looked up and commented:

"As you say, Tom, there is sufficient strong emotion relating to these events to cause reactions of extreme violence. But as you correctly wonder, why should Guyard's death have occurred so very many years later. I can readily accept that the two of them lived all their lives so near to each other and yet were so consumed with guilt that they could not exchange a friendly word in all that time. It is often the way with country people; they can hold a brooding, deep resentment of their neighbours which results in silence between them, often for generations. Sometimes the latest generation of children doesn't even know what the original dispute was about but this does not stop them from hating in their turn."

"Quite apart from the problem of the elapse of time," Tom continued, "I just can't see how Casson—and let's just suppose for argument's sake that something happened which caused him finally to explode—would have had the strength to carry out a murder such as you described to me."

"I would have thought it impossible without the help of a third party."

"It's a bit of a long shot, I know. What if Casson's son was not killed in that supposed car crash. He could be a potential accomplice, couldn't he? I don't like to think that the old man was actually involved, of course. But what if the son is still alive and along with some bully boy mates he decided to pay back Guyard for causing his father such a life of guilt and misery."

"As you say, Tom, that is an unlikely scenario. But as I am not getting anywhere with the case, it is not one I can afford to rule out. In any case, it would be very easy for me to check up on the boy's accident. You said his first name was Michel, didn't you?"

Renard added the name to his notes which now extended to four closely written pages. Then he went on to say that there was another person about whom he would need to check up.

"It will be less straight forward than with the Casson boy but I think we need to know more about the little girl who was born to Guyard's wife and who was living with her and the German soldier, don't you agree? It will be difficult but not impossible. After all, we have her mother's name and we know fairly precisely when the child was born."

Tom felt there was something else roaming around in his mind which he should pass on to Renard. The more he tried to pin it down, however, the less accessible it seemed to become. He determined to let it emerge of its own accord, if emerge it ever would.

"You know, Tom, you have done really very well. It seems that you are far more likely to elicit information from Casson than I or, come to that, any of my colleagues would be. He evidently trusts you whereas we represent authority and his instinct will be to keep us at arm's length. That would be particularly true if we need to delve further into those dark days he has already opened up to you about. It's not a popular topic. We don't discuss collaborators; we want to forget the retributions, the malicious testimonies and the undoubted personal vengeance that went on. Suffice to say that even after the spate of spontaneous killings that went on at a local level was over, the French Government found it necessary to charge a hundred and sixty thousand people with being collaborators. It was De Gaulle who brought all that to a stop and since then the French nation has thrown a veil over that period of our history. More of a shroud than a veil in actual fact. What I am proposing is that you take first line responsibility for contacts with Casson. Would that be acceptable to you, Tom?"

"Of course. In any case I freely admit the whole business of the Occupation, the Resistance and the aftermath of the war fascinates me. So anything which gives me licence to indulge that interest is welcome. Jenny thinks I am obsessed by it all and I guess she is not too wide of the mark. I don't think I'm alone in this though. I reckon that it's a topic which enthralls a lot of my compatriots who come to settle in France. It's something to do with being in the very place where all those desperate events were played out. The war was tough for people in England but we were not occupied. Enemy troops didn't march up and down our streets, take over our pubs, requisition our houses. I wonder also at the bravery of the young British men and women who were parachuted in to give a hand. I just cannot comprehend how they managed to escape the attention of the Germans. Not that they all did by any means of course. You will probably think me childish if I tell you that sometimes when I am eating alone in some busy restaurant or other, I pretend that I am here under cover. The group of people over by the bar I cast in the role of German soldiers, others become French collaborators. When I am playing this silly game, it becomes obvious at once that I would stick out like a sore thumb. It's not just the language either. Our gestures are different. The way we hold a knife and fork is different. We dress differently."

"We all have our little games, Tom. I will keep mine to myself at least for now. You are right though. It must have been nigh on impossible for your compatriots to remain inconspicuous. I expect the ones who were in this area tended to stay out of sight in the Morvan forests. I don't imagine they would make a habit of tripping off to town to the restaurant."

That was it! Tom's elusive butterfly of a thought had at last been pinned to the board. Of course, that was it! The English in the Morvan!

"Casson told me more or less as an aside that there were British officers in the sector he and Guyard were in. What will interest you in particular is that he said Guyard became a sort of liaison chap with them. Casson remembered him showing off the English he was picking up. It may just have been a smattering or a few phrases he had assimilated parrot fashion but . . ."

"But," Renard interrupted, "it shows that he did have some awareness of English! Who knows if he didn't carry on after the war learning more and more."

Tom thought that Guyard and Continuing Education was a very unlikely combination but he could see how keen Renard was to establish an English connection and it pleased him that he had been able to supply this morsel of information.

"We really must get those papers back from the lab boys this afternoon, Tom! I've got such a powerful feeling that this is critically important to the case."

"We ought to arrange our diaries for the next few days, plan ahead a little, Jean Luc, before too much comes along to interfere with my availability. Already I know I can't be around on Wednesday evening when I have to pick up Jenny and I have a strong suspicion that it is this week that I am expecting a young couple to come out here house hunting."

Tom grabbed his Blackberry which Jenny had given him for his last birthday to encourage him to become more technically competent and was able to confirm, after a few false starts, by consulting his calendar that the couple were due to arrive on either Wednesday or Thursday depending on how they got on with the agent in Avallon they were seeing before him. It was not entirely impossible that if they found what they were looking for through the other agent, they may not make it as far as him. Still, he wouldn't know that before the middle of the week and he would have to keep his diary free for them until then.

"While you have got that wretched piece of technology in your hand, shall we try to pencil in a few likely dates and times for paying a call on your compatriots?"

Tom explained his potential dilemma later in the week and the policeman was gracious enough to accept the situation with understanding.

"I think we should leave the Parsons until we are sure that the husband has returned to the nest. Ideally, I would like to do the same with the Browns but as Monsieur Foulkes seems to have taken up residence at their house, I fear we cannot wait until Friday for Monsieur Brown's return. So shall we go to the Walkers' house followed by a visit to Monsieur Nigel Barnes this afternoon and then visit the Brown place tomorrow, let's say in the afternoon? This will leave us time to look at the 'Guyard Papers' together tomorrow morning. What do you say?"

Tom assured Renard that would be fine with him and laboriously and with a few false starts made the appropriate entries in his Blackberry. The Commissaire once more tutted his disapproval of such newfangledness. Tom thought that he was evidently happier with good old fashioned pen and paper, just like he was if truth be told, and wondered to what degree the policeman avoided all new technologies. He had certainly never given the impression that he had any regard for the skills of his technical colleagues.

Renard declined Tom's offer to knock them up a cold lunch, claiming that he needed to chivvy up his technical support staff so as to be absolutely sure that what he was now terming 'The Guyard Papers' would be delivered to him as promised later in the afternoon. They agreed to re-convene in front of the Brown's house at half past three.

In actual fact, Renard had in mind to revisit Guyard's house and saw no reason to share his intention with Tom. There was nothing he could put his finger on but he felt a strong need to look over the scene of the crime once again. Perhaps it was no more than a hope that just by being there in that room something would occur to him. On the way there, he intended to have a chat with the officer whom he had left as his look-out. He wanted to know if his man had spotted any comings and goings between the Brits that he felt his boss should know about. Without letting the look-out become aware of his concern, if that was possible, he also was most interested in his number two Duvallon's movements over the weekend. Armed with that information, he would be going on to Guyard's house where he had ordered Duvallon to meet him. He was looking forward to putting his young colleague on the spot by asking him what the hell he thought he was playing at.

19

"Knowledge advances by steps, and not by leaps"
(Miscellaneous Writings of Lord Macaulay)

Renard was glad to see that Duvallon had got to Guyard's house ahead of him. The young officer had not emerged from his car and appeared to be writing up notes on his pad. Rather than approaching Duvallon's car, Renard strolled across to the farm gate which still had the scene of crime tape wound around it and, leaning against the gate post, waited for his colleague to join him.

When the young man was half way between his car and the gate, Renard bellowed at him:

"I reckon you have got a fair bit of explaining to do, my lad! What the hell is going on?"

"I'm sorry, Sir. I'm not sure what you mean," was Duvallon's uneasy reply.

"You don't know what I mean? Putain de bordel, for God's sake don't add crass stupidity to your unprofessional conduct, your total lack of any sense of discretion and your criminally inappropriate behaviour over this weekend!"

"Perhaps I should remind you, Sir, that the law no longer considers it a criminal offence for a person to have a preference for same sex relationships."

"Don't lecture me on the law, you cheeky little sod. I am not talking about whether you are a woofter or not . . ."

"Sir!" Duvallon cut in angrily, "I don't think our superiors would approve of such inappropriate language . . ."

"I don't suppose they would," Renard interrupted in his turn. "I don't suppose they would approve of one of their investigating officers getting pissed with and shacking up for the weekend with one of the witnesses in a murder case either. With a witness I might add who, as far as we know, could yet turn out to be our culprit. I don't give a toss whether the witness in question is a screaming old queen or a serial shagger of women. I don't even care which end of the ballroom you personally prefer. What I do care about is my officers' professionalism. What pisses me off more than you seem capable of realizing is that your behaviour could well have compromised the case. What is beyond any doubt is that your position, at least with regard to this witness, is not professionally acceptable."

"Sir," was Duvallon's terse response.

"You do know what I am talking about, don't you? In case you don't, let me spell it out for you very clearly. What I am weighing up at this very moment is whether to inform—and I mean 'inform' and not 'ask'—our superiors that you have been taken off the case. There would, of course, have to be an inquiry. You might like to ask yourself whether you would like to have your precious 'orientation' discussed with a panel of senior officers regardless of what the official line on homosexuality happens to be."

"If you don't mind me saying so, Sir, that sounds rather close to sexual harassment."

"To hell with harassment! I'm talking about your career, you stupid little cretin!"

"Yes, Sir. But if I may say so I did not discuss the case with Nigel—with Monsieur Barnes, that is."

"Forgive me if I find that hard to believe. Merde alors,you spend the whole weekend with the bloke and the case doesn't come up at all? Désolé mon petit, I'm sorry my little friend, pull the other one!"

"Honestly we didn't. For the record, as well, I would like you to know that there was no sex. There could have been I expect but there wasn't."

"What did you talk about then if it wasn't the details of the case?"

"Mostly about music. We listened to a lot of music. His paintings. He went on a bit about his splitting up with Tim.

He told me about his life before he came to France. I didn't have to say very much at all. He's hard to shut up once he gets going. I certainly didn't mention anything about the way the case was going. He didn't ask either, I have to say. I didn't talk about any of my colleagues. Your name didn't even come up in conversation."

Renard was quite unreasonably disappointed by that last piece of information despite his previous admonishments. He felt calmer now that he had blown his top at the young man. He began to wonder if Duvallon's transgressions were, in fact, so serious as to warrant being taken off the case what with possible suspension from duty to follow, not to mention all the bureaucratic rigmarole consequent upon such a course of action. He had also served long enough in the force to know that some of the mud aimed at Duvallon would inescapably land on him personally and he could do without that. It was this final selfish consideration which tipped the balance although, when Renard announced his decision, the young man put it down to his superior's generosity.

"Much against my better judgement, I've decided, for the time being at least, just to give you a personal warning. Keep right away from Barnes from now on, unless you're in the company of another officer, preferably me. For God's sake maintain a professional distance between you and anyone who may even remotely be involved in the case."

"Thank you, Sir. Much appreciated."

"Just watch your step, that's all! Now you can do something for me if you will. I'm getting totally pissed off with the way those half wits—if you'll forgive the expression—in the labs are dragging out examining those papers we found behind the grandfather clock. Go and see the bastards and don't leave without the originals or at least, as second best, make sure you get a complete set of photocopies. When you get them, give me a ring to find out where I am—I'll probably be interviewing some of the Brits. But check first and bring the bundle of papers directly to me. While you are in there, you might like to see Frédo and ask if anything else has occurred to him since I last spoke to him. You might also find out if anything more has come through in response to my enquiries about our Brit friends. What I have got so far is far from complete. It's all very unsatisfactory in my book."

Duvallon was musing over being restricted to being a messenger boy and wondering how long that would go on, when his boss barked:

"Well! What the hell are you waiting for? Fous-moi le camp! Bugger off! Don't forget I need these urgently."

"Certainly, Sir. On my way, Sir!"

The young man trotted to his car only pausing as he opened the door to turn and blow a kiss in Renard's direction.

"Cheeky little tosser!" the Commissaire said to himself but not without the suspicion of a smile forcing itself on to his features.

Renard stood admiring the views of the Morvan which was looking at its very best in the fresh clear air which had followed the overnight showers. Guyard's place was ideally placed to take in the rolling tree clad slopes interspersed with fields which even in the heat of the early summer were still bright green. There was even a babbling stream beyond the farmyard to complete the idyll. It was a God given spot alright. He breathed in the clean air deeply and turned reluctantly towards the front door of what until a week ago had been the lifelong home of a man who, he now knew, thanks to his English friend's coaxing out bitter reminiscences from another old man, had been guilt ridden and isolated for all of those years.

He pushed open the door and let the sunlight stream into the dark interior.

"My God," he thought "these people live like troglodytes."

It seemed to him that the advances they had made over the centuries from being cave dwellers to living, or, in his terms, existing, in rooms such as this had been minimal. The only example of any concession to real modernity was the oversize television which contrasted sharply with the heavy, dark and ancient furniture. If one discounted the grandfather clock and the over decorative carved front of the sideboard, all the rest was functional and basic. The double bed to the left of the front door was, like the rest of the room, on the filthy side of being humanly acceptable. Nothing other than the mutilated body had been moved since his first visit. The fibre suitcase which he guessed had usually been kept under the bed still lay next to the old stove, its contents strewn across the floor. The upturned drawers were scattered about the room. He supposed that some dealer would buy up the house contents as a job lot for next to nothing, recouping ten times his outlay just by selling the clock. Inevitably, in due course, the property itself would be sold, probably to a non-French buyer these days, and would be subjected to extensive renovation and modernization. Then, the only trace left of Guyard would be in the minds of local people who would remember him merely as 'the old chap who was murdered'. There would also be, of course, a file on the case gradually mouldering away in the cellars at Headquarters. That thought tugged him out of his reveries. Unless he got on with it and made some real progress, that file would remain open and the case unsolved. He would not like that to be the outcome because he would deem it to be a personal failure on his part and, no matter what Guyard may have been culpable of in his past, he owed him the quietus which, in Renard's mind, could only come when the guilty had been found and punished.

He moved around the room, noting with distaste the blood stains and the holes in the table top made by the nails. From time to time he stooped to pick up some item from amongst the debris which had been scattered across the floor. He would turn it over, look at it and then discard it by dropping it back onto the tiles. He did not know if he was looking for anything in particular or whether he was just hoping that by being here in the room and by handling these scraps that had belonged to Guyard, he would have some sudden insight. At length, he sat on a chair at the table, taking care to place himself as far as he could from where the butchery had actually taken place. He looked over towards the cooking area feeling slightly nauseous at the disregard for hygiene the old man must have had. The dark red tomette tiles, elsewhere in the room merely grubby, were thick with black grease in the cooking corner. Then he noticed that the rear leg of the all-purpose kitchen cupboard, the leg almost hidden in the dingy angle of the room, was propped up on three or four folded magazines or papers to counteract an unevenness caused by a sunken tile. If he had not been sitting down, he would not have noticed this. Standing, one could not see the rear leg of the cupboard. It struck him that he had stood throughout his previous examinations and that, in all likelihood, the murderer had done the same. It was probably of no significance but as he had drawn nothing but blanks during his visits so far, he decided to fetch a mat from his car so that he could kneel without ruining his trousers. Belatedly, he thought he had better don a pair of examination gloves as well. At least they would offer him protection against the accumulation of sticky grime that had built up, probably over years.

By slightly tipping the kitchen-dresser forward, he found it easier than he had feared to extricate the papers. Once he had gently scraped away the patina of grease and mouse droppings from the top sheet, it was possible, with care, to unfold the wad. At once he recognized that the papers were in fact old copies of calendars obviously purchased from the fire service, the Sapeurs Pompiers, who visited all the houses in the area selling these in the weeks before Christmas. Renard had in front of him calendars going back over a period of four years. The current version he noted was hanging from a nail in the door which led to the rear scullery area.

He was slightly disappointed at how few entries in the calendars Guyard had made. When he thought he had learned to decipher the shorthand the old man had employed, he was able to work out that 'D' or 'Dent' indicated an appointment at the dentist; 'C' or 'Clin' stood for a visit to the clinic at the Medical Centre. He took 'Av' to indicate a trip to Avallon and these appeared regularly each month. Less frequently, there was an entry 'Aux' which clearly referred to excursions to Auxerre and was sometimes followed by an 'H' for, Renard supposed, 'Hospital'. There were other one-off scribblings which for the most part consisted of one or two capital letters often with a time marked next to them. Renard supposed that these could refer to people who had called upon Guyard or, indeed, to whose houses he was scheduled to go. It would be interesting to work these out since they would give a fair idea of the contacts that the old man had had over the last five years. To judge from the entries in the calendars there had been precious few such encounters. He would give that task to Duvallon or perhaps even one of his brighter uniformed officers to work out. He was turning over the pages of the earliest of the calendars when he came across an item for July 6th, some five years ago, which was unlike the other entries as it was rather less cryptic. It read 'Taxi 8.30. Av dep 9.25. Gare du Nord d 13.15.' There was a briefer 'Av 17.25' written against July 13th.

Renard reacted rather like a bloodhound picking up a scent for it seemed immediately probable that these brief notes revealed Guyard had made a trip to England lasting a week. Common sense told him that the Gare du Nord serviced a whole swathe of northern France, Belgium and the Low Countries as well as London. Just to be sure, he telephoned his headquarters in Auxerre and asked one of the desk officers to contact SNCF and Eurostar to verify what trains had been scheduled to leave Avallon and the Gare du Nord on July 6th five years ago at the times indicated on the calendar. He packed the calendars in a plastic evidence bag and went out into the sun drenched yard to await the call back. He got the confirmation he had been anticipating within ten minutes. The 9.25 departure from Avallon was one of the two daily through trains to Paris Bercy and, more interestingly for Renard, apart from a couple of RER departures for the Paris suburbs and a Thalys to Amsterdam at 13.18, the only train scheduled to leave the Gare du Nord around the time

Guyard had written up on the calendar was a Eurostar bound for London. Bingo! His suspicion that there was an English aspect to Guyard's death had now turned into unshakeable certainty. At last he felt he was not stumbling around in total darkness. A small candle had at least been lit.

CHAPTER . . .

20

"A skulk of foxes"
(From a list of collective nouns)

His spirits lifted by the small, but to his mind significant, discovery he had made at Guyard's house and his inner man fortified by a passable 'Steak frîtes' at a roadhouse on the Nationale Six, Renard drew up in front of the Walker's house to discover that Tom was already there. He wondered idly at the annoying punctuality of the anglo-saxon peoples.

"Hello once more, Tom. I trust you have had lunch."

"I'm fine thank you, Jean Luc. I'm raring to go."

The policeman ran an appraising eye over the house. It was a typical Morvan farmhouse built of pink granite with the dwelling area to one side and the barns at the other. The hands of those who had originally constructed these buildings had been guided by practical considerations and so, inevitably, the working areas, the barns and stables, were far more spacious and grand than the rather poky living quarters. Here as with so many other such gentrified buildings, however, the huge barn doors had been replaced by double glazed entrances to what were now generously proportioned sitting rooms. A row of Velux windows let into the roof attested to the grain lofts above the dwelling itself having been converted into bedrooms. A lane ran diagonally up over the hill facing the house and there at the top, at what he knew to be a crossroads, Renard could just make out a thin plume of smoke which he suspected came from the cigarette of his no doubt very bored look-out man. He had chosen a good spot as the Commissaire had realized when he had had a chat with him earlier when he was en route for the Guyard place. From there you could just about see all the Brits' homes.

185

Renard thought that unless they were not at home, and he had preferred not to forewarn them of his visit so that was a possibility, the Walkers were being singularly reluctant to emerge to greet them. After all, given the remoteness and tranquility of the spot, they could not have failed to hear the two cars arrive.

Before opening the iron double gates and approaching the front door of the house, Renard thought it wise to apprise Tom of his slight worry at his presence at the forthcoming interview.

"I think it would be a good move if we were to kick off all these interviews by reassuring the Brits we are questioning that you are bound by the same rules of confidentiality and discretion as I am. They are very likely to be reticent anyway. It's a natural reaction to being questioned by the police. But I don't want them clamming up altogether because you are in attendance. I shall be bringing up some very personal, even difficult things which they will not appreciate a neighbour and compatriot being let in on. So let's try to put them at their ease as much as we can."

"Of course. Don't forget though that I already know quite a bit of a personal nature about them from when I sold them the house."

"Well, Tom, you're about to hear some really personal stuff about some of them, stuff they absolutely wouldn't wish to broadcast! Right. Let's go and knock them up."

They were already at the door and Renard's hand was raised to knock, when it opened and Peggy Walker smiled a rather thin and nervous welcome.

Renard had to review his assessment of Peggy Walker's apparent age which he had adjudged to be in her early forties when they had met briefly at Tom's party. Now in the bright sunlight, the lines on her tanned face and neck were more evident and made her look at least her chronological age. He guessed that she was paying the price of too much devotion to sunbathing over too many years. Her predilection for white clothes and her rather fiercely blonde hair contrasted sharply with her deep tan and this gave her at least a superficial attractiveness. He would certainly have given her a second look if he had passed her in the street but he doubted that he would have given her a third one.

"Come in, please do. Harry is in the lounge watching T.V. I'll give him a shout in a minute."

Tom noted that he had not been invited to deliver the habitual peck on the cheek. There was no offer either of a handshake for the policeman. Nor, indeed, did Peggy enquire if they would like something to drink which was unheard of at the Walkers' house. Tom couldn't remember a previous occasion when a glass had not been thrust at him even, almost, before he crossed their threshold.

The encounter was beginning awkwardly or so Tom felt. He recalled Harry's previously expressed anger at his participation in the enquiry and he wondered if it was that or simply Renard's presence which was causing the palpable frostiness of their reception. He felt it necessary to attempt a spot of glasnost.

"We are sorry—if I can speak for both of us—to disturb you in this way. It's no more than a formality I'm sure, Peggy. And in any case the Commissaire will be seeing all the Saint Val Brits."

"So you say, Tom. All the same, it is not at all nice to be interviewed in your own home by the French police. Even you, chummy as you are with them, should recognize that."

Renard had caught the gist of what she had said and when Tom had given him a confirmatory translation, he responded rather abruptly.

"Tell Madame if you please, Monsieur Fox, that it may not be 'nice'. If she prefers, I could easily arrange for the interview to take place at the station. That, I am sure, would be even less agreeable. As for it being the 'French' police calling on them, would she actually expect it to be the British or indeed the German, the Italian or the Spanish police for that matter? Please explain that we are in France."

So, Tom understood, Renard had opted for a confrontational approach and it was with a degree of reluctance that
he transmitted the message to Peggy.

She offered no reply and only a tightening of the lips and
a glint in the eye indicated that she had taken in Renard's
remark.

"So, Madame, if it would not be too much trouble, perhaps you could dislodge your husband from the television
set and then we can get this unpleasantness over with."

Peggy called out to Harry that he was needed and his response did nothing to lighten the atmosphere.

"This is just bloody typical. What a great sense of timing!
You can't expect the Froggies to understand. I'm right in the
middle of watching the Test match and Monty has just come
on to bowl. Christ!"

His disgruntlement was obvious enough to Renard and
Tom was able merely to paraphrase and avoid rendering
into French the offensiveness of 'Froggies' and the arcana of
cricket which in itself would have involved lengthy and baffling cultural contextualization.

Still muttering under his breath, Harry finally emerged
into the entrance hall and with a brief nod in Tom's direction,
growled:

"Well, seeing as you're here, let's get on with it shall
we?"

Renard suggested that they move somewhere a little more
comfortable and Peggy led the way into the kitchen. Once
they were seated at the solid oak refectory table, Renard began:

"I shall be asking the same questions of all your compatriots and so it would not be appropriate to imagine that you
are being picked out for special treatment in any way despite
what you may feel."

The Walkers glanced uneasily at each other.

"Firstly, I need you to tell me where you were a week ago
last Saturday evening from, let us say, ten o'clock until the
following morning at nine o'clock."

"For once we were here at home. It is very rare on a Saturday not to be out at somebody's house for a drinks party or a meal but that particular evening we were here watching television. We fancied a quiet night in because we knew we had a party of sorts coming up at our place on the Monday evening, didn't we Peg?"

"Yes, that's right. I suppose we went up to bed at around midnight and I came downstairs to make a cup of tea the next morning at nine-ish, I reckon."

"I presume you were alone all evening?"

"Correct."

"You will be able to tell me what you watched on television, of course?"

"If I remember rightly we watched a DVD that night. The latest Indiana Jones, wasn't it Peg?"

"Correct me if I am mistaken. My technical expertise is very limited. You can play and therefore watch a DVD at any time?" Renard queried.

"Of course you can. That's the bloody point of DVDs!"

"Indeed. It is a pity nevertheless. Because you see, as you were alone and you were watching something which you could have seen at any time of your choosing, I have to conclude that your alibi is rather thin."

"For fuck's sake, we were here together. Isn't that good enough for you? Do you think we are lying or something?"

"Unfortunately for you the testimony of either party of a married couple as to the other's whereabouts, or their actions for that matter, tends not to have much weight in a court of law. Besides it was with considerable consternation that I discovered something in your past which makes it more difficult than it should normally have been to accept at face value anything you say in support of each other."

"Oh shit!"

"Oh shit indeed, Monsieur Walker. There is that small matter five years back, is there not? Are the records lying or did you in fact not receive a six month sentence for a hit and run offence in which the victim suffered serious injuries?

And did you not, Madame, receive a suspended sentence for perjury for having backed up your husband's claim that he had never left the house that evening? Marital loyalty is laudable in normal circumstances but not when it comes to lying to the police and maintaining the lie under oath in a court of law. So you will have to forgive me if I feel justified in doubting your claim to have been at home together."

Silence ensued and Renard took the opportunity to remind Tom that anything he heard during their interviews was to be treated as strictly confidential.

When Harry spoke again, it was with considerably less aggression.

"We're neither of us proud of what happened. You can take it from me that we have punished ourselves over and over again. In fact, it is one of the major reasons that we came to live in France in the first place. We wanted a clean slate. We couldn't face our neighbours where we were before. But can't you see that we just panicked and once we had got into the big lie, we just couldn't back off. It's a whole different ball game being arse-holed from drink and having an accident and then trying to cover it up. Murdering somebody in that horrible way is something else altogether. Besides why would we want to kill the old boy? We hardly knew him except to nod to if we met him in the village."

"The whole question of motive is under investigation at the moment. I can tell you, however, that it is becoming increasingly possible that there is, if I can describe it in that way, an English connection. Could I ask if Guyard ever came to your house or did you perhaps visit him at any time?"

"I told you. We just knew who he was, that's all."

"There was that time though, Harry," Peggy corrected him, "when you went round to see him because his dog was barking all night and we didn't get a wink of sleep."

Harry looked daggers at his wife but confirmed:

"Oh yes. I'd forgotten about that. It must have been about six months or so back. I don't suppose I understood a single word of what he said but at least he shut the dog indoors at night after that. So there were no on-going problems."

"'As a matter of interest, would you say that he could follow what you were saying to him in, I presume, English?"

"Something must have gone in, mustn't it, because he took to keeping the dog indoors?"

"If the barking of the dog disturbed you so much, you must have been able to hear noises, certainly if they were loud, from Guyard's place?"

"I suppose we could, yes."

"And on the night in question, the night of his murder and assuming you are telling the truth and you were in fact at home, did you hear anything either of you?"

"No, nothing," they chorused.

"No car? Nothing like that?"

"We wouldn't necessarily have heard a car anyway. To drive to Guyard's place, you wouldn't have to come past here. You would drop down the lane behind Nigel's house."

"There was that car that went by earlier that evening though. Do you remember, Harry? Do you remember me wondering who it was? It's not often anybody drives by here that we don't recognize, you see Inspector. We are a bit off the beaten track here."

"Would you be able to describe the car?" Renard asked, ignoring the downgrading from Commissaire to Inspector.

"I didn't pay a great deal of notice to tell you the truth," Peggy continued.

"Nor me," Harry added. "If push came to shove, I guess I would say that it was dark coloured, perhaps even black. It could have been an estate. Something like a C5 or a Laguna maybe. I seem to recall thinking it was newish. I couldn't swear to it though."

"Could you describe the driver? Were there any passengers?"

" I couldn't tell you. I was doing some weeding out at the front and I only glanced up really."

"If anything does come back to you, I should be most grateful if you would let me know—through Tom here if it would be easier for you."

At that Renard closed his notebook and Tom, with some relief, assumed that this first interview was coming to a close. He had not enjoyed the experience in the slightest and he was much closer to understanding Jenny's original reservations about his participation in the case. He now agreed with her view that, certainly as far as the Walkers were concerned anyway, there was a distinct risk of their friendship with their compatriots being put at risk. What was eminently clear to Tom was that he personally would never again be able to view the Walkers in the same light. Even without Renard's admonition of confidentiality, he would have determined off his own bat not to lay the weight of his new found knowledge of the Walkers' past on Jenny.

When they had said their goodbyes and Renard had warned them he would probably need to see them again, they strolled off to their car. As it disappeared up the lane, Harry turned to his wife and said:

"What was it Nigel said on the 'phone earlier on? What was the phrase he used to describe them? A Skulk of Foxes wasn't it? Too bloody right. They're foxy alright. Fucking skulking around, sniffing out things that have got nothing to do with that poor old bastard, Guyard."

21

"Full well they laughed with counterfeited glee
at all his jokes, for many a joke had he."
(Oliver Goldsmith "The Deserted Village")

They decided to leave Tom's car outside the Walker's house and on the way to Nigel Barnes' rather more impressive home, Renard took the opportunity to remind Tom once again, quite unnecessarily in Tom's view, of the need for absolute silence about anything he heard during their interviews.

"After all, Tom, if it turns out that a person is not in any way involved with the crime which we are investigating then he or she has the right to keep any previous misdemeanours out of the public domain."

"Yes, of course, don't worry. I have taken that to heart," he responded a trifle peevishly. He continued in conversational vein.

"You know a lot of Brits give up on the experiment of living in France. It could be as many as half of those who initially intend to settle permanently change their minds. It generally comes to a head, or so the statistics indicate, after they have been here round about two and a half years. Those that make it past then tend to stay for a long time if not all their lives. Those who go back to the U.K. have often been a bit naïve in their financial expectations. They just hadn't recognized that it is no cheaper to live in France than in England. They suddenly find they need to earn some money to make ends meet. If you have to work, you are by definition no longer on a protracted holiday and that's what most of them were after in the first place. Even such a mundane thing as the novelty of shopping in French markets and shops wears off after a while. All those things which had made their holidays in France so idyllic and which had persuaded them to take the plunge and move here have evaporated. Now, I fear, Jean Luc, we may be in the process, by digging around among my Brit neighbours' past secrets, of providing yet a further impetus to repatriation."

"That is something we must risk, I am afraid. I have to say, however, that it is most strange that people, like the Walkers whom we have just visited, should settle in another country and make no apparent effort whatsoever to learn its language."

"Don't get me going on that one, Jean Luc!"

"I make the point simply to offer the thought that their reluctance to pick up some French could well be an early indicator that their sojourn here is provisional."

"You could well be right although Brits have a long-standing tradition of expecting locals to make the effort to speak English rather than learning the indigenous language. It's probably one of the last vestiges of our imperial past, I suspect. It's all part of an innate belief in our racial superiority."

"'We French are not innocent in that respect either. You should take a look sometime at the pronouncements of the Académie Française in its attempts to protect and preserve our language. I rather fear the fate of French as a truly international language is sealed though, especially now with the internet's insidious ubiquity."

"If English is flourishing, it is not because of us Brits, of course."

"No, of course it's America. I guess that the Big Mac is replacing your famous pork pie just as it is our Croque Monsieur. We should perhaps both quietly weep on our New York bagels and donuts."

"A desperate thought, Jean Luc!"

As they pulled up in Nigel Barnes' graveled driveway, they were greeted by the sight of Nigel skipping down the path towards them. He presented a vision that was sufficient to cause them both to abandon mourning their passing cultures. Apart from his cream moccasins, he was dressed almost entirely in mauve. His tie-dyed tee shirt did nothing to conceal the rise and fall of his generously fleshy belly and breasts which accompanied each skip. Above the rose coloured neckerchief, his florid jowls and cheeks were keeping time with his plump frontage. All that remained rigid about him was his luxuriant, white bouffant hair. That, they presumed, was lacquered securely in place. As he reached them, he came to a breathless halt. The after-quake of his embonpoint rippled into motionlessness.

"Willkommen; bienvenu; welcome!" was his greeting as he gave Tom a hug and offered his hand to Renard in such a posture that the policeman was not sure whether a shake or a kiss was expected. An extremely brief touching of the hands was all that he offered in return.

"Please come in, my dears. I expect you could murder a cup of tea, couldn't you?" he asked as he spun around in an essay at a pirouette and preceded them along the path to the front door.

Tom expected the Frenchman to gruffly refuse the offer of tea but he responded positively.

"Ah! The English and their tea! I would love to join you. Thank you."

As they installed themselves in the sitting room and Nigel was preparing the tea, Renard showed that he was impressed by the quality of the furnishings and the abundance of pictures and ornaments by nodding his head continuously as he looked around him.

"I can see why my young colleague was reluctant to leave this house. I have seen his poky studio flat and I can well understand he would enjoy such spacious and tasteful surroundings," Renard remarked to Tom.

"Not to mention that Nigel is a fine and adventurous cook and when he is feeling generous he is likely to produce a very handsome bottle or two from his considerable cellar."

Nigel re-emerged from the kitchen bearing a silver tray upon which stood teapot, sugar bowl and milk jug, also in silver, along with semi-transparent porcelain cups and sau-cers, apostle spoons and a plate laden with home-made fruit cake.

Renard leaned forward and picked up a teaspoon to ex-amine it.

"I have never seen such spoons in France although they may, of course exist," he said to Nigel.

"The little icons are meant to represent the Apostles. Not that you should infer that I am in any way religious. I don't think that you will find any other devotional artifacts in the house. Unless you count the odd piece of male statuary as 'objets de dévotion', that is," Nigel responded with a sly smile directed towards Renard.

He enquired how they took their tea and then without ask-ing served them each a slice of cake. Finally he laid an em-broidered napkin across each man's knee and sank into an armchair opposite them.

"Now, gentlemen, I expect you are here as inquisitors. Could we have our tea before the interrogation begins, Com-missaire?"

Tom was pleased that finally one of his compatriots had addressed Renard by his correct title. Nigel continued:

"I wonder also, Tom, if you would be kind enough to help me carry a few of Tim's things out as far as the gate before we start? We don't want to be interrupted by sordid domestic matters, do we?"

As they were drinking their tea and consuming the excel-lent cake, Nigel enquired:

"So how did the Skulk of Foxes get on with the Moids?"

The question left both men totally unsure what Nigel was asking and noticing their confusion, he sought to explain.

"I have my pet names for people. The other day I came across a list of collective nouns in a crossword solvers' com-panion and when I spotted 'a skulk of foxes', it just struck me as so appropriate for you two. After all, you are both called Fox in your own language and detective work involves a bit of skulking around, I would imagine."

"And 'Moids', Nigel?"

"That is what I call the Walkers. Promise me you won't let on to them, Tom. I want to keep that pleasure for myself. I just want to see their faces when I explain. Why 'Moid'? See if you can work it out, Tom."

Tom played around in his head with 'Peggy Moid' and 'Harry Moid' without getting anywhere at all. Renard was looking totally bemused.

"A little clue or two, Tom? Do you think, as I do, that Harry is rather a pain in the arse? You'll need to do a bit of an anagram as well."

It took Tom a good half minute to hit upon the 'haemorrhoids' and 'Harry Moid' play on words and considerably longer than that to explain the joke to Renard who still looked lost even after the explanation.

"Don't you think that all those hours soaking up the sun have made Madame Walker's complexion a tad leathery?"

Eventually, Tom came up with the play on words between 'pegamoid', a rather rare word for 'leathery', and 'Peggy Moid'. The mental effort and lateral thinking involved left him feeling that the jeu de mots was clever but not very funny. Jokes are never funny when they have to be explained. Nor are jokes in the least funny when they have to be translated, an opinion which persuaded Tom against attempting to decipher this one for Renard. He could see that his colleague was taken with the expression 'a skulk of foxes' because he repeated it two or three times and chuckled.

Tom was rather surprised that Renard was behaving in such an affable manner given the confrontational style he had adopted with the Walkers and, even more so, his anger that his junior colleague had spent the weekend at Nigel's house. When Tom returned from helping Nigel to transport Tim's pathetically few belongings to the front gate, he saw that the mood had changed. He understood that Renard was donning the formal habit appropriate to official questioning.

"So, Monsieur Barnes, if you are quite ready, perhaps I could ask you a few routine questions?"

"Of course. But please call me Nigel."

"Monsieur Barnes," he repeated, ignoring Nigel's invitation, "could you be so kind as to account for your movements late on Saturday and early on Sunday morning of the weekend before last?"

"My movements were perfectly regular but it is kind of you to ask," Nigel replied with a simper.

Tom explained the pun and, as he expected, Renard did not find it amusing. However, it did not deter him from remaining polite as he patiently repeated his question.

"As I recall I spent the evening here. I cooked a rather special supper that night. You see, Tim was still here then and things had been a little frosty between us. I thought that if I made a bit of an effort, it might bring him round. It didn't as it happened and after we had eaten he stalked off to bed in one of the spare rooms. I am afraid that I was rather distraught and I did severe damage to a bottle of Calvados. I fetched up falling asleep in the chair."

Tom thought there was a touch of moistness in Nigel's eyes and this was confirmed as he blew his nose loudly. If Renard had also spotted this sign of distress, it did not prevent him from pursuing his line of questioning.

"Given these sleeping arrangements, I assume it would be impossible for either you or Monsieur Foulkes to be categorical that the other person remained here throughout the night."

"But, my dear fellow, as I already told you, I was comatose. I very much doubt that I could have staggered as far as the front door let alone, as you are implying, getting to Guyard's place and doing him to death."

"The problem for me, Monsieur Barnes, is that, since by your own admission you and your friend spent the night apart, I only have your word for it that you were inebriated."

"I was not 'inebriated'. I was smashed out of my fucking brains."

"If I allow that was the case then you cannot vouch for Monsieur Foulkes' whereabouts, can you?"

"Well, I suppose I can't. But, believe me, disloyal, uncaring little shit though he may be, I can't see Tim as a murderer."

"In the final analysis, I am afraid that is just an opinion. It is not necessarily a fact. In any case I shall be speaking to Monsieur Foulkes and I will have the opportunity to form my own view of the young man. I have to conclude, for the time being at least, that neither of you has a sound alibi for the period which interests me."

"It's just a pity you are not asking me about this weekend because I would have had an unimpeachable witness."

Even this somewhat sly reference to Renard's junior colleague having spent much of the weekend chez Nigel failed to elicit an angry response from the Commissaire.

"Indeed. We are not talking of the weekend which has just elapsed however. In that connection, for the record, I have had a few words with Duvallon. I'm sure that you will understand that, until this whole mess is cleared up, it would be most improper for him to spend time at your house for any other purpose than police business. Lest, however, as my young colleague seemed at first to believe, you too suspect that I am being homophobic, I have to assure you that whatever the two of you choose to get up to after the case is closed is entirely your own concern."

Tom was impressed by Renard's gently but firmly stated position. He wondered if he himself would have been bold enough to be so clear and candid. He wondered also if Renard was expressing his true feelings or whether he was not in fact simply toeing a party line which was de rigueur in an organization such as the police where political incorrectness had become taboo.

"For the time being however," Renard added, "I expect you to adhere to the line of conduct I have described. I'm sure that as a man of the world you will recognize that Duvallon's professional status could be at stake."

"I, too, would like to say something 'for the record' as you put it dear Commissaire. I should like you to know that nothing sexually improper went on between us. I am not saying that Jérôme isn't a most charming and tempting young man but if I encouraged him to stay here with me over the weekend—which I admit I did—it was because I desperately needed company in what is for me a very difficult time. It gave me great solace to be able to look after him. It is not in my nature to be circumspect in what I say to people and it is highly likely that I came out with a few indiscretions about my past, about Tim and, even about my neighbours here in Saint Val. I remember telling him my little joke about you two 'skulks' for example. I remember likening Harry Walker facially to a Barbary ape I once saw in Gibraltar. I recall saying that he should beware of most of the Brit women in the village since they seem to me to be coming to the boil, coming to some sort of middle-aged stirring of the loins. I exclude Jenny from that, by the way, Tom."

"That is most kind of you, Nigel," Tom responded. "I was wondering if I'd been missing any tell tale signs in my wife."

Privately though, he was actually weighing up Nigel's assessment of his female neighbours. Certainly, to judge from Mandy's overt advances to him and, if what she claimed was going on in the Brown household was accurate, from Cheryl's dalliance with Tim, Nigel was not too wide of the mark.

"I can't believe that's true of Peggy," Tom blurted out realizing as he spoke that he was not excluding Mandy or Cheryl from those who may be 'coming to the boil'.

"You're probably right, Tom. After all if Harry looks like a Barbary ape, it could be that he shags like one as well. The poor woman's loins probably don't get the chance to stir. Is there something you are not telling me about Mandy and Cheryl, Tom? If there is, you know me, I'm always eager for a bit of tittle-tattle. Do tell!"

Tom was saved from satisfying Nigel's curiosity by Renard's intervention.

"Tom, what are you talking about?"

"I'm sorry, Jean Luc!" Tom apologized, realizing that he had left Renard out of the loop by not offering a translation of what he and Nigel had been saying. He paraphrased for his benefit, omitting any reference to his own wife's non-stirring loins but not forgetting to include Nigel's description of Harry Walker.

"Very good. That is very good. I like that. A Barbary ape with haemorrhoids. Poor man—and poor woman too from the sound of it!"

At that moment they all heard a car draw up outside. Doors were opened and slammed shut and, in seconds, the vehicle pulled away.

"Well, that's it then. The bunk is done. Farewell, Tim. You know I'm rather glad you are both here. Otherwise, I would not have been able to resist dashing out there and making a terrible scene. I would just have made a spectacle of myself and it would have served no purpose. Fuck it, all the same."

Nigel excused himself and made off to the kitchen to weep a private tear or two the others surmised. More to fill the ensuing silence than to express a seriously held thought, Renard enquired:

"You don't suppose Guyard was up to any funny business with any of the women do you, Tom."

"Christ, Jean Luc, the man was in his nineties. I suppose it's just about within the realms of possibility he could have been some sort of inexhaustible satyr but I couldn't see him appealing to any of the Brit women in the village. Without being unkind to the poor bugger, he was more than a bit on the feral side. It wasn't a great idea to stand down wind of him. As for getting up close enough to him to . . . you know! I just can't imagine it."

"No. You are quite right. It was a most foolish thought. I suppose I'm still trying to find a British connection. This was a step too far though, I admit."

Nigel returned from the kitchen bearing a bottle of Chablis Premier Cru and three large sparkling crystal glasses.

"Pray excuse me gentlemen. I am afraid I was temporarily overcome by thoughts of the solitude and self abuse which lie ahead. I need a drink and I would be very happy if you would join me. I know all about the old cliché of policemen on duty not drinking and all that bollocks but what the hell, I say."

"And I, too, say 'What the hell!' Monsieur Barnes", Renard responded.

"Tom, why don't you do the honours while I fetch us some nibbles?"

They settled down with their beautifully chilled Chablis and began to snack on the 'nibbles' which consisted of home-made black pudding sausage rolls and a bowl of fat olives.

"I must say this is rather delicious," Renard muttered as he ate. "However, if you will forgive me, I should continue with my questions. That, after all, is the purpose of this visit."

"Of course, I understand. Go ahead, Commissaire."

"We have established that, although it seems likely both you and Monsieur Foulkes were here throughout the time of the murder, this cannot be proved beyond doubt. Now, could you describe any contact you may have had with Guyard?"

"Rather sporadic, I would have to say. I don't think he came inside my house once. I guess I spoke to him a few times if he happened to be passing by and I was out doing a spot of gardening. On two or three occasions I called on him to give him some lettuces and some strawberries when we had a glut. I suppose I was doing the charitable bit to make myself feel good."

"Were your conversations protracted?"

"Good Lord no! He did invite me in to his house I seem to remember but I took one look and thought better of it. As you will confirm, I hope, Tom, I do try hard with my French but I am by no means fluent so we didn't say very much to each other at all."

"But surely, he was able to talk to you in English, wasn't he?" Renard asked seeking to bolster his sense that there was an English aspect to the crime.

"What? Guyard? I would not have thought so. But hang on! Now you mention it, I had quite forgotten and it shouldn't have slipped my mind because I was so surprised that I told Tim about it when I got back home. It was just one sentence. When I had given him the strawberries and we had exchanged a few platitudes, I was making my way to his gate and he called out after me 'Thank you very much for the strawberries, Mister Barnes.' His accent was pretty awful but as far as I remember the grammar was accurate."

"And that was all he ever said to you in English?"

"I am sure that was all. There was that other occasion though when I was chatting—or trying to chat to be more accurate—with Guyard at my gate and Tim called down from the vegetable patch at the side of the house asking me if I had seen the hoe. I was just about to reply that I hadn't a clue where it was when Guyard pointed to it propped against the hedge to our left. I didn't make anything of it at the time. I just thought it was a lucky guess perhaps. But now you are implying he had some English, I suppose he could have understood what was going on."

"Thank you. That confirms for me at least something which I have been suspecting for a while. Our Monsieur Guyard knew more English than he was prepared to let on about. The question for me now is to determine why that should be. I am most grateful, Monsieur Barnes."

Renard concentrated on demolishing a couple of sausage rolls and nodded his appreciation of them as he sank a mouthful of wine. He seemed content for the moment at having further established Guyard's secret language skills.

"I ought to go into your past a little," he said at last "but that would perhaps be rather churlish when we are sitting here enjoying your fine wine. I shall need to ask you a few things but that can wait for now."

"If you are looking for muck to rake then I am your man. But I expect you know that already," Nigel said with a sigh of mock regret.

"I am aware that you have a past. I am also aware that some parts of it have been, shall we say, unsavoury. I am very interested in the provenance of your finances and I should warn you that I am awaiting certain pieces of information from your surprisingly large number of bankers. I am sorry to answer your hospitality in such a boorish manner but such, regrettably, is the nature of my job."

Tom was anticipating that a second bottle would be produced. He was also looking forward to being let in on aspects of Nigel's murky history. In both respects he was to be disappointed since, on learning that Renard was digging around into his past, Nigel determined to serve no more wine and Renard himself got to his feet apparently content at this stage not to cause ripples in the mill pond of Nigel's old transgressions.

It was therefore with some reluctance that Tom followed Renard to the car, having agreed to help him look through the papers he had discovered and whose return from the laboratories he was awaiting with growing impatience.

They left behind them a wistful and somewhat anxious figure who, Tom thought correctly, would be seeking some temporary oblivion in drink.

22

"English tongue a gallimaufry."
(Spenser "The Shepherd's Calendar")

Tom, even after only two glasses of Nigel's excellent Chablis, would far rather have gone home alone to spend a quiet evening reflecting and, if he was honest, nodding off in front of the television. As it was, he was on a promise to receive Renard who, having despaired of Duvallon arriving with them, had driven into town to pick up photocopies of his famous 'English Papers' and to pore over these with him. At least, according to Renard, he would have a good hour or so to himself.

He was about to make a cup of system-joltingly strong coffee, when his mobile telephone rang. He resisted the temptation to ignore the call for the briefest of moments and then gave in to his essential dutifulness.

"Hello, Tom. It's Jenny here. I'm just ringing to see if you are alright. I've been trying to get you on the house 'phone all afternoon."

"Hello, Jenny. I'm fine. It's just that I have been out interviewing with Renard. Are things O.K. with you?"

Tom was of a generation which was happier using the telephone for utilitarian purposes rather than, like his children, being totally at ease chatting away at length about matters of no apparent consequence. Thus the conversation with Jenny quickly became desultory particularly as he sensed it would be wiser not to mention the antagonism shown by the Walkers. It would only confirm her worst apprehensions about his involvement with Renard. He did feel it would be safe to fill her in on the Nigel-Tim situation however and this was a sufficient titbit to keep her happy. He determined to tell her about Duvallon another time. At length, they exchanged perfunctory expressions of affection and hung up. Tom realized he was keeping a lot of information from Jenny and that he would have to get this sorted out in his own mind in order to prevent his self-censorship from becoming too much of an impediment to their usually candid relationship.

The telephone rang once more and Tom determined one of these days to master the technical feat of being able to read the incoming number before picking up the receiver. For now, though, he felt obliged to answer the call blind, as it were.

"Hi, Tom. Mandy here."

"Oh shit!" thought Tom but replied "Hello, Mandy. How are you today?"

"I am a bit worried actually, Tom. That's why I'm ringing you."

She went on at some length and Tom understood that she had still not heard from her husband, Tony. According to her she could never remember his being away for so long without at least a quick call to let her know where he was and how he was doing.

"Look, Mandy, I'm expecting Commissaire Renard any minute. Would you like me to tell him about your worries?"

"Christ, no! Tony would go apeshit. He would really get mad if he thought I had got the police involved. Don't mention it at all, Tom. I just wanted to talk to you. I thought it might make things seem less upsetting if I chatted to you."

She asked Tom how long he thought that Renard would hang around and when he told her that he was not at all sure and that it could be late, she signed off by saying:

"Pity. We could have got together otherwise. After all, we're running out of evenings when we are both on our own."

Tom did not know whether he was annoyed or flattered at her persistence but decided in the end that he felt a little of both emotions. He certainly wasn't going to risk seeing her after Renard had left. Not with the handy fisted Tony on the loose and, who could say, about to return home. He did agree though to give her a call the next morning to see if she had any news.

As he was caught up with the telephone anyway, he decided he might as well check through his messages. This he achieved with some difficulty. There were several calls from Jenny. The couple of house hunters he was expecting later in the week had called to say that they hadn't found what they were looking for yet and would therefore still hope to see him that week but not before Friday if that would fit in with his plans. They had thoughtfully left their mobile number unlike the goons of the previous week and Tom decided to give the couple a ring back in the morning. Finally, there was a short message from Nigel. He had evidently telephoned immediately after Tom and Renard had left his place. He sounded pretty upset and, if Tom followed what he was trying to say, needed to talk to Tom privately before Renard started to dig into his past. He asked Tom to give him a call the next morning because he was planning on downing another bottle and taking a couple of sleeping pills so he would not be in any state to talk that evening. This intention sounded a warning bell. But Tom convinced himself that Nigel was far too resilient a character to do anything silly. All the same, he decided that he would mention the call to Renard when he arrived, just in case.

Tom was finally able to devote himself to making the strong coffee he had planned half an hour previously. Scarcely had the percolator completed its cycle than he heard Renard calling from the front door to get his attention. When he had joined Tom, they voted 'nemine dissentiente' to accompany the coffee with a generous measure of Tom's best cognac.

"You have no idea, Jean Luc. The phone has been red hot ever since I got back here."

"On the contrary, I have a very good idea, my friend. You should see the mountain of paperwork piling up on my desk. I grabbed Duvallon and set him to work sorting through it all. I've never been much of a desk man personally. Anyway it will keep young Monsieur Jérôme out of mischief for a good while."

They had consumed their coffee and brandy with indecent gusto and in silent accord opted for another round of the same.

"I ought to tell you that Nigel has been on the telephone. He sounded a bit upset. He wants to see me before you give him the third degree about his past. Do you see any problem with that?"

"Not in the slightest. I think the general rule should be that you behave as normally as you can with your friends and acquaintances. If in doubt about what you should share with them or indeed if you hear something which you think is pertinent, get in touch with me."

"The other thing about Nigel is that he was promising to sink another bottle and take some sleeping pills. Do you think I should be worrying about him?"

"Well you are obviously—worrying I mean. Look why don't I ask my watchdog to call round on some pretext and make sure he's safely tucked up for the night? After all, Nigel seems to enjoy entertaining my officers and it will certainly give my man an opportunity to practice his interpersonal skills."

"This is probably a stupid question but I'm going to ask it any way. It's not the same poor chap on duty up at the crossroads all the time is it? He does get relieved by other officers, I hope."

"You were right. It is a stupid question. But since you ask, I am being very considerate. There are two of them. They do four hours on and four hours off. Their wives are probably glad to see the back of them for a while."

Tom thought that Renard was being a little cavalier with his men and did not envy them only four hours break, day or night, between tedious hours of duty observing and noting.

"Now Tom before going through the papers with you because, yes, the bastards finally handed them over to me, I would like you to look at some entries on a calendar and see if you agree that what they tell me is very significant indeed."

He removed the calendars he had discovered in Guyard's kitchen from a plastic envelope and pointed at the dates in question.

"Now! What do you make of that, Tom?"

"Well, it's fairly obvious they refer to train times. It looks as though the trains connect with each other and assuming that there was a train scheduled to leave the Gare du Nord for London at the time on the calendar, then I would say, my dear Jean Luc, that you have categorical proof that our friend Guyard, unlikely as it may seem, took a trip to old London town."

"Exactly, mon vieux, and I can confirm that there was just such a train departure. What do you think now of my insistence on an English connection?"

"I have to admit that it is becoming more and more plausible."

"Plausible? Plausible? Conclusive is the word you should be using, Tom!'

"There are a couple of possible slight reservations perhaps," Tom caviled, wanting, he knew not why, to temper Renard's enthusiasm.

"And what could they possibly be?"

"I admit that the entries on the calendar indicate the times of trains to London. They do not prove however that it was Guyard himself who was the traveler. It could have been for someone else. In fact, he could simply have been jotting down times for a journey that never actually happened."

"Well, yes I suppose that's technically true," Renard conceded reluctantly. "You have to ask yourself though what the most likely significance of the entries is. Clearly, they were written on Guyard's calendar which I found in Guyard's kitchen. For me it is self evident. In any case, whatever your objections, the basic tenet of my argument remains sound and that is there is an English connection to this case."

"I have to allow that."

"Do you know, Tom, I believe that your reluctance comes from a desperate hope that none of your Saint Val Brits is in any way involved? As far as I am concerned, and I assure you that I don't believe I am pissing in the wind, there is most definitely an English element to our crime. That being the case, it is highly likely that one of your neighbours is implicated in some sort of way."

"It is not for me to question the direction of your investigations. You are the professional around here, of course. But, to me, as a rank amateur, it does seem that what old Casson revealed about the way Guyard's wife was killed is important."

"I have not ruled that out in any way. I know I keep going on about this but I do have a major problem with understanding why, if the motive for Guyard's murder was, let's say, revenge, the killer allowed so many years to elapse before acting."

"That is a difficulty, I agree. But still . . ."

Tom thought it sensible to discontinue his objections to Renard's parti pris.

"No matter, Tom. Nothing is excluded at this stage. What we must do is look at these papers together and work out if they tell us anything. So what do you say to another coffee and cognac and let's get started?"

As Tom prepared a fresh pot of coffee and poured them another generous glass of his best brandy, Renard was spreading the papers out over the table.

"What I am doing, Tom, is trying to put them in some sort of chronological order although that is not always possible because some of the bits of paper are undated or have been clipped from parts of newspapers which don't bear a date on them. I've put them in the order which seems most likely to me but if you know better, just sing out and we will re-arrange them."

Tom leaned over the table next to Renard who had also risen to his feet so as to be able to survey all the pieces of paper. What Tom saw in front of him was a collection of twenty or so apparently random clippings from newspapers and magazines as well as four scraps of lined writing paper with brief notes penciled on them. It did not take more than a cursory glance to recognize that all the items were in English. He began to comprehend Renard's firm opinion that there was an English connection because whatever meaning might link the apparent randomness of the papers, Tom would readily agree that the very least they showed was that things English had patently held some sort of fascination for Guyard. He recalled also that what they were examining had been very carefully concealed by Guyard. Thus, for the old man at least, they must have held some significance beyond idle interest. Unless, of course, he had been going quietly potty for the last few years.

The four magazine cuttings seemed to Tom least likely to be of interest to them as they consisted of a photograph of the Beatles, a picture of what looked like an early seventies Austin motor car and two were of young women modeling thigh boots and mini-skirts. Apart possibly from the picture of the car, Tom thought they might well have been the sort of images a teenage girl or young woman in the sixties would have stuck on her bedroom wall. With Renard's agreement, he pushed these together to one side of the collection.

Tom spotted a half page which had been torn carefully from a tabloid newspaper. It contained for the most part an advertisement for Interflora. The rest of the space was filled with lists of births, deaths and marriages. Tom explained the purpose of such announcements totally unnecessarily Renard told him forcefully as he joined him in scanning through the list of names. They found no French names and none that appeared were the same as those of the people who now lived in Saint Val.

"It would have been too easy, I suppose, if the name 'Guyard' had appeared," Renard muttered more to himself than to Tom.

Nevertheless, Tom responded:

"You wouldn't have expected that anyway, surely. I mean, from the look of it, this dates from way back and we know that Guyard was alive here in Saint Val until a few days ago."

"Yes, obviously, Tom," Renard said to his colleague as though he were addressing a small and dull child. "I wasn't just looking at the deaths column. Suppose he had gone over to England and got married. Suppose a birth bore his name."

"Well it doesn't, does it? Nor for that matter do I spot the name Fox, Walker, Parsons or any of the other local Brits."

"At least there is a date to work on. Look '*Leonard Arthur James aged 82 years, a loving father and grandfather*' then there's a list of the children and grandchildren presumably, followed by '*passed away peacefully, June 14 1976*'."

"So how does that help?"

"It means that if we want to check these names we have a starting point."

"But we don't even know if any of the people in these columns are connected to the investigation in any way. Might it not be a long and probably useless exercise?"

"That could be so. But don't forget that Guyard kept this scrap of paper safe for over thirty years so the chances are that the exercise would not be, as you put it, useless. You must not imagine that police work is all smart arsed deduction and flashes of brilliance; most of what we do is sheer slog. It's not like they portray it in detective stories, you know."

Tom resented being reproved but had to admit that the likelihood the old man had kept the cutting for no reason at all was very slim. He turned to a smaller scrap of newsprint which contained a list of examination results of pupils at Alderman Smythe Community College, wherever that pillar of learning might be. Once more none of the eighty or so names on the list had any obvious relevance. Again, however, they had a date, the usefulness of which Tom did not, on this occasion, query. The introduction to the column of results included the self satisfied remark that '*This year's results show a 7% increase in the numbers of passes at Grades A-E over 1978 results.*' It was therefore fairly safe to assume that the list they had in front of them referred to 1979. It did not escape Tom's attention that, despite the advertised academic improvements, a disturbing number of young people were terminating their education with the grand distinction of a modest pass in a single subject. He wondered how many had not even made it on to the list.

Yet another newspaper report mentioned a teenage boy and girl, whose names could not be given because of their age, having received periods of community service as punishment for malicious damage and for attacking another youth.

A road widening scheme was described in a further article. This failed to prick Tom's curiosity as did the rest of the newspaper cuttings which covered a disparate range of subjects from the opening of a garage to a piece comparing the cost of living to average incomes.

He turned to the four small pieces of lined paper. In the order in which he picked them up to examine them more closely, they read:

'ASCC, New Poplar Road'
'Morrow and Sons'
'Temple Rise'

and

'Yellow Circle'

These meant nothing at all to him but he was able to point out to Renard, who himself had not spotted it, that the four jottings had unmistakably been written by a person who had been taught how to write in a French school. It was obvious to a non-Frenchman.

"So this is the lot, is it?"

"It would seem so."

After a moment or two of silent pondering, he continued:

"Well I have to say that nothing is screaming out of the collection at me. I rather fear that a long stint of slog and plod will be needed before we get anything much out of this lot."

Both men were feeling flat and Tom deemed it only proper to serve them another brandy.

"There doesn't seem an awful lot to go on with what we have here."

"Too bloody true there doesn't! I think you have hit the nail on the head. I would swear the wad of papers was thicker than this. I'm beginning to wonder if those plonkers have not given me the whole pile. Will you excuse me a second please, Tom. I'm going to give them a ring just to check? That's always assuming they haven't pushed off home already."

While Renard was busying himself with contacting his colleagues back at headquarters, Tom drifted out on to the terrace to smoke a cigarette. Even in Jenny's absence, the habit of not smoking indoors was so deeply ingrained that he went outside without thinking. As he looked around him, across the expanse of grass which took up half a day of his every week to keep trim, at the surrounding forest, he marveled for the umpteenth time at the sharp contrast between the sun-bathed cleared areas and the impenetrable dark which began a few yards beyond the tree line. Once again, he was struck by the contrast between the candour and light of the one and the brooding hidden menace of the other, images long held in the human psyche. He understood fully the predilection of writers of fairy tales for the wild woods, running with wolves and the atavistic menace they represented. For a moment he was able to put himself in the boots of rank and file German soldiers, especially after, in November 1942, they were ordered beyond the Demarcation Line to occupy the whole of France. For them, who were not even safe in the unforested areas, the resistance fighters were these wolves of the myths become all too real and deadly.

He stubbed out his cigarette and as Renard was now shouting angrily down the 'phone, Tom decided to light up another. He forced his mind away from the fanciful and tried to make some sense of the Guyard Papers, to discern some sort of pattern in them. There just had to be some common thread linking their apparent disjunctiveness. He began to think that Renard was right and that the key unlocking them all would only be found once a great deal of painstaking investigative effort had been made. There was an outburst of loud invective from Renard who was still on his mobile. Tom let his mind wander over the various pieces of paper. He felt he could do with Edward de Bono at his side as he quickly convinced himself that 'vertical thinking' was not likely to get him very far.

Perhaps if he had yet another brandy his capacity for laterality would be enhanced. It certainly seemed as if Renard would be in need of one. He had become apoplectic.

"I don't give a shit! Thank you for nothing," was Renard's parting shot as he terminated his call and threw his mobile on to the table. He accepted the offer of more brandy and waved his hand to encourage Tom to keep pouring.

"I need one of your cigarettes as well, Tom, if you don't mind."

"But you don't smoke, Jean Luc."

"I've decided to start," Renard retorted with a scowl.

"Well, by all means, please help yourself," Tom said, placing the packet on the table. "But, you know smoking is not a good thing to . . ."

"No," Renard interrupted. 'It's not a good thing either to be sent out to try to solve a murder with both arms tied behind your back. Ce sont des connards ! Des connards! Fucking idiots, couillons, that's what I say ! They can have my resignation in the morning. I've had it with the suits that sit on high, throwing banana skins under your feet, shutting gates instead of opening them. What do they expect? Merde! Merde!"

Renard made an inexpert attempt to smoke the cigarette he had taken but, after a couple of puffs, an explosion of coughing persuaded him to stub it out in the ashtray. That he burned his thumb in the process did nothing to improve his temper.

"Merde," he exclaimed, patently in cursing mode.

"Forgive me, Jean Luc, for asking. There seems to be a lot of 'merde' flying about. Just upon whom do you want it to land?" Tom enquired, although he had a fair idea who this might be.

"It's the powers that be in Paris. The Godfathers. We call them the Godfathers. They have been leaning on my regional boss to ease up on making enquiries to London via Europol. They even sent some gofer down to sift through the Guyard Papers and he's taken 'certain items', copies and all, back with him to Paris. No wonder they took so long letting me have the papers back. It wasn't the lab boys dragging their feet after all. When I finally persuaded them to put me through to my boss, he told me what was going on. He said he thought it was just possible there might have been some pressure from London which means, as far as I am concerned, that is precisely what bloody-well happened. I lost my rag. I told him that it seemed to me that the Godfathers were keener on keeping in with Scotland Yard than they were in solving the murder of a French citizen committed on French soil. I told him that I thought he was just like them and he had lost his sense of what we were here for. He got upset at that and warned me that I was talking to a senior officer. He said I would get into serious trouble if I wasn't careful. Well, you heard what I replied. I said I didn't give a shit—que je m'en foutais—and I meant it, Tom."

Both men turned to their drinks. Tom did not know how to respond and Renard was still fuming. After they had both drained down the amber liquid which by this point was slipping down with no hint of the burning sensation of the first glass, Tom broke the brooding silence.

"You still care about finding Guyard's killer though, Jean Luc. Unless I have totally misread you, there is no way on earth that you would give up on that."

"Thank you for that, Tom. It's very kind of you. It's hard enough to see our way through this case hamstrung as we are by those twats—quelle bande de cons!"

"You are very angry at the moment and that is very understandable. There is one thing, however, which should make you feel better, Jean Luc."

"What would that be, Tom?" Renard asked in a voice which revealed he doubted that anything positive could be gleaned from the situation he found himself in.

"Does it not occur to you that, if the authorities both here and in England want to gag you, your belief there is an English connection has been confirmed beyond any shadow of a doubt?"

"Yes, of course! You are right. I was letting my anger cloud my thinking."

"There is another thing too. If, as you say, you're keen to drop them in the soft and claggy, surely the best way to do that would be to solve the case despite their attempts to make things more difficult than they should be?"

"Again you are quite right. You are a good chap, Tom. I think I need to reflect a little on the best way to proceed from here. It would be a good idea if I left you in peace. We're in danger of finishing your excellent bottle of cognac if I stay here much longer. You must let me buy you a replacement, by the way. I'll tell you what we'll do," Renard continued after a brief pause. "I'll go away and try to plot out a possible way forward. I'll leave the Guyard Papers with you. You're more likely to make sense of them than me because of the language. We'll meet up again tomorrow morning here if that's acceptable to you."

Tom had been intending to call on old Casson next morning and when he explained this to Renard, the latter, perhaps harbouring a new respect for Tom, agreed it would perhaps be useful. In the end, as Tom was escorting Renard back to his car and feeling very relieved that he himself would not be driving into town, they decided to meet at the old man's place rather than at Tom's house between half past nine and ten o'clock in the morning.

As Tom went back indoors he had four things uppermost in his mind. First he must feed the dogs who had shown their hunger by not even threatening to chase Renard's departing car, preferring to stay close to the supplier of food. Second, the thought of feeding the dogs reminded him that he needed to deal with Casson's chickens properly. Third, he was looking forward with the same eagerness with which he launched into the Saturday Prize Guardian Crossword to trying to unravel the Guyard Papers. Fourth, he was worried about Nigel's state of mind and determined that, before anything else, he should check up on him.

Despite his inebriation and his reluctance to drive, therefore, he motored over to see Nigel, leaving the dogs happily attacking their bowls of food. He was glad to see that he had caught him before he had consumed too much of his bottle and Nigel assured him that he had not yet taken any pills to help him sleep. It seemed to Tom that he was almost pathetically pleased to see him.

"I'm sorry to arrive like this unannounced, Nigel. I didn't like the sound of things when we spoke on the 'phone earlier. I didn't want you doing anything daft."

"It's very thoughtful of you, Tom. There's life in the old dog still though. I'm too nosey about what's going on in the world to do anything silly. I am feeling pretty low all the same, I have to admit."

When asked what he would like to drink, Tom thought he had better stick to brandy and once they were settled in comfortable leather armchairs, Nigel began to speak frankly.

"I expect it is far from easy for someone like you to understand what makes someone like me tick. Nevertheless, I get the feeling with you that you don't let my silly posturings deter you from accepting the person you suspect lies underneath it all. I even think that you may like me despite all our differences."

"Of course I do. I enjoy your company and, for God's sake, you have a good brain."

"Yes that is something which would be important to you, Tom. I also have feelings however and these may be rather difficult to understand and to accept for someone of your persuasion. Tell me, just out of curiosity, how would you describe my relationship with young Tim?"

"Bloody Hell! That's a bit of a leading question, Nigel."

"All the same please try to answer it. I shall not be offended. I am too fond of you—and of dear Jenny too lest you get the wrong idea—for that."

"Well then since you put me on the spot, I think of you and Tim rather like a married couple although I have to confess that I fight shy of deciding who is the wife and who is the husband if you will forgive me for putting it like that. It's pretty clear that you are the financial provider. It's also obvious that you are very fond of Tim. Recent events make me doubt whether your feelings are reciprocated any longer, I have to say."

"What you say is exactly what I would have expected. It is not however strictly accurate. I'll try to explain. Help yourself to more brandy please, Tom. You see I am a homosexual after all is said and done although in my early years I did try a few conventional relationships which simply did not work. Later, after a series of rather unsatisfactory encounters with a variety of men, I met the love of my life. Thank God I did because I was on the way to total dissolution. He was older than me by quite a few years and I owe him everything. I don't just mean in financial terms although he was very well off and left me without any money worries at all. He taught me about many things, about art, about culture, about fine wine and foods. He taught me to be strong especially when he got cancer. He was so brave. Of course, I nursed him through to the end and then he died about eighteen months before I came out here. I couldn't stay in London. There was too much there to remind me of him. When he died so too, it seems, died any sexual passion I had. We were like a pair of swans, I suppose. When one goes, the other never seeks a replacement mate."

"That's very sad, Nigel. I am very sorry."

Nigel was close to tears but went on with his story despite that.

"No doubt you will be asking yourself how Tim fits into all this. I met him in London when I was getting the house ready to put on the market. I asked at the local pub I used if they knew of anyone who might tidy up the garden for me. A couple of days later along comes Tim. We got on together at once and when I discovered that he was holed up in some rat hole of a bedsit paying a ridiculous rent, I offered him free board and lodgings to get himself back on his feet. We never discussed it at any length because I didn't care to but I gathered he had been pretty close to falling in with some villains in the East End somewhere. Anyway, to cut a long story short, he moved in permanently and when I bought the place over here he came with me. For me, you see, one of the great cruelties of being gay is that one does not have children. I began to think of Tim as being my son. It seems that he does not want to be thought of by other people as the partner of an old tart like me and so he has gone. That I suppose is the punishment for the way I portray myself publicly, for the act I put on."

"So," Tom asked, "you were not a couple at all then?"

"If you mean were we sexual partners, we were not."

After a couple more drinks, Tom decided it was time to leave. He was sure that Nigel would not do himself any harm. As he left Nigel asked him to keep to himself anything he had told him as he wanted things to work themselves out naturally, whatever he meant by that. Nigel's confessions had revealed to Tom the man's deep secret sadness. Although Tom could not grasp why Nigel felt compelled to keep up his particular brand of often ludicrous charades, he had been granted some glimmer of understanding of what really lay behind them.

CHAPTER . . .

23

Tom awoke early to yet another perfect Burgundian summer morning. Despite his modest hangover, he judged it would be a good idea to get on with what he had set himself to do for it would get too hot later in the day for dashing around and even for strenuous thinking. It would be, in Jenny's words 'a God-given Pimms evening' but, before that, there would be the heat of the afternoon when everything became still, when the flowers drooped, when the Charolais cattle gathered together in the fly laden shade of any available tree and the French closed their shutters in the sun's face.

He needed coffee. He had some dim remembrance of Honoré de Balzac saying somewhere that coffee got ideas stirring and caused items stored in your memory to emerge at full tilt. He felt he could do with a bit of that. He needed a cigarette to add tranquility to the kick start effect of the caffeine.

Having set the wherewithal to satisfy these needs on a table outside, he installed himself in front of the Guyard Papers, poured a cup, lit up and prayed for an inspired touch of laterality. Almost at once, as though his brain had been at work on the topic throughout his sleeping hours, a couple of insights suggested themselves. The first, on reflection, seemed rather obvious now.

'ASCC' could be no other, he thought, than the initial letters of the school whose examination results constituted one of the press cuttings, the Alderman Smythe Community College. Out of interest, he went indoors to fetch the London A to Z. He quickly located 'New Poplar Road' and, at the east-

ern end of the road, the school in question was marked. This conclusion linked two of the documents together therefore. Tom felt he had made the first breach in the initial randomness of the collection of scribblings.

His second insight gave him more pleasure because of the cryptic element it contained. *'Yellow Circle'* could well be a reference to the London Underground map, on which he seemed to remember the Circle Line was coloured yellow. What is more the Circle Line served Liverpool Street which was very close to 'New Poplar Road' in Spitalfields. Could this mean that, assuming Guyard on his supposed trip to London was in fact heading for the Spitalfields area, the note was simply an aide memoire on how to get there? If he was right, Tom had tied in yet another item and chipped further away at the disconnected nature of the papers.

The next step he thought would be to decipher *'Morrow and Sons'*. Self evidently, it was the name of some business concern and he moved indoors, quitting the sunshine reluctantly, in order to sit at his computer and try his best to summon up the Yellow Pages on the internet. Using the instruction sheet which Jenny had prepared for him, he would be able, with luck, to enter search criteria which included a probable location as well as a name. He was rewarded almost instantly with the information that 'Morrow and Sons' was a firm of undertakers situated in Temple Broadway. He wrote down their telephone number.

Back outside with a fresh pot of coffee, he looked up Temple Broadway in the A to Z. He hoped that *'Temple Rise'* which figured on the last of Guyard's four jottings would be the name of a street close by. He was disappointed. No such street appeared to exist. On the off chance that work started early at 'Morrow and Sons' he decided to give them a ring despite the fact that it was still some minutes short of nine o'clock in France and, of course, an hour earlier across the Channel. His optimism was recompensed as his call was answered. He guessed that, because death obeyed no clock, long opening hours were to be expected.

"Good morning. Morrow and Sons, Funeral Directors. How can we be of service?"

"Good morning. I'm sorry to bother you so early. I'm ringing from France," Tom added as though this excused the untimeliness of his call.

"There is no need to apologise, sir. When the parlour is closed, telephone calls are directed to the house. It is part of the service to be available at all times of the day or night. How can I help you, sir?"

Tom was suddenly perturbed at the triteness of what he wanted to ask. After all, the man on the end of the telephone, one of the eponymous Morrows no doubt, would be expecting to deal with the much more profound question of funeral arrangements. He therefore determined to spin an expeditious yarn

"It is rather complicated, I'm afraid. As I said before, I live in France. It is to do with my brother who is much older than me," he added, unconsciously inferring that he himself was a long way off needing the services of someone like the Morrows. "Over the years, I regret to say that we have drifted apart. My great niece rang me yesterday to say that my brother had passed away. The hospital must have contacted her I suppose. The problem is that the last address I have for him is Temple Rise, Spitalfields."

"My goodness, sir, we have been out of touch for a while, haven't we? I am afraid that all the houses in Temple Rise were demolished some years back to accommodate the urban through way which was being made into a dual carriage way. In fact, that is where our premises are situated, sir, Temple Broadway. It would seem to me that the hospital which rang your relative is likely to be holding your brother's remains. If I could have his name and yours as well, we should be happy to contact the hospital on your behalf and report back to you."

Tom saw that he was getting out of his depth and in any case, he had found out what he wanted to know.

"That is very kind of you but I feel I owe it to my brother's memory—especially having neglected him for so long—to contact the hospital myself. I shall, no doubt, use your services and I will get back to you in due course."

"As you wish, sir. If I could just have your name, I will make a note of your having been in touch."

Tom was relieved that his number would be withheld from his interlocutor and he felt able, if not entirely morally comfortable, to give him a straight lie.

"Of course. My name is ..er.. Fish. Michael Fish."

"Just like the weather forecaster, sir? How very strange."

"Yes, isn't it? Well, thank you for your help. I mustn't keep you any longer."

With that, Tom replaced the receiver and cursed himself for the ludicrous ineptness of his untruth. Nevertheless, he could tick off one more query from his list.

In addition, he had stumbled upon an explanation of the newspaper clipping about the road widening scheme.

Tom began to have a suspicion that everything was beginning to fall into some sort of meaningful pattern. He just needed to get it into the front of his brain.

The next step until such time as that pattern began to take some sort of shape seemed to Tom to be to look at the two sets of names contained in the examination results in one cutting and the list in the announcements of births, deaths and marriages in the other. If the same name cropped up in both, it would merit closer scrutiny.

To his considerable chagrin, he reckoned it was time to set off to meet up with Renard at Casson's place. He did not wish to be late as he was not at all sure what the old boy's reaction would be if the policeman arrived ahead of him and he did not want him to disappear back into his shell particularly in view of the detente of his last meeting with him. He would just have to wait until later in the day to carry on with sleuthing his way through the Guyard Papers. At least, what he had already achieved was enough to strike a blow in support of—what had Renard called it?—'smart arsed deduction' and, perhaps, if he were not flattering himself too much, of 'flashes of brilliance' too. It would be interesting to observe Renard's reaction to his insights.

Happily, he arrived before the Commissaire and, in fact, had time to bawl out to Casson that he had come to call on him and that he was going to see to the chickens first. He had just collected the dozen or so eggs he came across in the barn and was scattering a few handfuls of corn in the yard, when he heard Renard's car coming down the lane.

To his surprise, Renard emerged from his vehicle bearing a large bag of cat biscuits.

"Good Lord, Jean Luc, I hadn't got you marked down as a cat lover."

"I'm not. I can't stand the bastards. Dogs neither. But I can stand even less the thought of all Casson's cats starving away in the barn. Make sure you tell him that I have fed them. My real concern is to get on the old boy's good side in the hope that he will stop thinking of me as some emissary of Satan."

"I'm sure they survive very well on rodents. In any case, I'm not convinced that your 'love your cats, love me' tactic will get you anywhere."

"You are probably right. I'm relying on you to smooth the way for me as well though."

"I wouldn't want to take bets on that working either. We can certainly give it a go though."

Tom turned the handle but the door, as previously, was locked.

"Jean François, open up will you? It's only me, Tom."

"No it isn't 'only you'. You've got that bloody copper in tow."

"There is nothing to worry about. He—I—well both of us in fact want to have a little chat about Guyard and to see that you are alright. We don't want to talk with a locked door between us, do we now?"

Renard mouthed to Tom that he had a couple of bottles of Saint Bris tucked away in the boot of his car and wondered if they might serve by way of a passport. Tom shrugged and nodded to indicate that it was anybody's guess but then why not give it a try.

"Jean François, 'the bloody copper' has brought a couple of bottles of white with him. What say we crack them together?"

"Beware of Greeks . . .," he heard the old man mutter. Tom was mildly surprised by the classical reference and then chastised himself for his own presumptions. Why after all shouldn't a man like Casson have a passing awareness of the classical period? Then he heard the bolt being released and the lock turning.

By the time the door had been fully opened, Renard was back beside Tom, the bag of cat biscuits in one hand and the two bottles in the other.

"Interrogating the poor bloody cats after he's finished with me, is he? Well he will get bugger all out of them, bribe or no bribe. You can't bribe me either. Just so long as you know that. Come on in then. We can't hang round on the doorstep all day."

He shook Tom's hand and then, encouragingly in Tom's view, he did the same with Renard.

"I wanted to see you because Tom here has explained how anxious you are about the Guyard business. I want to try to put your mind at ease if I can."

Casson motioned to them to take a seat at the kitchen table and hobbled off to the pantry to find glasses and a corkscrew.

"Bit of an impossible feat that, isn't it?" he remarked as he returned to join them. "Coppers invading your house wanting to grill you and 'putting you at your ease' don't sit well together."

"Jean François, the Commissaire isn't invading your house. He's here with me more as a friend than a policeman. He certainly has no intention of grilling you, as you put it!"

"Tom is perfectly correct, Monsieur Casson. If it helps at all, could I start by saying that whatever may or may not have happened between you and Guyard during the war is of no concern to me and my colleagues unless there is a direct connection with Guyard's death? That business of the shooting of Guyard's wife is awful, terrible. But it is over and done with."

"Maybe for you and your pals. It will never be over for me."

"I accept that and I can only say that I understand how appalling it must have been bearing this sense of guilt all of your life. All I can repeat is that your involvement all those years ago is of no interest to the police whatsoever."

Casson raised his glass and took a ruminative sip.

"At least your wine is bloody good, I have to admit that."

Tom sensed that this was as much of an acceptance of him as the policeman was likely to get. The ice, if not broken, was beginning to crack and he decided to try to ease Renard into a dialogue with the old man.

"I was telling Jean Luc here that you believed Guyard knew a bit of English. He found that very interesting, didn't you?" he said turning to Renard.

"I did indeed. I can't explain why exactly except to say that in my view it could have a bearing on his death. How proficient in English do you think he was?"

"I'm not the man to ask. I know nothing about foreign languages. Hell, I'm not too bright at my own language," he added with a cackle. "The only bits of English I know are all swear words. That poofy bloke came round one evening with a bottle and wanted me to tell him some French swear words. He insisted on teaching me a few English ones in return. It seemed to give him a good laugh hearing me try to say them in English."

"By 'that poofy bloke', I expect you mean Nigel Barnes?"

"That's the one. It takes all sorts, I suppose," he mused, staring straight at Renard as though to include him among the 'all sorts' one had to put up with.

He sighed deeply, took a long drink of his wine and then went on:

"I did hear tell, mind you, that Guyard was taking some English classes in Avallon. It seemed a bit unlikely to me but I couldn't vouch for it personally because he and I had as little as possible to do with each other. You'll understand why from what Tom seems to have passed on to you from our chat of the other day."

"Would you know if he ever travelled to England?"

"I have no idea. The old piece who used to cook for him might be able to tell you although knowing Guyard he probably kept her in the dark about what he was up to as well."

"There is one specific period of around a week in early July five years ago when he may have made a trip over the Channel."

"I couldn't tell you about that. What I can say is that every so often he would take off for a few days. I once saw him myself in the village with a suitcase waiting for the bus. No idea where he was off to and I've never much cared either."

"Can you think of anybody who might have wanted to kill Guyard?"

"Apart from me, you mean?"

"I didn't mean you at all. I believe if you were going to get him back for what he trapped you into doing in Cissey that awful day, you wouldn't have waited more than sixty years to do it."

"You would find it hard to discover anybody who liked the bloke. He was a miserable, crusty old bastard. That's a long way though from hating somebody so much you would want to . . ."

Casson tailed off and Renard wondered if the old man was picturing the murder to himself. If he was, then he would surely not conjure up the true horror which he himself had been obliged to witness. The policeman was now fully convinced that not only was Casson incapable physically of being the perpetrator, neither had he displayed any inkling of that black cruelty of spirit which would be necessary to visit such unspeakable punishment on a fellow human being.

"I wonder if you would be aware if Guyard has any family, Monsieur Casson?"

"I don't think there are any in these parts. If there are, they are estranged. Not that it would be surprising if he had upset any family he might have had. He certainly alienated his neighbours. There was that little girl he had with his wife, of course."

"Yes. I was coming to that. I believe you said to Tom the child was collected by the wife's relatives?"

"That's what I was told."

"You didn't discover who these relatives were nor where they lived, did you?"

"No. I didn't want to get involved. It was the guilt I expect. I just wanted to run away from it all."

"I can understand that. So I guess you don't know the child's name either?"

"I'm sorry. All I recall is that Guyard's wife, the one I . . . we . . . the one who died in Cissey that day, was called Cécile."

"We are going to have to check through the records. To give me some sort of starting point, I suppose that the child's birth would have been registered here in Saint Val."

"Your guess is as good as mine."

"Where were Monsieur and Madame Guyard married, can you tell me?"

"It sounds strange hearing them referred to as Monsieur and Madame Guyard. I got used to thinking of him not as a married man but as a crabby old bachelor. That's what he became, I suppose. They were married here in Saint Val at the Mairie and then we all went on to the church afterwards. In those days there was a little hotel and restaurant in the square. They decked out the barn behind the hotel. There was a meal and drinking and dancing until almost midnight. It was a wonderful day even though the war was on. Everyone seemed determined to forget all that for one day at least. Even the boches relaxed the curfew that night. I was still pals with Guyard in those days of course. That would have been in the August of 1943. Christ, if only we had known what was ahead of us all."

Tom could see it in his mind's eye like clips from a black and white film. All the black robed widows, the soberly dressed grown-ups, the awkward teenagers, the over-excited children were gone now. Only Casson, with his memories, survived.

When Casson held up the bottle to offer a refill, Renard put his hand over his glass to register that he wanted no more. Tom followed suit. They made their departure leaving the old man to the Saint Bris and to his remembrances.

CHAPTER...

24

"Remember me when I am gone away."
(Christina Rossetti "Remember" 1862)

The two men paused when they reached Renard's car. They perched on the bonnet, Tom to smoke a cigarette and Jean Luc to raise his face to catch the sunlight

"I don't understand how they can live in permanent penumbra."

"They live like troglodytes, I always say."

Tom's mobile rang but when he recognised that it was the Parsons' number, he decided not to answer. He was rather desperate to share with Renard what he had been able to glean earlier from the 'Guyard Papers'. Somewhat to his disappointment, Renard did not seem to be as impressed as he had hoped. He had been rather pleased with his interpretation of 'Yellow Circle', whereas the policeman simply grunted when he explained his thinking.

When Tom had finished his feed-back, Renard summarised the findings as though to fix them in his own mind and made one or two suggestions of his own.

"You are quite right. The next step is to see if there is any overlap between the names featuring in the examination results and in the birth, death and marriages columns. Perhaps we could look at those now."

"I am afraid I didn't bring the papers with me. I've got them set out on the table at home. I'm sorry," Tom explained although he had left them at his house with the quite deliberate intention of reserving for himself alone the challenge of continuing to decipher the documents.

Renard gave a loud sniff of annoyance and then continued:

"It seems to me that what we have in the papers is a set of notes for a journey. They take us all the way from the station in Avallon to the East End of London. That part we can take as read. Once we crosscheck the lists, who knows, we may have the names of the people Guyard was travelling to meet up with. What we know already from our first glance through is that we are not going to find any blindingly obvious link with people here in Saint Val. That does not mean though that a link does not exist. We just have to find it."

"There are still some of the papers that don't seem to fit with the 'journey' notion. I mean, for instance, what's all this stuff about the cost of living? What are the pictures of the Beatles and those models all in aid of?" Tom wondered.

"They may become clear as we proceed. The papers that those connards thought fit to remove might have helped. We shall probably never know now."

Renard sank into disgruntled pondering.

"You know, Tom, I think we have reached a point where we are not going to be able to make much progress without doing some basic record searching. How have you ended up for free time this week by the way, Tom?"

"It's not too bad. I have to be on hand to collect Jenny from Montbard on Wednesday evening. It looks very likely that I shall have some potential clients arriving on Friday. This couple looks promising unlike that peculiar pair from last week and I do have to try to earn a euro or two, you know. Apart from that I'm all yours."

"I'm just sorry that I can't find a way to get you some money out of my people. It's no more than you deserve."

Tom shrugged to indicate that financial reward did not matter but secretly he was very pleased that Renard thought him worthy of such consideration.

"So! As I was saying, the time has come for a spot of good old basic fact finding. It seems likely that any further requests for information from the U.K. will hit a brick wall.

In the meantime, therefore, I propose concentrating on the French end of things. I am going to try to track down what happened to the little Guyard child. That will mean my getting into parish records and soliciting 'Brigitte's' help to dig out whatever the vaults of the Mairie might hold. It might prove to be rather time consuming. I still haven't verified the circumstances of Casson's boy's death either and it needs to be done if only for the sake of tidiness and elimination. We still need to see the Browns, the Parsons and Monsieur Foulkes but those will have to wait until tomorrow if not later, I think. I wonder if I could ask you to do something for me, Tom?"

"Of course. Fire away!"

"How would you fancy driving in to see my cousin Lemaître? If I went, I would be pretty much obliged to make it an official visit and keep notes and so on. He is very much more likely to be indiscreet about his clients, past and present, if he is talking to you on your own. You probably know that notaires have to keep records of their dealings for a hundred years. His cellars must be a treasure trove of local information. I want to know anything you can find out about Guyard. Try to have a look at the Titles of any property he owned over the years. See if there is a will. Did he lodge a copy of his marriage contract with Lemaître? While you are talking to my cousin see if he knows of any scuttle-buck about Saint Val. Does he know of any great family rivalries? That sort of thing. You get my drift, I'm sure."

"'I'll see him as soon as he has a free slot. He's a very busy man as you know. I'd also like to carry on with those papers. I can certainly do a comparison of the two lists of names."

"By all means, although I'm not at all sure we will be able to get very far without the cooperation of the authorities over there. Do you know just to get up everybody's noses, I've half a mind to take a couple of days leave this week and bugger off to England on the quiet? I would need you to come with me, of course. It's a thought isn't it?"

Tom's first reactions were entirely mercenary and practical. It would not be financially prudent to miss out on his impending clients. How would he have time between Jenny's return home and the arrival of these customers on Friday to get to London and back for a sufficient period for it to be worth their while? Who would be footing the bill for their fares and accommodation? This would be the first thing that Jenny would want to know in any event.

"I suppose it might have to come to that, Jean Luc," was all he said in reply, concealing his venal concerns for the time being.

Lunchtime was approaching and by mutual unexpressed consent, the two men went their separate ways, Renard to sample once more a plate of roadhouse style steak and frites and Tom to prepare himself a hearty cheese and country ham sandwich. He rather thought there might be a slice of apple tart lurking in the fridge but he would give wine a miss on this occasion.

When he got home, he gave Lemaître a call and was not surprised to learn that he did not have a free moment until six o'clock. From previous experience, Tom realised that it was more likely that he would not actually get to see him much before seven that evening so much did his appointments tend to run over. At least this would give him an afternoon free to have another look at the Guyard Papers.

He had no sooner replaced the receiver than the telephone started to ring. Instinctively, he picked up again, before even thinking who might be calling.

"Tom? Tom? Thank God, I've got you at last! I've called you I don't know how many times. You never answer your mobile either!"

Tom's heart sank as he heard Mandy's accusatory tones. Who the hell did she think she was berating him for his telephone habits? Jenny was one thing but one passing snog, which he was beginning to regret quite keenly, didn't entitle Mandy to have a go at him like this. Jenny at least had served a long enough uxorial sentence to give her some rights.

"Hello Mandy! What a surprise! To what do I owe the pleasure?"

"Tom, I just don't know what to do. You remember I mentioned to you that I hadn't heard from Tony since he left for Magny Cours. I still haven't heard; not a dicky bird. I was only mildly concerned then. But it's been four days now. Four fucking days without a word from him!"

"If you're that worried there's only one thing you can do and that's to get the police involved."

"I don't think Tony would like that very much. I've told you about him and coppers before."

"I don't see what else . . ."

"I know it's asking a lot. I'd do it myself if I had the language. I wondered if there was some central information service you could ring to find out if he has been in an accident."

Tom had no idea whether such a centralised body existed. Regretfully, however, he could see no alternative but to try to help Mandy out particularly now that she had begun to weep gently down the line. So much for the afternoon he had mapped out for himself.

"I'll see what I can do, Mandy. I'll get back to you as soon as I hear anything. Of course, if, in the meantime Tony gets in touch you will let me know, won't you?"

Tom was rewarded by Mandy ceasing to weep with a suspiciously sudden mood swing and he would have sworn that she sounded positively perky as she said farewell and blew him a kiss down the telephone wires. He wondered, not for the first time by any means, at his inability to read what really made women tick. Had she genuinely been making a play for him over the last few days? If she had been, then how could she be so upset that Tony had not reported back to base more dutifully? Then again, was she actually distressed by his silence? Tom was dimly aware that there may be some play acting going on but he could not put his finger with any certainty on what elements of her performance were honest and real and what were merely staged. He sighed and wondered who he could ring to find out what misadventure, if any, had befallen Tony.

Having decided to contact the Sapeurs Pompiers who were so much more than just fire fighters and who he was aware had first line responsibility in the event of road accidents, he was passed between depots which more or less covered the route as far as Magny Cours. He even telephoned the main hospital in Nevers which he knew to be the closest large town to the racing circuit. As a last resort, he rang the emergency department of the principal hospital in Dijon. It was to there that severe cases were rushed, often by helicopter. None of them had any record of a Monsieur Parsons or indeed of any accident involving an English person over the last few days. More than one of them, however, had earnestly recommended that he get in touch with the police services since they had a much broader remit, including, it was suggested, road traffic infractions, as well as other misdemeanours, they added darkly.

Tom supposed that it was just about possible that Tony had been banged up somewhere and he did not see, despite his undertaking to Mandy, how he could reasonably avoid making contact with the police. Perhaps the most discreet way would be to ask Renard if he could make a few judicious enquiries on his behalf. In that way, perhaps, Mandy need never know he had chosen to disregard her strictures.

When he got through to Jean Luc, the latter was not entirely happy at being interrupted in mid discussion with 'Brigitte'. He heard him making his excuses to the Maire and during the ensuing delay he imagined he was stepping out of her office to continue answering the call.

"Yes, Tom? What is it? Have you had a breakthrough with the papers? I can only give you a minute. I'm with the Maire and she is due to go off to a meeting at the Maison du Parc in half an hour."

"No, I am afraid I haven't even got to the papers yet. I have managed to get an appointment to see Lemaître this evening though."

"I'm delighted to hear that. I hope you are not telephoning just to tell me that, Tom."

"No, of course not!" Tom spluttered indignantly. "I need your advice and perhaps a bit of help too."

He explained that Tony had apparently gone missing and that Mandy had charged him with trying to find out where he was. He stressed the fact that she, speaking for her husband, had told Tom not to involve the police.

"Is there any way, Jean Luc, you could do a spot of unofficial digging around? I'm sorry to lay this on you but Mandy is upset and anxious," he explained. "But is she really so very upset and anxious?" he asked himself privately.

"Very well since it's for your lady friend, leave it with me, Tom. He's something of a mystery man, our Monsieur Parsons, isn't he? First off he appears to have no records at all in England and now he has disappeared. Maybe he has just gone walkabout but that would be a bit suspicious in itself especially as he knows I am intending to have a chat with him. Or if something has happened to him that too could be relevant to our case. Is he just being a naughty boy or is he in fact a victim? Yes indeed, as I say, Tom, leave it with me. I'll keep you in the picture. Ciao."

Evidently Renard's initial tetchiness at being interrupted had been dissolved by his inbred mysteriarch tendencies.

Tom telephoned Mandy to let her know that thus far he had drawn a blank but that he would keep trying. He reassured her that it was unlikely that Tony could have had an accident because he believed he had contacted all the emergency services he could think of but judged it prudent not to mention his call to Renard.

"You're a sweetheart, Tom," she breathed. "I'll tell you what! If the bastard hasn't got in touch with me before this evening, if he's off amusing himself, I shall expect you to come and share a bottle with me. I need some company and I can't think of anybody I would rather drown my sorrows with than you, Tom."

When he explained he had a prior engagement, she wanted to know who he was seeing. He asked himself once again why she imagined she had the right to expect him to account for his movements to her. However, he consented to tell her that he was due to meet the notaire.

"Well that's alright then. Just so long as it is not another woman. I'll expect you to call in on your way home. I'm not going anywhere."

With that Mandy rang off before Tom had a chance to turn her down, leaving him scratching his head as to why it was any of her business whether he was seeing some woman or other or not. She was behaving disconcertingly like a wife. He began to sympathise with Tony. If she had become possessive towards Tom after one inebriated kiss, no wonder the poor bastard had felt the need to do a runner for a few days. He toyed idly with the thought that Tony had indeed gone off with a female or whether that was in fact what Mandy suspected. With her contacting Tom so frequently, was she maybe using him as a way of getting in a counter strike before any infidelity on Tony's part was in fact proven? He found it all very confusing and he admitted ruefully to himself that he would never understand the complexities of the fair sex.

CHAPTER . . .

25

"And lawyers talk of titles and descents;"
(Michael Drayton "England's Heroic Epistles" 1597)

It was the work of but a few minutes for Tom to identify two sets of family names which figured in both the list of examination results and the announcements of births, deaths and marriages.

Among the girls' names was a Susan A. Vickery who had accumulated an impressive fistful of passes while in the deaths column there was one Jeanne Louise Vickery who had passed away *'after a long illness bravely borne'* on June 12th, 1976. Elsewhere in the two lists, Tom came across a boy who had achieved lesser results than the girl and who was called Gary Sexton. This matched up with the announcement of a wedding between John Anthony Sexton and Avril Manderton which had taken place on June 10th, 1976.

Neither of the names 'Sexton' or 'Vickery' was particularly rare nor did either seem to have a clear link with the inhabitants of Saint Val. Despite this, Tom determined that when he had some time on his hands he would see what the piece of software for tracking one's ancestors that Jenny had bought him for his last birthday would reveal about these people. He had never used the computer package before so he was not at all sure whether it would be helpful or not. It could do no harm, however, and by using it he would please Jenny who, he knew, was disappointed he had left it gathering dust on the shelf. He would need to allow himself plenty of time for the exercise. He found new software baffling, time consuming and therefore very irritating. Two hours at least would be needed in his estimation and he would have to be off on his way to see Lemaître long before then.

He made a hand written note of the names he had found and jotted down a reminder to himself not to ignore the three year gap in the dates of the two lists. By now the dogs were staring at him fixedly so he decided to feed them. He couldn't stand being stared at like that. They looked like a row of grieving mourners. This was reason enough to put off having a struggle with the software package. Besides, he reckoned he should leave himself time for a good long shower and a change of clothes. He thought he had better take a light sweater with him because after such a clear, hot day as this, he might find the evening chilly. If he did call in on Mandy on the way home, he supposed that it would be less chilly at her place.

When he got to Lemaître's office, he was lucky enough to find a parking space right in front of his door. That was one consolation, he thought, for having such a late appointment. He was about to 'ring and enter' when the door was opened by Mathilde, one of Lemaître's array of easy on the eye assistants, who was just leaving for home.

"He's expecting you, Monsieur Fox. Just take a seat for a minute or two. He's just finishing off with his last client," she said as she sashayed away up the street, quite aware of Tom's approving stare at her rear view.

He did as he had been bidden. He wondered how many hours he had sat here, often on this selfsame chair, waiting to see the notaire about some aspect of a house sale which they were handling together. As ever, he asked himself what imperative of interior design demanded that all notaires' 'études' had this look of fading elegance. He thought he knew how it was achieved. All the information technology was housed in areas out of the clients' sight; filing cabinets were hidden away too. The furniture on public view was antique and solid with a reassuring patina. He thought he knew why the image was important. The furnishings gave a clear message that the office was long established and therefore well practised in the arcana of the law and, above all else, it was utterly sound. This was no place for smart arsed Johnny-Come-Latelies.

Ten minutes into his reveries, Tom was relieved to see the door of Lemaître's inner sanctum open.

"Good evening, Monsieur Fox. I am so sorry to have kept you waiting," was Lemaître's greeting.

He was never other than formal and almost excruciatingly polite, at least when other people were around. Tom felt ever obliged to behave in a like manner.

"Good evening to you, Maître Lemaître." Tom had got over the desperate need to giggle at this silly name which had so afflicted him at their early meetings.

The notaire ushered the elderly lady out into the street, asking her to be sure to transmit his best wishes to her family and not to hesitate to call upon him if she had any worries or problems, however slight. His formal politeness could tend to the unctuous in Tom's opinion.

"Come into my office, Tom. It's been a long day. That last one has been here for over an hour. Her late husband was as rich as Croesus and she insists in coming to see me almost weekly. Since he died she has taken it upon herself to protect his wealth on behalf of her two sons. It's like a crusade to her. I wouldn't care if they weren't such a pair of idle sods. Still it keeps her feeling pious, I suppose, and it keeps my money rolling in. But, it has been a long day all the same. Will you join me in a whiskey, my friend?"

"What a splendid suggestion, Charles. Thank you."

Charles Lemaître took a bottle of Chivas Regal from the bottom drawer of his desk and poured them both a generous measure in cut glass tumblers which had been innocently masquerading as water glasses next to the jug on his desk.

"How are you getting along with my terrible cousin?"

"I'm enjoying working with him. I like him very much and we seem to be developing an understanding. In fact, I'm here at his suggestion."

"Please do tell!"

"It's about our murder victim, poor old René Guyard. I've managed to prise a little bit about him out of old Casson. Do you know him, by the way?"

"Casson is a client of mine."

"Well, then, you will no doubt be aware that he and Guyard although not on the best of terms in recent times were close in their early years. They couldn't avoid it as they were brought up in a small village together. To cut a long story short, something very dramatic happened towards the end of the war which drove them irrevocably apart. What I—that is to say we—want to know is as much as you can tell us about René Guyard."

"That won't take me very long, Tom because, in truth, he wasn't very forthcoming. Naturally, being his notaire, I am charged with putting his affairs in order for inheritance purposes. Notably, I shall have to account to the authorities for any tax liabilities which he, or more exactly his legatees, will most certainly have. To put it very simply this involves my assessing the value of his estate, on the one hand, and, on the other, distributing the balance of that estate, after tax, to his inheritors. Under normal circumstances, I, acting on behalf of the family, have six months to complete this task. It is possible to apply for an extension in the event of unusual complexities and it is beginning to seem to me that this may be one such case. The first part of my duties will be relatively straightforward and, in fact, my clerks are well on with this work. I have had full bank statements from the Crédit Agricole; there is a paid up life insurance policy which he had already left with me for safe-keeping; and then there are his properties."

"Properties, you say? I thought there was his house in Saint Val and that was it."

"Far from it, my dear Tom. In addition to the Saint Val place he lived in, he owns—or rather owned, I should say—a large town house here in Avallon which is divided into four apartments for letting purposes; there is the farmhouse you showed people around a short while ago and which he asked me to sell just before his death. He only signed the Mandat de Vente on the Friday before he died. And finally, there are a number of parcels of agricultural land and forty five hectares of woodland over towards Quarré les Tombes. I have made a preliminary estimate of their value and, give or take a few percent for updating the figures when we actually come to probate, we are talking of a sum approaching seven hundred and fifty thousand euros."

"That much?" Tom wondered in some amazement.

"That takes care of the properties. The bank tells me that he had a few thousand in his current account and in a savings account there is a sum of just over five hundred thousand euros. The rents from the apartments have been going into that for years."

"But . . ." Tom began to splutter.

"Wait, Tom. I haven't finished yet. The pièce de résistance is the life insurance. I am able to tell you it is fully paid up and is worth slightly more than eight hundred thousand euros."

"'Shit!" was all that Tom could find to say.

"Shit is the word I would use to describe the rest—his furniture and so on. I'll be arranging for that to be taken to the dump."

"'But that adds up to . . .'"

"Just over two million euros less my fees of course and a fairly sizeable deduction for taxes, we reckon."

Tom was staggered.

"But he lived like a church mouse. I had no idea he was so well off. Just to think Jenny occasionally got me to take him cooked meals. Sometimes she would deliberately prepare an extra pie or bowl of stew so that I could take it round for him. We were worried he may not be getting enough to eat. I feel really embarrassed now you have told me all that. He must have thought we were such condescending idiots."

"If I know anything of peasant mentality and don't forget I deal with it on a daily basis, I am sure that he was very grateful to you. Your generosity only helped him to accumulate his wealth more rapidly. He probably did think you were fools but that would not prevent him from welcoming what you did for him."

"Does Jean Luc know about this fortune?"

"Not at all. You are the only person outside my office and the bank people who is in the picture."

"I must tell him. That is if you have no objection naturally. With sums at stake such as you have described, we could be talking of grounds for murder."

"People have been killed for far less than that, for pitifully small amounts in fact. So yes please do share the news with him. I don't suppose it matters if it gets around. It might even be fun just to see who turns up here claiming to be a long lost relative."

"Talking of which you said that your duties with respect to Guyard were twofold."

"Indeed. As you now see I am pretty much where I need to be with establishing the size of the inheritance. As I said that is the easy part in this case. Finding the legatees, even if any still exist, will be far trickier."

"Oddly enough that is precisely what your cousin, Jean Luc, is engaged on at present. He's been seeing the Maire of Saint Val. He's been digging around in parish records. I ought to tell you as you have been so frank with me that there was a child who would have been born in the middle of the war, a little girl."

Tom went on to share with Lemaître everything he had learned from Casson about the events in Cissey and about the subsequent whisking away of the baby girl.

"Jean Luc is trying to find out what the child was called and what became of her."

"Please tell him that if he gets anywhere, I would be very grateful if he would share it with me. By the same token, if my research turns up anything he will be the first to be told. It seems we are all engaged on the same quest."

"Only our motives differ."

"There is one small item which is puzzling me. I had quite forgotten about it until I took the Guyard file out of store. I thought it was a bit odd at the time but then decided it was just Guyard being a touch quirky. When I had prepared his last will and testament, I asked him to come in and sign it. The beneficiaries are not specifically named. The instruction reads something like *'to be shared equally among my surviving relatives consonant with French Law'*. My clerks witnessed it and I and the bank manager were appointed as executors because, quite simply, there was no one else. When he arrived he was most insistent that I attach to his will a sheet of paper which he himself had written or so he said. I explained to him that the paper didn't have any legal force in itself. It would be the actual will document which would prevail. However, he insisted and, for the form of things, I got my clerks to witness his signature on the piece of paper as well as on the will. It is not particularly unusual for people to want to have private papers and the like attached to the will—often they want them to be given out at the time of the reading. This one was odd only in that it was written in English and as far as I could tell in Guyard's hand."

Lemaître went on to explain that he would be less surprised these days at having to deal with papers in English simply because there were so many more British people living in the area than had been the case back then, thirty years ago, when residents from across the Channel were very thin on the ground indeed. Tom was not listening however. He was buzzing with excitement. This could be a major clue! He was scarcely able to croak out his request to Lemaître.

"Would you be allowed—would you be willing to let me have a photocopy of that piece of paper?"

"Of course and in return could I ask you to do me a translation of it into French when you have a moment? That would tidy up the file a little and none of my monoglots in the office is up to the job."

Tom nodded his assent and waited impatiently for Lemaître to return from the rear office with the photocopy. He could not wait to meet up with Renard and share with him the treasure he was sure he had unearthed.

CHAPTER...

26

'For you dream you are crossing the Channel . . .'
(W.S.Gilbert "Iolanthe")

When he returned to his car, he took out his mobile 'phone to
ring Jean Luc to arrange an immediate meeting. He was disappointed only to get Renard's message service. His technical
naivety had ensured that he had never mastered the technique
of sending text messages. He would not have had a clue how
to begin. He could only witness with a mixture of awe and annoyance the facility with which his children seemed constantly
to be 'texting' each other and their friends. He had just about
learned to manipulate the main functions of the main 'phone
in the house but he had always been very reluctant to try to access his mobile message service. Nevertheless, he thought he
had better have a try. Not only might there be something from
Renard, there may also be a word from Jenny whom, he was
conscious, he had once more been neglecting.

He stabbed haphazardly at the keys on his telephone.
Eventually, by some miracle of the order of monkeys at type-
writers eventually reproducing the works of Shakespeare, he
was invited to dial '888'. The lady at the other end of the line
informed him *'Vous avez sept nouveaux messages. Pour les
écouter, faites le un.'* To his dismay, the earliest message was
from more than a month previously. He waited patiently for
he did not dare to attempt to scroll on to the most recent calls
lest the system cast him out and force him to start all over
again. Eventually he got to the last three which consisted of
a rather frosty communication from the receptionist at his
dentist's informing him that he had missed an appointment;
one from Jenny who sounded very cheerful and 'was only
touching base'; the last one was from Renard telling him
that he had gone to Dijon overnight to chase up some war

records and that he would ring him the next day to arrange a get-together. As a footnote he said he had no news about Monsieur Parsons.

Like a small child frustrated at not being able to show off a new toy, he felt deflated at the prospect of the delay in transmitting his fresh information to Renard. It had almost slipped his mind that he was on a promise to call on Mandy on the way home. It was a promise he had been intending to break. Now, however, at something of a loose end he felt he had no justification for such ill mannered absenteeism.

As he drew up at the Parsons' house, it was as dark as it was likely to get with a fullish moon illuminating the balmy night. It was not quite bright enough for him to see his watch but it must be getting late he guessed. Nevertheless he felt he ought to see Mandy what with her worries over Tony.

"Tom, at last! I'd almost given you up. Come in," she said with a kiss on the juicy side of mere friendliness. "There's a bottle of Côtes du Rhône on the side. Would you mind opening it? I'll just put these things next door."

Tom opened the drawer in which he seemed to remember she kept the corkscrew and was suddenly struck by what a strangely intimate gesture this was. As he turned around, he noticed that she was lugging a suitcase into the sitting room. He wondered fleetingly if she had heard bad news and was preparing to go off to Tony.

"Oh don't worry. I'm not going anywhere," she explained, reading his thoughts. "Still no news about Tony. I was just gathering a few old clothes together to get rid of them."

"I haven't heard anything either. They all promised to give me a ring at home if they had any news."

Tom chose not to remind her he had not been home for a while. He did not wish to appear less than diligent in his enquiries about Tony's whereabouts.

"You know, Mandy, I really do believe that if you are seriously worried about Tony, we should call in the police."

"All things being equal, I would agree with you, Tom. But they are far from equal and, before you ask what that means, that's all I can say on the matter. It is absolutely out of the question for the French police to get involved. I am just going to have to ask you to accept what I am saying. You haven't gone ahead and contacted them already, have you?" she added with a look of stark alarm.

"No. Of course not," Tom lied.

Jenny always claimed to know when he was lying but Mandy was not perhaps as perspicacious as his wife because she seemed to readily accept his denial. Tom thought that Mandy was looking tired. She must be genuinely worried.

"I ran into the Walkers earlier on," she said favouring Tom with a brave attempt at her vivacious smile. "If you'll take my advice, I should watch out for that pair. They were spitting venom about you and your copper friend. Harry kept on saying something about fucking skulkers or something to that effect. I told them you were just doing your best to help the police find Mister Guyard's killer and that there was nothing wrong in that. I hope I didn't defend you too enthusiastically. After all, we don't want them twigging on to how much I . . . how fond of you I am, do we?"

Tom certainly agreed with her on that. He could just imagine the Walkers in their present vituperative frame of mind being all too eager to spill the beans to Jenny.

"How are things in the Brown household?" Tom asked in an attempt to re-orientate the conversation.

"I popped round there for coffee after I escaped from the Walkers. Cheryl is being pretty tight lipped. I gave her plenty of opportunities to talk but she wasn't for opening up. If you ask me though, what I said earlier about them is pretty obviously true. Tim was painting the end wall of the barn. It was just for all the world as though he were the man of the house. When the coffee was ready she called him in to have a break. She told him not to overdo it. It was all so lovey-dovey. There was an atmosphere as well. I don't exactly know how to describe it. It was as if they had an understanding which excluded anybody else somehow. However much they may be trying to keep it secret, it's as plain as the nose on your face. Those two are lovers."

Tom wondered briefly if Mandy lived in some dream world where life was exclusively made up of dalliances, affaires and high passion.

"Well, if you are right," Tom replied "I can only feel sorry for the injured parties. There's Nigel all alone and miserable as sin. There's Steve. What's he going to feel like when he comes back on Thursday night to find a cuckoo in the nest? What about the Brown boys?"

"At least Tim has been saved for womankind. Quite frankly he was wasted on that pompous old queen. Steve has only got himself to blame. He treats her like an unpaid domestic. As for those boys, I don't give a toss about them. They are just like their old man. They walk all over their mother. It'll do them good to have a spell of deprivation. Little twats!"

Tom had always been aware, or now he so supposed, that Mandy was ever ready to fly the flag for women. He had never grasped, however, that she was such a committed child hater. Perhaps, he thought, she was over compensating for her own childlessness.

By now, they had worked their way through the bottle. It was decision time. Tom rose to leave.

"Tom, you know you can stay," Mandy said "but I am not going to demean myself by issuing another invitation for you to turn down. I just want you to know that I think you are a smashing bloke. If things had been different . . . Well, who knows. In any case, we may not have chance again so before you go, just come here and give me a proper kiss."

Whatever the kiss was, it could never have been described as 'proper'. It had all the ferocity, mouth searching, stroking, holding and warm lubricity that would normally have been a prelude to passionate lovemaking. Instead of that, she put her head against his chest. He was aware that she was weeping silently. Tom had to flee or he would be lost.

"If we don't get the chance again, please remember this moment. I know I shall. Good bye, Tom."

With that she pushed him out of the door and he heard it lock behind him.

Tom was still dazed when he got home. He thought she had referred to the evening as a last chance because Jenny was due to return the next day. He was soon to learn that it was much more than that.

Despite his fears that he would not be able to sleep, he dropped off as soon as he hit the pillow. He did not surface until the telephone on his bedside table rudely ripped him from his slumber. It was Renard calling to arrange a time for them to meet. It was agreed he would pick up some crois- sants and they would talk over breakfast at Tom's house.

As he showered and dressed, he remembered the previous evening as though it were some dream. It had never really happened, had it?

When Renard arrived he was as buoyant with news as Tom. However, he gracefully let Tom share what he had learned since their last meeting before he launched into his account. He was as astounded as Tom had been to hear how wealthy old Guyard had turned out to be.

"Mon Dieu, these peasants never cease to amaze me. This is far from the first time that I have come across someone living in the depths of the countryside like a destitute almost and when they die, they turn out to be filthy rich. They spend nothing. That is the key. My grandfather used to say that such people were so mean they would nip a fart in two."

What interested him even more, of course, was the copy of the paper written in English which Guyard had insisted should be attached to his will. Tom produced it from the folder he had now thought it wise to open as he was begin- ning to accumulate quite a lot of material. He spread it out on the table in amongst the debris of their breakfasts and, as they read it through in English, he provided an impromptu French translation for Renard. This obliged him to look at it with more care than when he had first scanned through it.

It read:

> *I wish this statement to be attached to my will and to be held in the Central Registry of Wills along with that document.*
>
> *As described in the main body of my last will and testament, everything which I own in France on the day of my death is to be divided equally between my surviving descendants.*
>
> *The principal purpose of this codicil is to instruct my notaire, Maître Lemaître of Avallon or his successor, not to exclude from their searches for any such descendants the likelihood that they may be resident outside France or more specifically in London, England. Certain circumstances prevent me from naming the person or persons to whom this codicil is relevant. However, I earnestly request that all diligence be exercised to fully carry out my instruction.'*

The paper was signed and dated and bore the signatures of the two clerks who had acted as witnesses.

"Why didn't my dolt of a cousin show me this much sooner?" was Renard's first reaction.

"You can't expect him to remember what's in all of the thousands of documents he has stored away. He told me he'd forgotten about the paper," Tom answered, feeling he had to come to the defence of a colleague whom he admired and who had not, in his estimation, anything doltish about him.

"True. But you would have thought he might have remembered when it has to do with a client who is the victim of a murder. Still, I have to say that this little piece of paper is the final proof. Not that, as you know, I needed any more convincing. We have a definite English aspect to the case. I just wish we had had it sooner, that's all."

"There is something which has just struck me. From my knowledge of the wording of wills, and I have helped quite a number of my British customers to draw up a French will, I don't think the word 'descendants' is used. I think they talk about 'heirs' and 'rights of succession' but I can't recall seeing the actual word 'descendants'. Guyard seems to have been trying to be quite specific."

"Which may mean that he is pretty sure he has descendants. The papers you are looking at are pointing us firmly towards London."

"The other thing worth noting is that his codicil is written in very good English. So either he was virtually fluent himself or he had some help in drawing it up. I certainly didn't even know it existed so it wasn't me who helped him and none of the Saint Val Brits we have spoken to so far, even if they had the skills, has ever mentioned being asked to give him a hand."

"Talking about the cuttings, Tom, have you made any more progress? Any more insights?"

"Well as I have already said, there is a definite steer towards the Spitalfields area in East London. That is clear from a number of the papers in the collection. I had a look at the names in the two newspaper cuttings. There are two sets of names which appear in the examination results as well as the births, deaths and marriages announcements. I've written them down. 'Vickery' and 'Sexton' don't have any obvious connection with Guyard but I guess it would be worth a shot at tracking them down as we have no other likely names to go on."

"For my part, I spent hours talking to your esteemed Maire and dredging through parish records. I had a look through the microfiches in the Sous-Préfecture. I didn't think I would get a result at one point. I got there in the end though. I can confirm that René and Cécile Guyard née Martin had a baby girl born in September 1943. She was called Jeanne. I went through the census lists and found several Jeanne Guyards but none of them fitted for age. I tried Jeanne Martin as it seemed more than possible that if the family had taken her in they would have reverted to the mother's name. I can tell you that there are literally thousands of females with that name.

I had a result finally though. I limited my search by date of birth and by sticking to the four departments that make up Burgundy. When I thought I had the right one, I asked one of our chaps in Nevers who used to work for me—he's a bright lad and very thorough—to go to the address I had from the census. There were new people in the house and they knew nothing about the family. However, by a great stroke of luck they suggested my bloke talk to one of the neighbours. According to him she is as ancient as the hills but as sharp as a button. She told him that she thought the family had all died out except—except, and listen to this, Tom—except Jeanne who had gone to England when she was eighteen or nineteen to be an au pair. As far as the old bird was able to say she didn't think she ever came back. Certainly not to the old house as it had been sold on by then."

"You know, Jean Luc, I get a feeling that everything is knitting in together. With what I found out about the Guyard fortune and his instructions pertaining to his heirs, who it seems are likely to be living in England and are in line for a real packet of money, we have both a possible motive and your famous English connection."

"I hope you are not mocking me, Tom! Even you, the self appointed Defender of the British, cannot deny that my original hunch was bang on target."

"I wasn't on a mission to defend all Brits! It was just that I couldn't imagine any of my neighbours in the village being involved. And my hunch may well have been vindicated as well, it would seem!"

"We shall see—although you are no doubt correct," Renard continued. "I hadn't quite finished though. I think I mentioned I drove down to Dijon to look through some of the Military Records there. I met up with a guy who must be the world's expert on the history of the Resistance—certainly in this area anyway. He steered me in the right direction. You'll be interested to know that I found both Casson and Guyard mentioned. The dates all fit with Casson's account. There was a passing mention of reprisals and a summary execution in Cissey. No names of the victims were quoted though. As an aside, as I know you are interested in this sort of thing, Cécile's cause of death was marked down as 'misadventure'. Just that. Nothing else."

"What was it you called it? 'The shroud of secrecy', wasn't it?"

"I think so. Where was I? Oh yes! This helpful chap I came across dug out a list of British soldiers who were sent over to work with the Resistance. By a process of elimination and best guessing, he reckoned that the one that Guyard was ordered to act as liaison for could well have been a Captain Grey."

"It's unlikely but I reckon it's just possible your Captain Grey may still be alive and kicking. Of course, he may not have made it through the war. If he did, it would be fascinating to talk to him to get a first-hand account of those days. I don't suppose it would help the investigation, mind you."

"You never know. The most important thing though is that it should be blindingly clear to anyone that a lot of the answers to our questions lie in London. I checked with my boss before I came on here to your place and he is still adamant that England and London are strictly off limits. As far as I am concerned there is only one answer."

Tom had to wait to discover what Renard's 'only one answer' might be. The latter had gone silent however and Tom thought he would use the opportunity to remind him that Tony Parsons was still unaccounted for and that his wife 'was at her wits' end with worry' although the memory of their steamy embrace caused him to think that this might be something of a hyperbole.

Renard seemed not to register what Tom was saying to him and, at length, he breathed in deeply and squared his shoulders, as though he had come to a difficult and possibly decisive conclusion.

"Putain de merde. Ces couillons leave me no choice."

Tom knew what was coming and began to prepare his counter arguments.

"I am going to have to go over to London. There is no other way this bloody case is going to be solved. I can feel it in my bones. Everything I have learned after all these years being a policeman is screaming it at me. So I am going to go the first thing tomorrow morning. And, Tom, you are going to have to come with me."

"But I don't see how I can. My wife isn't back from England yet. I keep saying to you I have to collect her at Montbard tonight. I've got some clients on Friday. In any case the old bank balance is pretty thin. It will be even thinner after Jenny's trip, I expect."

"Mais, mon vieux, sans toi à Londres je serai foutu. I'll be useless on my own in London! We'll be there and back before you know it."

"We won't be 'there and back' before my wife knows it though. What do you imagine she would say if I told her I was off to London—when did you say?"

"Tomorrow morning. We could take the train via Lille."

"Jesus, Jean Luc! She will scarcely have got back herself."

"You will have had the night together and you could tell your wife to deal with your clients on Friday," Renard continued, ignoring Tom's worries..

"Now you are joking! She can't even abide me being an Estate Agent. There is no way on God's earth that she would agree to stand in for me. Besides she knows sweet Fanny Adams about the business."

"Put them off until Monday then!"

"I am not sure they are still going to be around next week."

"Ring them and find out, Tom! Surely you can do that!"

Though he knew only too well that Renard would take it as a sign that his resistance was starting to crumble, he nevertheless did as he said. Somewhat to his surprise, his clients were extremely affable and agreed to see Tom the following Monday at ten in the morning. They added that they were looking forward to it as they were determined to find a place before they went back to England and they had had one dis-appointment after another so far.

"I'm actually telling the truth when I say that I am not sure I have enough in the bank to fund such a trip."

"I shall be picking up the tab. So don't worry on that score."

"What will your Godfathers say, Jean Luc?" Tom essayed as a final line of defence.

"They will no doubt give me the push," he said with a shrug.

Faced with such a show of brave insouciance, when Renard was certain he was putting his career in real jeopardy, Tom felt he had no option but to fall in line.

"Good fellow! I think the train leaves at six minutes after seven in the morning. I'll see you on the platform at Mont-bard. Pack a bag, bring your passport. You won't need a book to read. We shall be too busy."

Clearly, Renard had been at least half decided on this course of action in advance of their conversation and had already looked up train times.

Renard made to leave and his parting shot was:

"Don't be late. See you in the morning."

"You will if I'm still breathing after I tell Jenny what's happening," Tom muttered to himself.

CHAPTER ...

27

"Ah! That war didn't do any of us any good," said
Mr Stillaway. "Nothing's been the same since."
(A.G.Macdonell "England, Their England.")

The TGV arrowed its way through the flat countryside of
north east France. Renard had pushed the boat out and bought
them first class seats. Both men were deep in thought.

Tom was replaying the scenes he had had with Jenny when
he broke the news to her that he was off to London 'for a
couple of days'. In the face of her displeasure, he had found
himself employing the same arguments Renard had used to
convince Tom to accompany him in the first place. She did
not seem to find them as persuasive as he had however. At
the heart of her anger, he knew, was her uneasiness at staying
in the house alone despite the presence of their three dogs.
But Tom had not been able to share this with Renard who,
he thought, in his present gung-ho mood would not understand. She said she found it extraordinary that he felt it more
important to go off 'gallivanting' with 'that French policeman' than to stay with her 'with some homicidal maniac on
the loose in Saint Val'. When he suggested that she should
have someone to stay over with her, she was not mollified.
Nevertheless, he had pressed ahead with his proposal and
telephoned Mandy. She did not reply. Since he felt it was
important to get Mandy to be with Jenny, as much to ease
his own conscience as to offer her genuine protection, he excused himself and drove round to the Parsons' house to leave
a note. To his considerable consternation, he found the gate
locked and all the shutters closed. He could not recall the
Parsons ever having shut up their house in this way and had
to conclude that Mandy had gone away somewhere. Perhaps
that is what she had been intimating when he left her the

previous evening. He felt sure that she would have contacted him if she had discovered that something had happened to Tony and discounted this eventuality. He returned home and suggested that Jenny ring Peggy and Harry Walker which she finally and reluctantly agreed to do.

It did nothing to appease Jenny when she was given very short shrift by Peggy who had gone so far as to indicate that 'it is possible to go off people, you know'. It was made manifestly clear that their friendship was being audited and, as it stood at that moment, it did not look as though the books would balance favourably. She was offered neither overnight accommodation nor even the promise of company.

Out of desperation, he rang Nigel who agreed joyously to feed Jenny royally and to put her up in the guest suite during Tom's absence. Jenny was not enthusiastic but when Tom explained that Nigel doubtless needed someone to see him through his loneliness, she grudgingly accepted the arrangement. In fact, before they had retired to bed she had come round sufficiently to enjoy Tom's humorous version of the Barnes-Duvallon affair and when, the next morning, she dropped him at the station, she was charm itself.

For his part, Renard was mulling over their progress in the case and sketching out in his head a probable agenda for their time in London. From time to time, however, he found it impossible to avoid weighing up the likely reaction of the 'Godathers' to his flying directly in the face of their express orders. When he saw that Tom had closed his eyes and seemed to be napping, he tried to do the same. He may well have dozed briefly but he came round as the train slowed down smoothly at Marne la Vallée—Disneyland, their first stop. He was certainly awake when the train stopped once more at Roissy-Charles de Gaulle Airport. Tom was watching the alighting passengers struggling with their suitcases and idly wondering to what far flung destinations they were heading.

"Next stop Lille Flandres," he remarked to Renard.

"We'll have time to have a drink there before we cross over to Lille Europe for the Eurostar," was the response.

In fact, they descended on the Irish pub next to their platform and Tom treated himself to a pint of Guiness which Renard refused despite Tom's claim that it would begin to get his taste buds attuned to foreign climes. He opted for the relative familiarity of a pastis.

They spoke very little on the Eurostar train since it was very crowded and they were aware that they were closely surrounded by English and French speakers who would have been able to listen in to their conversation. It was as if the approach of England made it more important to maintain discretion. Tom was amused to note how excited Renard became as they got close to and then passed through the Channel Tunnel. He was making no attempt to pass himself off as what Mark Twain called 'an old traveler' and Tom found that engagingly refreshing.

When they at last reached St Pancras and Renard had made Tom explain who John Betjeman was, they took a taxi, on Tom's advice, to Somerset House. On the way, the Commissaire rang Duvallon and asked him to put a note on their superior's desk informing him that he was in London. He advised him to stand well back as there was likely to be quite an explosion. Duvallon said he would let Renard know what the reaction was like.

Just in case his boss decided to contact the authorities in London through the 'Godfathers' in order to rein Renard in, he told Tom that it would be a good notion if they sought their information as private citizens.

"Let us pretend that I am looking for a long lost relative of mine who came across to England probably in the early sixties and you are here to help with the language," Renard proposed.

"That's not far from the truth of the matter anyway. All we are doing is substituting you for old Guyard."

"If they ask me for proof of identity, I shall pretend to be a distant second cousin of Guyard's or something like that."

"If we don't get anywhere with them, as a last resort you could always try flashing your warrant card at them—even though it is French."

"In which case, and we are obliged to go 'official' despite the risks, you may have to appear to be from Scotland Yard helping me out."

Tom's enthusiasm for a touch of subterfuge did not extend as far as impersonating a police officer. It ran through his mind that there were serious penalties for that sort of thing. For the moment, he decided to say nothing to puncture Renard's boyish enthusiasm. It may not, he prayed, come to that.

When the taxi dropped them off at Somerset House, they could see no indication of any Records Office. They enquired of a young man who emerged from the front doors with a pair of ice skates slung by their laces over his shoulder.

"The records haven't been kept here for yonks, mate. I think you have to get them off of the Internet these days," the youth said airily and vanished along the crowded pavement.

When they double-checked what the young man had said with reception, they had confirmation that if they wished to look at paintings, examine decorative art or view exhibits from the Hermitage they were in the right place since the building housed the Courtauld Gallery, the Gilbert Collection and the Hermitage Rooms these days. You could even skate on an ice rink for God's sake. What they would most definitely not find here any longer were the records of Births, Marriages and Deaths. The girl on reception echoed what the youth had told them when she advised them that people 'go online for that sort of thing nowadays.'

"God, I'm sorry, Jean Luc. It must all have changed since I've been living in France. I've been over there more than ten years now. I should have known all the same."

"It's no good beating your breast about it, Tom," Renard said magnanimously though he was patently far from happy. "The important thing is how to proceed from here. We are certainly not going to get anywhere stood outside this Somerset House of yours with our overnight bags, twiddling our thumbs."

"Perhaps it would be a good move to check into our hotel. They are bound to have Internet access there. At least we can verify from the net where we have to go to get our information."

"Okay, I agree. We'll be able to get rid of our luggage so we don't look so much like a pair de sacrés touristes égarés, a couple of lost bloody tourists," Renard said, just about maintaining civility for he was kicking himself that he had not got Tom to do more basic research before dashing off full pelt for London.

The greater strain on his equable temper however came from his aversion to new technology and he had grave misgivings about his ability to access anything on the web. The strain would have been irresistible had he been aware that his English colleague was entertaining similar doubts.

"I'm sure I'll be able to cope," Tom silently reassured himself building up self confidence by shutting out of his brain the fact that he generally called upon Jenny to sort out 'this technical computer crap' as he referred to it.

They took the Underground from Charing Cross to Russell Square where they had reserved rooms at the Albion Hotel. It proved to be one of those hotels which had originally been constructed in more opulent and ambitious times and was now struggling to maintain the décor of its former grandeur. It was having some success as it fell just above being seedy. Tom gave their names at reception and they were accorded adjoining rooms with en suite facilities.

"It is very important that we have internet access in at least one of the two rooms. Is that possible?" Tom asked.

"Of course, Sir, all of our rooms have WiFi. You will need to get the codes from me of course so that you can connect up your personal computer and that is all there is to it."

"You mean there are no computers in the rooms already?" Tom asked.

"Well, no, actually there aren't, Sir," the receptionist replied with a smile which did not totally hide his conviction that he was dealing with a pair of bumpkins.

"Well, we have a problem in that case. You see my laptop was stolen at the railway station," Tom lied in an attempt to show that he was not a total mesozoic.

"All may not be lost, Sir. We have a few laptops in stock for such eventualities. It will be possible for you to hire one of these from us if you wish."

"Oh that would be most useful. How much do you charge may I ask?"

"I'll just have to look that up, Sir. Thankfully we don't get many guests whose laptops have been stolen especially at railway stations so I don't have the prices at my fingertips. Now, let me see. Ah yes," he continued as he consulted a typed list below counter level, "here we are. I am afraid the daily rental is £35 per machine, Sir, and there is a £250 deposit against the return of the computer in good working order."

Tom consulted Renard who raised his eyes heavenwards but agreed to the hire.'

"Just make sure that the price covers the services of some geek to get the bloody thing up and running, will you?"

"We can do that for you, Sir," the receptionist responded to Tom's more politely framed enquiry in English. "Rachel is due to come on duty in fifteen minutes. I'll ask her to pop up to your room with the laptop and to get you launched. I'll hang on until she has got you up and running. Could I have a bank card, Sir?"

Renard handed over his Crédit Agricole card aware that it was getting quite a bashing.

"Thank you, Sir. Of course, the card will not be debited for the deposit on the computer unless—", he tailed off leaving the pair to conclude the sentence for themselves. "Here are your keys. You are on the first floor. Have a pleasant stay, gentlemen."

They had time to settle into their rooms and have a quick wash before Rachel arrived bearing a Toshiba laptop.

Tom summoned Renard to his room and they watched the young woman who was all smiles and rapid efficiency as she set up their link to the internet. The very speed with which she manipulated the machine only increased Tom's apprehension at the task that lay ahead of him.

When Tom explained that neither he nor his French colleague were experts in computer technology, she advised them to keep the laptop in stand-by mode when they were not actually surfing the web.

"In that way you won't lose your connection. You don't get charged for being online so you might as well stay connected if you find it easier. There is one thing I should tell you. Because this is a free service, we don't guarantee that you have a secure connection."

Tom didn't understand what she meant by this and smiled dimly at the young woman.

"Well if you are happy I will leave you to it. I'd better get back down to reception. Brian doesn't like hanging around too long at the end of his shift."

Renard pressed a handful of assorted coinage into the young woman's hand and to Tom's embarrassment, he noticed that he had given her euros and centimes. Still, she would no doubt be able to make use of them at some time or another.

They pulled an extra chair to the desk, stared at the screen tentatively, looked at each other and then at Renard's shrug and vague wave at the machine, Tom entered 'Somerset House' in the search box. To his joyful relief he got a response. As he expected, they were informed that Public Records were no longer housed there and the site went on to describe the current uses of the building which coincided with their earlier discovery. There was a useful suggestion directing them to 'General Register Office' but when Tom looked at that he was advised to visit local government area sites. This route did not seem a likely one as they were not sure what local government area they needed to look at. Nevertheless, he tried, by way of experiment, 'Westminster' and found himself in a morass of no doubt fascinating historical, statistical and tourist information which did not seem to help their cause in the least way. Tom began to have that familiar feeling of going round and round in circles. He put a damper on his growing anger and summoning what remained of his optimism, he began to examine other options and found he was gradually growing in confidence. At last, he had the common sense to type in 'Births, Marriages and Deaths' and was rewarded by being directed to www.familyrecords.gov. uk. When he got on to that site, he turned to Renard whose attention had wandered off to the picture hanging on the wall above the desk and exclaimed:

"Bingo! Here we go. Look, Jean Luc! Just look at all this information."

Together they scanned the menu of categories offered and Tom translated them out aloud.

   i. Births, Marriages and Deaths
  ii. Immigration
 iii. Military Records
  iv. Wills
   v. Census
  vi. More Topics—Parish Records; Emigration; Adoption.

"This is it, Jean Luc. There must be everything we need here!"

If the Frenchman appeared less than enthusiastic it was because he was asking himself if all of this couldn't have been done back in Burgundy thus avoiding the rape of his bank account. He also nursed an abiding mistrust of the technology they were addressing.

This was not alleviated when they drew a blank for 'Guyard'. But when Tom searched for the names of his British neighbours allied with their birthplaces which he had had the foresight to copy down from the deeds of purchase of their French properties, it was the work of but a few minutes to locate them and to engage Renard's full attention to the screen. He began to write down summary notes of what they found and regretted that they did not have access to a printer. They were disappointed when they could find no trace of either of the Parsons or certainly none that fitted with what they knew of Mandy and Tony. They simply seemed not to exist.

Next Tom looked for the names which he had found overlapped on Guyard's scraps of paper and, in very quick time, they had established a life history of sorts for families called 'Vickery' and 'Sexton' both of whom coincidentally had at one time lived in Temple Rise, Spitalfields. They noted down that a Terry Sexton had been born to Harold and Amy Sexton, née Lincoln, on February 2nd, 1963. Harold had been born in 1933, married Amy Lincoln in 1961 and had died of cardiac failure in 1999. Amy who was registered as being born in 1937 had died in childbirth from puerperal fever in 1981. She had died young, Tom thought, but supposed that for those days she was a rather elderly mother-to-be and, while tragic and indeed unusual in such recent times, the mode of her passing was probably not relevant to their enquiries.

As for the Vickery family he located a Susan born on August 25th, 1963 to George Vickery who was listed as being born in 1938 and who had died, the victim of a road accident, in 2008 just short of his seventieth birthday. Renard became very excited and stabbed his finger at the screen when the details of George's marriage came up. He had married a lady called Jeanne née Martin in January 1963. When Tom, now full of technical self confidence, looked up her record and cross checked against registered immigrations, they knew she had died of stomach cancer at the age of thirty seven in June 1980 but she had been born in France and she was the woman they were looking for. This was Guyard's daughter for certain. They had their link whatever this implied.

They were so stimulated by this discovery that they almost ended their searches there and then and it was almost as an afterthought that Renard asked Tom to turn to the Military Records section. There it was not difficult to unearth a Colonel Rupert Grey who had served in the Secret Operations Executive during the war and had been dropped into Central France at the relevant period. Tom was able to check back through the census returns once he had gathered details from the births and deaths records for Rupert. These told him that although Rupert himself had died in 1997 at the good age of eighty seven, he had left a son, Richard, who was born in 1942 which Tom calculated must have been shortly before he was sent to France. Through him they discovered there was a grandson, Samuel, who was born in 1970. When Tom interrogated the latter's records in the latest census returns, he learned that he was listed as being a police officer. He pointed this out to Renard who pursed his lips thoughtfully.

The two men felt suddenly exhausted but euphoric because, although they still could not see why Guyard had been killed, they had at least managed to link him to an English family. Renard suggested to Tom that his bank account, though terminally ill, could nevertheless stand an attack on the mini bar. Recklessly, Tom said he would pick up the drinks tab during their stay.

They were on their third miniature of whiskey when the telephone in their room rang. They were both surprised and strangely furtive since they had not given anyone their hotel or room number. It was Rachel in reception.

"Sorry to disturb you, Mr. Fox but there is a gentleman here asking for your French friend Mr. Renard. Is he available only I have been ringing his room and he doesn't seem to be answering?"

"Could you tell me who is asking for Monsieur Renard, please?"

"He says his name is Samuel Grey and that you will know who he is."

"I see. Just give me a moment please."

Tom turned to Renard and explained that Grey, the chap who had popped up during their searches as the grandson of the Rupert Grey who had served with Guyard, was downstairs in reception asking for him.

Renard said no more than 'Let's go' and was already striding out into the corridor leaving Tom to find the key and lock his door. Tom found himself obliged to break into a trot to catch up and then keep pace with Jean Luc.

Standing next to the reception desk, idly reading through a tourist guide, was a slender, tall man in his middle to late thir-

ties. His smart, sober suit, highly lustrous shoes, crisp white
shirt and the striped tie of, Tom imagined, some club, regi-
ment or public school, made him the very epitome of what he
had always believed a senior civil servant would look like.

"Commissaire Renard, I believe. And you would be Mr.
Fox of course. Allow me to introduce myself. I am Samuel
Grey and I am proud to be the grandson of Rupert who, as
you now know, many moons ago found himself in your neck
of the woods in the Morvan."

"But how the devil did you find us here? It's no more than
an hour ago that we even knew of your existence," Renard
spluttered.

"Perhaps we could step over there," Grey said, pointing to
a secluded corner of the foyer.

"I repeat how did you know where . . .?" Renard began to
ask when they were out of earshot of any guests and of the
receptionist who was making a poor attempt at hiding her
curiosity.

"'It is very simple, my dear Commissaire," Grey cut in,
"you have been searching for certain names, including my
own I have to say, on a government website. My electronic
surveillance people have standing orders to advise me at
once if they pick up people showing an interest in this particular combination of names. You were using a non-secure
site here at the hotel so it was child's play to locate you."

"But you also know who we are," Tom stated in some
awe.

"I have the chaps I believe Commissaire Renard refers to
as the 'Godfathers' to thank for that. I was told to expect you
in London today. Very pleased I am to meet you too, I might
say."

"That is very kind of you. I am very glad to meet you because there are several questions to which you may be able
to give us. . . ." Renard was starting to explain before Grey
cut him off in full flow once again.

"I'm most awfully sorry, my dear Commissaire Renard,
but this is neither the time nor the place to have the sort of

discussion which, I am sure, you have in mind. Here is my card. Could we meet outside Entrance A—it's marked on the card—at, let us say, half past ten tomorrow morning? I am sure that I shall be in a position to be of some help to you. Until the morrow, then?"

Without waiting for an answer, Grey gave a crisp bow and strode off to the front door of the hotel. Tom rather thought that if Grey had been wearing a hat, he would have raised it as he bade them farewell. He had a formal, self assurance which Tom found slightly cowing. It was an Englishman to Englishman thing he supposed since Renard did not seem to in the least abashed. In fact, Tom heard him mutter under his breath 'pompous oaf, you give me arse ache!'

28

'Qui ne gueule pas la vérité, quand il sait la vérité,
se fait le complice des menteurs et des faussaires'
Author's translation 'Whosoever does not bawl out
the truth when he knows the truth, makes himself
into the accomplice of liars and fraudsters.'
(Charles Péguy 'Lettre du Provincial' 1899)

When they arrived five minutes ahead of time, Sam Grey
was already waiting for Tom and Renard outside Entrance
A of his departmental building and suggested that it might
be agreeable to stroll along the Embankment to the 'White
Lion' and introduce the Frenchman to the delights of English
ale. He also informed them that the pub served half decent
traditional English fare at lunchtime.

"You see, Commissaire, I really do believe that a disser-
vice has been done to the reputation of English food and
before you return to France I should very much like to put
the records straight."

"I am afraid you may be hard pushed to persuade me
brought up as I have been in an epicurean French family,"
Renard responded, preparing himself to defend to the death
the primacy of French cuisine among truly informed lovers
of fine food. "I shall be returning to France when I have a
few answers and not before," he added belligerently, seeking
to make sure Grey understood that he would not be diverted
from his purpose.

"He is quite right, you know, Jean Luc. You can't beat
a well prepared pie or a roast. As for the range of puddings. . . . Well, you just wait and see," Tom added as he felt,
in his turn, nationalistic culinary pride rising in his breast
and wishing at the same time to smooth over any unneces-
sary antagonism.

But Renard remained firmly uninterested in this talk of food and drink which was unusual for him given his devotion to the topic. Now, for sure, he was single mindedly concerned with discovering whether Grey would be true to his word of the previous day to be of help to them. The fact that he was lugging a well filled brief case was promising, he thought, and so Renard swallowed his disappointment at not being invited into the inner sanctum of Grey's office in favour of neutral and rather public territory.

Once they had settled themselves into a dimly lit cubicle at the 'White Lion' and Grey had brought three pints of what appeared to Renard to be brackish, headless cold tea to the table, the Frenchman could not restrain his impatience any longer.

"Forgive me, Monsieur Grey, if I reinforce the fact that, at the moment, I am less interested in the reputation of English food and drink than I am in the efficiency or otherwise of your police service," he began, a touch petulantly in Tom's opinion.

Tom was amused by the look of disbelief which crossed Renard's features when he reached across to pick up his glass only to discover that it was body temperature. He raised the glass to his lips as keenly as if it were a poisoned chalice and the first reluctant, tentative sip elicited a facial expression akin to a cat's backside.

"I expect that this is the first time you have tasted real ale, Commissaire," Grey remarked as he too noticed Renard's discomfort. "I guess it is something of an acquired taste. Stick with it. I think that by the end of the glass you will be won over."

Renard had very grave doubts that he would be capable of getting anywhere close to the 'end of the glass'. He rather suspected he would start to retch as a prelude to succumbing to ptomaine poisoning and unconsciousness. He pushed the glass away from him and fixed it with the apprehensive stare of one faced with a king cobra. His strabismus became more pronounced. He decided the only circumstance that would induce him to consume the noxious liquid would be if Grey came up trumps with all the information he needed to move his case towards its conclusion. That alone would constitute a categorical imperative for such a life endangering response of gratitude on his part. He was dumbfounded to see that the two Englishmen had already sunk a good half of the foul potion and, not only still in the land of the living, they were actually smacking their lips with enjoyment. He wondered briefly where this apparent masochism came from. Perhaps it was just one more 'maladie anglaise'.

"As I made up my mind to do after we met yesterday, I have brought along a selection of what our transatlantic chums refer to as 'mug shots'. Perhaps you would like to look through them and see if any of them resemble the people in Saint Val," Grey suggested as he pulled a manila folder from his plump briefcase.

"Avec plaisir," Renard responded holding out his hand for the folder.

"I should explain," Grey continued not yet releasing the folder, "that these photographs are all we have of a particular arch villain's known henchmen. It is always possible that new people have been hired in for specific jobs he wants doing. Have a look through them anyway," he added noticing Renard's increasing impatience.

What Renard had before him was a series of photographs taken from the front and from the side of people who were holding cards with their prisoner reference number on them. Attached by a paper clip was a second sheet which bore a set of the person's fingerprints.

As Renard was taking a measured look at each photograph, Superintendant Grey addressed them both.

"You may be wondering why we are meeting here in this hostelry rather than in my office. I have overwhelming evidence that one of my officers has been bribed by Ackroyd, the arch villain to whom I referred, to supply him with inside information. I wanted to keep you away from any danger of his being made aware of your presence here in London.

It will be healthier for you if you can't be identified. For as long as he remains useful to us in feeding Ackroyd with the doctored information we want him to have, we will just keep him under tight surveillance. When the right moment comes though, I'll be sending him down."

"How do you know you have this mole?" Tom asked, intrigued at the duplicity which seemed to inhabit Grey's world.

"I knew we had stuff getting out of the office and it had to be one of my small team. I personally kept an eye on the most likely candidates. I couldn't leave it to anyone else. It took me a while but eventually I observed one of my men meeting up with Ackroyd's bent lawyer in a public house. They had got rather careless. Once I had a look at his bank account, I found sums too large to have come from a police officer's wages. So I knew I had my man. Subsequent events have confirmed the fact."

Renard nodded his understanding of Grey's predicament.

"Regrettably one has to deal with that sort of thing from time to time. It leaves a nasty taste," Renard commented.

"At one period the Met in particular was as leaky as a sieve. It was a real pandemic. Mostly it was officers who just couldn't cope with confidentiality. They couldn't separate out all the shady deals involved with getting tip offs from their narks from being loose mouthed in the wrong company. They were probably just muddle headed or too fond of getting pissed in the wrong pubs. There were others though who made a very handsome living out of feeding information to villains. They were villains themselves, in fact. Things are much tighter these days thank God!"

Renard closed the file, sighed and slid it across the table to Grey.

"Thank you for letting me look at those. None of the faces means anything to me, I'm afraid. I don't know what I expected. Maybe I was hoping that one of our Saint Val Brits would turn out to be one of the rogues from your picture gallery. A bit of simple minded optimism, it seems."

Because Grey was coping admirably with conversing in French, Tom was beginning to feel excluded from the dialogue of the two professionals. He had become, he sensed, supernumerary. He was especially piqued that Renard had not even thought to pass him the mug shots so he could examine them. Superintendant Grey was more sensitive.

"Perhaps you should flip through the photographs, Tom. Something might ring a bell. I expect you know some of the people who have visited your neighbours, some of the people they associate with perhaps?"

"A few certainly. Not many though, I have to say."

Tom began to leaf through the folder as Renard with a grimace of repugnance took a second taste of his beer.

When he got to the fourth photograph in the collection, Tom's hands trembled with excitement.

"Fuck!" was his monosyllabic reaction.

The policemen looked at him waiting for him to explain his expletive.

"I wouldn't ever forget this face. I met this man in Saint Val. I was told his name was Ted. He was with a woman. They got me to show them round some houses."

"Have a look at the last photo in the folder, Tom," Grey suggested.

"Fuck!" he repeated. "This is the woman who was with him alright. What was her name? I nicknamed the bloke, Ted, the 'Bear'. That's it! I called her the 'Weasel' She gave her name as 'Wendy'."

Tom checked the names on the two records. They read Wendy Alyson Mason and Edward McIntyre.

" 'Wendy' and 'Ted', the short form of 'Edward'!"

Grey showed no surprise.

"These two have records as long as your arm. His are mostly for violence. We are certain he is Ackroyd's enforcer in chief. He collects protection money for him. He roughs up Ackroyd's tarts when they step out of line. There's one he went too far with. She's alive but she won't ever work the streets again. We know it was Ted but we can't pin it on him. The girl is just scared out of her wits. She'll not grass on any of Ackroyd's mob and they know it. As for the woman Wendy Mason, she's Ackroyd's long term girl friend. She mostly runs his string of girls but she has a deep violent streak as well. We've had her for living off immoral earnings. We thought we could get at Ackroyd himself through her but she was happy to take the rap herself. She seems potty about the bastard. She's got a couple of convictions for grievous. She smashed a glass in a girl's face just because she thought the girl was making up to her man. Once she took a knife to a bloke who was bad mouthing him. She took his finger off."

"Messieurs," Renard said softly, "I have no doubt whatsoever we are looking at our murderers."

"They certainly look the part. I thought they were a bit scary when I was showing them around houses but looking at these photographs they have real menace in their eyes," Tom agreed.

"The business of the finger amputations clinches it for me," the Commissaire added. "Happily, we may well be in a position to absolutely confirm that they are Guyard's killers. Before leaving for London, I took the liberty of 'borrowing' the records of the fingerprints we lifted at the murder scene. I have them here in my bag, in fact."

Renard beamed at the two Englishmen.

Grey replaced in his brief case all the sheets of mug shots except those showing their two suspects and reached towards Renard to take from him the five sets of fingerprints which had been brought over from France. One set, he noted, had been marked in pencil 'Bonne' and another was labeled 'Boulangère'.

"I take it that these prints belong to the housekeeper and to the bread lady?" he asked Renard.

"That's correct. The other three are marked 'inconnu' as you can see."

"So we have three sets of unidentified prints," Grey said, stating the blindingly obvious, Tom thought.

The Superintendant rummaged in the depths of his attaché case and emerged with a fold-up magnifying glass and proceeded to peer closely and carefully at the prints which were spread out before him. Tom thought that he would like to look at all the contents of the bag to see what other treasures it held and he remembered having the same sensation when their family doctor had called to see him when, as a child, he had measles and the doctor had rested his bag on Tom's bed. Renard, in the excitement of anticipation, forgot himself and took a large gulp of beer without any outward sign of distaste.

At length, Grey straightened up and passed the magnifying glass to Renard.

"Of course, we'll need to get an expert to look at these for confirmation. But for my money, these two", he said, pushing the third one aside, "are definitely the prints of Mason and McIntyre."

"I agree," Renard muttered after, in his turn, closely perusing the prints. "Is there any way you can get one of your chaps to do us a rush job on them so we can be one hundred and ten percent sure of our ground?"

"No problem. I'll just make a call."

They heard Grey telling a colleague to dash round to the 'White Lion' to pick up the sets of prints and that he would need them back within the hour along with a written assessment of his findings. Above all he was to say nothing to any of his colleagues.

"And in the meantime, gentlemen, what do you say to another pint and steak and kidney pie all round?"

Renard demurred at more beer and requested a half pint of lager to accompany their food.

While Grey was at the bar ordering their lunch, Renard leaned closer to Tom and said in a low voice:

"It looks like we have our killers. I am not very clear on a motive though. I can't believe those two animals went over to France and randomly picked out old Guyard as their victim. There is something we are not being told. How did the

Superintendant know to bring those particular mug shots along with him?"

"I have been thinking back to anything that might have been said while I was showing them those properties. What struck me as peculiar is that they made it clear to me more than once that they were only interested in buying a house in Saint Val. Nowhere else was of any interest to them at all. The other thing was that they kept on asking if they could see houses that belonged to English people. I told them that this would probably mean paying a higher price than would be the case if they bought from French owners. That didn't seem to bother them in the slightest."

"It seems to me they could have been using you to find some English person they were looking for. They were picking up on your local knowledge perhaps."

"But if they were after one of the English residents of Saint Val, presumably acting on orders from their boss, Ackroyd, why did they do for Guyard?" Tom wondered aloud.

"There could be a clue to that in the manner of Guyard's death. Frédo and I were speculating about the reason why the death was so drawn out. It seemed as though the old boy was being tortured to death. We thought it could have been motivated by revenge or by a desire to extract information from him."

Tom had forgotten and was going to ask who the hell 'Frédo' was but thought it was probably not the right moment.

"If they were using me to identify somebody in Saint Val perhaps that is also what they were trying to torture out of Guyard," Tom mused.

"But who, Tom? Who is this somebody they seem to have been hunting for?"

"I don't know. Certainly all our work yesterday on the computer and all our dashing hither and thither around London didn't turn up the name of anybody in Saint Val."

"That's true. All we can say categorically is that we know why Guyard was driven to visit London and the reason for his fascination with England and the English. We know why he had all those cuttings."

Renard suddenly went very still. After a moment or two, he breathed in deeply and said:

"Mon Dieu, I am being inexcusably stupid. I know where the answer lies!"

If Tom thought he was going to be let in on Renard's sudden illumination, he was disappointed.

Grey returned to their alcove with his colleague in tow. He dispatched him to do his work on the prints with an encouraging slap on the back and a strong reminder that rapid results were expected.

"The barman will give me a call when our lunches are ready," Grey remarked as he slid back on to the bench next to Tom.

"Superintendant . . ." Renard began but was interrupted by Grey.

"Please, I don't believe we need to be so formal. My name is Sam."

"Superintendant Grey," Renard persisted, seeking to maintain their relationship on an official footing, "I believe there is something which you are keeping from me and which I absolutely need to know. I am asking you now in all seriousness to be open with me."

Renard's eyes locked on to Grey who stared back equally fixedly. Once more Tom began to feel extraneous. It seemed that the two professionals were no longer aware of his presence let alone sensitive to his equal commitment to a resolution of the case.

At length, Grey responded.

"Commissaire Renard," he said echoing Renard's form of salutation to indicate that he was aware the Frenchman's desire to keep to a formal relationship, "I am being as open as my position and my sense of duty permit me to be. I can assure you of that."

"Yet you seem quite at ease withholding items of evidence in a murder enquiry which my 'sense of duty' impels me to bring to a conclusion."

"Our senses of duty seem to have collided head on," Grey retorted uneasily.

"As far as I am concerned, Superintendant, by not giving me those items, what you are doing is tantamount to colluding with the crime."

"I resent that remark," Grey began but seemed to control his ire and continued 'Look, I fully understand your position and I sympathise totally. I also know however that you are here in London in direct contravention of explicit instructions from your superiors."

"The sacré Godfathers. All they know or care about is procedures and protocol. I want to put a pair of brutal killers away for a long time. It is justice I seek and, as far as I am concerned, je m'en fous, fuck the niceties of politics."

"You must be aware that your job is at risk. In fact, for all I know, you may already be an ex-copper and in that case neither you nor Tom Fox, who is a civilian, has any authority to continue the investigation, above all here in the United Kingdom."

"'I think, if I may, I should like to put a word in edgeways here," Tom intervened. "I may be no more than a civilian, as you put it, but from my perspective you both appear to be highly dedicated and motivated officers. Surely there must be some way in which both your senses of duty can be reconciled? It will help neither cause if you get stroppy with each other."

"I apologise if I have been impolite," Grey replied. "You do not understand that by giving you the truth that you are seeking I could quite well be putting at least one more life at risk although there is probably less danger of that, I must confess; now that we have been able to take certain measures. I am very happy to collude with you in getting our friends, Mason and McIntyre, back across the Channel on to French territory so that you can arrest them and, as seems likely, convict them. Nothing would please me more than to think of those two slammed up in a French jail. If you could throw away the keys it would be so much the better in my book."

"That would be very useful and it is something we could discuss. Perhaps I should say that I am fairly certain that I know what is going on and what your problems are."

Grey thought for a moment and then conceded:

"It would not surprise me in the least if you had worked it all out."

"I am going to test out my hypothesis on you by putting a few questions to you. If you do not answer, I shall take it as a 'yes'. Do you agree?"

Grey was silent.

"Well?" Renard persisted.

"I am playing by your rules. By not answering, you may take it as a 'yes' response. Therefore when you ask me if I agree and I do not reply then . . ."

"I can take it as an affirmative. You do agree. Okay, let me see then."

Renard paused and looked at Tom with a small gleam of triumph in his eyes

"Did Ackroyd send his thug and his tart to get rid of someone who contributed to his being convicted and sent down?"

Grey did not reply.

"So, he was after exacting revenge and at the same time sending out a reminder to others that just because he was in the nick, it did not mean his power and influence had been diminished."

"Is that a question or a statement?"

"It's a question."

"Then our agreed protocol demands that I do not reply to that question."

"In short, what we are dealing with here is your Witness Protection Programme, is it not?"

Grey did not reply.

"Au fait, I suspect that you are the national chief of that service and as such you were able to get agreements out of the Godfathers in Paris. They would have been aware that one day no doubt you would be in a position to return the favour. That is neither a question nor a statement by the way. I am just thinking aloud."

"Nevertheless, to stick to our rules, I shall not be replying."

Both men were now smiling, amused by their silly game and also perhaps relieved that the cat was out of the bag. Tom now saw the rest of the story as clear as a bell and could not help blurting out:

"And the people you are protecting are Tony and Mandy Parsons. It has to be them. When we all thought that Tony was off to the motor racing at Magny-Cours, he was in fact getting away to a new safe house. You remember I told you that their house in Saint Val seemed deserted just before we left for London, Jean Luc? I would wager that Mandy had been given the all clear to follow him."

"In order to round things off," Grey added, 'you will need to tie Guyard into the plot, surely?"

Both men were stumped partially. They knew of his family links from their endeavours of the previous day but realized this did not in itself account for his murder. And then Tom said:

"Sam, if I may call you that . . .?"

"Why not? It is my name after all."

"Well then, Sam," Tom continued "and this is a question to which I think we shall need a proper answer, we know that Guyard and your grandfather, Rupert Grey, were brothers in arms in the Morvan at the end of the war. Did something happen that bound the two of them together so to speak?"

"You deserve an answer to your question. After all you have very nearly got all the other answers on your own. René Guyard saved my grandfather's life. He had been shot during a raid on a German fuel dump and was bleeding rather badly. The raid did not go well and everyone was getting away as quickly as they could. Guyard came back for Rupert and carried him to safety. He made sure he got proper medical treatment. From time to time ever since then we have kept in touch. In fact, he came over for the funeral when grandpa died five years ago. Grandpa made my father, Richard, and me, in my turn, promise on our honour not to turn him down if he needed a favour. 'My family owed him,' he said."

"So," Tom picked up the thread, "when you were looking for a safe house for Guyard's relatives, the old boy prevailed upon you to find them a place close to him. Don't you see, Jean Luc, that's why he was forever hanging around the Parsons' place."

"He carried a great burden of guilt about his family because of what happened to his wife. He was trying to pay back in some sort of way. I suppose he did pay by going to his death without revealing their identities."

Renard felt he needed to summarise for himself the family links between Guyard and 'Tony' and 'Mandy' so that he was sure he had got all the ramifications clear in his mind.

"Excuse me, Tom and . . . er . . . Sam, if I just run through all this again to be sure that I have it right. We know that Guyard's daughter, Jeanne Guyard, reverted to her mother's name, Martin, and was brought up by relatives who lived in the Nevers area. The girl left France in when exactly?"

"In 1961," Sam Grey supplied the date and added "She came over to be an au pair."

"A year or so later she married . . ." Renard consulted his notes from the previous day, "one George Vickery who was born in Spitalfields in 1938. She must have been pregnant already or about to become so as there was a daughter born in the summer of 1963. This child was Guyard's granddaughter, of course, and she was called Susan Vickery. She became the woman we know in Saint Val as 'Mandy Parsons'. To carry on the family tree, Jeanne, Guyard's daughter died of cancer in 1980 and her husband, George Vickery, we discovered, passed on eighteen months ago. His death certificate quoted 'death by misadventure' and referred to some road accident or other."

"If I might break in here, Jean Luc?" Grey asked. "He was the victim of a hit and run accident. We are pretty sure that the driver was one of Ackroyd's men but we were never able to prove it. We found the car abandoned on some waste land. It turned out to have been stolen in King's Cross. It's a racing certainty that Ackroyd was trying to put the frighteners on

'Tony' and 'Mandy', as you know them. Carry on, my dear Commissaire, you are doing very well."

Renard was not sure there was not a slight mocking tone in Grey's voice. You could never tell with these bloody English. Nevertheless, he ploughed on.

"'We found out from our research that this Susan, alias Mandy, got a bunch of decent examination results in 1979. We picked up on the fact that at the same series of examinations, a Terry Sexton achieved rather poorer results. These two got married in 1986. This Terry must be the 'Tony' who is married to our Saint Val 'Mandy'.'"

"And I suppose," Tom suggested, "the leak in your organization was able to steer Wendy and Ted in Guyard's direction. When they couldn't get him to spill the beans, they tried to locate 'Tony' and 'Mandy' by pretending to be house hunting and by pumping me for information. Our old friend Guyard turns out to have been something of a hero, doesn't he? What a terrible way to go. Once they located the old chap, they were going to make damned sure they sent a very clear message to the Parsons. He never stood a chance."

"None whatsoever," Renard continued. "Once they got to him he was a dead man. It was just his wretched misfortunate that they were not only on a mission. They happen to be a couple of raving nutcases into the bargain. I can just picture them. Each of them outdoing the other in acts of barbarity until they were sated. God almighty, I would even wager that hideous woman keeps a collection of fingers as trophies."

"The old chap had always been absolutely adamant that the 'Parsons' should be kept totally in the dark about their family connection with him. A lesser man might not have insisted on that especially given his lonely existence," Grey commented.

Tom reflected that he himself may well have been fortunate to have escaped the murderous attentions of the killers. He also thought that he had been very slow on the uptake in not recognizing sooner the semantic link between 'Parsons', 'Sexton' and 'Vickery'. He would explain this to Renard later and in order to prepare himself he rehearsed the nearest equivalents he could think of on the spur of the moment— 'Pasteurs', 'Sacristain' and 'Vicaire'.

"He was a hero alright. So what are we going to do about his murderers, Sam?" Renard asked.

"As I have already said to you, Jean Luc, it would do my heart good to think of them rotting away in a French prison. In that way they would be beyond the reach of Ackroyd so he wouldn't be able to use his influence to make their life inside any more comfortable than it should be. There is the added advantage that McIntyre would perhaps be more ready to shop Ackroyd if he knew he couldn't get at him. That would be a prize indeed if I could nail him for being the guiding hand behind the murder as well. His woman won't ever give anything away though. You can count on that. At least though, it would really and truly get up Ackroyd's nose knowing that we had her under lock and key across the Channel and that would be a source of immense joy to me. The trouble is getting an extradition order is such a long winded process and I really do not want to give them any time to make themselves scarce."

"Alors, how do we get them on to French territory short of drugging them and bundling them into the back of a van?" Renard asked. "That wouldn't look too good in court."

"I suggest that I use my bent officer one last time before he gets banged up in his turn. Through him, I will let it be known to Mason and McIntyre that 'Mandy' and 'Tony' have been moved to one of the Channel ports in France. We'll need to pick one that is easy to put a secure net around. I'll make it clear that we have put them temporarily in a hotel just outside the port. I will have a word with your Godfathers so that you can have all the manpower you need for the operation and I will insist that you are to be in charge, Jean Luc."

"A sting! That all sounds good to me." Renard responded.

From behind the bar they heard a call of 'Thirty Seven' which indicated that their meals were ready to collect. The three men fell upon the steak and kidney pies as though they had not eaten for a week.

They ate with gusto and in silence as they digested the food and plotted the sting. Their absolute attention to the food was only interrupted by Grey's man who returned and confirmed he had a good finger print match. When they had finished, wiped their mouths and leaned back in contentment, Renard said:

"That was excellent. I promise you, Sam, I will tell all my French pals that traditional English food well cooked compares favourably with anything produced by our French chefs. I may even have to pop over to England from time to time so that I can work my way through the menu here."

Before they departed, they agreed that Dieppe would be ideal since the port area could be contained so easily and unobtrusively. Sam Grey handed Renard and Tom each an envelope.

"You could have done with this bit of evidence earlier, Jean Luc, but my hands were tied by my need to protect my witnesses. I had it removed from your bundle of cuttings. I had to make sure that 'Tony' and 'Mandy' had been got away from Saint Val safely. It will, I believe, complete what you need to secure a conviction. Your envelope contains something more personal, Tom."

Renard's envelope held a newspaper cutting which announced that Ackroyd had been sentenced to fourteen years in prison for manslaughter. The article went on to state that it was largely thanks to the eye witness accounts of Mr. and Mrs. Terry Sexton who had witnessed Ackroyd stabbing a man, who subsequently died of his wounds, in a fight outside the Blue Fountain Club, that a conviction had been secured. The judge had declared that were it not for the fact that the victim had also been carrying a knife, he would have felt it proper to instruct the jury to consider a murder verdict. The report concluded by saying that Mr. and Mrs. Sexton had been taken into the Witness Protection Programme for their own safety.

Renard began to grin broadly as Tom translated the cutting.

"Je suis d'accord avec toi. I agree with you, Sam. This bit of paper I must have originally found hidden in Guyard's place completes the circle of evidence. I really believe we have them especially with the finger print evidence and what's more, with your support, Sam, I don't imagine there will be any difficulty at all in persuading my Juge d'Instruction that I have a water tight case for him to put to the court."

Tom's envelope held a short note signed '*From the girl you know as Mandy.*'

It read:

'*My dear Tom*

Please forgive me for pestering you so much in the days after Tony had left and I was waiting to follow him. I needed to find out as much as I could from you what the local police knew about us.

I enjoyed spending time with you and although I ask you to believe I love my husband, it was not hard for me at all to keep up the charade.

In fact, if I ever do decide to go off the rails, I'll be sure yours is the first door I knock on.

Love'

Tom wondered what he would do if she did come knocking.

29

"If you don't go to other men's funerals" he told
Father stiffly, "they won't go to yours."
Clarence Day "Life with Father" 1935

There was high cloud cover over the Channel as the fast ferry left Newhaven bound for Dieppe. In two hours the boat would dock in the French port and already the teams of policemen were moving into their appointed positions.

Grey had ensured that two policemen from the Sussex force were among the customs officers who were checking passports at the English terminal. They were able to inform Grey and, through him, Renard that their targets had driven through on to the docks in a dark blue Vauxhall Vectra. The registration number was disseminated amongst those officers who needed to know it including one of Grey's men who was entirely trustworthy and who was masquerading as a ferry loading operative. He confirmed that the two were on board and that their car would be amongst the first dozen to disembark. A female officer had been enrolled to clear tables in the bar lounge and, in between railing at the sexist attitudes which had presided over the allocation of her role, she kept a watchful eye on the pair. Her subsequent notes would reveal that the man consumed two pints of lager and the woman had two whiskies and a packet of cheese and onion crisps during the short crossing.

On the French side of the water, a dozen gendarmes were in place. Of these, four were marksmen armed with precision rifles. They were strategically placed, one on the roof of the Harbour Master's office, two in lorries with canvas sides and, forming a final killing point just in case the targets made it as far as there, the fourth was outside the harbour area itself secreted behind an unmarked police van. They had been instructed that if it looked as though they might make their get-away, on Renard's command, they were to shoot to kill if necessary but to maim if possible.

Renard had had a passing thought that he had it in his power to have them shot down like rabid dogs but he knew that he would only issue the order to fire if things had gone badly wrong with his plans to take the pair into custody alive.

He intended to read them their rights and to arrest them personally. To cover all angles, he had arranged that Grey himself would be present to give Mason and McIntyre the English version of what he was telling them. He didn't want some sly lawyer getting them off the hook because they could claim they didn't understand what was going on. The long exit route from the port ran alongside a tall wire fence parallel to the public road to the town centre on the other side of the fence. They had arranged that the usual two lanes of disembarking traffic would be restricted to one. One of his men would open up the second lane ostensibly to speed up the off-loading process just as soon as the Vauxhall got to his position along the exit route and direct it into a slip lane. The following traffic would then be immediately directed back into the original single lane. This was as much as they could do to keep the public out of harm's way and to distance them from the villains' vehicle. Similarly, despite his protestations, Tom had been kept well clear not only because of the danger a shootout would present but also because Grey had advised that it would be better to protect Tom's anonymity in case Ackroyd sought to continue his vendetta of killing. He was, he considered, more likely to visit his vengeance on a civilian than on the combined might of two nations' police forces. He might not be above sending them a very nasty message though and that nasty message may well take the form of an attack on Tom.

The longest part was the time it took from first sighting the ferry on its approach to the harbour to the actual disembarkation. When the vehicles began to emerge, it all happened very fast.

The target car was herded away from the other traffic and three police cars, one of them containing Renard and Grey, screeched to a halt in the form of a triangle around the Vauxhall. Hands holding revolvers poked out of each police vehicle.

Renard spoke quietly to Grey who then shouted his words in English at the two villains.

"You are entirely surrounded. We have sharpshooters with their rifles trained on you. Open your doors! Get out of your car! Lie face down on the ground."

The man and the woman looked at each other and it seemed to Grey, reading her lips through the car window, that Wendy said to Ted that it was a 'fucking set up' and that they had been conned. He was sure that all Ted replied was 'Yeah'. As they seemed not to be reacting to his commands, Grey, at a nod of agreement from Renard, repeated them in an even louder bellow and assured them they were as good as dead if they did not comply.

This time they responded and did as they were ordered. Once they had been cuffed, searched and hauled back to their feet, Renard stepped forward and formally put them under arrest. Grey repeated the formula of words in English. Ted made no response. The woman pulled forward against her cuffs and tried to spit in Grey's face but fell short of her target. The prisoners then set off in separate cars on the four hour journey to Burgundy. Renard had arranged that at each intersection, the local police would clear the way and hold back cross traffic so that the two vehicles could make their journey at speed and without stopping. He joked with Tom and Sam Grey that provincial police were good at that sort of thing because for most of them the highlight of their year was organizing the passage of the Tour de France through their patch of territory.

The whole process of arrest and dispatch seemed to have happened in the wink of an eye.

The three of them, Tom, Jean Luc and Sam, shook hands and gave each other a hug of congratulations. Then they were given a lift by the local police across the swing bridge as far as 'Les Trois Corsaires' restaurant on the town quay. In anticipation, Renard had asked for a bottle of Moët to be put on ice and had ordered an 'Assiette de Fruits de Mer' which he insisted had to include a spider crab for each of them.

"I'll show you bloody Brits what food really is," he promised himself.

*****

A few days later, the three men reconvened outside the rather neglected church in Saint Val which seemed a million miles from London and even from Dieppe. Guyard's body had been released and they were there to be at his interment.

When they stepped into the gloom of the church and their eyes had adjusted, they were surprised to see so many mourners. Of the English only the Walkers were absent by choice and the 'Parsons' were not able to attend since they were still in hiding. Tom thought that many of the villagers were there mainly out of curiosity. Guyard had after all not been an easy man to get to know and there were good reasons for that as Tom now knew. Above all, Tom was glad to see that Casson was there.

When the short funeral mass had concluded, the congregation went in single file past the coffin which rested in front of the altar. Each person dipped a silver shaker in the bowl of holy water held by the priest, shook a few drops on to the lid of the coffin and passed it behind them to the person next in line.

The coffin was then placed back in the hearse to be taken to the cemetery. The mourners some bearing wreaths or bunches of flowers followed on behind the hearse to the burial ground which, typically in France, was some way outside the village itself. Tom fancied he could see evolution at work among the assembled locals. A brachycephalic, squat sturdiness appropriate to a labour intensive existence evident among the more elderly was giving way to a taller, upright spriteliness in the younger generations. Life was changing for French people, he thought.

After the cool penumbra of the inside of the church, the sun now seemed brighter, the sky a deeper blue and the heat more intense than when they had been waiting in front of the church for the service to begin. Tom, Jean Luc, Sam and a few others were wearing dark suits and black ties and, as they walked, the dust rose from the lane to cover their shoes and the legs of their trousers. It all seemed rather Sicilian to Tom, a sensation which would have been even stronger if the body had been carried in a glass sided carriage drawn by black beplumed horses instead of a somewhat incongruously modern Mercedes.

The cemetery looked down from the hillside between a cleft in the wooded hills towards further rolling slopes and forests. In so far as 'a good place to be buried' made any sense, then this, thought Tom, was one such spot.

The priest said a few words and before the coffin was lowered into the earth the assembly followed the lead of 'Brigitte', the mayor, wearing her tricoloured sash of office, in singing the 'Marseillaise'. Tom had always found he was easily moved by the French anthem and the inexpertness of the singing on this occasion, only added to its poignancy. A tear or two formed in his eyes and he was not alone in this. He heard Jenny at his side sobbing.

When the anthem was over, some stepped forward to cast a handful of earth into the grave. Others simply shuffled a bit and then moved off uncertainly. Sam Grey took two guardsman—like paces forward, stood at attention for a moment then bent and placed a wreath against the piled earth. He stepped in reverse back to his original position, stood at ramrod attention once more and gave a military salute.

Before they left, Tom and Jenny looked at the card on the wreath Sam had lain next to the grave.

It read:

'To our heroic grandfather with our love and grati-tude.' It was signed *'Mandy and Tony'*.

Tom had the thoroughly unworthy thought that once Le-maître had sorted out her grandfather's will, 'Mandy' would have even more reason to be grateful to old Guyard.

Postscript

"In every parting there is an image of death."
(George Eliot "Scenes of Clerical Life")

It seemed superficially as though it was Guyard's brutal murder which initiated the series of upheavals in the lives of the expatriates of Saint Val. In retrospect though, if the gruesome event played any part at all, it was an indirect one. The most one could claim was that the sudden death in their midst caused them to recognize their own mortality in such a way that a need to put right those elements of their lives which were unpalatable to them more urgently shaped their decisions. A wave of carpe diem-ism spread rapidly through the small community.

Harry and Peggy Walker believed that their criminous past had become common knowledge in the village although Tom had revealed nothing to anyone other than Jenny who, he thought, deserved some sort of explanation for the Walkers' animosity. Their belief that their history had become common currency, however mistaken it was, caused them to realize that they had never really felt at home in a French village which in truth had been no more than a bolt-hole to which they had dashed in search of secretiveness. With this apparently gone, they saw no reason to remain. They sold their house to a French family and moved on. Significantly, they did not use Tom's services for the sale nor did they tell any of their neighbours where they were going.

Cheryl Brown and Tim Foulkes found a rental cottage in the Cévennes and moved there with her children. She kept in touch sporadically with Jenny who thought she seemed happy and somehow more self assertive than in her previous life. Tim had started a gardening business and they seemed to be making ends meet. As for Steve Brown, he returned to Saint Val from time to time mostly for long weekends and on each

292

visit he idly planned to sell up. He spoke to Tom about putting the property on the market but never quite got round to it.

The English couple whom Tom had put off until his return from London fell at once in love with Nigel's house and offered him a good price. When Nigel drove away from his home in Saint Val for the last time, he shed a tear or two and sang 'Onward Christian Soldiers' fortissimo. He was able to afford a fin de siècle town house in Dijon where he could be with Jérôme Duvallon who had abandoned his career in the Gendarmerie in order to pursue further law studies in the Faculté de Droit in Dijon. On their occasional shopping trips to the city, the Foxes would meet Nigel for lunch and hear the latest highs and lows of his new domestic arrangement. Tom fervently hoped that, if it really was a father-son relationship Nigel was hoping for, Duvallon would be happy with his role.

'Tony' and 'Mandy' did not, of course, return to Saint Val. There was an ongoing risk to their lives even though the pair who had been after them and who had killed Guyard were languishing for the foreseeable future, he, in the prison at Joux la Ville and, she, far away in the women's section of the correctional institution in Lannemezan. There would certainly be others on the prowl. Where the Sextons, alias the Parsons, were, or even what their new names might be, remained a mystery to their former neighbours.

Jean Luc Renard tendered his resignation but this was refused. He stayed in regular contact with Tom and they sometimes met up for dinner, occasionally as a foursome as Jean Luc had met a young woman on whom he seemed particularly keen. Every now and then, he called to see Casson with a decent bottle. The old man seemed to the policeman to have reached a plateau in his life where he showed no signs of further ageing and gave every sign of enjoying his chats with Renard.

The sale of Nigel's house was Tom's final transaction as an Estate Agent and, now that he had time on his hands, he not infrequently wondered whether he and his friend, Renard, would ever again get to go skulking together.

Lightning Source UK Ltd.
Milton Keynes UK
02 August 2010

157768UK00003B/107/P